Praise for earlier novella, **Body Freedom Day: When a Clothed-Minded World Unraveled:**

"...an excellent counterpart in both form and subject to Edward Bellamy's 'Looking Backward' (1888)"—Lee Baxendall, founder of The Naturist Society

"...one of the best and most concise accounts of [the U.S naturist movement history] now available."—The Sundial

"It displays a wry sense of humour...it is told at the personal level and mostly by anecdote, and so is easy reading...I recommend it."
—Duncan Heenan, British website reviewer

"[Ward tries] to ferret out just why people have been so bothered by their bodies."—Mark Storey, N magazine

Strange Days Indeed

Strange Days Indeed

Memories of the Old World

Stuart Ward

Desert Sage Books

Copyright © 2007 by Stuart Ward

ISBN: 978-0-9771754-1-3
Library of Congress Control Number: 2006904458

Published by:

Desert Sage Books
13715 Thrush Road
Montague, CA, USA 96064

Printed in Canada by Friesens
on Roland Enviro Edition 100 Natural
100% post-consumer recycled paper

In memory of my parents
who showed me the wilderness

A note to the reader

This work straddles the line between fiction and nonfiction. The writing is a blend of popular history, fictionalized autobiography, and flights of pure fancy. Please note that—barring the narrator's made-up family, friends, and ancestors—all quotes, dates, names and organizations mentioned before the year 2007 are real.

Editor's Forward

Humanity today stands poised on the brink of staggering breakthroughs. With dazzling advances in technology and quantum leaps in consciousness, we're entering unexplored realms in which things unheard of ten years ago are fast becoming routine. Of tomorrow's breakthroughs one can only wonder.

Would it be unrealistic to suppose future advances might include developing the means to teleport objects through time? I submit the following manuscript—purporting to be precisely that—for your perusal. I'll let you, the reader, decide its provenance.

My name is Green. I run a modest home-based book-publishing business. I print mostly self-help, biography, popular culture, but I also publish, shall we say, unusual subjects others might hesitate to take on. I keep a Martin Luther King quote perched over my desk:

Human Salvation Lies in the Hands Of The Creatively Maladjusted

It was undoubtedly my reputation for sometimes printing offbeat works that led a man to my Berkeley, California door one October day. He was dressed lightly, considering the sharp chill in the air. A determined look burned in his eyes, like one on a mission; I'd seen it before. *Now what?* He held out a thick blue book with bright gold lettering and solemnly handed it to me.

"I think you might want to publish this."

"Looks like I'm too late," I joked. "It's already printed."

He had the grace to smile. "Check the title page."

I flipped open the cover. "*Strange Days Indeed,* by Zet Quimby. Intriguing title, odd name, but…?"

"Oh, right; I meant check the copyright page."

I turned over the title page—and did a double-take.

"Okay, what's the joke?" I asked.

"No joke; at least not that I can figure. Want to hear the story?"

Curiosity peaked, I said sure and ushered him into my home office. I offered him a seat by the fire blazing in my fire-view woodstove and a steaming mug of yerba matte. *This ought to be good,* I thought. There could be no reasonable explanation.

The page had read "Copyright © 2061."

"My name's Samuel, Mr. Green, he said, warming his hands around the thick mug. "I know this'll sound nuts, but this book found *me*." He took a sip of tea.

"I was up at a secluded lake in the High Sierras last weekend to get back to nature a while. Now, call me weird, but I like to lose my clothes whenever I can. I'm no nudist per se; just an old hippie who likes going naked when the weather's nice."

I thought *oh boy, I get them all.* But his sincerity gave me pause.

"The weather was clear at first, so I promptly ditched my clothes. Then it clouded over. Rather than get dressed—I'd been chained to work clothes all week—I kept warm by taking a brisk walk along the small lakefront path. I sensed I was the only one there so late in the season and wouldn't startle anyone for being out of uniform, as it were.

I came to another beach clearing and spotted a sign-bearing tree at the far end. Curious, I walked over. The sign, barely legible, hand-painted, read:

Posted - No Nudity

"Now, standing there naked as a jay—the same squawking

about me—staring at this sign in the middle of nowhere telling me my lack of clothes would not be abided gave me pause. I looked across the lake and then I remembered: forestry used to lease lake-front lots there for a dollar a year to vacationers who built simple cottages on them. Decades later, Forestry ended the arrangement and the structures were removed.

"I could picture it: maybe ten summertime dwellers and most were okay with the occasional day-tripping skinny-dippers on the lake's far shore. But a few got up in arms and posted this sign—probably others too, long since pulled by rangers, taken as souvenirs and used to feed campfires. Chuckling and thinking, *no problem now*, I strolled back to my spot. The sun had come out again. I ate a sandwich—baked tofu with avo, tomato, alfalfa sprouts on rye. (I'm a vegetarian, I should add; no dead critters in my meals, thanks.) Afterwards, I felt a rare contentment: full belly, sun shining, no clothes, no worries. I went into lotus position and looked out over the sparkling blue waters, musing how people could get so bent over others shucking their clothes, even right in the heart of nature.

"It was funny, but also vexing. A friend of mine had just been ticketed for nude sunbathing in Hawaii—you believe that? 'Come to Paradise' they tell you. 'Sun your Buns in Hawaii,' the tourist shop bumper stickers beckon. Then they slap a fine on you when you try to! It's like *The Emperor's New Clothes* in reverse: people acting all ecstatic in their clammy, constrictive swimsuits, frolicking in the waves, while a kid on shore blurts out, 'Look, Ma! They're bathin' with their *clothes* on!'

I took a deep breath, feeling my new swim trunks had just been insulted somehow; I usually only skinny-dipped in the tub.

"Anyhow, my mind was in a quandary over the absurdity of humans' seeming inability to accept their own bodies. With the sun shining down and lake water gently lapping the shore, I slipped into a deep meditation. I envisioned how nice it'd be if we lived in a peaceful, body-positive world, one where clothing was always optional. Time seemed to stop. I don't know how long I was gone, but I was brought back suddenly by a sudden *poof* sound at my feet."

"Don't tell me—the *book*," I said.

"The book." He looked chagrined at my quick deduction and obvious disbelief. "I wouldn't have believed it either if it hadn't happened to me," he admitted. "But I tell you, this book—not there a second before—suddenly appeared on the ground.

"And how many joints did you say you'd smoked?" I know; it was mean.

Samuel ignored the dig as if not even hearing it. "The thing just manifested," he said in wonder, gazing at the dancing flames through the stove door's glass. "Unbelievable as it sounds, it simply *manifested.*" He turned and fixed me with a gaze of such earnestness I had no doubt *he* believed that was what happened. "Listen," he said, "just glance through the book; tell me what you think. I'll make it interesting: I'll bet you a dinner—winner's pick—you'll want to *re*-print it."

I was always up for a new read, especially one with a friendly wager attached. I said he was on. He left with plans to return in a few days for my verdict. I finished work I'd been doing and picked up the book. Funny, I hadn't noticed before: the binding material was unusual; the paper had an unfamiliar feel...

I settled in my favorite chair by the fire, fresh mug of tea in hand, and began reading. The introduction stopped me cold— there was that 2061 date again. *Preposterous.* But then, in marked contrast, the first few chapters appeared plausible: a speculation on both the advent of clothes and man's meat-eating habit; a thumbnail history of modern nudism, recent body liberation trends; the return to healthier diet—generally how people re-connected with nature—along with the writer's offbeat life relating to the subjects explored.

Then dates began spilling into our future again. The writer would have us believe our future was his past, like, "I remember back in 2014..." *Right.* The work was obviously the product of someone's overactive imagination. I tossed the book aside, thinking it might have fantasy value, and moved on to other things.

The next day, though, I found myself again thumbing the book's odd binding. If only to satisfy my curiosity, I tried tracking the supposed author. After a thorough online search, I netted one Zet Quimby listed in the entire country. Phoning and actually catching him home and answering (a rarity in our age of communication), I explained my reason for calling. He was intrigued, admitting he was in fact something of a nudist and natural-food nut, but denied having written any book. I thanked him and tried tracking the listed publisher, Peace Planet Press. I found no such publisher. Their supposed location, Ocean City, Idaho, I found nowhere in the atlas. *Ocean City, Idaho?* The state is two hundred miles inland. I know I should have known better, but I called the U.S. Copyright Office; I gave someone there a good laugh.

Despite myself, I began to wonder. The book seemed too much effort for a prank. What if future humanity actually did discover the technology for teleporting inanimate objects through time and space, and this book really was a voice from the future? A wild thought I couldn't entirely dismiss, try as I might.

Shifting focus, I gleaned the book again. My grey matter stirred as I began looking at dress and diet through the writer's quirky perspective. Regardless of its avowed source, I decided the book maybe had more than fantasy value at that.

When Samuel returned, I told him of my research efforts and puzzling outcomes. If he was surprised, he didn't show it. I said I was indeed interested in re-printing the book, but on the condition I add this explanation and disclaimer. Though it dismayed him I couldn't bring myself to accept his story at face value, this satisfied him—as did the meal I sprang for later: he chose Italian.

Cy Green,
Editor-Publisher,
Jumpin' Junipers Press

Editor's Note:

The discerning reader will note phonetic spellings on certain words, such as *tho, altho, enuf* and *nite* for *though, although, enough* and *night*. Also, words like *bodyfriendly* and *skinnydip*. To believe the book's origin, these are the accepted form in the future, reflecting English-speaking humanity's having at least become more rational in its spelling.

INTRODUCTION

WHY ARE THOSE PEOPLE wearing so much clothes, Grampa?"

I could guess which picture he was looking at without looking up from my potting. "Well, that's a long story, Zak.

"Couldn't you tell me a short story?"

I laughed. "Not easily, no."

"Was it a costume party?"

"No, I'm sure it wasn't."

My four-year-old great-great-grandnephew was pouring thru the tattered photo album that'd survived the shift intact. Our extended family was out puttering in the solarium, enjoying an unseasonably warm November day on our island village.

It was too nice a day to wear clothes, so we weren't.

The album brimmed with family photos, some going back to the 1870s. The black-and-white picture I was sure piqued his interest showed a family reunion of my great aunts and uncles on my father's side, circa 1900. Standing woodenly by a lakeshore on a nice—if not downright hot—day, they were mysteriously draped in reams of heavy dark cloth. Every younger person seeing that photo invariably asks the same question.

"They sure look like they'd be happier without all those clothes on, don't they?" he said more than asked.

I agreed absently as I transplanted a batch of velvety tricolor violets to a waiting flower bed.

I heard him turning more pages. "Now *they* look happy," he said. Curiosity peaked, I shuffled over. I was right. He was gazing at a 1930s-vintage photo of Zep, my great-uncle on my mother's side, along with friends: They were wearing *no* clothes, peacefully sitting on rocks beside a creek, faces wreathed in smiles, as if safeguarding some wondrous secret. He flipped back to the first picture, returned to the second, flipped back to the first again. "How come *they're* wearing so much clothes?"

I stopped work awhile and tried explaining how things were in the old world, how Uncle Zep and friends were the rare exception; that, apart from bathing and playing a favorite grown-up game in the bedroom, most everyone kept their bodies covered, hidden from each other and themselves, regardless of weather or place.

"Huh? Hide our bodies? That sounds silly. Why do that?"

I'd thought about that question plenty over the years. "There were lots of reasons. Like I say, it's a long story. That's just how things were."

He had a sudden thought, as if hoping to explain their odd behavior. "Were they playing hide-and-seek?"

I chuckled. Maybe Zak was maybe on to something. "You might say that—but they weren't having much fun at it. It was a serious game. So serious, people who didn't play by the rules could go to jail."

"*Yow!* That doesn't sound like any fun. He flipped a page. Who's *that* man?" He pointed to a photo of Chester, an overweight distant cousin of mine, logger by trade. He was munching on what looked like a double-cheese hamburger, a pack of cigarettes protruded from his shirt pocket, a bottle of beer stood beside him, and concrete jungle of a city looming beyond. I'd almost thrown the picture out; it reminded me of a time I'd hoped to forget. Now I was glad I'd kept it, as it showed what a paltry lifestyle many people led then. I couldn't have asked for a better example of decadent living.

"That sorry reprobate was one of your distant relatives."

2

"What's a *wepobrate*?"

"Let's just say he was one foolish man who didn't know better than to come out of the rain. He died in his fifties, well before his time, from lung cancer, sclerosis of the liver, or heart disease—one of the above. That thing he's eating? Oh...you probably don't want to know."

"Yes I do, tell me."

"Well...remember now, you asked. It's a sandwich made of ...well, made of ground-up cow."

Zak's whole demeanor changed; he looked stricken. "*He ate animals?*"

"I'm afraid so." Most all of us did back then, myself included, for a while."

"You did, too? Why? Did they let you?" I could tell he was in shock, and I regretted telling him, even tho he had to learn sooner or later. I had no choice now but to try and explain.

"No, they didn't have any say in the matter. People killed them first, and they didn't like that at all. We thought we had to, for health reasons, that plant foods alone weren't enuf. You were thought weird if you didn't eat them. Like always wearing clothes, it was just the way things were." I sighed, remembering how peculiar life was then; I hadn't thought about the old world in a while. "People back then didn't care if animals had feelings or not—I suppose they liked to think they didn't. They just knew they liked eating them, so they paid others to kill them where they didn't have to see it and bring their cut-up bodies to grocery stores."

He looked at me with a pained understanding. Zak had piercing blue eyes that quickly saw to the heart of things. I suddenly felt like someone who'd survived an unspeakable past of flesh-eating cults. "You sure lived in strange times, didn't you, Grampa," he concluded. I agreed. "Hey, mom, what's for dinner? We're not having *animal*, are we?"

"No... Oh, what's he been telling you *now*?"

Later, Zak's questions still weighed on me. Why *did* we wear all those clothes? Why *did* we eat animals? We've lived so long in a freebody and vegan culture, it's easy for young ones to assume we've never lived otherwise.

I resolved, then and there, in the spirit of understanding bygone eras—and indulge my writing penchant—to commit to pen and paper my recollections of those peculiar times. I wanted to explain to current adult generations why, amid other absurdities, being naked was deemed a crime; tell how freer spirits coped with it; and explain why some felt the need to devour part of an animal carcass before thinking they'd had a real meal.

The way I saw it, both age-old cultural habits stemmed from the same profound disconnect from nature.

Somehow mankind took a grievous detour from living the way we were meant to on our fair green planet and had a helluva time finding the way back. Lots of people, tho, acquiescing to the sad situation, didn't think anything amiss—which is what made our journey so...*interesting*.

With both clothes-wearing and meat-eating habits deeply ingrained in most of our cultures, we dealt with the hypnosis of social conditioning—what Deepak Chopra called "...an induced fiction in which we have collectively agreed to participate." In discouraging moments, I felt humanity was like a terminal cancer growth infesting the face of the planet, or a runaway train barreling towards oblivion. In upbeat moods, I realized each of us had had it within their power to transform the situation and turn our world around by the way we chose to live—by what we felt and what we thought, what we wore and what we ate. It could be a damn slow process trying to transform our poor, beleaguered world, but we knew it was a matter of time before it got back on track and became the peaceful world it was meant to be. That's what kept us carrying on.

I chose to focus more on outer body liberation than inner, for many reasons—but I didn't attribute any more importance to securing personal body freedom than saving the animal kingdom

4

from mankind's ignorance. Suffice it to say: Difficult as it was resisting the ingrained flesh-eating ways of the world, it was even trickier trying to live free of mandated clothes.

I suspected I was undertaking a fool's errand, hoping to make sense of it all. We harbored such murky, contradictory, downright weird feelings about our bodies and what we ate that I may as well have tried explaining how each drop of water in the ocean affected the other. The way we lived was incomprehensible, like walking into the middle of a millenniums-long serial matinee—*Story of Humanity, Episode 4,684*—and racking our brains trying to make sense of it all. We'd sit thru it, determined to get something out of it if only because we'd already paid the admission price. I suppose my quixotic nature enjoys the challenge of hoping to explain the impossible: *Avast ye, windmills!*

My family had been hounding me to put some of my recollections down on paper, anyway. I decided to tie two projects together and add my personal experiences to the mix. As I lived thru much of the period I write about, I can tell first-hand how the world changed for me and my relations regarding food and dress and our general relationship towards nature. Beyond that, I'm an armchair historian and draw on research—and, at times, psychic intuition—to fill in some of the blanks.

At age 112, I may forget what I was going upstairs for, or where the stairs are—hell, sometimes if we even *have* an upstairs—but, strange to say, I can recall parts of my life like they were yesterday. It has always been my mixed blessing to vividly relive certain episodes in my life. Revisiting the past rekindled sweet memories—and bitter outrages at a long-gone corrupt order. By writing, I think I vanquished a battalion of old demons. (Here I should add I don't purport to remember conversations verbatim, but I strove to recreate their essence.)

Others, of course, have already written brilliant analyses on growing body freedom. There's Joshua Birdfeather's *When A Clothes-Minded World Unraveled* (Kumquat Press, 2032), and the classic work, *Transparent Planet,* by P. Zanluv (Lightyear Press, 2037 edition). And the wave towards vegan diet is ably covered in Sarah Poundworth's standard, *Food at Last* (Enzyme Publishing, 2042). But I'm certain to be adding a unique perspective to the body of literature here.

You see, my family, in a peculiar case of genetic extremes, was forever divided down thru time on matters body-related. Those on my mom's side historically leaned towards a more natural mindset, enjoying getting free of clothes, reveling in the wildness of nature, and eating whole, plant-based foods. Those on my *dad's* side, on the other hand, favored wrapping like mummies, devouring critters by the barnyard-full, and had no use for nature beyond something to exploit. That these two lines ever got together only showed how love could conquer all.

Here's the thing: *I inherited both sides.*

For the first half of my life they engaged in perpetual civil war inside me, dad's side winning. My repressive genes claimed the day growing up (even while longing for release from my oppressive jeans). A natural nudist as a toddler, I learned all too soon to repress the urge to ditch clothes on even the hottest day; I came to feel secure and decent only when cocooned in cloth. I became terrified at the mere thought of others seeing me naked *(don't look; I'm hideous!)*. You'd have concluded, and rightly, I thought myself grossly disfigured somehow, even tho I was normal looking, if a bit lanky—not unlike a stretched-out figure in an El Greco painting. The predictable result: I became an enthusiastic, if guilt-ridden, closet nudist. And, linking nudity to sex as I did, I dragged sexual inhibitions about by the ton as well.

My dietary leanings were similarly schizophrenic. (Mom, the family cook, had broken away from her own family's tradition of healthy diet, conceding to Dad's tastes.) Some strange part of me

6

relished eating dead animal: *Hand me the knife, paw; I'll kill the critter myself. Don't he know he's our dinner?* I loved fried chicken and craved sirloin steak, and roast beef, done medium rare, was—to use a phrase apropos of the times—to *die* for. I lived for junk food too, inhaling Twinkies, fried potato chips and sticky buns; I gobbled sugar-loaded cereals awash in cow's milk like a condemned's last meal and downed gallons of Royal Crowns like I was always dying of thirst. Another part of me, tho repressed, loved to munch on apples, snack on nasturtium plants—stems, leaves and flowers—and savor crunching down on a single round hazelnut. My second all-time favorite dish was a huge Fisherman's Wharf crab salad, which, minus the unfortunate dead crustacean, was veggie heaven.

Respect for nature? That's where dad departed from *his* family norm. Growing up in a big city, I learned to make the best of the nature-starved, compulsory-dress environs. But I always sensed it was an artificial habitat, always longed for the sanctuary of wildness that I learned about early thru our family's annual, month-long visits to the West's pristine wildernesses.

Along with the photo album, some of my relatives' bedraggled journals and scrapbooks survived the shift intact as well—crammed full with faded news clippings, letters and email printouts—even a few of my scribbled notebooks. From these I refreshed my memory and gleaned anecdotes and quotes to further illuminate those improbable times.

Those peers still alive, who were there and know only too well how upside down, inside out and bass-ackwards things were, maybe don't want to be reminded—and I wouldn't blame them. But then, making sense of the past often allows a keener historic perspective, freeing you to marvel at your place in the time stream. And those not yet born, now blessed to be living in epochal times of planetary restoration, can't help but bring out of these remembrances of humanity's recent dark ages a fresh appreciation for our glorious green Earth.

If at times I seem like an old know-it-all, I don't mean to be; I suspect picking up the quill sometimes brings out the frustrated professor in me. And I beg the reader to make allowances if I approach my subjects in a scattershot way. My mind *is* a bit of an anachronism—throwback to a vanished era—and one considered a bit odd even then.

Zet Quimby
2061 A.D.
Earth Haven, Mount Shasta Isle

How idiotic civilization is!
Why be given a body
if you have to keep
it shut up in a case
like a rare, rare fiddle?
—**Katherine Mansfield**
English short story writer,
1888-1923

Life is a tragedy of nutrition.
—**Arnold Ehret**
Fasting and diet pioneer
1866-1922

Man in his misguidance has powerfully interfered with nature.
He has devastated the forests, and thereby even changed the
atmospheric conditions and the climate...These and other things
are serious encroachments upon nature,
which men nowadays entirely overlook...
—**Goethe**
German poet and dramatist
1749-1832

ONE

To be naked is to be oneself.
—John Berger, Ways of Seeing

THERE WAS A TIME a tyranny of clothes ruled the world.

Clothes weren't bad, of course; clothes were clothes. It was people who *insisted* we wear them, whether or not we needed to, or wanted to, that could put a crimp in our day.

Imagine a delightful summer day: white sandy beach, bright blue ocean, playful breeze, gentle sunshine; the air charged with sweet sensuality. Every fiber of your being dictates shucking any clothes, becoming one with sun-drenched earth and letting the elements work their magic.

Now imagine not being allowed to.

Of course, you've probably already done this, having studied archaic cultural norms in school and all, but if you're like most, you might still find it baffling. How could there ever have been such a time you couldn't even *swim* naked—not unless in total privacy? A time when, short of such isolation, others would think the only possible reason you'd be naked where others might see you was to "make a shameless exhibit" of yourself.

You've no doubt heard the old chestnut, "What we and our fore-

11

bears forbore for baring was unbearable."

Well, it's true.

Cloak-thy-bod laws were enforced everywhere, except a few scattered beaches, mineral springs and resorts—and even there people might sometimes feel more heat than sun alone provided. Otherwise nice people gave others strong disincentives for trying to enjoy the day unwrapped beyond the privacy of home, no matter how fine the weather, no matter how pleasant the surroundings, no matter how innocent the intent.

"Nude" was a four-letter word: It rhymed with crude, it rhymed with lewd—it rhymed with rude, dude. 'Twas to be eschewed, forever booed and misconstrued. No matter your mood, your attitude, or size of brood, you knew that you'd beware the prude who wanted you zoo-ed for going nude.

People inclined to go bare usually settled for disrobing only in secluded spots—if fortunate enuf to have such nearby. If not, then only within their homes, on vacations to special or remote places, maybe discretely on rooftops and furtively in their yards, under cover of nite—someplace where neighbors and busy bodies couldn't see and make them feel uncomfortable for being naked and possibly even call the police.

Life was a masquerade and costumes were compulsory.

Others, less attuned to the simple pleasures of communing with nature directly, disregarded the wisdom of their bodies and absently accepted their cloth prisons. During hot weather they might grumble, knowing they'd be cooler without unneeded covering, but there's the rub: they *were* thought needed; it was simply the way things were.

We'd always worn clothes, hadn't we? Clothes were our second skin; we felt too naked, naked.

For most, the idea of being without clothes in public went so far beyond the pale of accepted behavior it beggared belief.

We flitted between parallel universes: bare butterflies when alone and with lovers; pupas wrapped in cocoons while in public.

✳

How did humanity come to wear clothes so compulsively? How could people become so self-conscious about their physical beings they invariably felt the need to conceal them?

A sage once said, *the cause of anything is everything, and the cause of everything is anything.* Much as I'd like to reveal the exact causes of our wrap-happy world in a neatly-tied package, the puzzle of our past is vast and intricate, with a slew of missing pieces: Many factors leading to our obsessive dress habit stretch far past the mist of recorded time. Trying to pin precisely how we came to be such obsessive-compulsive clothes-wearers—to the point it became effectually illegal not to wear them in public—is a slippery slope indeed.

Naturally, there are a few *duh* reasons we first adopted clothes. Beyond that, tho, we're left to speculate, theorize, and point out some of the most likely contributing causes that piled up, overlapping, over the ages to understand how we ever got so damnably addicted to duds.

✳

[By kind permission, I borrowed some of the following list from Melody Foxworthy's out-of-print classic, *Clothes Thru History: Friends & Foes* (Serendipity Press, 2041). Others I came up with myself. An old man has time to muse on such things. You'll note how meat eating was in many ways connected to clothes wearing.]

Nineteen Reasons
We Wore Clothes

1. First and foremost, clothes served as protection from the elements—even as they do today. Logically, people covered up when it was cold, wet or windy, or so hot the skin needed protection, and thus maintained body comfort.

2. Primitive man began dressing to show tribal rank, resourcefulness, signs of distinction and wealth. In a pecking-order world, clothes were crucial for showing who was who in the human zoo.

3. Some theorized earliest primitive man gradually mutated from an early hairy-ape state to almost bare-skinned to avoid insects infesting his former thick matt. Losing this natural built-in coat, he needed to replace it, and hence primitive clothes in the form of fashioned plant matter and the hides of animals. (One might wonder about such earliest clothes being called *hides*.) Possibly they first killed them in self-defense and then realized their furs and hides gave body protection and devouring their flesh provided sustenance. (My Great-Uncle Ziggy was an exception to the rule; he was so hairy he weighed an extra ten pounds sopping wet.)

4. People have always loved to decorate their bodies, whether out of creative urge, desire to attract others, plain vanity, or whatnot. Such tendencies, combining with other factors, might have resulted, over time, in people universally accepting clothes-wearing as matter-of-factly as they did eating animals. Forgetting to dress became like forgetting to make a fashion statement or like…well, forgetting to dress.

5. For a people weathering the Ice Age over thousands of years, clothes-wearing likely became genetically hard-wired. These thickly-garbed tribes were often more aggressive for dealing with

harsh climates. Not living where food grew on trees and bushes, they killed and ate animals and wore their hides for survival. They sometimes expanded and migrated to warmer climates, where they easily overwhelmed the more peace-loving, minimally-dressed food-gathering tribes. They assimilated them, impressing on them their own diet and dress code, and, over time, the default appearance of humans segued from naked to clothed (and the default diet from vegetarian to omnivorous).

As you see, the reasons for our former discomfort over nakedness were myriad and inextricably combined. Like an onion, we keep peeling away more layers:

6. As mentioned, among the first clothes were animal hides and furs, and, for untold ages, clothes were literally "to kill for." Is it possible clothes-wearing was, on one level, emblematic of a person's hunter prowess, and this vibration came down thru our genes (and into our jeans), keeping even later cloth wearers more prideful and aggressive for wearing them? *"I hunted down five stores and beat out two other shoppers to snag these Levis; I tell you, the competition was fierce. Tell the truth: do they make my butt look fat?"*

7. Once realizing we were in many ways different from other species, pride made us want to distance ourselves from the rest of creation, proving ourselves dominant and superior by covering our bodies with the skins and furs of *their* bodies: "We are not animals!"

8. Clothing served to provide a mutual shield from one another's undoubtedly abysmal hygiene standards.

9. Clothes proved a deterrent to over-impulsive and irresponsible matings.

10. In some eras, a naked person was viewed as a wretch so poor he couldn't afford to clothe himself: no one wanted to encourage that conclusion—lest some well-meaning soul take pity and offer the person the shirt off his back. Possibly this attitude was partly a carryover from times when only slaves went naked, or nearly so, and not by choice.

This barely covers half of the likely reasons clothes wearing became more than a fashion statement:

11. Clothes served to help muster a sense of dignity during eras when dignity could be a precious commodity indeed. Our bodies, tho amazing, beautiful, and precision creations, might appear comical or unsettling or astounding for their sometimes dramatic and exaggerated configurations—or lack of drama: anything that didn't fit a society's ideal norm might provoke unwanted attention in the form of rude smirks, bald astonishment or outright ridicule. By covering up, people felt a modicum of propriety and thus stood a better chance of being taken seriously.

But in the process of seeking privacy and security in clothes, humanity over time developed negative body attitudes. The syndrome: *my body is unsightly and therefore must be kept covered.* This led to wanting to dress up, to gild the lily, as it were, and redeem one's otherwise unacceptable body thru pricey apparel and painful shoes.

12. The more we wore clothes as a matter of course, the more emerging clothing merchants and fashion traders gleaned a *huge* captive market in the offing. They scrambled to reinforce the habit, preying on our vanity, constantly impressing on us how spiffy variously touted body coverings made us look. ("It's *you!*") They guaranteed themselves fabulous fortunes in the process— even as many on my dad's side of the family would. Eventually,

styles of cover-up were calculated to change from season to season and year to year, necessitating going out and buying yet more clothes lest one be thought unstylish. The French, destined to become global arbiters of fine clothing design, began marketing apparel fashions in 1678.

13. In our peaceful, quiet villages, nestled in nature, with no more than a hundred or two dwellings in most, it's always inviting to forego clothes in nice weather. But in the old world, the mega-villages of cities were super-compressed habitats for *millions,* living on top of, underneath, and beside each other. Mix in it being the primitive machine era, with surreal scenes of loud, toxic un-Earth-friendly energies assaulting one everywhere, fraying the nerves and deadening the body's sensitivity. People sought refuge behind solid walls—and solid clothes—to keep a semblance of centeredness and security amid the hectic scramble.

Wanting to go naked in such unpleasant conditions was viewed as a sign of madness. Poor Great-Uncle Zip: suffocating in his clothes one muggy New York City heat wave, he tore them off and jumped in a handy fountain, refusing to dress when asked. He spent the next three days in a mental ward for "observation;" he observed them back.

14. Life was a crazy masquerade, often filled with aversion or at least dis-ease towards seeing one another's uncovered bodies, unless lovers or sport team buddies. (*"Good to see you, John! ...eww, I didn't want to see* that *much of you."*) Wearing costumes hiding our real, vulnerable selves gave people a better chance to muddle on thru—an incognito everyday negative forces had to work to penetrate.

15. Industrialized life pulled us further and further away from our once-intimate relationship with nature. It became something to be conquered and over-exploited for individual gain, rather than

revered and worked for the common good. It got to the point city people on vacations could barely relate to relatively unspoiled nature beyond superficial "scenic tours," behind glass, behind clothes, behind schedules. Someone once wrote "The manner in which people choose to clothe themselves speaks the truth of how they perceive their ties to nature." The more separated from nature we became, the more separated from each other we felt, and the weirder—and more compulsively—we dressed (and ate). In trying to distance ourselves from our primitive origins, we distanced ourselves from the very source sustaining our lives.

A few more:

16. It was often a hostile world. When people battled each other, wearing clothes helped protect the body from harm and made it easier to tell who the enemy was (assuming each side dressed differently). In more recent times, it was still hostile, tho usually on a subtler level, wherein people vanquished each other with deadly looks and barbed comments. Altho most people no longer needed steel or hide armor, they kept wearing clothes as shields against indifferent or unfriendly—or *too* friendly—vibes of others.

17. The kind of clothes one wore were identification badges of one's station in life amid a rigid, materialistic, class-conscious society. Chimney sweep, bricklayer, banker or lawyer, there were different costumes for different classes—and for different professions within each class. In a time when appearance and status took precedence over substance and heart, clothes *did* make the man. Proud people were passionate over propriety and pigeon-holing each another.

18. Some believed it was the influential ruling class that led the way to our dress mindset in the first place. Their pride and vanity in dressing, wanting to show the world they were people of sub-

stance—*some*body, not just *any*body—created pronounced body attitudes and dress habits. Such puffery eventually trickled down to the slavishly emulating lower classes, wanting to show *they* were somebody too.

This brings us to the last and one of the more profound and controversial factors in the advent of mandatory dress, which, wanting to explore it in some depth, I saved for last: religion, morality and the control of the populace:

19. Over time, mankind struggled to become more genuinely civilized and understand what he glimmered to be a mysterious rhyme and reason to life, possibly some divine underpinnings to existence. He sensed maybe there was a divine creator, an intelligent force—some grand design at work of which he was part. His less sophisticated mind used two-dimensional, *either-or* thinking—in contrast to the more comprehensive *both-and*—to try understanding his existence, in time drawing hard lines between one's "higher," spiritual self and "lower," earthly self, thus creating a chronic battle between flesh and spirit.

Today we realize the importance of harmonizing all parts of our being. We appreciate the value of each to the other in becoming our fullest, most integrated selves. Then, we'd gone covered in public so long most people couldn't keep a handle on the pleasurable flood of keen sensations and lusty appetites aroused (or revulsion and mortification evoked) when nude or seeing others nude. Religious leaders feared that when people listened to their bodies they wouldn't listen to God. And maybe rightly so, as possibly humanity was going thru some evolutionary adolescence of raging hormones: Initiates for the priesthood might've lost resolve to be celibate if pretty parishioners came to mass revealing the glory of God's creation.

Some saw it differently: When naked, they reasoned, we were in closer attunement with our bodies and environment, and so felt more integrated and empowered. We went our merry ways, happy in our skins, indulging our sensual appetites freely. More rational-thinking people refused to listen to the religious leaders, purporting to know what God wanted us to do (for, apparently, God *really* wanted us to cover up). They dismissed such leaders as materialistic bureaucrats and charlatans—wolves in sheep's clothing—who'd hijacked once genuine, spirit-based religions and corrupted them to get their thumbs over people in a grab for naked power (or, in this case, clothed power).

But rebels from this perceived scam were a minority. Influential people, in on the ruse or too trusting and naïve to realize they were helping perpetuate a rank deception, appeared to respect and obey the edicts of God's supposed mortal spokesmen; most of the common people followed suit—literally.

The upshot: We left our earthly paradise, repressed the rich stream of sensuous stimuli the human body is receptive to. We smothered ourselves in animal skins and coarse cloth (and much later, dubious "miracle" fabrics, concocted in laboratories). In the process of desensitizing the body's capacity for feeling, we lost attunement to the wisdom of our bodies. (The extreme in discomforting ourselves thru dress was the hair-shirts worn by certain religious devotees to "mortify" the flesh—tho the outfits of many lay persons often appeared to serve a similar purpose.)

Earthly desires and, by extension, nakedness, were *bad.* Some religious sects taught us to feel shame at the sight of our own bodies. Full-length mirrors were scarce.

Bathing was frowned on. In early Colonial Philadelphia, you could be jailed for bathing more than once a month. The reasoning: to bathe, you had to get naked; being naked, your sexual appetite was fueled, which promptly led you to run amok. My own distant ancestor, Rayon Mather, was one so punished: "Methinks it seemeth Ungainly, nay, well-nigh Idiotic," he groused from his jail journal in 1615, "to punish one's Godly desire for Cleanliness such wise."

Some speculated that early Christians began viewing bathing as sinful in reaction to the orgies raging away in opulent bathhouses during the Roman Empire's decline while Christians were being slaughtered in the coliseum for noontime entertainment.

Tho I wasn't as much of a *conspiracy theorist* as some—one suspecting underhanded plots afoot by ruling forces were behind everything—I couldn't help but think that the often-corrupted powers of church and state *knew* they could better control, oppress and manipulate the citizenry by exploiting the tendency of people to cover their bodies. Take away the freedom to be our essential physical selves by making clothes mandatory, tell us feeling good was bad, make our bodies indecent, and we were thrown off-center, putty in the hands of lord high muckety-mucks bent on trying to run our lives.

If true, if some, in efforts to control others intentionally made us feel so ashamed of our bodies we felt the need to conceal them, the deed was surely one of the most brilliant brainwashings ever foisted by man onto fellow man. Under the guise of pious morality, corrupt and greedy powers had succeeded in no less than crimping the freedom and comfort of our own bodies, and hence, our very lives.

Most difficult for people not alive then to understand is why some could be so selfish. There was usually enuf for everyone, if they'd only worked together and shared. But we didn't have enuf social conscience and concern for the public good to appreciate this. Without the cooperative spirit we've since cultivated, people who could consolidated power over others—the peasants, the little people, the great unwashed masses.

They apparently viewed us as no more than dumb beasts for not catching on to their hoodwinking. We let ourselves become disempowered, clueless how to turn things back around. They kept a stacked system guaranteeing the perpetuation of the deception, a foul divide-and-conquer game, pitting one against the other in a scramble to play ball with them to get a share of the spoils. Entire populations were thus checkmated by each other and kept from working together for positive change.

Living in a too-often confusing, strange and scary world—its foundation seriously off kilter—we allowed oppressive controls over our lives if it offered a semblance of security. But we paid dearly for them, and a daily reminder was mandatory dress.

At times, it appeared body coverings served—as much as any other function—as tokens of the few tattered shreds of our mortgaged pride left after our self-respect had been mangled and compromised into acquiescence by high-handed forces. On one level clothing came to symbolize bandages—fancy or plain—covering our grievously wounded personal integrity.

Such manipulators often acted in ignorance, of course. They were caught in a runaway snowball effect thousands of years in the making. But some knew exactly what they were doing: The sly monkeys put down the human body *in the name of decency*: the Creator's handiwork was judged indecent and thus had to be shielded from offended eyes. They told people white was black and people believed it—or at least wouldn't dare debate it if they wanted their family's next bread ration from the church bakery. Or wanted to avoid the town pillars clamping them in the town pillories.

Long story short: they had us covered.

❋

No doubt there are countless other factors that rendered our natural state unseemly over the course of time. Suffice it to say, whatever rational reasons humankind once had for wearing clothes soon drowned in a sea of irrational ones. What was first fashioned to make us feel more comfortable and protected, devolved into becoming virtual prisons, albeit soft ones, for every *body*.

As I said, I don't know the whole story; I doubt anyone does. The subject defies easy analysis. (For a different take, read *Addictive Dress and Other Peculiar Habits,* by Rufus T. Merriweather. Guttenberg Press, 2033.) Somewhere along the way, due to a complex accumulation of cause and effect over long millennia, Earth's more "civilized" cultures embraced compulsory-obsessive clothes wearing and, more often than not, attendant body shame.

Eventually people were left feeling vulnerable without the security-blanket of clothing. We adapted raiment as our armor against an unkind world, to such a profound degree we felt incomplete without them.

We muted sensitivity to our skin, the largest organ of the human body and crucial sensor for attuning to environment.

We became strangers to the land.

TWO

Clothes make the man,
but nakedness makes the human being.
—**Kevin Kearney**

FAST-FORWARD TO the start of the 20th century and people in industrialized nations went about incredibly over-wrapped. Swathed from head to foot, individuals were in seeming denial they even *had* bodies, or at least feeling somehow apologetic for the fact.

This, tho ironically, America had a dedicated skinnydipping President at the time, Teddy Roosevelt.

Things had eased up some since Lady Gough's 1836 book, *Etiquette,* advised, "The perfect hostess will see to it that the works of male and females authors be properly separated on her bookshelves. Their proximity, unless they happen to be married, should not be tolerated." Even so, in 1900 the word "leg" wasn't spoken in polite mixed company—not even referring to furniture: Great-Uncle Algernon once showed a guest the door after the visitor commented on the "fine legs" of the parlor piano while in the presence of my Great-Aunt Minerva. Boston once refused a shipment of navel oranges because the fruit's name was deemed "too immodest." Men went beside themselves at the flash of female ankle. (A full century later, Minnesota still had a law in their books making it illegal to dry men's and women's underwear on

25

the same clothesline, tho it's doubtful it was enforced by then).

Women bustled about super-swathed in petticoats, girdles and whalebone corsets. Proper fashion dictated women wear copious yards of cloth even when ocean dipping, risking drowning from the sodden outfits pulling them under.

Great-Aunt Minerva had a close call one day at Cape May, on the New Jersey coast. She'd wanted to show off her new beach costume that was all the rage. She decided to be adventurous and actually wade into the surf. Before she knew it, a rogue wave knocked her over and pulled her out into deep water, turning her woolen outfit into an instant leaden anchor. She saved herself only by tearing off the now-dratted outfit while thrashing underwater. Staggering to shore, sputtering for air, bereft of all adornment save her sopping black stockings, she was so mortified she never set foot in the ocean again.

By the 1910s the stuffy Victorian era was fading fast. With swimming becoming popular, women took to wearing more practical, form-shaped, one-piece tank-tops, close to the outfits men wore in water, with upper legs covered. Skirts rose to mid-calf, yet were so tight at the knees women could barely walk at more than a mincing gait without tripping.

In 1913 the modern bra was invented. New York debutante Mary Phelps Jacobs couldn't deal with the constriction of her corset and how it showed beneath her plunging neckline. With the help of Great-Aunt Zoë, then working for her as maid (before marrying up), Jacobs designed the first modern bra. She stitched together two lace handkerchiefs and a bit of pink ribbon. "The result was delicious," Jacobs said. "I could move more freely, a nearly naked feeling…"

Future designs wouldn't be so body-friendly. Grandfather Elroy worked as quality-control supervisor in a Boston garment factory, Apparel Nonpareil Amalgamated. It made some of the more tortuous brassieres. "Coddle the body and weaken the spirit," could have been the company's motto. Elroy persuaded the boss to hire his eldest son, Anatole—my dad—in the 1920s. Grandfather showed him the ropes of the garment industry that served dad well in later building his own clothing empire.

While things improved—World War I brought more women into the workplace, creating the need for more practical, less constrictive clothes—we remained under the sway of irrational body-suppressive coverings and the insistence they always be worn in public.

Even men could be arrested for removing the tops of their swimsuits at the beach. Such an incident might well have gone something like this at a sometimes less than completely law-abiding Coney Island beach in 1915:

"Oh, my! Look, Gladys. Stanley over there just removed his costume top."

"The rogue! Oh, but he is a fine specimen...er, don't you think so, Aunt Augusta?"

"Humph. Oh, he's a fine specimen, all right. Why, have you both lost your senses? I'm appalled you're encouraging such scandalous behavior. I'm fetching the constable this instant. 'Fine specimen,' indeed!"

The good thing about a situation becoming so abysmal was it often inspired people to do something to remedy it. The light at the end of the tunnel glimmered years earlier, with the German birth of modern nudism.

☀

Germany had come under body-oppressive Christian influence later than other European countries, enabling its people to preserve more of their rich pagan earth religions and natural ways of living, which included minimal dress. Despite this, the country became so heavily industrialized, by 1900 it held more large cities than the rest of Europe combined. Such a technocratic departure from natural living inspired mutiny among the more nature-loving, everyday Germans.

A burgeoning *lebensreform* or life reform movement was born. Assorted rebels, many from middle class homes, rejected the decadent bourgeoisie order to one degree or another and returned to their ancestors' ways. Often leading the charge were the *Wanderogel*, or wandering birds. German youth, rejecting the dehumanizing industrialization, poured out into the countryside in droves, living like gypsies, hiking and singing, camping, eating simply and shedding unneeded clothes. (The globally popular International Youth Hostel organization, offering shelter to intrepid young travelers, grew directly from this movement.)

People re-attuned to nature's elements for health and wellbeing, increased camaraderie, and spiritual nurturing. Enthusiasts variously adopted simpler, body-friendlier clothes; followed basic, plant-based and raw-food diets; took air, water and sun baths; soaked in mineral baths and sweated in saunas; forsook alcohol and tobacco—generally reawakening their ancient mystical bond to the land.

Meanwhile, the medical establishment, which many had similarly rejected, believed in strong drugs and drastic invasive surgeries—pills and procedures—for curing what ailed you. While such doctors often shone as life-savers once illnesses and injuries were full-blown and life-threatening, they were astonishingly ignorant about the value of preventive healthcare, especially when it came to something as basic as healthy diet. Members of the new movement, having had a bellyful of such doctors—loaded for bear and battling maladies like military campaigns—believed in working peaceably with nature in order to foster the body's self-healing capacities.

Natural health pioneers like Adolph Just, Carl Schultz and Arnold Ehret harnessed methodical thinking to re-discover ways

28

to regain and maintain robust health. Twenty-four doctors had abandoned all hope on the malady crippling Ehret, an inflammation of the liver. He dumbfounded (and no doubt mortified) them, first by curing himself—after careful study of fasting, conscious diet and exercise—and then went on to hike and bicycle about the countryside like a marathon man.

The naturist, or nature-cure, movement adopted health practices and lifestyles sharply at odds with society's entrenched ways and industry's vested interests. Departures from the norm included fasting, herbal healing, chiropractics, massage, yoga, colon cleansing, color-light healing, magnetism, meditation, mineral and steam baths and—the main subjects of my ramblings—body acceptance and cruelty-free diet.

Many German nature-cure proponents, fed up with the decadent heavy-handedness around them, skedaddled to America—same as my own ancestors—joining the flood of emigrants to a land exploding with opportunity and in such flux oppressive forces were handicapped in getting a thumb on any new popular movement. They brought with them new-found alternative values, health discoveries and dedicated enthusiasms for working with nature and passed the torch of knowledge to receptive Americans, many recent immigrants themselves.

Natural proponents eventually locked horns with the entrenched American medical system—no less preoccupied with pills and procedures than their German colleagues. The importance of diet was dismissed to the point it might just as well have not existed. A "well-balanced diet" meant eating equal portions of everything.

Most nature-cure proponents on both sides of the ocean adopted certain alternative values while otherwise maintaining accustomed conventional lifestyles. However, a tiny minority of reformers adopted a radical lifestyle all their own.

Called *naturmenschen* or natural men, such men, women and children rejected any and all ways of living, thinking and being for

29

which they found no valid reason to conform—regardless of how accepted they were as everyday norms. Besides mandatory dress, they rejected meat, dairy, alcohol, and tobacco. What clothes they did wear were unconventionally loose-fitting. They forsook white sugar, coffee, black tea and bleached flour. Some became raw foodists, rejecting cooked foods in favor of exclusive diets of raw fruit, seeds, nuts, grains, legumes and vegetables. They refused the medical system's pharmaceuticals and vaccinations, the draft board's summons, the enrollment of their children in public schools, and advocated feminism and communal living.

Any 1960s generation peers reading this might about now be experiencing déjà vu: *at the turn of the old century, these people had become proto-hippies.*

One such natural man was Bill Pester. He migrated from Germany to the balmy Palm Springs, California area in the early 1900s. Pester grew a full beard, let his blonde hair go long and lived simply in a palm log hut by a flowing stream. He spent much of his time naked, played guitar, went barefoot in town and ate only the raw food growing in abundance around him. "Man was intended to live in a state of nature," he wrote. "All man's troubles, sickness, anxieties and discontent come from departure from nature... I have little use for money, and I am not bothered by politics or religion as I have no special creed."

Fifty years before the Haight-Ashbury, he became the first California hippie.

He was also the first of the Nature Boys, what grew to be a flower-child fraternity of long-haired, bearded, Southern Californian nudist raw food enthusiasts of the 1920s, 1930s and 1940's. One of them, Gypsy Boots, went on to play at the Monterey Pops and Newport Folk Festival, on the same bill as The Grateful Dead and Ravi Shankar; in so doing he linked the German naturist movement to the budding American hippie coun-

30

terculture destined to emulate their ways—albeit with psyche-delics and a theater-of-the-absurd twist.

Another member, eden ahbez, actually walked across the United States *four* times. He felt inspired to write the haunting 1948 international pop tune hit "Nature Boy," recorded by Nat King Cole. In sweet synchronicity, the song's acceptance helped lay the groundwork energetically for the generation then being born and destined to become nature-loving hippies.

❀

Most nudist historians trace the beginnings of modern organized nudism to 1903 Germany, with the publication of Richard Ungewitter's book, *Die Nacktheit*, or *Nakedness*. A contender to being the founding proponent was Dr. Heinrich Pudor, a German sociologist and scholar. Simultaneously, yet another German, Paul Zimmermann, opened a clothesfree facility, Freilichtpark, near Hamburg, for those open to the then-radical idea of spending their vacation in the nude. *Early proponents often encouraged an all-around healthy lifestyle, eschewing meat, tobacco and alcohol, as well as unneeded clothes.*

Nudism revived popularity in getting free of clothes that ephemerally bobbed to the surface throughout history, for various reasons. Ancient Greeks, for instance, deemed being nude an empowering privilege of high-status males, for exercising, partaking in sporting events and doing public rituals. Slaves, women and barbarians were forbidden to be naked.

The rallying point this time was more democratic: throwing off cloth restraints to regain health and rejuvenate the human spirit. Letting sun, air, water and earth be experienced directly; when not possible outdoors, indoors, in gyms and pools. *What a novel idea,* people must have thought. Advocates argued the attire of the day restricted circulation, irritated and chafed the skin, and caused further body discomfort by excessive heat buildup, which in turn increased bacteria-breeding grounds, promoting diseases.

An over-bundled world of compulsory clothes had compromised the body's precision ability to self-regulate and self-heal.

Europeans giving nudism a try either liked or rejected the attendant fruit-and-nut diet regime; mineral baths; saunas; and abstinence from meat, alcohol and tobacco; but they *loved* getting naked. They discovered a keen renewal in relaxing and mindfully shedding their clothes amid pleasant surroundings—like snakes shedding skins. They found the spirit-lifting exhilaration of communing directly with nature, together, free of cloth interference, to be grand therapy indeed.

Among them was my Great-Uncle Zep, revisiting his old homeland in Germany. On hearing about the budding colonies, he dropped in on one on the outskirts of Munich. Afterwards, he wrote of it, "Though my German had grown rusty, I think I communicated better with people there, just for being naked together in natural surroundings, than I ever did any bushel-full of clothed people back in Missouri. Didn't care for the peculiar food, though; they almost booted me out for trying to wrangle a sausage-and-eggs breakfast."

Uncle Zep was so enthused by nudism he later tried starting his own nudist preserve back home—minus the raw food. Unfortunately, the good people of the "Show Me" State only wanted to be shown so much; they got him closed down on some flimsy pretext before you could say "seersucker suit."

"I guess they showed *me*," he rued.

Nudism faced fierce resistance in Europe until after World War One, when it gained droves of enthusiastic converts across Germany and Switzerland. Citizens impoverished by the war sought affordable recreations: getting naked in the woods was free

32

and an innocent pleasure. It was health-restoring too. The devastating inhumanity of the war and attendant mechanization frenzy of a rapidly industrializing world stirred a desire to get back to nature to heal, free of societies' blasted trappings. During the 1920s nudism spread to France, England and Czechoslovakia.

Of course, the more radical minority, who moved to the countryside and adopted living food and holistic healing practices as well—bonding with kindred spirits who likewise rejected artificial living wherever it lurked—took the nature cure to more profound levels.

☀

Back in the U.S., the 20s found the day's youth eager to throw off more restraints of stuffy society, adopting simpler, body-friendlier wear. College deans had a cow when coeds revealed their calves (sorry).

My Great-Aunt Zyla, always a firebrand, bobbed her hair, took up smoking, and was among the first to dare wearing the new leg-, arm- and shoulder-revealing, one-piece bathing suits She promptly got arrested for indecent exposure, along with others, in a well-publicized Chicago beachfront bust in 1922. "One of those lugs wrestling us into the paddy wagon tried starting a petting party so I kneed him and how," she wrote.

Laws were soon changed to accommodate more relaxed dress standards at water's edge.

The nudist movement crossed the Atlantic to North America in late 1929, by way of recent German immigrant Kurt Barthel. While ephemeral pockets of freebody cultures had previously cropped up in various Utopian communities around the United States for a century already, Barthel's efforts were acknowledged

as the beginning of modern organized nudism stateside. He started up his fledgling nudist organization twenty years after settling
in New York City and becoming a naturalized citizen. In delicious
historic irony, the tendrils of nudist interest grew here at the same
time as the great stock market crash—people were losing their
shirts even while they were "losing their shirts."

Resistance was even more fierce in the U.S. Ninety-nine percent of Americans had never even *heard* of the concept of nudism.
As it turned out, the first "nudist camp," Barthels' Sky Farm, in
New Jersey and eighty kilometers from New York City, earned the
acceptance and respect of local police as "a damn fine crowd" by
working with them from its inception.

Other retreat camps, either in less liberal-minded regions or not
trying to work with the surrounding community, didn't fare so
well. Five deputies—Great-Uncle Stanley among them—stormed
one early rural camp in New York State in 1930, jumping out of
the bushes with pistols drawn, bearing arms on bared arms as it
were, as if in mortal fear of the naked people. "We drew straws at
the station for who would go," Stanley wrote. "I swan, I'd never
seen such a sight: people parading about in their birthday suits,
not a speck of shame. I'm telling you, it was scandalous—I've got
a batch of 8 x 10 glossies to prove it."

There was a word for such people as my great-uncle—*gymno-
phobiacs*: people who had a fear of nudity, their own, and, by
extension, that of others. Gymnophobia of some stripe or other
was so rife people didn't even know they had it. If they did, they'd
probably have organized and adopted a bumper sticker statement:

**I'm Gymnophobic and I Vote
So Cover your Ass**

That our bodies were more than instruments of physical pleasure and procreation, assimilation and elimination—also the earthly temples of our souls and as such worthy of honor and accept-

34

ance—seemed utterly lost on our more self-alienated culture. That said, tolerance by the public of the multiplying nudist preserves grew after court battles and attendant publicity and nudist literature won over converts and sympathizers.

By 1938 there were at least eighty-one active nudist groups across the country. Alas, Zep's was not among them, but one his cousin Zane started with his wife in Georgia was: Roxy's Rest & Rejuvenation Retreat, or The 4R, lasted seventy years, until it was sold and the grounds converted to clothing-optional condos.

Maybe 20 percent of the groups had problems with local authorities: raids in early years and later, with restrictive legislation, passed or proposed, designed to render various nudist clubs illegal. So long as they kept beyond view of the disapproving, leering, not-sure-what-to-make-of-it public and tried to meet the community half way, they had a good chance of being left alone. Not always, tho. Nudist colonies could feel like Old West fortresses under siege by Indians outraged over white people's invasion of their hunting grounds: nudists fought off war parties by a perma-dressed public outraged by the naked invasion of their textile-happy domain.

While alcohol was not allowed (and would be generally banned in such places until the late 60s), American nudism apparently made no definitive call on meat-eating or tobacco use.

Most individuals joined colonies to experience the relaxation and exhilaration and health benefits freedom from clothes allowed. But people had myriad and overlapping reasons for joining, as I realized on gleaning William Hartman's 1970 classic study, *Nudist Society*. Among them:

- To enjoy freedom from conventional lifestyle—a way to safely rebel from a spirit-deadening conformist society
- To gain a fuller self acceptance

- To gain a sense of well being thru the super-attunement to one's body nudity allowed
- To enjoy sports and recreation in the buff
- To socialize, free of clothes-created status, with like-minded spirits
- To experience the aesthetic joy of seeing fellow humans in their totality
- To foster a morality not dependent on shame and guilt
- To allow their kids the freedom to be more accepting of themselves and others
- To get that prized all-over tan
- To have a safe zone to pursue going nude in nature

Uncle Zep, who had to drive clear to Texas from Missouri after his own nudist camp bit the dust, had his own reason for joining: "I just like socializing naked with others in nature; what's 500 miles?"

Memberships were kept secret and people mingled on first-name-only basis out of concern for job security and reputation back in the clothed world. Nudity was often mandatory inside the compounds, a policy as extreme as compulsory dress outside perhaps, but understandable when you considered: in a culture obsessed with mandatory cover-up, naked people rendered themselves extra-vulnerable and as such felt uneasy among those secured behind the often-desensitizing armor of clothes.

Uncle Zep again: "I wasn't ashamed of my body or anything, but when fully dressed visitors were given tours thru our grounds as prospective members, you could tell which ones had no intention of ever shucking their duds; they just wanted to drink us in, like we were a carnival peepshow or something. It was mortificatin'.

"Finally we told them, "come on in, but you gotta take your duds off first. *That* fixed their wagon."

In 1931, my dad's older brother Horace was busy building his fortune with an imported line of fancy Italian suits. In the same year, the American Sunbathing Association was launched to help publicize, organize and legitimize the daring new lifestyle in the United States. Its adherents appeared to be less than Uncle Horace's ideal customer. Of the movement, he reportedly once spouted: "Why would a body want to go naked? What kind of tomfoolery is that? If the good Lord meant us to be naked, we'd be b—...*oh, never mind.*"

Meanwhile, there was new resistance to Germany's by then flourishing nudism: "One of the greatest dangers for German culture and morality is the so-called naked culture movement. It takes away women's natural shame and robs men of their respect for women, so destroying the conditions for real culture"—so warned the emerging Nazi regime.

☀

Back in America, hucksters and racketeers tried cashing in on the newborn freebody trend with prurient slants in ads and publications and further gave nudism a bad name. It was difficult maintaining a sense of integrity amid such a leering, condemning culture. Nudism would be equated with lewd behavior—or at the least certifiable weirdness—in the public mind's eye for generations to come. The concept was so alien and morally frightening in America that before a court victory in 1937 one didn't have the legal right to even *advocate* the idea; such talk was deemed risking social disorder.

Grandfather's black sheep cousin Axel started up his own pseudo-nudist magazine, *Shameless Hussies Go Nudist*. It folded after two issues. It might have lasted longer, but the hussies Axel photographed were even more shameless about their pay demands.

Men continued risking censure when daring to go without their tops at East Coast beaches—including my Uncle Zeeman. He enjoyed heading over to Coney on his one day off from sewer-pipe-fitting in the Bronx: "Things are depressing enough without people telling me I couldn't even enjoy the sun on my chest," he wrote to a cousin. In 1934 he was one of eight men there fined a dollar a piece. The magistrate told the culprits, "All of you fellows may be Adonises, but there are many people who object to seeing so much of the human body exposed."

Next year, Uncle Zeeman was among forty-two topless men mass-arrested at Atlantic City and fined *two* dollars each. They were dryly informed, "We'll have no gorillas on our beaches."

Men gained the legal right to be topfree later that decade, something many women wouldn't *begin* to gain for another sixty years or so. The reason? A male-dominated society made rules to favor men. The female body as handmaiden and nurturer of human life is powerful; keeping it rigorously covered slowed women from embracing their natural strength and causing men to lose any unfair advantage.

Many males had so sexualized women's bodies they didn't want to see women's breasts unless wanting to be aroused. And if breasts didn't meet their standards of desirability, men *definitely* didn't want to see them. Studies suggested women could be as sexually attracted to men's bare chests as visa versa, but no matter; it was a man's world.

Some women, like Aunt Zeta, challenged that presumption.

During the 1950s, Aunt Zeta one day dared to go topfree at a Kansas country club pool. Men protested, shocked by her effrontery, demanding she cover up. She refused, holding her ground, telling them "*I* don't particularly like seeing your hairy chests and beer guts, for that matter, but I wasn't complaining, was I?" She offered a compromise: "I'll cover up if *you* do." The men thought the notion laughable and reported her to the manager. He kicked her out, trotting out the tired old rationale aimed at protecting the newly brainwashed from getting confused: "After all, there are *children* here."

"Oh, right, what was I thinking?" was Aunt Zeta's parting retort, the way she told it. "God forbid children should ever see a breast." (Breast-feeding was *not* popular then.)

The United States' comfort zone when it came to the unadorned human body expanded at a glacially slow pace. While nudism took root to varying depths in practically every civilized country, in America the seeds of body freedom found rockier soil. Could it be because Europe had gotten rid of its super-strict Puritans to America at our nation's inception? Perhaps Puritans over-reacted to the corruption they left behind by swinging the pendulum of acceptable behavior too far the other way, learning to distrust sensual feelings. *One bath a month?* In any event, nudism in the United States was kept rigorously contained within walled and gated communities for decades to come.

World War Two forced changes in dress habits. Fabric shortages spurred government restrictions, forbidding extravagant ruffles and full-cut sleeves on women's wear, as well as an order to reduce fabric in women's swimwear ten percent. A halt to production of zippers and metal fasteners, in order to redirect metals to war needs, inspired the wraparound skirt. War's end brought out the women's two-piece bikini swimsuit, as if celebrating peace by liberating the female body a bit more.

The bikini was promptly banned in Italy, Portugal and Spain, and generally banned from Hollywood films until the early 1960s. Cousin Zinny, vacationing in Spain, nearly got herself arrested wearing her plaid bikini at a Barcelona beach: *"Por favor, senorita, no pladista tourista nudista!"*

❄

The 1950s was considered the golden era of nudism, such as it was. Perhaps it was the ending of another unspeakable war that again inclined people to seek simple pleasures amid nature and rehumanize. What easier way than by shedding the restrictive trappings of society in the guise of clothes?

Aunt Zeta and Uncle Yancy, longtime vegetarians, retired in 1953 after selling a successful Midwestern pottery business. They bought a shiny new Airstream trailer to pull behind their trusty Studebaker and moved back to Florida. They toured the state's flourishing nudist parks a year before dropping anchor at Home at Last, near Sarasota. "Five hundred acres of body freedom, complete with a café, two lovely swimming pools and a boating pond to boot," Aunt Zeta wrote in her diary,

> plenty big enough to forget about the overdressed world out there. The sunshine is too divine for words. The café offers vegetarian specialties and the dress code is always casual. I love it! There are plans in the works to start a vegetable garden to supply our own produce, and Yancy and I are starting up a pottery class. I told our poodle Toto I *knew* we weren't in Kansas anymore.

In the 50s, a major court victory for freedom of the press and the nudist movement was won by one Illsley Boone, Kurt Barthel's pick to become the American leader of the movement and for thirty years its most dynamic, colorful, and often controversial proponent. Enjoying playing David and Goliath, in one issue of his *Sun* magazine he defiantly refused to airbrush out genitals from his nude photos—the only way the post office would handle such illustrated nudist literature. When the post office refused to mail the offending magazines, Boone enthusiastically appealed. In 1953 the D.C. District Court overturned the decision. From then on the mails carried nudist magazines, depicting people as they *really* were.

"Can you imagine?" people no doubt cried. (This question was asked a lot in those times, perhaps indicative of how imagination-challenged we could be.) Actually, before then, that's all people could do. Except for the stray photo of Ugandan bush people in *National Geographic*, few knew what fellow members of their own species looked like in unselfconscious, normal, everyday living conditions.

Unfortunately, such relaxing of the law prompted body-objectifying pornographic magazines to flood the market as well. Some skin mags, like *Big 'Uns,* and *Bigger 'Uns,* devoted themselves to women with large breasts. Those into astrology believed the United States' endless preoccupation with breasts stemmed from our nation's sun sign, which influences group personality, being Cancer, the "ruler" of breasts.

In any event, it took little stretch of the imagination to see the advent of a ubiquitous burger chain's neon yellow arches as giant, glorified cartoon boobies thrust skyward across the land.

THREE

I suppose we acquire most of our feelings
about our bodies too early, and in ways too complicated,
to make them easy to account for.
—**Charis Wilson**

A CENTURY AGO during the 1950s and 1960s I was busy growing up in San Francisco—or trying to.

Home was an 1890s vintage, four-story row Victorian in posh Pacific Heights. One of four siblings, I had my own room, replete with four-meter ceilings, wainscoting, dumbwaiter panel and generous alley view. On a good day the window got seventeen minutes of sunshine.

Just saying the word *nudist* could be dangerous around our house. My dad Anatole was the direct product of staid and staunch Victorian sensibilities, by way of migrating British ancestors who helped found the Massachusetts village of Stoneham in the 1630s (and were undoubtedly part of the prosecuting team in the Salem witch trials a half-day's horse ride away). He was a firm believer in the virtues of keeping bodies securely covered in mixed company.

Moreover, he was CEO and majority stockholder of Anatole's, a posh, upscale clothing chain he'd founded in the 1940s with one store and built into a clothing empire, after going public and shoe-

43

horning outlets into every la-di-dah shopping center ever to gen-
trify aging cities. He saw his business as a service to help the rich
dispose of their bothersome wealth thru his enticing raiment.
Clothes were his bread-and-butter; people going without them
meant lost sales: the idea of nudism going mainstream was
unthinkable.

"You better hope that loony fad never catches on, son, or you
can kiss Harvard good-bye," he told me one evening in the living
room. I looked up from my crosswords; I'd been stumped on a
seven-letter word for 'they find clothes unbareable' until then. His
forehead creased like an accordion, right temple vein throbbing as
it did whenever he threatened to get excited. He'd just read a semi-
tongue-in-cheek article in some magazine on how nudism was
finding popularity in certain sunny climes. A compulsive worrier,
he was a dog with a bone.

"Can you imagine people actually wanting to run around without clothes?" he asked.

I was fifteen: My mind promptly reeled thru a full-length feature—*World without Clothes*, starring Brigitte Bardot, Gina
Lollobrigida and a cast of thousands—and was out the door
munching my third box of popcorn in the second he paused for
breath.

"We'd be in the poorhouse before you knew it. "Our stock
would plummet to nothing. We'd have to rent out our vacation
homes just to eat." Altho dad owed his entire fortune to people's
constant desire for new and different ensembles to flatter their
notable personages, he'd grown up poor in the 1930s. Somewhere
in the back of his mind he was afraid of hitting lean times again.
He was forever telling us, "We stuffed cardboard inside our shoes
to keep the rain from leaking thru the holes in our soles," as if it
were such a fond memory he wished everyone could experience
the joy.

In contrast, I grew up with my feet super-shod in spit-shined,
hardboiled dead-cow wing-tips, so polished I couldn't look down

on sunny days without getting blinded; there was no hope of rain ever getting thru those babies without sabotaging them in the tool shop. I wore slacks with creases so sharp I could open mail on them. My upper torso was usually swathed in one of a dozen virgin-wool Pendleton shirts, ferreted from a walk-in closet so crammed with clothes it took too long to find anything and I usually wore whatever I grabbed first. Dad wanted us to have all the advantages he never did; he insisted on it.

My mom, Zera, tho a certified clotheshorse, had a more relaxed attitude towards nudity. She'd obviously strayed from her family's naturist bent, finding she'd definitely preferred clothes, even tho having a trim figure and not feeling ashamed of her body. She'd cover up around us beyond our toddler years, and see to it we were suitably dressed. But her obedience to the unwritten dress code was more out of compliance to society's iron-clad insistence one went about dressed rather than any moral belief nakedness was bad.

Unfortunately, dad's word was the law in town, and acquiescent mom generally kowtowed to it, along with the rest of us. His negative body attitude got the lion's share of press in my impressionable mind and somehow shaped in me a circus-freak self-image. My quirky mind drank in the energies behind thoughts and feelings and attitudes, and—imagination running amok—intensified them out of all proportion; I was a human energy magnifier.

While I'd outwardly adopt dad's strict, "life is tough and you've got to get used to it" attitude, I inwardly cultivated mom's low-key, "life's a bowl of cherries but watch out for the pits" spin on things.

Mom's love of fine apparel is probably what cinched her attraction to dad, pulling her further away from her family's freer-minded leanings. At the over-strict summer nudist camp she'd been packed off to in Florida as a kid, she'd been outright forbidden to wear clothes. Maybe she acted out the rest of her life wearing clothes all she could, taking a kind of guilty pleasure in it like others did in *not* wearing clothes. I'm guessing, tho. She rarely discussed her upbringing. I only learned of this wrinkle of her past later from one of her older sisters, who confided in me. "Your mother finally rebelled against that nudist regime one day," she told me. "She did a *reverse* streak, daring to run, fully clothed, across the camp grounds. Boy, did she get in Dutch for that!"

For whatever reasons, mom adored clothes. A watercolor painter by hobby, she had an artist's eye for color, form and texture. She'd offer dad innovative ideas for new clothing lines over the years, and he used some with great success.

※

My parents both loved unspoiled wilderness. They were no more than unwittingly complicit in society's cavalier disregard for the environment: People chopped down virgin forests for toilet paper; car owners dumped tons of poisons in the air to drive half a block for a quart of cow's milk; and our government tested the latest deadly bomb upwind from communities, assuring townspeople any fallout from ground zero was harmless, forty years later claiming it a coincidence half a town's citizens were sprouting extra toes.

Many lived so packed in sprawling cities they couldn't step outside their own front door without energetically feeling they were stepping onto a busy freeway. Earth's poopulation had more than doubled in the first half of my life; by 2007 the planet supported close to seven billion people, and urban dwellers outnumbered rural dwellers for the first time. We had a herd complex, probably a genetic carryover from prehistoric times, when there was safety in numbers from all the wild beasties and hostile neighboring tribes and challenging climates. Vast expanses of unspoiled nature went begging, while others were so super-populated they sometimes reminded me of a pet shop's water bowl of coin turtles I once saw as a kid: The poor little turtles endlessly clambered over each other in an unending struggle for the limited dry island in the middle.

Humans in cities were little different: We kept wound up, scrambling about and trying to create a semblance of comfort zone for ourselves thru endless conveniences, in the process making the environment so polluted with noise and fumes we redoubled our efforts to cope with it. Our hunger for solitude was such, people often settled for staying inside their homes to enjoy any quiet, all but abandoning hope of enjoying any relaxed solitude in the fresh air and sunshine—the long, drawn-out travel maneuvers to flee the madding crowd were daunting. People might exodus from town on weekends to get a nature fix that hopefully tided them over the next urban-saturated week.

We displayed a profound lack of environmental awareness thru the sea of toxic substances we let flood our lives. Some men actually used benzene, a toxic substance derived from coal, for aftershave. Others took kerosene and petroleum jelly as internal medicines. We routinely added poisons into everyday items: mascara, food, children's toys... I shudder to recall how as a child I chewed mindlessly on toys undoubtedly laced with lead—worse, how our entire family drank tap water from ancient leaden pipes. As people later learned, absorbing too much lead wreaks havoc on the nervous system, affecting development. What toys didn't have lead had PVC, another swell "better-living-thru-chemistry" substance not exactly human-friendly.

By the early 2000s the nation's Environmental Protection Agency estimated we disposed of nearly half of the nation's sewage sludge as fertilizer, once banning its disposal in oceans and rivers in 1991. Tho nutrient-rich, it was also loaded with pathogens, germs, viruses, heavy metals, and chemicals. It fouled the air and polluted downstream waters, resulting in nearby residents coming down with gastrointestinal ailments, headaches, and burning eyes and lungs. (The practice was banned in 2009, I learned, after checking an old almanac.)

We sometimes even dumped poisons right *in* our home environments. A notorious case in point: New York State's Love Canal.

This toxic chemical dump was named after the 1890s speculator, William T. Love, who'd begun digging a power-generating canal between downhill bends in the upper and lower Niagara River, before losing funding and abandoning the project. The sixteen-acre rectanglar pit left made a handy dump site years later for Hooker Chemical Corporation and the U.S. Army—the company alone admitted burying about 21,800 tons of various chemicals in it over the decades—before the site was filled over with a thin layer of dirt and sold to the local board of education for one dollar. Wanting to get their money's worth, in 1955 they promptly built a grade school and playground smack on top of it. The school didn't have a basement, only because when they tried digging one they ran into chemicals. Oops. They decided on a slab foundation instead.

Children reported being burned just touching the ground in the schoolyard, and the place could stink to high heaven. In the early 70s, Lois Gibbs, a shy mom with a high-school education, knew something was very wrong. She grabbed her sling and went after Goliath after doing some research and drumming up neighborhood awareness. Responsible bureaucrats stonewalled her (or what was a bureaucracy for?), denying there was any provable connection between several residents coming down with life-threatening diseases—some who'd never been sick a day in their lives before moving next to the festering brew of toxins, containing at least twelve known carcinogens. It took years to see justice done, but finally the government permanently evacuated a thousand families.

Multiply that tragedy by thousands—if not tens of thousands—worldwide, and you can appreciate how mankind had a wayward talent for fouling its own nest.

And eating dead food.

✳

Mom, a typical gullible housewife, was lured by the siren song of animal products and so-called convenience foods then flooding food markets. She'd grown up semi-vegetarian, but had acquiesced to dad's preferred diet, which reflected the mainstream dietary wisdom: eating dead animals was important for healthy, strong bodies. She duly served various poor creature's select remains and generous glasses of bovine fluid every day. Our freezer section was crammed with parts of unfortunate animals: We were always ready to have a cow.

She bought canned fruits, vegetables and meats by the ton, along with box mixes that you "just add water!" to. An over-trusting soul, she believed splashy ads' claims of providing wholesome nutrition, when in fact we were scarfing the skeletal remains of the original food stuff, after the living enzymes had all been sucked out and the residue "fortified" with synthetic vitamins (a fraction as effective, if at all). Why would they do that? For the sake of long shelf life. Multinational corporations were out trying to corner the food market and it was impossible without first desiccating the food. Why'd we go along with such madness? Hey, it saved time in the kitchen, and our wise government gave its blessing.

Canned goods by the hundred vied for space on our groaning pantry shelves. I'd absently stare at them, their jumble of colorful labels conjuring abstract images in my mind, feeding my imagination if not my body. We gobbled bleached spongy white bread by the cart full—all but void of nutrition but a *great* substitute for modeling clay. If *it* was the staff of life, it was a balsa wood stage prop for a children's church play. We stocked packaged snack foods so embalmed with unpronounceable preservatives their useful shelf life *still* hasn't expired.

Fried strips of pig muscle marbled with fat and chicken embryos constituted part of a good nutritious breakfast. I didn't know what was good for me if I didn't eat my fried chicken livers or braised cow's tongue, dad said. Sandwiches featuring ground-up, seared cattle muscle were the all-American snack. (I don't mean to gross you out here, but, crazy as it sounds, this is actually what we ate.) If we are what we eat, it's a wonder we didn't grow hooves and sprout fins and feathers.

As I mentioned, people rejecting such bloody faire for exclusively non-animal food sources were looked on with more than faint suspicion.

☀

How could such a sorry situation come about? The question's worth exploring. Like I said, our now-archaic meat eating habit tied into the same profound disconnect from nature causing our over-attachment to clothes. And, the same way we tried tuning out the outer discomfort of the unbodyfriendly apparel we wore, so we tried tuning out the internal distress created forcing animal remains down our gullets.

Some said it was natural to eat animals: many animals in nature ate each other, didn't they? And, after all, weren't we part of nature? Such thinking ignored the fact humans were entrusted to be wise and loving stewards of Earth—imitating carnivorous beasts' violent habits of devouring each other didn't set well for fulfilling that trust. But not everyone knew we were meant to be planetary stewards then; in fact, damn few did.

Some religious scholars believed that until humankind defaulted from the plan in the Garden of Eden, life on Earth was a peace-able kingdom. Its human inhabitants subsisted solely on the fruits and nuts of the trees and the wild grains and vegetables. They held there was no violent taking of animal lives for food, or even pur-loining of milk meant for their young. They said it was only after we blew the plan that we stooped to flesh-eating—and developed a widespread cult of animal sacrifice in pathetic efforts to regain God's favor after having royally blown it. As an outgrowth of this ritual, killing God's noble creatures and consuming them regular-ly became an accepted way of life. (Cynics would say that meal prayers were often a distant echo of such ritual sacrificial pleas.)

If one didn't buy the Adam and Eve story, there were plenty of other explanations to go around: One, that primitive man slew ani-mals for survival—for their meat and for their skins. He hadn't yet learned how to plant seeds to grow foods his body could thrive on, and, as mentioned, wild food sources could be scarce. Eating the flesh of other beings could keep him alive. While he'd eventually learn to cultivate the soil and harvest bountiful crops, by then meat had become a deeply acquired taste, with powerful survival associations; he saw no need to stop. And mankind was still enuf in primitive reptile brain to take greater satisfaction in violently killing his meal than peacefully harvesting it.

Or this one: Thru the ages, decadent royalty, whose coffers overflowed from taxing the populace to the bone, had to live dif-ferently from their subjects somehow, or what good was it being a king or queen with gold to squander? They dressed royally, they lived royally—and they ate royally, having a constant parade of animals slaughtered for their glutenous feasts. (They also processed royal flour to make their bread loaves more "refined" than the coarse brown faire of peasants.) Many of royalty lived short lives for the degenerative diseases brought on by such "rich" diets causing them royal pain. But that didn't deter the have-not peasants, hungry for power and wanting to "live like kings," from emulating their eating habits. If you could afford having pigs to slaughter, or cows or pheasants, you'd arrived, baby, leaving your fellow plant-grubbing peasants behind.

Fast forward to recent times. More spiritually attuned beings concluded lusting after dead-critter faire was not only barbaric and unnecessary, but also wasteful, selfish, and a veritable form of slow suicide: only animal products had dietary cholesterol, which the body repelled, and only plant foods had fiber and complex carbohydrates, which the body thrived on.

Theirs was a minority-held viewpoint, subject to mean-spirited jokes and cruel derision. Meat had become an acquired taste among the mainstream in more affluent western cultures—all but genetically hard-wired in people's DNA, it seemed. As strange as it sounds now, the devouring of decomposing animal flesh and reproductive fluids in their many guises was associated with prosperity, health, and virility. People had still to shake off their distant ancestors' cavemen mentality.

Those starting to see the light had their work cut out for them. In their struggle to shake free from resonating with the death vibration everyone else seemed hunky-dory with, they were all but guaranteed a character-building challenge. They had to deal with others' reactions to their passing on eating animal remains "I slaved all day in the kitchen to make": everything from concern you'd waste away to nothing and die of starvation and take your children with you, to outright mockery—you'd swear people suddenly had fangs and claws, the way they could assume wolfish grins and predatory gleams on challenging your non-violent diet.

The majority never saw the wisdom in surrendering their carcass cravings—that is, short of quadruple-bypass surgery after clogging their arteries with enuf inassimilable animal residue over time. The meat, dairy and egg industries, either in blind faith or by willful deceit, successfully reinforced humanity's exploitative food habit—no less than those benefitting from compulsory dress reinforced man's body alienation. They'd convince people, thru moneyed influence in government, institutions, and school lunch programs, that animal-based foods were actually *crucial* for optimal health—"part of a complete, well-balanced diet."

Again, those refusing to eat dead animal and the robbed milk and eggs were viewed as flakes, heretics, and defectors from the faith. As Gabriel Cousens put it in his book, *Spiritual Nutrition,* "Because most people are normally banging their head against the wall, we [vegetarians] are considered abnormal because we choose to stop."

❋

I was the youngest of three brothers and a sister. Our family was what you called emotionally buttoned-down. We rarely spoke our deeper feelings, and, for sure, never talked about nudity—let alone ever *were* naked together. We saw each other naked only by accident. One time I walked in on my sister fresh out of the shower and she wouldn't talk to me for a week; I felt nearly as embarrassed (altho a little fascinated).

Being the youngest in a divide-and-conquer, pecking-order family, I wasn't allowed much air time to speak my mind, so I stopped trying. I didn't start talking in earnest until I was nearly five. I'd say *no* a lot and that was it:

"Zet, finish your bacon."

"No!"

"Then go to your room."

"No!"

"Don't you want your ice cream?"

I nodded.

Eventually, writing became my way of self-expression. I could talk to paper; it was always the perfect listener. It never told me I didn't know what I was talking about, never made faces at me, never laughed at me and told me my underpants were on backwards. Before learning to read and write, I saw books as good only for building blocks, the black sea of hieroglyphics inside them so much unintelligible gibberish. After learning, I got happily lost in Hardy Boy adventures, and writing freed me to articulate my thoughts and feelings and rare imaginings.

Music was my other lifeline. I'd learned to play simple tunes by ear at age five and was soon pounding our old upright piano like my life depended on it. I discovered that with music one could express naked feeling, bypassing words. Nebulous feelings I couldn't begin to put on paper, let alone speak, poured thru my fingers and onto the keyboard. During a later five years of piano lessons, I resisted learning to read notes; I found it more fun trying to figure out a song I heard in my head than deciphering all those mad, caffeinated dots on paper. My ears were sponges, soaking in musical sounds from everywhere and wringing them back out on the keyboard.

For awhile I'd try duets with my brother Clyde on violin, but soon abandoned that, as he took pleasure in leaning over and screeching agonized notes like alley cats locked in mortal combat into my ear, just to get a rise out of me.

Much as I loved writing and music, my fondest child memories are of going camping summers.

We lived in a city largely bereft of greenery except for a few giant swaths like Golden Gate Park, created as if to compensate for the paucity of nature elsewhere. Soviet Premier Khrushchev, on visiting San Francisco in 1957, commented "You have a lovely city, but where are your trees?"

Visiting wilderness was always a treat. In nature, I naturally felt more...*natural*. Each summer mom and dad took us on long road trips in our 1950 woody Plymouth to majestic state and national parks. One of them—Big Basin—provided my earliest pleasant memory: I was toddling along a creek-side trail dappled in sunlight, impossibly-tall giant redwoods looming above us, their thick canopy filtering sun rays swirling with dust motes and alive with butterflies; I inhaled the rich earthy fragrance of the woods and listened in wonder to the creek's rippled murmurings of magical realms that stellar jays jealously guarded with their squawking at our approach.

Dad let his hair down camping. He played a mean harmonica around the campfire at nite, as he had done when he was young and footloose. After adventurous days hiking, I'd get lost in the rich glow of the fire embers as he waxed fancy playing tunes like "Red Wing" and "There's a Long, Long Trail."

While camping I felt such an affinity with unspoiled nature and its riches I never wanted to leave. I suspect dad, given his druthers, might have preferred staying there too, if he weren't so busy draping humanity.

Back home, our family kept a semblance of connectedness with nature thru a patch of sandy earth in our backyard, where we grew carrots, chives and nasturtiums; plus kept a menagerie of pets: parakeets, hamsters, goldfish, coin turtles, salamanders, a chipmunk and a black-and-white cat named Aloysius.

The chipmunk, Frisky, did time in a tall, home-made wire-mesh cage that at least gave him room to dart around in. Later I brought home a female chipper from the pet shop to keep him company, hoping they'd produce a litter. They either stayed platonic or Frisky was so un-frisky by then he needed chipmunk-Viagra, and, unfortunately, no pharmaceutical giant had pounced on the market possibilities. She stayed skittish of human contact, but I could feed him dried cantaloupe seeds. He accepted them one at a time thru the cage's mesh, on his haunches, until his cheeks bulged and he scurried down to his nest to stash them and scrambled back for more.

Sometimes I let them out and watched them scamper about my bedroom floor. Freedom (of a sort). Thinking back on it, their tasting liberty beyond the cage was maybe similar to my sampling freedom from clothes: it happened so rarely it felt surreal. Like the heavy rain pounding on the car roof suddenly stopping while driving under a highway overpass, or grade school miraculously letting out early.

☀

I soon realized the importance of clothes beyond hiding our nakedness. Louisa May Alcott noted, "...clothes possess an influence more powerful over many than the worth of character or magic of manners." Despite this growing awareness (or, more likely, because of it), I was never too impressed by the fancy duds that put food on our table. Why should people treat me better than the next boy because I wore finer clothes? Were we that superficial? *I am not my clothes*, I told myself, but with less and less conviction as time passed. Oh, sure, I'd enjoy the cushy feel of pristine socks and the oddly appealing chemical scent of brand-new shirts. New clothes could be a treat to wear the first day of school—once you got all the pins out; new clothes could make you feel like a new person. And you could snuggle inside them on a cold, rainy day like they were your best friends.

But clothes could be a pain. A melting glob from a long-anticipated double-scoop cone of highfalutin hazelnut ice cream plopped down on my new shirt and suddenly the feast was interrupted by vigorous efforts by mom mopping up the mess and berating me to be more careful. It left me staring balefully at my troublemaking cone: feeding-frenzy interruptus. And if you couldn't even wipe sticky fingers on them, what earthly good were they?

Besides, I had an ultra-sensitive nervous system. I bridled at unnecessary clothing muffling my skin receptors, hemming me in, stifling my ability to regulate my body temperature and feel air currents. Plus I always got tangled up in them while learning to dress myself, becoming an alligator wrestler loosing out to a beastly sweater, feeling helplessly pinned down by futilely trying to poke my head thru an arm sleeve. Plus with my indecisive nature I often wasted my first precious waking minutes switching from one outfit to another in utter frustration, dissatisfied with all of them, no doubt unconsciously wishing I didn't have to wear *any* of them.

Mom later told me I'd thrived on being naked during my toddler years, playing the unabashed nudist whenever I could. At some point, beyond which it was no longer cute or acceptable to be freebody, I was dragged, kicking and screaming, into compliance with the clothes-minded world, the same as everyone else. "I had to keep an eye on you," she said, "or you'd be pulling off your clothes two seconds after I put them on."

Knowing resistance was futile, I acquiesced to clothes-wearing as the way of the world. In short order I learned to seek sanctuary inside them from the often less-than-friendly energies floating about. When I was older and saw futuristic illustrations of spacemen in their suits, protecting them from unsupportive Martian atmosphere, I thought, *that's how clothes work here on Earth*. We could more or less breathe the air, but between the unbodyfriendly environments and the psychic atmosphere of an alienated population oozing about like poison gasses from a chemical plant spill, protective shields were a welcome item.

I paid a high price for my clothing dependency, tho; perhaps a higher one than most others. Even as I found a kind of security in clothes, I came to feel more and more cut off from my body, more a stranger to my physical self. My skin receptors basically numbed out and I felt disconnected from my body. Clothing, no matter how enticing its rich colors, soft textures and nimble fit, became, to me, like Alice in Wonderland's Cheshire cat, who first charmed me with his dazzling smile, then, once totally captivating me, his giant bushy tail impishly erased the trail leading out of the dark woods.

Sensitive nerves and genetic predisposition aside, my eventual passion—at times, *obsession*—for wanting to live free of clothes whenever I could possibly stemmed from two early-life events. I nearly choked to death at birth but for the quick action of the doctor: the umbilical cord was wrapped around my neck three times. (This went a ways towards explaining my later lack of fondness for ties and turtlenecks and why I'd feel garroted when barbers cinched hair-guards about my neck.) Then there was my earliest memory, at age one or two: I lay sweltering in my crib, alone in a dark room, smothered under acrylic blankets, encased in thick one-piece jammies with built-in plastic-sole booties, wondering why I was being tortured.

I was to spend decades trying to shake off discomforting physical restraints of any stripe. I couldn't wear a watch or rings. Ski boots? Forget it.

As a child I'd vent, singing a silly sing-song ditty to the classic snake-charmer tune: "There's a place in France where the ladies wear no pants…" It was a comfort imagining people *some*where not having to wear pants: no wedgies driving you mad; no worries getting trousers dirty playing in the mud; no belts cinched so tight you couldn't breathe, or so loose pants slid down; no fear of trousers' metal-toothed monster attacking your penis and putting you in mortal shock, echoing the trauma of circumcision.

☀

At age seven I engaged in an act of rebellion against staying covered; the repercussions would color half my life.

I was standing by a swing set in the backyard of Karen, the

sweet girl down the block. We'd been best friends since toddler days in the local playground sandbox. It was a warm summer day. In the spirit of full disclosure, I pulled down my pants; I think I longed to feel the warm sun all over me as much as show her how I was different from her. In return, she, being shy, had agreed to show me her bellybutton. That moment her dad, a hard-drinking lawyer, spotted us from the kitchen window. He roared an oath—giving me early warning—and chased me out of his yard like a raging bull. I didn't bother with the closed yard gate; I jumped up and flipped over the two meter plank fence like a gymnast going for the gold, racing home up the block's steep uphill like it was downhill and a dozen vicious hounds snapping at my heels.

That nite, after heated words between our fathers over cocktails at our house, they'd decide we should never play together again. They'd never cared for each other, having clashing political views, and I later realized we'd become pawns in their efforts to spite each other. Karen and I heard the showdown—they were like trumpeting bull elephants, threatening to charge each other. We were hiding out in the pitch darkness of the front hall closet, squeezing room for ourselves amid the cushioning coats; sweaters, and rain gear jamming the clothes rack and hangers and collectively emitting a peculiar bouquet of scents.

We marveled at a blue glow-in-the-dark Mr. Peanut keychain piece I held out in my palm. It was given me earlier that day by a towering, monocle-ed, cane-sporting Mr. Peanut at the local food market as part of a promotion. Our minds swam in the pale glow of the tiny talisman, trying to block the unpleasantness raging outside, as if hoping to hold childhood's fleeing innocence at bay by immersing ourselves in the key fob's cool luminescence.

While losing a cherished relationship was wrenching enuf, any remaining shreds of positive body acceptance I'd yet clung to were snatched away too. I'd already developed a vague, uneasy feeling my body was bad somehow: now it seemed unspeakably nasty. And it got weirder.

Not long after, dad took me for a swim at San Francisco's prestigious Olympic Club. Then an exclusively men's club, bathing suits were *verboten* in its venerable indoor pool. Naturally shy and by now convinced nakedness was evil, I freaked out having to come out of the locker room butt naked—nostrils assailed by chlorine, every sound bouncing off the tastefully stark, toupe-colored walls—and expected to splash in the water with a bunch of strange naked men. Dad most of all: we'd never been naked together. He didn't look like he was enjoying it much, either.

For years I'd wonder why he ever took me there. I was sure getting mixed signals: first I was bad being naked, and then I was in trouble if I *wasn't*.

A few years later, a male friend and I, both ten, hiked over to a secluded wooded area of The Presidio—the City's other large tree preserve—and shucked our clothes. We leaped about the pine grove, screaming like banshees. You'd think we were two hungry coyotes taking down a deer. Looking back, I think we were simply in jubilant rebellion from having to wear clothes.

The only conclusion I later drew from these two opposite experiences: *I* wanted the choice of being naked or clothed, not have either one forced on me.

FOUR

Few, if any, survive their teens. Most surrender to the vague but
murderous pressure of adult conformity.
—**Maya Angelou**

DURING MY TEEN YEARS, with hor-
mones racing like a raging river at spring snowmelt, I re-sensis-
ized to my body after having lived more or less apart from it for a
decade. I gourmandized newly-awakened taste buds at Italian
pizzerias and my ears lapped up music on the radio like the answer
to life's every riddle lay in its rhythm, rhyme and harmony.

I longed to further indulge this soaring sensual awareness by
sunbathing naked. I wanted to feel the sun's delicious rays, free of
clothes, in the intoxicating weather San Francisco could lavish on
its denizens. I wanted to do it from the security and convenience
of home, but the back yard was out; ditto the front deck. I was
resourceful, tho: From an attic-bathroom window I could climb
out onto our gabled roof, which safety abutted the adjoining
house's gabled roof. I discovered a sloping spot where a dormer
window's outcropping blocked being seen—barely—by scores of
potential eyes from a tall apartment building looming across the
street. I peeled off my clothes and, awkwardly canted on my towel,
allowed my sun-starved skin to drink in the sunshine. The smell of
the hot roll roofing commingled with the Coppertone suntan

lotion I slathered on myself like a self-basting human on slow bake.

Even as I experienced a thrill liberating my body and feeling the sun drenching me with its penetrating warmth, the frantic excitement running thru me for breaking the taboo was so strong I might have just as easily have downed a quart of espresso coffee on an empty stomach.

Had dad discovered me, I shudder to think what would've happened:

"Get inside, you. No son of mine is going to make a shameless exhibit of himself on our roof. You're grounded for life. Now put some clothes on... Now put some more on. And some more... Where the hell'd you get that J C Penney shirt? Wearing the old man's low-brow competition, eh? You're grounded for two *lives."*

***

I was soon shown two secret treasures destined to transform my young life. For some unfathomable reason, an older, bullying neighborhood boy named Butch one day led me to his secret hideaway in his apartment building, located two doors down. Maybe it was a gift I had for prying secrets out of people without even trying.

Accessed from the six-flat building's garage, the place lay at the end of a labyrinth involving gritty determination to reach: Once ducking in the garage undetected thru an alleyway side door, you climbed thru a narrow, horizontal plumbing-access panel opening located a meter and a half up a wall while trying to hold up the fifty-pound panel with one arm; crawled on hands and knees over cement for three meters, flashlite in hand, careful to avoid broken glass; maneuvered yourself over a bare hot water pipe spanning the center of a small window-like opening without getting burned; dropped down and stepped, hunched over, three meters along a low-ceilinged, dirt-floor chamber; and, finally, clambered up a small ceiling opening leading to the fortress proper.

There, stashed inside the dark cloistered vault like a bank depository, was a fat stack of vintage nudist magazines. I couldn't have been more impressed if they were a leaden stack of gold ingots. I'd only stolen glimpses of *Playboy* magazines before (in which women took off their clothes for the camera to excite wonder and admiration in men and horny boys everywhere), and never had had time to leisurely peruse any.

As I gingerly leafed thru my first copy of *Nudist Adventure*, I think it was, I tried shutting out Butch's snickers at my wide-eyed astonishment; my eyes were blinded by the sudden bonanza of dazzling curves and rich skin tones that lay hidden underneath women's perpetual coverings. It was an exotic world of swelling breasts, like twin scoops of ice cream with cherries in the middle; of backsides like cleft peaches clinging to branches; of mysterious thatches of curly hair crowning the places their sculpted legs met... I staggered at the beauty that was the female body.

And felt a mysterious new sensation stirring inside.

Butch warned me, on pain of death, never to reveal the place to a living soul, and to never go there without him. It was understood the magazines stayed.

Then, miraculously, he moved away three weeks later. He left behind the fortress, of necessity, *but the magazines too*. (I'd thought of him like an adult, being older, but he obviously didn't want to take a chance spiriting them on board and then explaining his exotic taste in reading material after his mom unpacked his stuff while he was in school.) Waiting a judicious period after the moving van and family rolled off—seven minutes—I giddily claimed the hideaway as my own.

The chamber, one-and-a-half by three meters, was the otherwise enclosed under-staircase cavity of the apartment building's first-floor run. Replete with candle in wine jug, vintage rugs, thin mattress, blankets and pillows and the aforementioned nudie mags, it was possibly every city boy's dream hideaway. The innermost vault of the Great Pyramids of Egypt paled in comparison: it wasn't next door and accessible to a curious and privacy-hungry thirteen-year-old.

In a fit of whimsy, I dubbed it Dipsy Doodle Detour. It became my select neighborhood set's inviolate refuge, a sanctuary where we felt blissfully safe from meddlesome adults. Apartment tenants would trudge up and down the thickly-carpeted stairs sloping over our heads, invariably causing certain tread boards to squeak. We'd break out in muffled laughter, probably leading tenants to complain to the manager about mice in the walls. But our secret place was never discovered; we were in another galaxy.

Together in the hideaway—steeped in sweet-musty scent of long-stored cotton sheets pilfered from home—buddies and I eagerly poured thru the magazine treasures by flickering candlelight and EverReady flashlights. We were pirates, deliriously fondling gold pieces from a laden brass-bound chest: There was *Modern Sunbathing, Sundial, Nude Living...* Some of the photos were in color, others in glorious black and white. Instant connoisseurs of the female form, we savored them all. We oohed and ahhed our votes.

It was a new universe that met our eyes, one inhabited by amazingly naked, happy-looking girls and women enjoying sunbathing, dancing, gardening, eating, volleyball, beauty pageants, all kinds of things, without a stitch on. The boys and men in the pictures, not wearing clothes either, looked happy too. Clothing appeared nonexistent except for the occasional cowboy hat, Indian bonnet or sombrero.

What made these magazines special was how the people in them looked so relaxed and accepting of their bodies, going about happily undressed in real, everyday life, not doing posed cheesecake shots under artificial studio lighting and throwing the camera *you-naughty-boy* looks. One picture I still remember: a congenial group of three or four mixed teens, one girl with WE LOVE

ELVIS! painted on her back along with a guitar sketch, standing around a clubhouse, looking like normal teens except for being utterly naked.

Even tho budding hormones eclipsed any possible academic interest this wannabee sex maniac might have had in the wholesome benefits of living out-of-doors out-of-clothes, I was struck by the purity and goodness the nudists radiated. A tiny mustard seed found root in me, an inner voice saying *this is the way it should be*—even as it was all but drowned out by the manic choruses of *oohh-oohh*s, *hubba-hubba*s, and *oh-mamma!*s.

☀

In amazing synchronicity, a fetching new neighbor my age moved into that apartment building's now-vacant flat. Fresh from Texas, Dawn had blossomed early and was a self-proclaimed sex-pot. And—sweet savior of horny youth—she took a fancy to me.

I promptly showed her my hideaway.

Concerned for fire safety, I'd earlier upgraded the one-candle illumination with electric lighting by running a long extension cord in from a garage outlet and hoped no one would wonder where it led. I liked muted lighting, and a three-watt nite-lite panel did the trick. As the newly installed keeper of the hideaway, I told the neighborhood gang I wanted exclusive use of the place until further notice. They kept away, but not without snickers and the inevitable sing-song, "Zet and Dawn, sitting in a tree…"

By dim turquoise light, casting a magical, otherworldly glow on us, Dawn and I shared worlds of sweet pleasure perhaps only curious fourteen-year-olds can know. Over time, we graduated from first shy kiss to making out like the world was on fire, to heavy petting, to playfully undoing and pulling off each other's clothes, to lying down naked and making out with feverishly renewed ardor.

We never went all the way; we didn't want to. At that age, in that era, making out and petting, naked *and* prone *and* in a snug, safe hideaway, was already triple-heaven; who could ask for anything more? We leisurely explored each other's bodies—terra incognita—to our hearts' content—chastely keeping clear of genital touching. Sometimes we fell asleep together, naked in each others' arms, the scent of her hair like wildflowers after a rainstorm. Her breath sometimes smelled of garlic; my initial dislike of the pungent scent transformed to a turn-on as I linked it to our swirling thru a wonderland of pink passion.

Once, while she was sleeping, or pretending to, the mood lite off, I discovered a new, irresistibly pleasurable sensation. By thrusting my pelvis against Dawn's backside and sliding along her bottom, an exquisite excitement grew inside me—especially in my penis. Suddenly I orgasmed for the first time, spurting all over her back. My mind reeled in mixed shock and delight, heart pounding, trying to grasp what had just happened; I never knew peeing could feel so good. After a while she awoke, or pretended to. She said, "Hey, what...?" and stopped. She no doubt felt something wet and sticky on her lower back, but decided not to call me on it. I never volunteered to explain, too confused and ashamed for having involuntarily peed on her.

It was the only time that would happen in our continuing trysts; I learned not to let myself get too excited, coming as close to the precipice as I dared in our naked make-out sessions without leaping off the edge—until later, alone: I'd discovered a fun new solo pastime I pursued with noteworthy dedication.

Part of me was in paradise with Dawn, but part of me was still burning in hell. You'd think maybe I'd have felt all right being seen by one so intimate with me, especially since Dawn wasn't shy about her own nudity, having a far healthier body acceptance— and an attractive body that thrived on appreciation from the right callow admirer.

But no, my body shame went deep; my closet-nudist status

remained inviolate. I didn't know how to be myself naked with another beyond groping in the dark. I'd feel like a bug under a lifted rock whenever Dawn, looking for a stick of Beeman's gum, might accidentally-on-purpose shine the flashlite on me. *Don't look; I'm hideous.* My body was normal, mind you, no gross deformities, no missing testicle or extra toe, yet I felt unaccountably ashamed of it. My perpetual salute to her charms didn't help any; it struck me as grotesque somehow, like an injured foot swelling to unsightly proportions—a foot that wanted to pee on her.

Our year of blissful teen pleasure ended with the second major bust of my home years.

We'd taken our act on the road, as it were, after I told my parents I wanted to sleep down in our basement rumpus room for a change; the piano had been moved there, lending plausibility to my ruse. At nite she'd slip in via a side door leading from a handy private corridor off the street. I forget what excuse she gave her mom, if any, to go out, but her mom was liberal-minded and trusted her daughter's judgment. The place sported a comfy old blue corduroy couch we took for a spin. Dawn and I didn't dare get naked there; the place was a billion times riskier for getting caught than our secure fortress. But we'd lay together under a blanket, various hooks, zippers and snaps undone for comfort, while pawing, cuddling, and kissing. She sometimes drifted off to sleep a while before slipping back home.

Dad, no dummy, suspected something was up. One nite he came down the stairs so suddenly it left me no time to wake Dawn up, let alone spirit her out. I leaped up, ran over to the doorway and tried desperately to divert dad into the hall with some top-of-the-head prattle or other. I'd hoped against hope Dawn would hear us, wake up, and make good her escape. Alas, Dawn was a heavy sleeper and Dad wouldn't be fooled. He made an easy end-run around me, zeroing in on her and waking her with a nudge. At that point I slunk off down the basement hall, stunned we were suddenly busted after a whole year without incident.

I could only imagine what she must have felt: waking up and seeing my dad—craggy old man with dragon breath and rumpled hair, wearing his immaculate purple satin bathrobe—standing there one meter away, peering down at her, and me nowhere to be seen. Ever chivalrous, despite the circumstances, dad asked her if she wanted an escort the fifteen meters to her apartment in our abysmally safe, stolid neighborhood. She declined with a dispirited murmur and left, no doubt thinking me a no-good dirty rat-fink for leaving her to face the music alone.

What could I have done? Tell dad, *"Shh. She's sleeping. Isn't she a vision?"*

"She is that, Zet; sleeping like an angel. Sorry, didn't mean to disturb you, son. Have a nice nite."

In my dreams.

He caught up with me in the laundry room—an appropriately dank and hellish place, complete with flickering, ice-blue flame hissing inside the base of the gas water heater.

"Where did we fail you, son?" he opened with.

This isn't happening. No, please say this isn't happening.

"Don't you love your mother and me?" he wanted to know, pressing a red-hot iron of guilt into my ridiculously malleable mind.

Why are you asking me this? I screamed silently. I was numb, speechless; the room spun.

"I thought we raised you better than that," he pressed. "You've let us down," he lamented.

I nearly fainted.

The next day, my parents and Dawn's divorced mom called a summit meeting by phone, and dad decided on the same solution as with Karen and me six years earlier: we shouldn't see each other again.

No longer cowed by parental edicts, Dawn and I would still rendezvous to fool around—mostly over at her dad's home when he was away on business trips—but it wasn't the same. My newfound world had dissolved in an instant, paradise lost, replaced with a helpless sense of futility for having sensual feelings at all— and a fresh truck-load of guilt.

☀

At least I could still exercise some authority over my own body: Full of low-key daring, I quit wearing underpants.

As I said, once puberty hit I became keenly re-sensitized to my body. My crotch felt irritated, smothered and wedgied in briefs (no boxer shorts in our family); I wanted to give my newly-appreciated equipment room to breathe.

I spent the mid-60s weathering regimentation at a teeming high school: our class alone had over five hundred students. I'd felt painfully self-conscious dressing and undressing in the gym locker room before; now I worried I'd bring extra attention to myself and be deemed weird for breaking the time-honored dress code of wearing pants under pants. But body comfort was worth risking censure. I suppose I should've been thankful I wasn't expected to wear pants between my underpants and my overpants: *Look, Quimby's not wearing any middle pants. Weird!*

I also dreaded having to shower after gym classes. I was dependent on my textile armor to hide vulnerable, unexamined feelings. It was impossible for me to run the gauntlet of openly showering with thirty raucous, indifferent or equally terrified peers without tender emotional sensibilities getting mangled. Decades later, when I read about how some teens chose to shower in their underwear, or suffer their dried sweat the rest of the day sooner than undergo the nude regimentation of public school showers, I understood all too well.

I turned the tables on the school system's custom a few years later, using fear of open showering to get my junior college degree. By my last semester I'd royally resent having to take P.E. I didn't, and so didn't qualify for my humble associate-in-arts diploma. Deciding I wanted that degree after all, I hatched a plan. I went to the college dean, explaining my status and asking for a waiver.

"You needed that half-unit of P.E.," he told me in his posh office, reeking with tenured authority. "Yet you say you had no medical excuse. I'm sorry, but I don't think I can help you. Suppose you tell me why you think I should give you one."

"Well," I said, feigning embarrassment, "I'm *gay*. It was just too ex*cit*ing showering with all those guys." (I think I might have batted my eyelashes at this point.)

His authoritative demeanor crumbled: I might as well have said I was a contagious leper. He hastily assured me he'd okay a waiver and rushed me out of the office: *I shook his hand.*

In that homophobic era—before a modicum of understanding and tolerance evolved for those with unconventional sexual proclivities—it was that easy. I wasn't proud of my ruse…hell, yes I was. I'd always thought I was one who, as Shakespeare put it, hadn't "the craft to color," and the dean had bought my act.

❋

I was thankful for a handful of friends in high school. Whether they liked me for the way I was, or despite the way I was, or both, we were all discovering ourselves together. There was Richard, Gail, Kate, Jennie and Sam. (They'll get a better introduction later on.)

Unlike many of my classmates—Richard was cross-country,

Sam was varsity basketball and Gail made state finals in tennis—
I had zero athletic ambition. But I enjoyed running like a gazelle,
on my own, away from school grounds, stretching my wings while
venting my inexhaustible supply of teenage angst. One year I
found myself pulled to run in the City's annual Bay-to-Breakers
race.

The footrace spanned the town's eleven kilometer width. It was
a straightforward race then; anyone trying to run the race naked
then, as they did later, probably would have been nabbed for indecent exposure the first 50 yards.

I had enuf stamina, barely, to finish the course, along with
16,000 others, placing somewhere around 15,997[th]. I think I beat
out three of the seven participating septuagenarians. *The
Chronicle*, listing each runner's time and placing the next day,
goofed on me, placing me in the top 200. My school's long-distance coach spotted my outstanding, albeit fictional, time, and
hounded me to go out for the long-distance team. I declined.
When I ran I wanted to *go* somewhere, not run in circles, and I
didn't want to "beat" anyone; I was pretty damn uncompetitive,
actually: winning at something left me empathizing too much for
the disappointment my vanquished opponent felt to enjoy my personal victory.

※

Believe me, the 50s and early 60s were not the body-friendliest time
to grow up in—rock 'n' roll, beatniks, and Hula Hoops notwithstanding. Not for me, anyway. Things were worlds better than during the world global conflict in the preceding decade, for sure, but
now we had escaped into some weird neverland in efforts to recov-
er from the shock war had unleashed on our collective psyche.

At least I'd discovered thru the nudist magazines that there was
a world of unabashed naked people out there—*somewhere*—hav-

ing naked fun in nature, even as I stayed imprisoned in the City, in my wingtips, Levi's and Pendletons, gilded in guilt and feeling like a gelding. It gave me hope the world could actually be a nice place to live.

But while I now knew there were people totally comfortable with their bodies, living blithely without clothes in nice weather, I was still clueless there was a world of different *food* out there as well—tasty, easily digestible, plant-based food that didn't involve cruelty to animals. Oh, sure, I knew about the hole-in-the-wall "health-food" stores in town, with their shelves of strange supplements and their cabbage-and-kohlrabi-juice cocktails at the Formica counters. My friends and I used to put them down as too weird for words—one in particular near our neighborhood: Arnold's Health-is-Wealth Shoppe.

One day we made a bet over who would chicken out first standing in oncoming traffic. I lost, deciding I'd rather be out a few coins than road kill. We'd agreed that whoever lost had to go in Arnold's and drink a large glass of spinach-beet-garlic juice. (We tried to think up the grossest combination.) "We'll be watching thru the window to make sure you do." I went in, hoping the clerk wouldn't recognize me as the one who threw a pork chop smeared with ketchup thru the door before bolting, a month earlier, just to gross the place out. He prepared my order without comment. But as he took my money he did favor me with a *"are you sure you want that?"* look. Actually, it wasn't that bad, considering; my taste buds felt they'd entered a weird parallel universe of taste sensation. But I made a great show of wanting to retch to my watching buddies.

Even tho part of me enjoyed that drink, I pretty much marched lock-step with what passed for food to the industrialized world's peculiar way of thinking. I regularly blew my allowance at a nearby Mel's Drive-in, scarfing down seventeen-cent cheeseburgers and greasy thirteen-cent French fries, washed down by twenty-cent vanilla malt milkshakes. And then I wondered why my face broke out.

One time we received a visit from Aunt Zelda—okay, here I should explain a couple things. First, I had a *lot* of aunts and uncles, on both sides of my family: dad was one of seven, mom one of twelve. As the observant reader may have noticed, everyone on mom's side had names beginning with Z—as if maybe we were characters in a play by someone with a Zorro complex, wanting to carve Zs everywhere with bold strokes of his pen. The truth lies in a long family tradition, one I didn't learn about myself until many years later.

I was shocked (and intrigued) to discover that ancestors on my mom's direct line were almost turned back at Ellis Island as undesirables: Apparently, on the way over, after interminable days of nearly asphyxiating down in the crowded passenger hold, they dared to take a deck-side nude sun-and-air bath; they were used to nudity at home, and hoped no one would mind. People did. But for the intercession of a kindly immigration officer named Zachary, their huddled masses would've been sent packing back to the Fatherland and maybe I'd be writing this in German. In eternal gratitude to the official for getting them in to the New World, they vowed to name all their future children with names starting with a Z.

Dad, thinking it too cute to name his kids with the same first letter, had protested naming *any* with a Z; hence euphonious names like Clyde. But he relented with me, if only to please mom, who'd worn down his resistance by then.

"All right, but *'Zet'*? What the hell kind of name is *'Zet'*?" he'd wanted to know, as mom later told me.

"Well, what kind of name is *'Anatole'*?" she'd replied. "I just like it, that's all, don't ask me why. It has a zip, a zest, a certain *je ne sais quoi*. It evokes a feeling, like a blend of *zebra* and *zephyr*."

Dad finally conceded, mumbling how "I married a loony-tune, and zat's ze truth."

Anyway, Aunt Zelda was visiting from Florida. She sported a

tawny tan and radiated such vitality I wondered if maybe she wasn't one of that exotic breed known as a nudist. I didn't dare ask, tho, especially in front of dad. It would've sparked as explosive a situation as if I asked if she'd voted for JFK. (Dad was an arch Republican, who mourned for our nation the day he was elected.)

Dad absolutely forbad mom from giving me any ideas by ever sharing with me any of the crazy lifestyle her nonconformist relatives led. But I'd find out anyhow, when I was eighteen and hung up over a world of things.

One evening, while dad labored late in the textile mines down in the garment district, mom came down to the music room where I was practicing piano; most of the bridge chords on "Alley Cat" were eluding my determination to figure out without buying the sheet music and laboriously deciphering the dot code. (Little did I know: that bouncy little tune was to become my theme song for the life I'd live in a few short years.) I took a break from my frustration. Mom was clutching an old envelope.

"Zet, I want to talk to you. I'm concerned about how you seem…well, uncomfortable with your body. Some of that's natural at your age, I suppose, going thru hormonal changes and all, but…well, you seem to be having an extra rough time of it. I know your father created some setbacks, the way he reacted over you and Karen, and then later with Dawn. I'm sorry now I didn't try to intercede.

I was staggered. Such frank discussions were unheard of at our house. She was bringing up issues I'd never talked to anyone about and liked to pretend didn't exist. I didn't know what to say; I said nothing.

She plunged ahead like she'd been deciding what she wanted to say for a while, and a dam was bursting inside her. "The way we raised you to conform to society's big bugaboo about nudity probably did more than anything to make you feel uncomfortable with your body; I'm sorry for that. All parents try their best, you know, but it's always on the job training, and society's rules are sometimes…well, nuts."

"Oh, you did okay," I mumbled.

Then she floored me. "Maybe it might help if you knew the truth about my side of the family." She looked significantly at the envelope before handing it to me. "You should know that you come from a long line of nudists."

"No—really?" I was thunderstruck.

As I lifted the flap and pulled out a pile of old snapshots, lost in a daze, she went on. "I sort of broke the pattern—obviously. But I remember how you were a natural nudist as a toddler, more than the others, and it broke my heart to have to make you wear clothes."

On top of the pile was the photo of Great-Uncle Zep, whom I recognized from an old framed portrait of him in the living room. But he was dressed in that; here he was unabashedly naked, sitting amid the happy group by a creek.

Mom laughed nervously, knowing dad would explode if he knew what she was doing. She looked around, as if to make certain he wasn't there. She leaned over and spoke in a hush.

"Zep was my favorite uncle. He never pushed his beliefs on anyone, but his enthusiasm was so contagious he won lots of converts to the nudist lifestyle."

The next photo was of Aunt Zelda, standing naked in front of her modest nudist resort with a blue ribbon and scissors for what looked like an opening day ceremony. That answered that question. For a second or two, I felt weird seeing her naked.

"Your Aunt Zelda was the co-founder of a Florida resort called Sweet Haven," mom divulged. "Under other circumstances, maybe I'd've helped Zelda run her place. Probably not, tho; I just loved clothes too much to want to not wear them for long—the feel, the fit, the colors... It makes me want to go shopping right now, just talking about them. No, I'd probably have worked Sweet Haven's reception desk dressed to the nines, and newcomers would've come in and gotten thoroughly confused, thinking surely they were in the wrong place."

She went on as I leafed thru the other photos in a daze. There were a few more of Zep and her sister's resort and one of a family gathering in Florida. "…and anyway, better late than never: I want you to know there's nothing shameful about the human body; really.

"Your dad's always meant well, but you can't imagine how frightful people's body attitudes were when he was growing up. He took you to the Olympic Club pool that day at my insistence; I thought it might help you. I realized afterwards you were left more confused than ever.

"I've wanted to have this talk with you a long time, but your father forbad it. You see, I finally had to go behind his back so I could live with myself. I know you'll keep our little talk a secret, won't you?"

"I can't even *imagine* telling him about this." I shuddered involuntarily.

"Good. Once you get out from under the home nest soon, I honestly think you might be happier if you looked into pursuing my family's lifestyle, see what it's all about. It wasn't my cup of tea, but I think it might suit you. Call it your old mom's intuition."

Quickly changing the subject after she realized I was blushing like a schoolgirl, she asked if I'd finished my homework. Before going to my room, I recovered my wits enuf to ask if we could get a copy of the group photo made and she agreed, with the proviso I keep the project secret. I'd stash the photo in a slit in the album's back inside cover and never show it to anyone until on my own.

It took a month before we tracked a mail-order photo lab that'd re-print the 5 x 7 black-and-white of Zet and his skinnydipping friends that still graces my family album.

FIVE

People today are still living off the table scraps of the sixties.
They are still being passed around—the music and the ideas.
—**Bob Dylan**

THE FIFTIES and early sixties witnessed fresh enthusiasm for getting naked more often. This included a low-key popularity of nakedness within nonconformist beatnik circles. But nudism largely remained body freedom practiced by the few, in segregated compounds, removed from everyday living, by membership only.

Of course, unorganized, isolated nakedness was not uncommon: Multiply that stray naked boy precariously perched on a rooftop by perhaps hundreds of millions worldwide—each seeking a secluded spot in which to enjoy being nude amid an over-clothed world—and you get an idea of the situation.

We were a planet of closet nudists.

Society had a long way to go before more than a tiny minority of people, viewed askance as eccentrics at best, found the idea of getting together socially, free of clothes, nothing but shocking, weird, or idly arousing. It was a bridge not crossed, a song not sung, a crazy aunt kept locked in the attic nobody talked about.

And skinnydipping on public lands? "Why, you could get

arrested for something like that!"
Come the hippie movement and the cavalry had arrived.

❋

Each generation has fresh notions how to live, often at odds with the proceeding one, taking for granted their elder's hard-won achievements, even while enthusiastically building on them as their own. My baby-boomer generation came of age at a dreary, war-haunted, rock-bottom, time-to-drain-the-pool point in time. A lock-step mentality of dull conventionality and blind obedience to a rigidified State prevailed, while an imperialist war raged far away my peer group was forcibly drafted to fight and die in.

One of an illustrious company of 77,702,865 Americans born between 1946 and 1964, I was ready to go to Canada if called. No way would I be part of a murder machine. But I lucked out with a high lottery-draft number—they'd called one thru 200 and mine was 211—and I was thus spared the ignominy of fleeing my country to avoid being ordered to take up a gun or rot in jail as a conscientious objector.

I came from venerable draft-dodging stock. Mom's Uncle Oswald fled Germany for America in the 1880s to duck being conscripted by the Kaiser to fight his imperialistic war in Russia. His father Otto had six other sons variously approaching draft age (plus four daughters) and lacked any abiding affection for the Kaiser. Solution: Great-Grandfather Otto sold the farm and moved the family to America.

They settled in Florida. Offspring married and raised flocks of kids. Some eventually got swept up in the nature-cure movement, spreading the gospel of natural, raw foods and cooperating with nature for health and happiness. Great-Uncle Zeus pioneered the first health food store in Tallahassee. He often locked horns with the medical establishment for recommending easy cures for shoppers' maladies that cut pill-pushing doctors out of the picture. They threatened to take him to court and close his business for practicing medicine without a license if he didn't quit dispensing free advice. Great-Grandfather Otto, a farmer all his life, took up growing fruit tree orchards. His son would cheerfully repel salesmen's pitches for chemical pest control and fertilizer.

Living in a sunny, humid clime as they did, many family members became de facto nudists, more for basic comfort than to embrace any "ism." "It just made sense," Great-Uncle Zeus wrote. "Without clothes, you stood a good chance of actually enjoying the climate; with, you only coped and kept peeling your sopping clothes away from the skin."

Mom, *not* a nudist, moved to San Francisco during the Great Depression of the 1930s, where she met dad in a Safeway store's produce section; they'd both reached for the same avocado.

Home was a half-hour walk from San Francisco's Haight-Ashbury, ephemerally the global epicenter of a grand cultural ferment destined to spark a leap in consciousness on the planet.

I came of age during the hippie culture's richest blossoming. I'd be won over almost instantaneously by the people daring to break free of the two-dimensional brittleness calcifying society, daring to reclaim their co-opted humanity, letting the chips fall where they may.

At first I'd believed the media's largely distorted reporting. One day in summer 1966, I walked the two kilometers over, cutting thru Golden Gate Park, trusty Yashika-D camera in hand. Ready to play tourist in my own town, I hoped to capture the funny furry people on film. Who were these malcontents with the audacity to make waves and threaten to upset society's nicely established system? These mysterious misfits with the temerity to rebel from our wonderful conformist order?

I strolled up Haight Street—Johnny Straight Arrow with a crew cut, head imperiously up his butt, one among the droves of your everyday people and the exotic new denizens milling the street. I soon spotted a group of three likely suspects for a photo, three cheerful longhairs sitting on apartment steps. I'd label it in my album "notorious hippies hanging out." Before I could snap a shot they raised their *own* cameras and pretended to photograph some blank-faced tourists aboard a stuck-in-traffic Gray Line bus taking pictures of *them*. I cracked up. I'd suddenly gotten my first glimmer of what the scene was about: Life was a play and we were all actors in it, willing or not. Chagrined, I put my camera away and relaxed into the scene some.

I wandered into a poster shop that caught my eye. Its artwork went beyond the pale of conventional sensibility, and for a moment shorted out my circuits. But if the front room was impressive, the curtained back gallery room, lit by ultraviolet blacklites, was staggering. There, an incandescent wonderland of intricate, inspired artwork, singing artists' surreal visions, drenched in brilliant fluorescent colors, leapt out from dozens of posters. They tickled me; they fairly gave off intoxicating perfume that melted my mind, the colors so vivid I could almost taste them: cherry red, electric lime, blueberry blue... I walked back out on the street, reeling in a happy daze.

As I'd only later learn and appreciate, I was a budding sensitive. Sensitives, depending on degree of attunement, can be intensely aware of other people's and object's energy levels and gain instant readouts on where others' hearts and minds are at. Even tho my hang-ups kept me from using my gift more effectively, I found myself making quick studies of the swirling energy currents along the fabled street—the exotic clothes, the psychedelic sign lettering, the music and the people—feeling my level of awareness soaring. Was it a contact high from the hundreds of psychedelic trips and stoned states of mind surging there, around the clock? If so, part of me approved, even tho it was two more years—until the very nite of Nixon's winning his first election, in '68—before I smoked my first joint, at 19.

Over several day trips that summer, before my senior year in high school started, I got increasingly complex readouts on the group energies. I saw plenty of what I later realized was run-of-the-mill nonconformist behavior, people flirting with letting go of the system's oppressive values.

But I also witnessed near-miraculous sights, sights that became forever etched in my soul's memory. Standing out like supermen and –women from the "weekend hippies" were genuine dyed-in-the-wool hippies, holy-stoned beings: flowing-haired, full-bearded prophets in biblical robes, staffs in hand, standing on corners bestowing blessings to every passer-by, fiery, unconditional love blazing from hearts split asunder; dazzling earth mothers in granny dresses, sunshine and flowers and visionary dreams pouring from compassionate eyes, yearning to nurture the entire world, gracing us with their presence.

They were so juiced and heart-centered, something stirred in the very core of me, and I leaned towards them as a flower towards the sun.

"Everybody's beautiful" was the message this seventeen-year-old ugly ducking heard, and I thought *where do I sign up?* Within two years I'd grow my hair long, *try* to grow a beard, start smoking pot, and begin transcendental meditation—all while still bunking at home. I was too shell-shocked by life to even consider running away from the security of the home fortress, bastion from the real world out there; although some of my peers ran away from clear across the country to join the scene I absently day-tripped in a half-hour stroll from home. But even tho I was hamstrung emotionally—more or less unable to access or convey feelings in conventional ways—my consciousness flew to other planets and back again. After a life-long slumber, I was awakening to life's infinite possibilities.

❀

Magic was afoot. A re-emergence of ancient wisdom and mystic knowledge flooded the hearts and minds of millions worldwide. Life was embraced as a miracle, worthy of celebration. The more courageous and valiant among us would come to rebel against anything and everything interfering with our living as free universal beings.

I hope you'll forgive the sudden royal "we." I indulgently allowed myself the conceit of basking in the reflected glory of my hippie peers and elders, aspiring to join their tie-dyed order, tho I'd be little more than a hippie wannabee all along, according to my own definition. But I was swept up in the spirit of things, the same as untold numbers in my Neptune-in-Libra, peace- and beauty-loving generation. I was on a contact high from the ocean of peaceful feelings inundating town, vibes one had to be either spiritually inert or metabolically challenged to *not* feel. (It wasn't all sweetness and light, of course; bad things happened; violent crime went on, the same as always. But to all evincing the slightest receptivity, the entire region was on a collective magic carpet ride, powered by the blessings of peace.)

Seekers of a better way of living left behind a dying order's empty food, conformist dress, poisonous drink and dubious medicine, the whole consumer society and its hollow, soul-destroying mechanization of humanity. Rejecting the artificial, people embraced nature and down-to-earth living again. We wouldn't fight their wars or cut our hair or shave our faces. (By the time I grew my hair long it was only a mildly nonconformist gesture, and soon long hair would become no more than the latest conformist grooming trend among the young; but for a while it was an incredibly daring statement, symbolic of boldly defying the prevailing clean-shaven, crew-cut conformity and blind obedience to a rigid state order and war machine.)

We refused to work jobs exploiting the worker and perpetuating a corrupt order (which, according to who you talked to, had you "working for The Man" at most any job). Many, dropping out of alienated lifestyles they suddenly found distasteful, often managed to get by on next to nothing, living off the fat of the land and kindness of strangers. Others carved out new work fields, doing things they believed in, on their own terms. Whatever the circumstances, people gave dedicated and enthusiastic focus to learning to live more naturally.

Forty years later I'd have a revelation: Tho unorganized and unlabeled—more likely because of it—*the hippie counterculture's organic way of living and reverence for creation was no less than a ten-thousand-fold magnification of Germany's turn-of-the-century, proto hippie naturmenschen movement, now spreading to a global level.*

Authorities—those dedicated groomers of *un*natural men—were not pleased.

I soon became part of one of the greatest generational clashes the world had ever seen. While one branch of the counterculture thrived in peaceable and creative pursuits—harmonious, Earth-friendly living and spreading good vibes—another branch "took arms against a sea of troubles," calling the social power structure out on its systemic corruption and hoping to force them to change. Or, if unable to, disable the machine any way they could.

Yet another branch, undoubtedly the most viable, integrated the two polarized mindsets, its pragmatic philosophy captured by the tongue-in-cheek advice, "Remember, kids, always keep a smile on your face as you smash the State." I took this to mean to keep a Gandhi-like calm even as you strove to correct injustices.

Alas, I was neither fish nor fowl. I was too hung-up, too much the sensitive artist, repulsed by gnarly confrontations and unpleasantness, to want to join the front line and help smash any state, thank you; too lacking in inner rootedness and clear mindedness to become one of the peace-and-love beings I admired.

I'd seldom enjoy social pot-smoking: Whenever the roach clip was handed to me, the "*'Ere, it's killer*" endorsement accompanying it—choked out like dying words of a prospector wanting to tell where the gold was hid—was something less than an enticement, along with the ungracious snort inevitably made as the person tried holding the hit and saying "'Ere" at the same time.

I felt like the fool on the hill of The Beatles song, who never showed his feelings. I saw the world spinning 'round—when I lay down and focused, I could *feel* it spinning 'round. I imagined a world without war, even if I was too hung up to offer more than a bubblegum peace. I did my own thing—wrote sheaves of poetry, rhapsodized at the keyboard, struck up deep connections with wilderness, and hitchhiked coast to coast and back again—trying to gain a momentum in my life, to shake free of a stymied past and embrace life.

I flirted with discovering who I was beneath the many encrusted layers of non-self. Like barnacles overtaking a boat's hull hampering smooth gliding on the waters, layers of illusion rendered me less than seaworthy. I could deal with only so much reality shock at a time, and so scraped gingerly.

While bolder, more together peers went full-tilt, digging personal changes by the fast shovelful, I scooped mine with a teaspoon, fearful of discovering *too* many of the illusions I'd invested so much time and energy into cultivating as real. I refused to believe I might have to tear down much of my reality-framework and start over if I hoped to be more than what Bob Dylan called "a neon Jesus, glowing in the dark."

My sister Sarah was the only other one in my immediate family who also heard the pied piper. She'd experiment with peyote, mescaline and psilocybin, write for the *Berkeley Barb*, join the Peace Corps from college and spend two years in Kenya, come back, help start an alternative health clinic, come out and join the gay liberation front.

We'd get high a few times together. Once we walked over to the Fillmore Auditorium two kilometers away with her girlfriend Sunny to hear the rock-jazz-blues fusion group Blood, Sweat and Tears. We immediately got stoned from the perennial joints being passed around the floor like mouth pieces by scuba divers short on oxygen tanks.

We rocked out in the vast, dim-lit chamber to the joyous wall of sound. When the group sang "And When I Die" and the brass spiraled upward, I began experiencing a metamorphosis, the music somehow transporting me to another realm. When they launched into "Spinning Wheel" I felt the whole universe suddenly opening and rushing thru me.

I peeled off my shirt in a burst of daring.

To my knowledge, neither of my brothers was ever even remotely tempted to smoke pot.

Clyde, who possibly missed his calling as a policeman, suspected I was partaking of the weed. One day, I came home from junior college classes to be confronted by him outside my room door. Doing his duty as a law-abiding citizen, in my absence he'd taken upon himself to search my premises for my stash. Sure he had me dead to rights, he glared at me in righteous wrath and held up the damning evidence: a clear baggie filled with...*pine needles.* (I kept them in my sock drawer as an aromatic sachet.)

My bursting out laughing didn't help future sibling relations any. He never found the stash, which was miniscule, as my ultra-sensitive system made for an astoundingly low threshold for any internal stimuli: one tiny pinner of Mexican leaf was good for three highs. I kept the stash hidden in the back of a certain plastic drawer in my cent-collection drawer bank—the one labeled 1909-S VDB. As that vintage was the holy grail of Lincoln-head cents and worth a small fortune, my fellow numismatic Sherlock might've had a clue had he'd spotted it. Imagining the worst, he no doubt thought I was the new neighborhood dealer, had a huge stash buried in my closet, and searched accordingly.

Clyde and my oldest brother Jason dismissed the psychedelic goings-on as so much drug-induced silliness mocking the established order and dead seriousness of life. Clyde would be astounded and dismayed, decades later, when some of his offspring became neo-hippies. He'd thought the 60s a one-time social aberration, stomped out of existence by the triumphant resurgence of conventional reality. He was reasonably sure the only possible counterculture left lurked in greasy-spoon diners. Imagine his dismay, then, when his daughter Susie quit college in the 90s to form an all-girls' punk-rock band, Tri-Dubya and the Dotty Calmers.

❁

As people of my generation parted company post-haste with old irrational ways—scrambling outside the box of limited perceptions and smug sensibilities with merry abandon—among the first to go were the guilt-ridden attitudes and exploitative dehumanization of the human body.

We rediscovered our bodies like long-lost treasures.

At nineteen, bursting with a newborn desire to get naked in nature, I hitchhiked over to a remote Marin county beach called Steep Ravine one day and dared to go ocean skinnydipping for the first time. While fear of being seen put a damper in my enthusiasm—even tho the entire beach was deserted—I managed to experience near-ecstasy feeling the swirling surf against my body, a soothing, tingling all-enveloping sensation that made me feel fully alive for the first time in ages. But it seemed so *illegal*, it was as if I'd gotten instantly addicted to some new mind-expanding drug. *("Psst! Wanna buy some Nood?")* Later, I enthused about the experience in my college's underground paper—anonymously, of course. Nudity and sex were still much the same to my still-virgin mind; the episode felt like an erotic experience, my writing a true confession for some pulp magazine:

They Called Me a Polymorphous Pervert
When I Made Love to the Ocean
But I Didn't Care
by Anonymous

We rediscovered a childlike sense of innocence in getting back to nature and feeling a nitty-gritty oneness with the earth element. If we went dirty and unwashed a while, earning the derisive label "dirty hippies," maybe it was only to get *grounded*, to reconnect with the planet and its essence, *dirt*, after having grown up in the too-often sterile and stilted middleclass lifestyle of the 1950s. Maybe we were intuitively emulating the belief of the City's namesake, St. Francis, that an unwashed body was a pious body. (In contrast, there admittedly *were* those who did seem to take some perverse pride in being as slovenly as humanly possible, thus helping provide currency for the derogatory label.)

Some felt the very word *hippie*, in and of itself was a derogatory label, a buzz word invented by conventional media to lump together and blur an incredibly diverse group of individuals who, to varying degrees, and for often very different reasons, chose to distance themselves from conventional society. It was inevitable a people striving to break free of a stifling order to embrace their authentic selves and discover a more relevant, fulfilling way of living would be summarily stereotyped by a conformist, label-happy world. The word did serve to distinguish a level of consciousness, of perspective, tho, and was offhandedly embraced by label-ees, employed with self-mocking humor, as in "What kind of hippie are you, cutting your hair for a job?"

87

An even more potent label bandied about within the countercul-ture, and for the same reason, was *freak*. The word became a term of endearment for people who, by virtue of letting their inner selves come out, warts and all, in a world that made it all but impossible to be yourself without first compromising yourself to the corrupted order, were indeed considered freakish. (It was a bit of a shock for more than a few of us, then, when decades later the word gained new currency to describe violent nutcases.)

Men's rough beards and long hair sent shock waves thru a clean-shaven, over-genteel world. Society in general, barring brief fads, had long been adverse to the hirsute look. In 1705, Peter the Great, trying to Europeanize Russia, actually taxed beards: whiskered men had to fork over 50 rubles a year for refusing to shave. Beard prejudice hadn't changed much since then.

In a fascinating reversal of logic, the same people insisting the rest of our bodies be securely covered fairly *demanded* to see one's face naked: You concealed your body inside clothes and you tenuously proved yourself a decent person; you let your head sprout hair and a beard and their minds scrambled to match you with the post office's FBI's Most Wanted photos. Such people considered beards and unshorn hair a sign of unseemly neglect, unrefinement, of lacking "clean-cut" gentility, although we made convenient exceptions for Lincoln, Jesus, Uncle Sam and Santa Claus. (Similar attitudes were expressed towards women choosing not to shave their legs or armpits or corral their hair into cropped cuts, embalmed with toxic hairspray.) The average man spent four months of his life shaving and nicking his face. Hippie sensibility deemed shaving and barbershop visits a waste of time, money and effort and let their heads go their merry hirsute ways.

☀

Not long after my first ocean skinnydip, I came back from my first solo backpacking adventure in the high Sierras in time to be best man at my brother Jason's wedding.   I was blissfully naked in the wilderness every day, hiking for hours. On day two, during a hike, I suddenly heard a distant but distinct voice saying "Quick, honey, hand me my rifle, I think I hear a deer." Rather than blow my non-cover by announcing my species, I took a chance and ran off like the startled animal he'd mistaken me for. Thankfully he didn't shoot. Maybe at the last he saw I was only a white-tailed human.

Back home, I brought back with me an effusive, wild joy communion with nature had instilled in me. Altho I dutifully bathed and donned a dreaded suit and tie for the church ceremony, I kept my hair bushy, risking offending anyone attending who favored the fleeced and shorn look. Sure enuf, mom's prim and proper best friend, Mabel MacGuckin, raked me over the coals in the church foyer after the ceremony.

"Why don't you get a haircut?" she demanded, livid, her eyes trained on my hair like a trigger-happy hunter—twin lawnmowers that would've put a marine-boot-camp barber's sheering determination to shame. I smiled wanly at her, not dignifying her words with a response. Like the Cat Stevens song, I felt a power growing in my hair, one that couldn't be ruffled by such small-mindedness; it was my freedom flag. Mom supported my right to forge my own lifestyle (if not the pot-smoking), thought Mabel out of line, and cut off relations with her cold. Like I said, the times were polarized.

Imagine: such anger over how one's *hair* looked.

✺

Uninhibited social nudity became commonplace in hippie circles, both in the seclusion of nature and sometimes amid the openness of city parks and fountains. Maybe it helped that we had another skinnydipping president in the White House: LBJ.

The advent of guilt-free body acceptance was extraordinarily captured in the tribal rock musical *Hair!* Having learned stage-craft at City College, I wangled a brief stint as substitute stage-hand for the 1969 San Francisco production. Cast members shed all their clothes at the end of one soaring number, bringing home the simple dignity and splendor of the unadorned human body. It was so hot back stage I felt like getting naked too, but I didn't dare. I suspect some of my more free-minded cousins might have, and thereby made the production's nudity more than a perform-ance. Each time the utterly juiced and naked troupe members strode by me as I busied with stage props, a surreal feeling swept over me; I tried, unsuccessfully, not to stare rapturously at the women's liberated breasts.

In more reflective moments I mused over how society appeared to be entering uncharted waters: *Naked in public: what a concept.*

Reflecting society's ongoing breakthrus in body freedom, in 1974 many of the nation's college students caught the wave and went streak-happy, daring to get naked in public, often running. In the exuberance of youth, they became obsessed with campus streak-ins, trying to outdo each other for sheer volume of naked partici-pants.

On March 5, during a magical spell of exotic weather, the University of Georgia, Athens campus was determined to beat out North Carolina. 1,500 nude students converged. Cousin Zor hap-pened to be there during his hitchhiking around the nation, and joined in. Over-reacting police, in part maybe deciding the campus was possibly getting *too* nude, in part reacting to a heated black student demonstration waged the same day against a visiting lecturer perceived as a racist, waded onto campus with tear gas, riot gear and gnarly attitudes, to disperse them. The students undoubtedly set a new record tho.

Zor nearly got arrested as an "outside agitator". "Oh, it was something all right," he wrote in a letter, "We felt like the whole world was going nude for a while—till the goggle-faced Martians landed and reminded us otherwise." Eleven days later, streaking students in Boulder, Colorado would number 1,200: close, but no joint.

I wondered if I would have dared join in. Other than in the shower room and the Olympic pool, I'd never been publicly naked beyond toddler years. The closest I came was getting naked in my college's piano-practice room, five years before streaking fever hit. Being naked, even in private, felt radical to me, and inspired more spirited renditions of "Feelin' Groovy" and "Sounds of Silence." I locked the door, tacked a sheet of paper over the small door window, turned off the overhead, got naked, and let it rip.

In 1969 John Lennon and Yoko Ono astonished the world by posing matter-of-factly nude on their *Two Virgins* music album, front and back. Among other things, they effectively protested the clothes-obsessed world and its all-pervasive body shame, which they clearly weren't buying into. Our college underground paper re-printed the picture on an edition's front cover, and the paper disseminated thru campus with the radioactive effect of a copy of a nudist magazine at a Baptist summer camp. On seeing it, I remember feeling a mixture of shock and admiration: two parts *how could they* and *why would they,* and one part *right on!*

The bolder among us learned to celebrate life free of many trappings of society. Women burned bras, freeing themselves of "booby traps"—or, as Dawn had called them, "over-the-shoulder-bolder-holders"—thus enabling fuller circulation of blood and lymph. Over-constrictive bras were thought by some to be linked to heart disease and breast cancer. Any comfort-compromising underwear—men's or women's—was suspect. And people bare-footed a *lot*, liberating poor over-shod feet, regaining a fresh connectedness with Planet Earth. Newly adopted clothes, besides being wildly cheerful—if not luxuriantly splendiferous—were often of natural, breathable fiber and generously unconstrained. I remember my color-thirsty eyes drinking in a feast of rich deep purple outfits many of the more free-spirited college coeds wore, along with their long, long hair, adorned with flowers and dabbed with intoxicating clouds of patchouli, cucumber and honeysuckle oil.

Meanwhile, the Madison Avenue world of fashion reflected the flirtation with greater body-acceptance thru the mini-skirt that rose shamelessly to mid-thigh, much to every hetero male's delight. Thousands of women around the world were arrested on indecent behavior charges—including my older cousin, Zinny, trying out the latest fashion while on vacation in Portugal: "You'd think they'd never seen legs before," she wrote in her journal. "They acted like I was *naked,* while I had on more than any woman ever wore at the beach."

Tens of thousands of schoolgirls were strongly reprimanded or ordered home to change; hems could be no more than a critical few centimeters above the knee: Exacting measurements were made, enabling so-inclined administrators to get a close-up of the offending flesh. And that wasn't even the later, more daring micro-minis and hot pants—often little more than loin cloths. The latter, originating with European street walkers, became briefly fashionable among daring "respectable" women with bodies to flaunt and/or statements to make: "It's my body; I'll wear what I want."

SIX

If slaughterhouses had glass walls,
everyone would become a vegetarian.
— saying

PART AND PARCEL to opening our eyes to ourselves and the planet we called home, environmental awareness took off as fast as clothes. A worldful of people had been scrambling at breakneck speed to keep the corrupt money machine in overdrive. The adverse affects to peoples' health and quality of life thru the attendant pollution of air, water, and earth had become so outrageous people started protesting.

Some of our political leaders, aiming for damage control, shared their storehouse of wisdom for safeguarding our human habitats. Vice president Dan Quayle tried clarifying the situation for us: "It isn't pollution that's harming the environment; it's the impurities in our air and water that are doing it."

Everyday people had a firmer grasp. Annual Earth Day celebrations, begun in 1969, raised awareness by showing ways to minimize our impact on the planet. Recycling, pre-cycling, alternative transportation, renewable energy sources, composting, and tree-planting all gained dedicated adherents. Attention was brought to bear on the growing greenhouse effect created by polluting industries and vehicles, overheating the atmosphere, causing the gradual melting of the polar caps, increasingly extreme weather patterns, and depletion of the sphere's ozone layer that protected us from excessive ultraviolet rays. It was hard to believe Mother Earth was a happy camper. The way we mindlessly destroyed the planet's life-support system and laid waste to precious resources, it was a wonder *she* didn't protest before she did, finally.

The Trust for Public Land, a conservation group, gave us sobering statistics in 2005. "Every day, America los(t) 8,700 acres of forests, farms, meadows and woods to sprawl. That means nearly 3.2 million acres of open land disappear(ed) every year." And it only got worse. A popular one-panel comic strip of the time, "Ziggy," captured the failure of some to grasp the bigger picture: a bearded, plaid-shirted lumberjack, axe over shoulder, spouts off to an ecology activist holding up a "Save the Planet" placard, saying something like, "The thing you environmentalists don't understand is that destroying the planet may be the price we have to pay to save the economy."

In the process of trying to turn things around, our efforts often went two steps back for every three forward. In 1990, for instance, hundreds of thousands gathered to celebrate Earth Day in New York City's Central Park; they left behind 154.3 tons of litter that took fifty park employees till the middle of the nite to clean up.

It became clear we were slowly killing ourselves and mortgaging our children's chances to live in a decent world. The wave of environmental concern sweeping the world brought pressure to bear on big business and government to stem the tide of planetary pollution. Results were mixed. Some businesses, seeing the light, responded and championed positive change by cleaning up their products and services, often at great expense.

Others, having too much money sunk in inappropriate technologies—and so little social conscience it could fit inside a thimble with room left over to hang out a **SPACE FOR RENT** sign—wouldn't lift a finger besides the middle one. Instead, they mounted expensive campaigns to green-wash their poisonous products, with television ads of animals frolicking and birds singing amid voiceover assurances the makers were working rapturously hand-in-hand with nature. They persuaded the dumbed-down and system apologists the only thing wrong was the damn militant environmentalists, out trying to disrupt the planet to make a fast buck. Them and the damn animal rights activists; and the damn ____. (One filled in the blank from any of a dozen maligned social conscience groups.)

The situation was so depressing that distancing ourselves from a lemming-like order, bent on mass suicide, and seeking out new ways of living appeared the only way to regain a semblance of sanity.

A cornerstone in building a more Earth-friendly way of life was bringing integrity back into our diets.

☀

Food at its best is medicine, nourishing our bodies, lifting our spirits, a shared communion celebrating life. Food had been organic forever until industrialized agriculture came along in my and my father's time, mucking with toxic chemicals. More at home in a skyscraper office crunching profit figures than tilling the earth, ag-biz-men degraded the purity of our food supply in their quest to industrialize farming and corner the food market.

Their de-mineralized, de-vitalized, chemically-laced fake-foods swamped us at every turn, threatening to sink our ship of health with every bite. Over-processed food, the lifeblood sucked out, left consumers with prettily-packaged remains, touted with bouncy commercial jingles and catchy slogans, fairly guaranteeing whatever money they didn't snag getting them hooked on life-destroying foods would go to their deserving cohorts in the high-tech medical world, who would try to arrest the damage done with their expensive band-aids that didn't address root causes, and, if that didn't work out, well, there was the deserving undertaking industry. (There was the Circle of Life and then there was the Circle of Strife.)

The whole foods movement breathed to life by the counterculture took matters in hand and alerted anyone not deaf to reason how poisonous their food supply had become. Until then, such industrial table faire was taken for granted as much as always wearing clothes—both matters were too far under the radar of mass consciousness to even be identified as problems. Now it became the mission of anyone wanting wholesome, unadulterated food in their diets to seek out the few natural food stores around. Such shops gave shoppers welcome alternatives to mainstream's fake food and dead-animal offerings by striving to stock only raw, organic, and bulk foods and herbs, supplying people foods with nature's vital integrity still intact.

Predictably in a greed-driven world, industries that once derisively laughed off more natural products, decades later would pretend to have championed it all along once they smelled money in it. They brought their prodigious powers of deception to bear, introducing products with the *appearance* of unadulterated foods. An entire new industry of watered-down offerings blurred the line and confused quality-seeking consumers. Triumphant shouts of "all-natural!" "no artificial ingredients or preservatives!" and "Whole Grain Goodness!" festooned the splashy packaging of what were still non-organic, over-processed food stuffs.

The pity of it was that many of these food makers actually *were* offering consumers something better than previous similar products, even if it was still worlds away from the living whole foods that their ancestors and descendents took for granted. Once the food industry saw organics taking off, they jumped on the bandwagon, and some of their less public-minded brethren sought to water down certification standards for what constituted *organic*.

✳

Plant-based protein diet became *de rigueur* within the peace-loving branch of the 60s counterculture. The thought of killing animals for our sustenance became repellent. (The more militant, bank-burning branch, in contrast, was too angry at the system to want to stop eating meat: it helped fuel their rage. Even one-time countercultural hero Ken Kesey, no militant per se, once said he was too mad to want to stop eating meat.)

The vegetarian movement represented a new threshold in human consciousness. Various peoples had reached the point they no longer felt the need to eat meat for sustenance and so left the age-old, violent omnivorous habit behind. People connected the dots: Those without the *stomach* to witness the cruel slaughter of animals no longer wanted to force their seared remains *into* their stomachs.

This was one reason; those studying Eastern religions endorsing non-meat diets learned there were *six* good reasons for going veggie:

1. Instills compassion towards the animal kingdom
2. Fosters personal health
3. Helps preserve Earth's ecology
4. Preserves human life
5. Helps feed the hungry
6. Inspires peace

The first two reasons grabbed me earliest. At twenty-one, I went veggie in 1970 fairly easily, along with six others at the little Berkeley communal house I briefly lived at before the song of the road beckoned. We'd decided to eat nothing moving faster than photosynthesis. I had zero-problem forsaking red meat, as I'd come to realize my digestive system protested sending it down meat to deal with, which often turned into a painful leaden lump. And it finally it dawned on me that if I couldn't kill the animal myself I had no business eating it. I'd never been a seafood fan either, beyond crabmeat and fried prawns and maybe fish 'n' chips—but I would sorely miss fried chicken and turkey a while.

Altho my dietary evolution was patchy, like most, I imagine, I began seeing the meat-eating habit as tied to a mainstream mentality incapable of extending compassion and sensitivity toward fellow sentient beings (beyond select pets and favorite wildlife). But Isaiah 66:3 put it plainly: "He who kills an ox is like he who kills a man."

Our resolve was, as communal member Gail put it, to eat "nothing with eyes." My older brothers once went fishing down at Crissy Field and came back with a dozen fish, snagged from the bay. They gutted them and, for some unfathomable reason, put the late fishes' eyes on *The Examiner*'s sports section out on the back porch. I'd looked at those shiny unseeing eyes in commingled horror and fascination, for a moment imagining they were catching the day's scores: *"Damn, Dolphins lost again."*

White sugar and flour were also verboten, dairy discouraged. Perversely, we tacked a garish poster of a hot dog in a bun slathered with mustard on the kitchen wall; it was akin to displaying a Playboy foldout at seminary school, reminding us what we were giving up. While I never felt any temptation to sneak off to McDonalds and snarf a Big Mac—unlike Bones and Charlene—white sugar was my downfall: I'd sneak in Hershey bars and Hostess Twinkies, gobbling them in the dark with guilty pleasure, while a current song lament poking fun at mixed success in keeping to a pure diet ran thru my head: "…but at night I'm a junk-food junkie…" I spirited the wrappers out, so they wouldn't be found and linked back to me. We could really turn food nazi on each other.

Even as we each had lingering animal-based- and processed-food cravings to wrestle with, we'd walk over to the little whole foods co-op with the eagerness of desert nomads approaching an oasis. Not just for the living foods the place teemed with, either. The store bubbled over with a down home ferment; one of people rediscovering the sweetness and savor of life, a people empowering themselves to break away from the artful imitation of life that had held us in its clutches like a python around a piglet, squeezing the life out of us.

Co-ops made a break from the shared-monopolistic order of the day: food consumers banded together as a non-profit service—for themselves and the public—cutting out retail middlemen and keeping food prices down to the bone and stocking only what the majority of members wanted. Our co-op was different from many of the time in two ways: the storefront ran on all-volunteer help; and we priced food items at actual cost—shoppers added a certain percentage on, according to whether and how much they worked the store. (Those who devoted at least twenty hours a month got a sweet deal: food at wholesale plus one percent.)

Food is personal and intimate. We feel that when eaten consciously, food is communion with the Divine; we were then beginning to glimmer this awareness. And beyond turning on to foodstuffs that actually *nourished*, rather than debilitated, us, our lives were further enriched by choosing food products grown, processed, distributed and sold by people mindful of this intimate role. We became part of a cultural renaissance making food a tribal thing, something each of us shared within the spreading network of like-minded beings. Emerging out of the depths of an unimaginably corrupt Babylon, we'd rediscovered the vital importance of wholesome food and turning each other onto it. (*"Forget that converted rice, man; it's heathen. Here, try some of this basmati; guaranteed to tantalize your taste buds."*)

The politics of food amazed us. Grasping how something so basic, so vital to our health could be sacrificed on the altar of greed, we realized how much the whole system was shot thru with rank underhandedness. The industrialization of food-growing, along with food processed to hell and gone, powerful lobbies and over-centralized distribution, all rendered the entire mainstream food supply suspect. Mountains of pesticides, insecticides, and chemical fertilizers were used to squeeze out bigger crop yields, but at an exorbitant cost: producing poisoned food (shamelessly riding on foodstuff's age-old reputation for wholesome goodness); establishing store prices laden with the hidden costs of subsidized water, fuel and transportation and attendant pollution of vast, centralized farms working the land to death; and driving countless smaller family farms out of business by locking in a system favoring purchasing only from such industrialized farms.

Money was tight in our bungalow. Dad cut me off from a generous living allowance after I quit school. It was just the wrong time to be in college, with the cultural renaissance on the streets teaching me more of what I needed to know. "If you can't make it on your own now, then the hell with you," dad said after grudgingly helping me move my stuff in and checking out my long-haired, bearded and bra-less communards, who he was positive were brainwashing me into becoming a hippie-pinko-commie-no good.

After an over-protected and privileged upbringing that sheltered me from the coarser side of life, I'd soon learn how the other half lived. It was reality shock and then some.

We complemented our basic stash of foods—brown rice, beans, millet, lentils and such—with the generous produce offerings from the supermarket Dumpster conveniently located across the street. The idea of routing thru a waste container for food attracted me about as much as the thought of opening a cadaver. But hunger was a humbling motivator, and the sudden quest for survival abruptly dethroned any over-genteel sensibilities. The store regularly threw out tons of perfectly good food (if insecticide-laden, chemically-fertilized produce could be called perfectly good). I was dumbfounded how wasteful the system was. While millions went hungry, others callously threw away edible food by the truckload. Uncompassionate corporate heads preferred tossing out cosmetically blemished and ripened food like so much trash than see it fill the hungry bellies of those who couldn't afford to shop in their stores.

Fortunately, backroom workers let us get away with our periodic Dumpster raids; I don't think my overweening pride could have taken being chased off for trying to "steal" their waste. (Years later, I'd experience having a malicious worker knowingly throw a box of discards right on top of me as I routed thru his Dumpster; *that* was humbling.) The workers probably earned paltry wages for all their sweat and knew how tough it was making ends meet. But I heard tales of other supermarkets sprinkling bleach or detergent over their rejected produce, to ruin it for gleaning. (In later times, such foods were often rerouted to free-meal kitchens, after gleaning advocates had appealed to the consciences of store owners, who realized they'd generate good will from it.)

❋

I've been a vegetarian now for over ninety years, vegan the last fifty-five. I've kept my meat-free diet intact the whole time, except for a few brief lapses: once when I reverted to poultry for a few weeks, thinking I wasn't getting enuf protein from plant sources; another, earlier on, when for the same reason I ate a bologna sandwich in a moment of madness—and that nite dreamed I was a pig being chased thru a slaughter house by a butcher with upraised clever.

As I said, my philosophy was if I knew I couldn't kill it, I had no business eating it. I was no hunter—or fisherman either.

At age ten, I caught a fish while out in a rowboat with my dad on Yellowstone Lake. I gagged at the campground table during dinner, trying to down bites of its fried carcass, after dad insisted I eat what I caught or it'd be wasteful. I couldn't appreciate the lesson in frugality then; I kept remembering how the poor fish frantically fought for its life, flopping about in the boat bottom, and dad yelling, "Put it out of its misery!" It was the first and last time I ever went fishing. Even so, for another ten years I'd disassociate my continuing animal-based diet from the abuse and life-taking reality behind it, which our meat and dairy industries were so good at disguising. Every body needed milk, steak grew hair on your chest, and chicken was finger-lickin' good.

Killing animals was so ingrained in America, the common slang word for money—*bucks*—echoed it. During the first half of the 1700s, skins of male deer, or bucks, were traded heavily on the American frontier—a quarter to a half a million each year. Buckskins soon became referred to as *bucks*. Hunters and traders reckoned earnings and rates of barter exchange with them. If a man said "I've got ten bucks," he meant someone had skins ripped off the carcasses of ten slain deer. By 1856, the word had become synonymous with *dollar*.

Some of my friends dearly loved their meat, and I tried not to pass judgment on their diet; they tried extending me the same courtesy. Relatives weren't always so accommodating. For decades after my diet switch, when visiting my brother he always asked me pointedly, "are you *still* a vegetarian?" like it was a lingering illness I'd perversely refused to shake.

I was fortunate in later coming to lead a relatively low-stress rural lifestyle. Cynics of the time might've said this life allowed me the luxury of cultivating such lofty sentiments. But even when I was living on the street, I'd refused to eat meat: Once, I spurned the ham-and-mustard on white bread offered me at an Arkansas food shelter, opting instead to try shoplifting energy bars—a prospect more appealing to me than eating flesh and perpetuating the taking of life.

Meat-eaters loved to rebuke vegetarians' argument against killing animals for the pain and suffering it caused. They'd say carrots felt pain too, when cruelly yanked from the ground. "Plants have feelings too, you know, har-har." Of course, there *was* some truth to that. Even tho plants lacked brains and centralized nervous systems, unlike animals, there was an energetic disruption involved in harvesting them. It was for this reason members of the Jain sect wouldn't eat root vegetables—only fruit, seeds and grains. I'd met vegetarians who agonized over how the needs of their existence caused distress for other life forms. But living almost invariably meant some harm to other life and the environment. (Just in the process of bathing and scrubbing one might be doing in untold microbes peacefully grazing on one's dead skin.)

As Gabriel Cousens pointed out in *Spiritual Nutrition*, "…plants are our natural food and are much lower on the food chain than flesh food, so a vegan diet works to reduce the amount of harm in a dramatic way." A plant-based diet minimized disruption.

I had such a sensitive system I needed to minimize all the disruption I could. A book that came out decades later, called *The Highly Sensitive Person,* would at last help me understand why. Its author, Elaine N. Aron, Ph.D., set forth that in every species there are sensitive, aggressive, and hybrid members, a judicious mix of roles to help the species survive. The sensitive ones—of which I had no doubt I was one, among the 15-20 percent found in the human population—were the canaries in the coalmines, as it were, the ones warning miners when the air got poisonous (in their sad case by dropping dead). I'd realize in the years ahead that meat, dairy, alcohol, and tobacco had all been slowly killing me. Whenever I found myself 100 meters behind a diesel semi on the highway, my car's windows up, I'd gag on the trace amounts of carcinogenic fumes streaming in my air vent. While such things affected me and other sensitive types sooner than sturdier warrior-types, they'd likely affect others eventually.

Many schools of thought floated about on why people ate meat. I've already mentioned a few. A spiritual one: defaulting from the divine plan and plunging into age-old confusion and violence. And survival: Before tribes became agricultural or found places where edibles grew in plenty, animals represented portable, year-round food sources. Caveman TV dinners: just kill and eat.

As mentioned, persistent as the notion was that we *had* to wear clothes, so too was it genetically hard-wired in us from early times: *meat equaled survival.* Ages after we'd obviated the need for devouring animals to get by, tho, kids in school yards told terrified vegetarian classmates they'd die if they didn't eat meat. Until science irrefutably disproved the idea meat was "high quality" protein and demonstrating it actually shortened lives, we believed we needed to eat animal products to be healthy. The idea of *not* eating slain animals and dairy horrified people. (Oh, our planet were upside-down indeed.)

Another explanation for meat-eating I base on Aron's contention there were warrior members among Homo sapiens: possibly such persons felt a stronger need for the raw primitive energy meat afforded to do battle with the world (and, conversely, sensitive members felt the least, or no, need). Because such aggressive members usually dominated society, they might've impressed their own preferences onto others until it became the common mindset.

Another factor: Some felt meat-eating related to how stressful our lives were. Like with cigarettes: if you lived a stressed lifestyle, a cigarette's nicotine offered relief by fogging the brain and numbing emotions, giving you a mini-holiday from the trying realities at hand. It was perhaps similar with meat-eating: its gross energy helped the body deal with stress by resonating with the low energy fields of such situations, rather than resisting them (or avoiding them entirely), thereby keeping from getting over-whelmed. The coarse vibration of the dead food matched the insensitivity or outright brutality of the scene, putting one into a kind of weird, low-grade energy homeostasis in an otherwise intolerable situation. As long as we bought into cultural violence being the natural state of man in our "dog-eat-dog world," we considered eating meat normal.

In later years, some women friends who'd once been on strictly plant-based diets, often for decades, told me they'd let a little meat, poultry or fish back into their diets, either out of health concerns or some indefinable yen. Some said they felt their bodies needed the amino acids meat provided to tip the inner nutritional balance somehow. Some, with greater protein needs than men (other things being equal) appeared to have a meat craving possibly related to their hormonal roller coasters and monthly bleeding out of nutrients, wanting to get an iron-rich, concentrated-protein fix, and nothing less than meat could do the trick for them. I wasn't sure about any of that, but respected their beliefs.

Some felt astrology had an influence: Those with fire sun signs—Aries, Leo and Sag—had fiery natures that somehow resonated with meat eating. And those living in colder climates felt they had a greater need for meat protein, as could those engaged in hard physical labor. And, of course, many ate meat as comfort food, identifying eating various slain creatures with warm fuzzy memories of childhood—like sitting around the family table at Thanksgiving, with the headless browned carcass of an unfortunate bird, its vital organs now replaced with further delectables shoved up its butt, the center of avid attention. (I'd remember one year, growing up, looking at the carcass during grace, feeling thankful I wasn't the turkey.)

What we ate, how we ate it, why we ate it, touched on deep, unconscious realms of our psyche, no less than why we wore clothes or lived in cities or watched "Leave it to Beaver" re-runs.

✸

What I found endlessly fascinating—no less than the wildly differing attitudes towards nudity—was the vegetarian-diet ladder and its many rungs.

Those forsaking red meat only were on the lowest rung of the ladder. The flesh of cows, pigs and sheep mostly—also that of animals such as deer, moose and buffalo—made the "do not eat" list. They held the unwieldy label of being pesco-pollo-lacto-ovo vegetarians. It infuriated some pure vegetarians how a few called themselves vegetarian for just giving up beef and then continued eating pig, lamb, poultry and fish—like they were vegetables or something. Tho they exaggerated, giving up beef *was* a giant step to anyone used to a lifetime of hamburgers, pot roast and steak; barbeques, meatloaf, and veal parmesan—a radical first step in bucking the tide of popularly ingrained diet. Such people did so usually out of health concerns rather than any empathy for the animal kingdom. To help people in transition, while supplying solid, tasty nourishment, various food companies crafted ingenious meat-substitute creations from processed soybean and wheat glutton, which looked for all the world like the hot dogs and hamburgers they'd given up and didn't taste bad at all.

Next step up the ladder was the pesco-lacto-ovo vegetarian, one who surrendered poultry as well as red meat—again an unwieldy title and big step for those accustomed to Thanksgiving turkeys and fried chicken picnics their entire lives. Since, ounce for ounce, chicken was as high in cholesterol and saturated fat as steak, it was just as well for health reasons one surrendered poultry along with red meat.

Then came the lacto-ovo veggies, who in addition to quitting red meat and poultry, eliminated sea foods—quitting foods like fish 'n' chips, tuna fish sandwiches and anchovies on their pizzas. (Here I should add there were often variations in what was eliminated and what was kept in one's diet. Some quit seafood and continued eating poultry; others quit dairy but still enjoyed seafood, and so on. Krishnas gave up all animal foods *except* dairy, which they went wild over at feasts. At what point one strove to buy only organic foods also varied; this step became easier and more affordable once the organic food movement exploded in the early 2000s.)

The next rung up was a lofty one, one the majority of vegetarians (including me) hesitated to go for: giving up all dairy and eggs and becoming a vegan. If giving up meat was tough and poultry and seafood tougher, abandoning all dairy—ice cream and milk shakes, California omelets, mayonnaise, rich cakes made with milk, butter and eggs, buttered pancakes, egg foo yung—could be toughest of all. So many processed foods contained milk or eggs or both, it forced eaters to finely examine their diet, ethics and the entire food system far more critically. Since a vegan empathized totally with animals—believing they had the same right to live free and dignified lives as humans—she not only forsook eating anything from animals (including honey), but also any products derived from them: leathers, feathers, wool, silk, sinew and bone. Out of new-found love for all of creation, they strove to co-exist as equals with the animal kingdom, even as we do now.

The next rung up was equally daunting: raw foodism. Adherents held that heat destroyed food's living enzymes, needed to digest the food and utilize the fullest nutritive potential of whole foods. With the food thus lacking self-digesting enzymes, the body called on its own limited supply, diverting them away from more vital tasks like cleansing the liver. Further, they believed cooking food rendered it foreign to the body, and that mucous formed as a result to protect the digestive linings from being poisoned by such cooked food. In the process, this mucous lining seriously blocked assimilation of valuable nutrients. Depending on how much cooked food we allowed in our diets, the thinking went, the amount of food actually assimilable could be miniscule, leaving us hungry no matter how much we ate, and hence one in three people pursuing affluent diets in America were at once overweight and undernourished.

A raw food regimen required a radical revamping of diet, thoroughly undoing an entire lifetime's eating habits. It also required learning how to sprout, juice, and blend raw foods into tasty, nutritious meals (or settle for relatively Spartan faire). Such a diet differed from the way 99.9 percent of people ate. Practitioners discovered it fostered a stronger awareness of life's spiritual basis.

Then, lest one thought they'd reached the dizziest height in dietary evolution, there was another rung, that unicorn of diets: the Breatherian. This practice involves an advanced yogic technique to recharge the body with cosmic energy from the either, sun and air, as well as a highly advanced breathing method. Various practitioners adopted it if only to prove that man is Spirit.

I'd hung out on the lacto-ovo rung for decades, feeling advanced for having climbed that high, thinking I'd arrived, but over time forgetting why I went non-meat in the first place. For 35 years, I failed to realize my arteries could get just as clogged as a meateater's by scarfing dairy and eggs, with their equally high fat and cholesterol content; or that most animals raised for their milk and eggs had a later date with the executioner anyhow, after being cruelly mistreated their entire lives.

There were long stretches I was a de facto vegan, as I could often take or leave dairy and eggs in my diet. (I'd gladly given up milk and butter at the start.) All along, tho, I felt vaguely guilty aiding and abetting the theft of mothers' milk from calves, and helping perpetuate inhumane treatment of cows and chickens—but not enuf to quit eating cheese pizzas and egg omelets whenever I wanted.

Once I toured a big dairy in Southern California. It produced a popular brand of yogurt, kefir and ice cream stocked in natural food stores across the nation. I was a fan of their products, thinking their fruit-flavored kefir ambrosia. Then, during the tour, out of the blue I experienced a powerful psychic connection with a cow—an experience that forever disabused me of the notion animals couldn't communicate with humans.

The tour group was up on a catwalk looking down at the cows in a long row, all hooked up to mechanical milking devices. The cows faced away from our tour group. Suddenly, one turned her head and looked up *right in my eyes*; I mean, we locked eyeballs. I sensed some mournful, beseeching plea from this creature— which it now dawned on me was an intelligent, feeling animal—a trans-species plea to save her from the impersonal exploitation of her milk supply meant for her young, who were torn away from her almost immediately after birth, to suffer a similar fate if female, and be butchered as veal after four months of tortuous existence if male. Even after that connection, I'm ashamed to say, I kept eating dairy products sporadically. I told myself that, after all, they weren't being killed in the process of providing me ice cream and sharp cheddar, not knowing otherwise.

I only grabbed for the vegan rung decades later, after getting caught up in the new wave of dietary consciousness flooding humanity and remembering why I'd become a vegetarian in the first place. I read how cruelly dairy cows and chickens were treated; millions suffering living deaths, treated as unfeeling products—and then systematically slaughtered once they quit cranking out maximum product. And I learned of the overwhelming scientific evidence from objective nutritionists that dairy and eggs were just as bad for one's health as meat-eating.

But becoming an absolute vegan was well-nigh impossible, I learned, so embedded were animal products in *everything*: from home insulation, tennis rackets and certain beers, to supplement capsules, marshmallows and car tires. I found I was reluctant to give up the warmth of my down comforter and jacket I'd treasured for years, in denial they were byproducts of animal slaughter. I kept using them, now mindful of their warmth's slaughterhouse origin, until leaking jacket feathers flew in my face one windy day. I inhaled one and almost choked to death, being forcibly reminded of the violent demise of my once-feathered friends. After that I gave my feathered items away.

Curious, I read up on how modern vegetarianism got started. England among Western nations had long been a relative hotbed for vegetarian diet—ever since 1847, when the Vegetarian Society of Great Britain sprang up (possibly the result of a positive influence by their largely-non-meat-eating colony of the time, India, which deemed cows as sacred—not happy meals). As early as 1909, the Society reeled with debates over the ethics of continuing to consume dairy and eggs. The majority wouldn't even consider it. *"What, give up cheesecake? Surrender soft-boiled eggs? You must be daft, man. I'll gladly give up my beefsteak and pork chops, even my fish 'n' chips, but, by Jove, you go too far. You blighters leave my eggnog and custard pudding alone."*

A Londoner, Donald Watson, along with Elsie Shrigley and five others, made the decisive break in November 1944, launching the first vegan organization. (Watson coined the word from the first three and last two letters of *vegetarian*—as if the deleted "etari" maybe meant *dairy and eggs* in some strange tongue.) Watson was still with us in his nineties early this century, living testimony to the wisdom of plant-based diets.

The movement took hold in the United States in the late 1940s, and the American Vegan Society started up in 1960 in Oceano, California, by one Rubin Abramowitz. Over the years, movement members came to avoid any products connected to the exploitation of the animal kingdom—or tried to. They took a stand against wearing furs, feather and leather, hunting and fishing, zoos, circus animals, animal experimentation, animal sports racing, and even questioned the age-old custom of keeping pets. Too often pets appeared token members of the kingdom that people lavished attention on almost as if to compensate for killing and devouring others.

The sentiment, now universally acknowledged, was, of course, that man could not live the most positive and fully interconnected life so long as he exploited and enslaved other beings—animal or human.

SEVEN

*The time will come when men
such as I will look on the murder of animals
as they now look on the murder of men.*
—**Leonardo DaVinci**

IT'S HARD TO IMAGINE how people's eating habits could have ever been so rapacious. We flinch at the thought of killing and eating our fellow animals the way people then were horrified at the thought of eating one another or a beloved pet or any member of the its same species. George Bernard Shaw, a dedicated vegetarian, summed up the sorry situation for the ages: *"While we ourselves are the living graves of murdered beasts, how can we expect any ideal conditions on this earth?"*

The same upside-down, inside-out mindset of a world gone nuts had us in its grip, and we had to fight tooth-and-nail to free ourselves from its clutches. In a land where the blind led the blind, sighted ones were castigated as looney or dangerous—anything to preserve the poisonous worldview that enabled the ruthless exploitaton of the Earth and its inhabitants.

We've learned to work hand-in-hand with nature since the shift;

113

the attendant vibratory increase and dimensional expansion sparked an empathic consciousness. We meet all our food needs now, amply and heartily, without resorting to killing our fellow sentient beings or exploiting them for their body fluids and eggs, their wool or their feathers. We realize, as did more and more aware people during the last days, that the millions of acres taken up for pasturing and growing grain to feed livestock could have fed the entire world's hungry directly, and at a fraction of the cost. We might've reduced far more suffering in the old world if only enuf people had become aware how optimal diet precluded animal products, and had let their compassion extend to other species with their equal right to live. Slaves to an irrational dietary habit, they kept signing their own death warrants with their forks.

American Indians had been relatively cool about it. Tuned into the circle of life, revering all creation, they respected the animal whose life they took for sustenance, considering their lives no more important than the animal's. More thoughtful ranchers showed something approaching a similar respect towards their livestock, giving them free range and feeding them well and, when the time came, offering a quick death. But ultimately, no matter how you looked at it, it was still the violent taking of life.

Humankind kept up a Conquer Mentality: We subdued nature for our needs and accustomed habits. Most livestock was penned in inhumane factory conditions, millions of animals never seeing sunshine or feeling earth—unable to *move*, even—in their artificially-lit, cramped mountains of tiered warehouse cages. They were shot up with hormones and given poisonous junk diets to keep cost down and mad-chemist substances to artificially stimulate growth and antibiotics to forestall diseases brought on by such an existence, and slaughtered before even such measures could no longer keep them alive. Factory farms were so huge, people living downwind could come down with respiratory illnesses from the concentrated stench of tens of thousands of animal waste. And some scientists held that the greenhouse effect was worsened just as much by the methane released thru cow farts as by vehicles' carbon exhaust.

To the hippie way of thinking, we ate death every time we ingested meat—and not just because one was eating the flesh of dead animals. We were taking into our bodies the mortal fear flooding the bodies of the sentient beings, their whole lives if mistreated, and especially when sensing their coming demise, or gasping for life if it wasn't a fast dispatch (which it often wasn't). Some Indian tribes refused to eat animals that suffered long deaths, believing the fear was a toxin tainting the carcass.

Absorbing such fear perpetuated a vicious cycle: *fearful, we killed; eating more fear, we wanted to kill more*, or at least have others kill for us. The jarring energetic disruption created by the daily slaughter of millions of creatures to fuel such unnecessary and unhealthy animal-based diets was part and parcel of a negative-spiraling constrictive energy rampant in the world. It reinforced the climate of fear and perpetuated the mangling of nature, its creatures and their homes.

❋

Our homes, too.

The same constrictive force manifested in a heart-wrenching insensitivity to the habitats we carved out for ourselves. Non-supportive and nature-starved residential clusters grew like cancers, often right beside droning freeways. People no doubt kept their bodies covered partly from aversion to the mere thought of being unprotected in such degraded, non-tranquil environments. Pave paradise and get naked in a parking lot? Not.

This isn't to say freebody enthusiasts always strove to pursue tranquil, harmonious lifestyles, tho. Far from it.

In a complex, topsy-turvy world, one's personal evolution of lifestyle often made uneven strides. A person might fight tooth and nail for equal rights for women and minorities, but taking him to task for driving gas-guzzling behemoths was a waste of breath. Others might bike to work or strive for zero-pollution transportation, but you didn't dare suggest taking away their double-cheeseburgers. Some dedicated their lives to turning the world vegan and letting God's creatures live out their lives, but you mightn't expect bouquets for pointing out their resignation to needless clothing. Others found it a breeze shedding clothes but might support a lavish nudist lifestyle by investing in the armaments industry. A world peace advocate might not have time to recycle. A dedicated recycler might be an electrical energy hog. An energy-efficiency nut may be addicted to porn...and around it went.

Progressively minded people tried to minimize needlessly impacting the globe. But we lived in such a strange world, overloaded with wasteful, nutzoid ways, you'd have had to have lived in the hills, grown your own food, made your own clothes, used alternative transport methods, and had your own energy system to avoid taxing the sphere's strained-almost-to-the-tipping-point sustainability. Indeed, many of my generation, and other generations before us, did just that—or tried to. They heeded the call to "head for the hills, brothers." Some dug in, persevered, and flourished. Others gave up after a season's flirtation with country living and returned to city life.

Where the rubber met the road, many were too hooked on creature comforts and the dazzle of city-based enticements to want to forego them. The lure of ready-made homes, with infinite running water and electricity on tap; nearby restaurants and super-stocked food markets; shiny chariots; pumped-up entertainment venues; and, of course, city-based jobs to fuel such a lifestyle all conspired to win out over any noble-minded notion of chucking it all for some will-'O-the-wisp rural life. That, or they couldn't find a way to support their basic needs out in the boonies; or rowdy neighbors ruined it, or they moved back to allow their kids a better social life.

Or so *they* could have a better social life. Building communities in the boonies often meet with sketchy results, leaving residents the feeling they were hermits united in some unlikely refugee camp rather than part of any viable social unit.

Untold numbers remained rural dwellers, tho. And others fled to small towns—under population 10,000, in my book. (Some, in a fascinating denial of reality, referred to a teaming anthill of 100,000 inhabitants as a "small town.")

For myself, small-metropolitan boy that I was, I'd go country in due course, knew it the moment I gazed on the July 1969 cover of *Life* magazine when it came in the mail. I was 19, still living at home, but yearning full-bore to live amid the sweet peace of nature. The cover: an extended family photo of hippie types, drenched in a rough-hewn, grounded integrity and sporting fringed buckskins and granny dresses, posing in front of their backwoods commune. They looked as if they'd carved out the good life. I said *that's for me*. I'd spend the next ten years seeking a country commune to call home, an oasis of kindred nature-loving souls, working together to reclaim paradise amid a purgatory planet.

Those who did relocate to rural spots and towns of course found the fresh air, clean water and relatively quiet atmospheres, with room to breathe, lent themselves to feeling closer to nature, more in tune with her natural rhythms. As the big-city need for protective textile armor faded, people naturally came to feel safe going without clothes.

Those counterculture types who chose for various reasons to stay in big cities kept grounded thru meditation, yoga, tai chi, and walking barefoot on grass. They availed themselves of opportunities to shed clothes: at home, health clubs, or on weekend getaways. Amazingly, they were centered enuf to feel one with Earth even while smartly dressed in the midst of a teeming megalopolis. *More power to them*, I thought in admiration; *no way can I do that. Give me country or give me death*. Of course, many—especially in later years—were only putting in day appearances for their jobs, commuting two hours each way from their exoburb havens. There, they might live on five acres of rural tranquility and tackle much of their work home online or while ensconced on commuter rails, sipping stevia-sweetened mattes from stainless steel thermos cups.

※

The hippie counterculture had swelled to epic proportions, transforming my life and that of countless others. But it appeared to definitely run out of steam by the mid-seventies. On one level, it had all been a dream (perhaps even as the reader reading these words is in a dream). People had regained their senses after having experienced phenomenal St. Anthony's fire hallucinations by the universeful: they cut their hair, re-adapted to wearing painful shoes and choking ties and re-joined the "real world."

Many expectations of instant societal transformation and how to bring it about had proved absurdly unrealistic and hopelessly naive. But on a deeper level, the new ways of feeling, thinking and being that had suddenly flooded human consciousness were as real as the gentle spring after a cold winter. Like herbal teas, rich infusions of music and art and everyday, upbeat living had steeped inside humanity's teapot of former prosaic awareness, now giving it a more complex, full-bodied flavor. What had often been a black tea and coffee culture—caffeinated, with a kickass bite—was now blending with exotic ginseng, sassafras, and red tea, with hints of knik-knik, licorice and ginger root. The tidal waves of expanded consciousness released had forever altered the flavor of life on the planet.

Spiritual historians later mused on whether perhaps the whole hippie phenomenon had been divinely orchestrated. Their speculation: Those receptive had been *suddenly* gifted with visions from above, allowed a peak into the future and the light at the end of the tunnel thru which much of humanity was stumbling blind. Given to see with certitude the inevitable transformation of a strife-torn existence to our current peaceful planet, people's hearts ignited, inspiring them to herald the grand coming attractions to an anguished world—a world numbed out for seeing life as a series of grade-B horror flicks, mean-spirited comedies, and feel-bad dramas.

Such historians concluded the 60s era was a season of visions, a rarefied window in time when our local universe's spirit circuits opened wide and poured in rivers, allowing the "mystic crystal revelations" sung about in *Hair!* to any and all receptive. The historians pointed to how The Beatles' animated feature film, *Yellow Submarine*—depicting a bleak, frozen black-and-white world melting into one kaleidoscopic with music and joy—reflected the historic change afoot.

On this subtler, nonmaterial level of understanding, beyond the drugs, beyond the long hair, beyond the bare feet and sexual experimentation, the counterculture's core driving force—visionary thinking, unconditional love and transcendent being—never went away.

It only shifted gears.

The freedom-loving seeds had been sown far and wide. Dissemination was unwittingly aided and abetted by a mocking media—the very force bent on trivializing the movement into a Ringling Bros. Circus sideshow: *"See the furry freaks, folks, only fifty cents! Tofu crumbs for tossing, only twenty-five cents more."*

But truth won out, revealing the lies and half-truths perpetuated by the snake-oil hucksters trying to run the show at our expense, determined to drag us down into the tarpits of their own self-destruction. The seeds of positive awareness, planted by millions, had found receptive soil the world over and were soon to sprout changes in the lives of open-minded peoples everywhere.

❋

Even emotional wrecks like me, with a yawning chasm between the way I was and the way I wanted to be. Like I said, I never considered myself more than a hippie wannabee. "Peace and love" sounded great. I wanted it in my life, even if I was fairly clueless how to manifest it.

Inspiring as the holy-stoned people were I'd see and sometimes rub shoulders with—who reminded me by their example of the way life *should* be—I felt too crippled inside to do more than faintly echo the merry chorus of peace they sang to the world.

I wasn't your more stereotypical hippie either: never wore Birkenstocks; never learned to play guitar or hackysack—even throw a Frisbee properly. When I heard a radio spot touting an upcoming rock festival in New York that was destined to make cultural history, I thought: *What? Travel clear across the country just to hear some rock bands? Ya gotta be kidding.*

As for pot smoking, I'd always had a pronounced right-brain side that made more than one pot puffing peer advise me, "You don't *need* pot, Zet; you're spacey enuf already." (Apparently, many of my compatriots constantly fought the stranglehold of their left-brains.) At first the friendly weed served me well, helping me reintegrate brain circuits and defrost frozen feelings, round some hard edges. I later wished I'd quit it after my initial foray with mild leaf, but sometimes I was a slow learner.

And peer pressure was a bear. During a time when everyone was primed to show how cool they were, one didn't want to be perceived as uncool at any cost. Pot was the holy communion in the Our Lady of Cosmic Love Church or the social glue in the Wayward Order of Stoned Stragglers—depending on the company.

So I inhaled a toke as the joint or bong or soapstone pipe made the rounds, but rarely enjoyed anything close to what could be called a high. Often it was just the opposite: People may as well have asked me, "Hey, wanna get low?" While cozying at my older college girlfriend's apartment, she tried to get me in the mood by constantly handing me lit joints attached to her flamboyant, orange-and-purple-feather-festooned roach clip. She hoped enuf hits would transform me into a love machine. But I was already emotionally out on a limb, and each dutifully held hit only stranded me out further, virtually guaranteeing I'd be a dud, not a dude.

It took the later, super-potent hybrid "killer" buds—which could easily disintegrate what functional left-brain ability I *did* have and leave me a zombie puddle of shorted-out neurons, fizzing and popping in utter chaos—to finally convince me to quit. I'd realized preserving my comfort zone was more important than my declining the roach clip netting me paranoid, *are-you-a-narc?* glances. Twenty years later in Hawaii, a thoroughly respectable-looking woman approached me on a Big Island beach one day. I still had long hair and a beard and fit the stoner stereotype, I suppose, tho I'd quit partaking by then. When she asked if I knew where she could get some bud, I swear, I really thought she meant the *beer* at first (Bud, or Budweiser, was a ubiquitous beer brand); I hadn't realized how far the popularity of pot-smoking had spread beyond countercultural realms. I told her I had no idea, at once amused by our apparent lifestyle reversal and taking umbrage for her daring to ask me—the same way she probably would've had I asked *her* 20 years before.

To my understanding, one original school of hippie thought held the belief that, at best, mind-expanding drugs served only as temporary tools to jumpstart one on the road towards enlightenment. A sort of enema to unclog constipated thinking and jammed feeling blocking the spiritual circuits, an aid to clear a channel for developing natural highs thru things like meditation, yoga, dance and conscious diet. Tho many continued occasional pot use for pain relief and mellowing out from end-time stresses, glorification of drugs was never intended. Too often, the "Give me *drugs!*"

mindset was furthered by those missing the boat, mistaking flash for substance, trippy hallucinations for enlightenment—people seeing the writing on the wall but too stoned to read the message: *"Oh, wow, I think the first letter's a 'k'—or something. But what's a 'k' anyway? It's all Maya anyway, man."*

There was yet another reason I quit smoking herb. The pretty plants, whose leaves each formed a rich green, splayed high-five, plants once prayed over and sang to as they grew before being merrily harvested and freely shared among kindred souls, too often became fenced, guarded cash crops, grown by gun-packing sleazoids; a commercial product, moved down a distribution chain of cash-hungry middlemen, forever fearful of getting burned, busted or bumped. Not good. Before quitting, whenever I inhaled the smoke from such pot into my body, I was enuf of a sensitive to unconsciously tune into any such bad energies clinging to the leaves, which could really put a royal damper on efforts to get high; I wasn't conscious enuf to neutralize such energies with a blessing.

✺

Obviously, the blinding blur that was the late 60s and early '70s radically shaped and changed my life—as it did legions. Even as the material trappings of the hippie phenomenon were co-opted and swallowed whole by a moribund dominant culture; even as the shiny, magical quicksilver love force split a million ways, its beads reconfiguring in new disguises and new places; even as Crosby, Stills & Nash supplied us a reality check with the song "Long Time Gone" that it would be a long time before the dawn, I knew strong medicine had been released; medicine so strong it would nourish my spirit to the end of my days. I was sure my life, and others', rather than drab ordeals, could be, should be, some day *would* be, rare bejeweled adventures.

✳

Among the bumper-crop of watch phrases home-grown in those times—"Do your own thing," "Everybody's Beautiful," "Make Love not War"—were two I took to heart right away.

One was "You Are What You Eat." I empathized too much with fellow sentient beings to encourage their lives being ended so I could eat a dubious burger. There was plenty of tasty food around that didn't involve killing to eat. I was happy to live on plant-based food; it was cheaper, digested easier, and tasted better, once I learned a little culinary know-how. The animal-food industries— deceptively touting their bloody, exploitative offerings as essential to health, gobbling up our lands and water and polluting the environment to supply the multitudes of duped customers with the next slain-flesh fix while they giggled all the way to the bank— would just have to write me off as a customer.

The way I saw it, if those championing meat-eating imagined fricasseeing Fluffy or barbequing Lassie, they would've had a clue how some people felt about killing *any* animal to eat. If cats and dogs deserved to live out their natural lives, so did cows, calves, pigs, lambs, turkeys, chickens, tuna and holy mackerel: all life was sacred.

But the same people horrified to hear how Nazis stretched the cut skins of their human victims to fashion grotesque lampshades complemented each other on their fine taste in leather jackets made from some poor murdered cow's hide. Or wallets made from their unborn young. To practically worship some animals and regularly devour others and wear their skin and fur did not compute. About the only way many flesh-eaters could live with their diet was to numb themselves to the reality of what went on in slaughterhouses, to go into denial that animals had feelings or rights to live, maybe hold fuzzy hopes they lived decent lives and never knew what hit them at the end. And people, including me, who'd keep eating animal byproducts, thinking eggs, cheese and ice cream didn't involve mistreating and killing animals, never realized how once the cow or chicken's "useful product life" had ended they were promptly dispatched for fryers and burgers.

As time went on, more people—small minorities yet—realized that, from an enlightened, trans-species perspective, *all* sentient life forms were entitled to live. It dawned on us that the way we killed and devoured animals was little different than cannibalism, that the species-chauvinistic slaughtering of fellow beings for food was essentially the same as human beings killing each other, for all the needless hurt, pain and misery it unleashed into the world.

Seen from afar, a visitor from a neighboring galaxy wanting to check out the vibrational health of our world with his energy meters before paying a vacation visit, would have concluded the planet had a widespread cancer growth, for all the virulent killing of animals going on—leave alone the ongoing human slaughter. He might've decided to go elsewhere for his interplanetary vacation, mumbling *"Can't trust those holographic brochures worth a nano particle. 'Charming paradise of a planet,' my third eye."*

On a cheerier note, the other motto I resonated with was "If It Feels Good, Do It."

Despite my noteworthy hang-ups, replete with persistent repressions, stupendous delusions and impressive confusions, I knew all along—as did everyone but dedicated gymnophobes—it was easier feeling good naked. Scoffers of the time no doubt argued *all* nudity was sexual—some maybe claiming even taking too much pleasure in a bath or shower was an autoerotic experience—that it was only hedonistic escapism and unalloyed kinkiness to enjoy being naked beyond bed and bath.

But wanting to feel good, feel vibrant, is natural in the best of times. In times fraught with pain and sorrow, feeling good could spell the difference between life and death.

An amorous pastry chef with a flair for the poetic might have said making love is the frosting on the cake of being naked: One carries the sensual joy of having the five senses wide open to profound depths by sharing heightened sensations with someone special in an alchemy of commingled bodies, hearts and minds.

But simply enjoying the simple pleasures of nudity and the enhanced sense of supreme wellbeing it fostered had much to recommend for itself.

I always asked myself: *Why limit such a feel-good thing to sex?*

More and more were asking the same question.

EIGHT

...clothes make the man—
into a victimized pawn of the State.
—**Lee Baxandall**
Founder of The Naturist Society

MANY OF US FOUND the idea of getting naked more often appealing now–solo and together, indoors and out.

One time a person maybe skinnydipped and nude sunbathed and that was it. Starting in the late 1960s—and taking off in the 1980s, 1990s and early 2000s—nude *anything* garnered dedicated enthusiasts: camping, running, lunch-hour sunning; canoeing, driving, horseback riding; aerobics, dance, yoga sans pants; cooking, dining, free rock-climbing; sailing, surfing, back yard turfing; hiking, biking, recumbent-triking; housework, computer work, any kind of work, Burke...

"Anything fun can only be funner nude" was the growing sentiment. Various people became so body-attuned clothes only interfered with fully enjoying their chosen sports, hobbies and pastimes.

For example, my cousin Zor was passionate about nude skydiving. He felt such a rush soaring naked thru the air it left him euphoric the rest of the day—like he'd come down to earth as a new-born. His enthusiasm sometimes blurred his concern on *where* he came down. One time he didn't allow for strong wind currents and missed his target, landing in the middle of town, narrowly avoiding a mini-park's nude Poseidon sea god statue, with welcoming upraised trident.

"Look, there's a naked man coming out of the sky!"

"Now *that's* something you don't see every day."

"Bet it's a stunt; wonder what he's promoting."

"Hey, that's Zor, he's not promoting anything; he just likes to dive naked. But I don't think he meant to land here…uh, hope he misses that trident."

In time I became fond of nude creek-exploring. I loved wading in the living liquid ribbons of water with sandy bottoms on soft summer days, upstream and down, discovering magical swimming holes around the bend. Some sites were complete with sunny mini-beaches and sun-drenched boulders to sit on and drink in the beauty and warm up after the latest bracing soak. Canoeing, inner-tubing and rafting were fun too. But, for me, there was nothing like becoming one with the creek: no paddles, no river waders, no nothing; like a fish, just you and nature, seamlessly merged.

I'd come to relish freehiking too, *sans* footwear. Not getting naked while ambling thru pristine nature could feel like leaving your coat, hat and shoes on while visiting in a friend's home: it was rude. Hiking naked thru fields or beach or majestic cathedral of redwoods, I no longer felt apart from nature, but a part *of* it.

※

Once, decades earlier, it wasn't in nature I enjoyed a nude stroll, but right in the city.

It was the mid-seventies and I was living in Seattle's Capitol Hill district after scraping rent money together doing temp work. I felt a bit more self-accepting and grounded in my body, having by then tenuously discovered the joys of sex and how it helped me feel grounded and happy in my skin. My last partner, Suki, had been refreshingly frank in her body acceptance, and some of it rubbed off on me. But I was a long ways from cured: I'd still feel indecent and illegal naked in public, for sex and nudity were still pretty much one and the same to me.

The year before, I regrettably found myself living on the streets in Seattle. One nude-worthy summer nite, while shambling aimlessly near downtown, I came upon an office building's plaza fountain, lit up and splashing away. No one was around. Daring to do the unthinkable, I stripped naked and got in the inviting water. I felt indescribably liberated. (If a late office worker had stuck her head out the window and inquired what I was doing, it might have been an awkward moment—especially since, in the excitement, I'd grown a raging hard on.)

I'd begun daring myself to act on more of my impulses. And so, one exotic August morning in 1974 I felt inspired to do the unthinkable again. It was Sunday, all the shops were closed, and it appeared everyone was staying in, savoring the languorous weather privately. I looked out my window: not a soul on the street; no moving cars. It felt like the sweet solitude of the country had transplanted to the city. The sensual splendor of the day beckoned me like a goddess planet longing to be felt by her children; to wear clothes would only have disappointed her.

Leaving my ground-floor apartment door unlocked so I wouldn't have to carry a key, I stepped thru the near side door and stepped out onto 11th Avenue's sun-drenched sidewalk barefoot naked. I moved hesitantly, like a baby taking his first steps. I could have been walking on the moon for the utter surrealness of the feeling. As I inhaled the morning's rich air and felt the sunshine enveloping my body like a lover, a giddy sense of reclaiming paradise right in the middle of town washed over me—tempered with the certain knowledge I could get arrested any second for my quixotic efforts.

I saw no one. The neighborhood felt vacant. It was eerie; I *knew* there were hundreds of people around within shouting distance. But Seattle folks liked to cocoon away their Sunday mornings inside their castles and out back in their private gardens.

I got bolder. I ventured a block up to Broadway, the hill's usually-bustling main thoroughfare: it was empty as a classroom three seconds after recess bell.

I felt like The Last Man on Earth. Had I miraculously become the sole survivor of some disaster? No, suddenly I heard distant traffic. I instinctively dodged into a storefront alcove. I needn't have bothered. There was no passing traffic; nobody; just me: nude pedestrian, out for a morning stroll in a sleepy city with its blinds drawn. In another alcove I ducked into after hearing more traffic sounds I realized I couldn't get into window shopping: My mind went blank staring at the sales displays for Wrangler jeans and Jockey underwear promising comfort fits.

I headed down Denny and over to the water reservoir park, across from my apartment. I walked along the concourse ovaling about the fenced-off body of water, a path sometimes popular with joggers.

No one.

By the time I reached the far end of the reservoir, I felt I was guaranteed not having my naked reverie uninterrupted. Then I looked up from my careful stepping over the rutted dirt—into the dumbfounded eyes of a shiny-badge-ed uniformed guard, six meters away. He just stood there as if in suspended animation, brain synapses temporarily shorted. Before he recovered from his astonishment, I hotfooted it away, now oblivious to any sharp rocks, and scurried home, heart racing. Busted, or damn near.

The surge of endorphins I felt being nude a good twenty minutes in a high-density, compulsory-clothes zone was unlike anything I'd ever experienced beyond lovemaking. Even if only one person saw me, I'd breached the Forbidden Zone, traversed a parallel universe, created my own Salvador Dali painting: *Melting Reality.*

Rarely had circumstances combined to allow such a golden opportunity. I'd learn decades later that it was the year of the streak and that I'd only tuned in to the wild epidemic of streaking going on all around the nation's campuses. It would be ages before I dared take my urban nudifying the next step.

In the meantime, I'd enjoy being naked in nature and at home whenever weather and circumstance merited.

❋

The most common way people segued into freebody being then, including me, was thru semi-public nude sunbathing and skinny-dipping. Bathing "suits," as such, were a modern development of the nineteenth century, created in response to greater numbers of people of mixed genders gathering at the water's edge. Before these modesty suits—"shame suits" some called them—swimming nude or in your "skivvies" at most was the norm, especially for men.

As it happened, my great-grandfather, Rufus, an up-and-coming clothing Boston merchant, had a chance to get in on the ground floor on this new item of apparel in 1868, but spurned it. He and his wife Beatrice always took cold baths in the morning when the well-water felt the most bone-chilling cold, believing it faintly immoral to enjoy the sensation of warm water on the skin. He was appalled by the notion of encouraging losing one's dignity by "donning some infernally ridiculous outfit in which to go splashing about in the water like a popinjay."

Fast-forward thru a century of mandatory swimwear, and many of us began to feel being un-naked in water was like taking a bath with your clothes on.

We felt inspired to return to time-honored ways.

During my early 20s, years before my Seattle adventure, I'd taken mom's advice and made my first faltering step towards socialized nudity.

It was at a place called Mirabel Beach, along Northern California's Russian River. There I discovered droves of people, many your hippie-type, enjoying the hot summer day and placid river's cool water without a stitch on. *Welcome to Paradise, Zet*, I told myself, staggered, a virgin once-removed. I had to reign in frenzied excitement to avoid heart seizure for the mind-boggling sight of a dozen naked women lolling in the sun and splashing in the river: Set among the men and children like exquisite diamonds in a rare necklace of naked humanity, they made me feel there *was* a heaven on Earth.

I joined suit—or unsuit—hastily, as I suddenly felt self-conscious in my clothes, like an idiot for suffering needless wrap on such a summer-drenched day. Divesting of my vestments, I strolled naked timorously along the river beach, partly feeling a liberated rush of coming home to myself and partly feeling acutely self-conscious and hoping not to get an erection. I didn't, but even tho part of me felt a childlike innocence in being naked among naked others, another part of me was inwardly drooling; my mind all but dehydrated.

Being among such sensuous and, to me, erotic splendor, was as painful to me as it was delightful, and not just because I was a late-bloomer hoping to catch up with where I thought I should be in life experientially.

While there were many influences leading me to lose touch with my feelings—repressive upbringing, alienated society, callous environment—always masquerading in compulsory cloth costumes didn't help. Hidden behind clothes, it was too easy for me to become someone else, someone others *wanted* me to be, or not be, and eventually my heart froze up.

Over time, all but disconnected from deeper feelings, I'd let myself become an animate *object*, a compliant human automaton in a mechanized world that too often dismissed genuineness and authenticity as desirable qualities—unless they could be exploited for gain. I was like a person of color in a racist world, learning to hate myself and others in the same boat of a dog-eat-dog world. I'd learned to objectify myself, and, in turn, objectified others.

Clothier advertisers may as well have effused: "Treat yourself to the luxury of our emotion cover-alls and let it wrap around your mind and feelings. Feelfree®, made of luxuriant, 360 thread count, long-staple Egyptian cotton in a dazzling array of colors, so silky soft you'll forget your feelings are wearing anything at all!"

Once naked among others, outer disguise shed, it wasn't as easy pretending to be someone other than who I was. Inside, I still felt wrapped up like an Eskimo on a freezing winter day. I couldn't *begin* to remove such clothes. Alice's hookah-smoking Caterpillar was looking me dead in the eyes and asking, "who *are* you?" Like Alice, I didn't know.

My real self was encrusted under layers of illusion I mistook for actual self. That day the shock of realizing how unreal I'd let myself become hit me with hurricane force.

Immersed in society's pretend-world illusions, I wanted to flee from anything threatening to expose my artificial self for the rank fraud it was: I'd have made the ideal poster-boy for why public nudity should be kept taboo. In a world that hid from itself, fostering mountains of illusion and denial for selfish gain and control, public nudity only messed things up.

Painful as the episode was, things got a little easier after that. A series of experiences conspired to force me to confront the mortgaged me. I glimmered some of the more obvious lies I'd bought into—that my body was shameful, that sex was dirty, that I always had to follow the prescribed program, no matter how arbitrary—and began to deal with them. Free beaches, where dress conventions were turned upside down, were free therapy workshops. There, with natural and artificial human worlds colliding, I processed gut-level feelings towards my body in relation to others and began healing.

I doubt most first-time free-beachers experienced as extreme a reaction as me. (I hope not.) Like I said, I leaned towards being an exaggerated reflection of whatever societal energies my super-impressionable psyche soaked in. For better or worse, I was a mockingbird, embellishing and magnifying the dominant squawks heard in the human forest. Having grown up in dying Victorian woods, if you will, filled with dying trees tottering in the wind, I'd learned some odd squawks indeed—dirge-like screeches and wailing skirls of a bygone era. Then, on flying off on my own and visiting healthy, living forests, I heard new, happier tunes, more like my as-yet-unlearned innate inner melodies. I scrambled to upgrade my repertoire.

✺

In the early 1970s Mirabel Beach was but one of hundreds, if not thousands, of similar spots around the United States—one of hundreds of thousands around the world—to which people flocked to enjoy being naked together in nature.

Skinnydipping fever had hit America.

Formerly low-key and tranquil skinnydipping spots were soon

overrun by droves of new enthusiasts—plus attendant beer-swilling, low-life voyeurs. Complaints to authorities from disgruntled locals armed with binoculars poured in, and suddenly once-tranquil spots were in danger of being barred to the bare.

"Gladys, I'm telling you, there are people actually stark naked down there on the beach."

"You're imagining things, Harold; nobody would dare."

"Here then, look for yourself; the binoculars are set on high-zoom."

"Where? I don't see any...oh, my God, you're right! I wouldn't have believed it. Not a stitch. How can they be so shameless? What's our country coming to, Harold? Harold, where are you going?"

"To call the sheriff, what do you think?"

"Good! Oh, my God, what a hunk."

To the rescue: Lee Baxandall. In 1975 a popular free beach—so-called for one being able to enjoy it nude—in the Cape Cod National Seashore was threatened with being put under textile lock. Baxandall garnered grass roots support, organized a giant nude beach demonstration and kept the beach clothing-optional—one of many phrases he coined. His efforts spread to coordinating with West coast free-beach activists, initiating a National Nude Beach Day, and documenting information on nude-swimming areas nationwide.

Little did I know that while I was making remedial breakthrus in body acceptance in my fretful little world, others were busy educating the public on this very issue, rallying support for the peaceful, non-sexual nude use of select natural public spots.

Baxandall's and others' efforts expanded, and in 1980 he founded The Naturist Society. He had his own printing business and wasn't worried about getting fired for becoming an outspoken nude advocate. *The Naturist Society's first quarterly issue of*

Clothed with the Sun accurately prophesized a naturist culture would *"...one day decisively break through the wraps of the decadent clothes-compulsive regime."*

The Society's major credo: nurturing positive body acceptance of self and others thru non-sexual social nude gathering, wherever and whenever possible and appropriate, and in the process gain an increased sensitivity and respect for each other and the environment.

The Society resurrected a semblance of the German nature-cure vision held by its proponents some 70 years before. But new efforts labored under a powerful handicap: the United States was a super-urbanized technocracy of complex, speeded-up, artificial lifestyles, profoundly disconnected from any sort of harmonious Earth living we've since come to enjoy. And the country had no deep-rooted earth religions to fall back on, as had the Germans, to regain a full sense of natural being. We were left to borrow from the age-old Native American reverence for Earth, indelibly imprinted in the land on the subtle level, and dig deep within our genetic memory to reactivate our ancestors' ancient ways, long before they pulled up roots and moved to America.

Earlier nudist organizations, notably the American Sunbathing Association, had fought tooth and nail to secure legitimacy and gain participants for *walled* nudist enclaves and clothing-optional resorts. Pushing the envelope for the right to be naked in select *public* places was a whole new ballgame. It was loosely akin to Southern blacks sitting down at a white lunch counter during segregation years and hoping to be accepted rather than arrested.

Skinnydipping enthusiasts had been isolated from each other. They were powerless to protest any high-handedness by authorities deciding to clamp down on public nudity at various beaches with long freebody traditions. The Society served to pull people together and champion the right to mindfully shed clothes if they so chose—and help the legions of my fellow neurotics accept their biologic reality.

Proceeding in the spirit of compromise and accommodation with the clothed world, The Naturist Society gently pressed for body freedom rights. The growing membership proved a vast spectrum of nude enthusiasts existed, with votes and dollars; otherwise upright citizens could no longer be dismissed as a weird lunatic fringe.

Suddenly there were people who believed they were entitled to enjoy their scenic public lands intimately, not once-removed by unneeded wrapping. They realized there were times clothes served no earthly purpose beyond making shekels for the textile industry, fueling bent imaginings, and sparing the body-phobic from having a cow.

NINE

Heaven is under our feet as well as over our heads.
—**Thoreau**

AFTER YEARS OF aimless if quixotic drifting about—seeking my elusive commune, losing my citified mindset—I finally settled down. Once I'd lived to become part of a thriving commune and be among kindred spirits; at one point I'd even bought my one-way train ticket to join The Farm in Tennessee, but changed my mind at the last, doubting I could adapt away from my accustomed West Coast culture or fit into their communal beehive structure.

Then several years of homeless living—discovering survival challenges I never wished on anyone—buried my finer nature. Now I had to learn to live with myself again and slowly exfoliate callused feelings before I could live with others. Years of sensory overload and utter lack of privacy had built in me an absolute craving to have my own land more than ever, a place to heal and take stock of my life, learn to listen to my heartbeat again and become one with Nature.

Even tho dad had severely disapproved of the way I was living—I'd thrown away any chance to do the old man proud—he took pity on me when he found out I was living like a derelict and sent me a five thousand dollar check. I wasn't too proud to accept it.

"No son of mine is going to live like a bum," he wrote in the accompanying letter. "I don't care what; you use this money to get settled somewhere." He'd written in a halting hand, as his health had begun to plummet. Between his help and the pittance I'd squirreled away apple picking in Washington State and kept in my boot, I could now afford to buy a small country parcel. From a funny old man I bought an old car, a refugee from the wrecking yard with a little life left in it, and went land hunting.

I yearned to live in the kind of places we'd visited as kids: wild nature, with its balm of solitude and riches of undisturbed earth; pure air and pure rushing streams and teeming wildlife. What I could afford was far from the redwoods and crystal streams of my vision, but I knew I'd learn to love whatever I found, so long as it was peaceful and mine to do with what I wanted.

Come October, I snapped up six hectares of high-desert land—juniper, sagebrush and lava outcroppings—dirt-cheap. Nestled in the foothills of majestic Mount Shasta at the top of what-was-then California, the land was bordered on two sides by national forest land. Despite having a 200 meter deep water table, requiring some of the area's sparse residents to haul water in instead, the parcel drew me like a magnet. The low down of $750 and $25 monthly installments left me with plenty to build a quick temporary shelter before the first snows flew and stock it with basic necessities. I built without measure tape, level or square. I'd only built a shelter once before, in the New Mexico high desert, but carpentry ran in our family and I learned fast. I felt a keen primordial satisfaction throwing boards together: like a bird building a nest.

I knew the region as special, not only for its scenic grandeur but for being a natural power point of some sort, an interstice of the electro-magnetic grid work of Earth energies, or some such. Like its sister volcano, Japan's Mount Fuji, many deemed Mount Shasta a spiritual mountain. There were days it emanated such a majestic force I didn't doubt it a bit.

Many chemically sensitive people, having experienced crippling reactions in their old, toxins-ridden home environments, picked the region to move to, as it also had a reputation for being relatively nontoxic. The refugees' former environs—awash in chemical-sprayed lawns, air pollution, compromised food and water supplies, its locals drenched in gag-able hairsprays, perfumes and outgassing dry-cleaned clothes—finally made them run for their lives. The Mount Shasta region was a relative sanctuary of clean air, pure water, and alpine wilderness, with organic food stores and alternative healthcare providers. I was more chemically sensitive than most myself and suspect I was instinctively drawn here in part for that reason.

Some claimed Mount Shasta was the third-eye chakra of the planet; I wasn't sure about that, but I *did* notice my dreams took a decided turn for the exotic even before I arrived, once I'd decided that was where I'd settle. In a visionary cartoon the mountain kaleidoscopically swam around a circle, while out the middle came the voices of the folk group Peter, Paul and Mary singing "This Land is Your Land."

Years later, I'd observe newcomers' imaginations going into overdrive as they gushed about towering Lemurians dwelling inside the mountain and fleets of UFO scout ships hidden inside the giant lenticular clouds that sometimes hovered over the mountain. I understood; the mountain activated something in people.

A beguiling assortment of local people claimed to channel every spiritual master under the sun (and no doubt a few from *over* the sun). Tho I too had my head in the clouds, at the same time I'd struggled to get my feet on the ground. Claims of such exotic spiritual excursions only drew ho-hum reactions from me, tho I'm sure many were authentic, gifted channels. Even if some claimed to be the reincarnation of Saint Germain or to channel his sister's cleaning woman, tho, that was well and good; it struck me as a harmless byproduct of the mountain's intense energies. Only when others took such questionable claims seriously did I wonder if maybe we weren't kidding ourselves and getting hung up on the astral plane—especially if one convinced others he had a direct pipeline to Melchizedek, who was encouraging people to support the channeler's dedicated efforts with generous cash donations, credit cards welcome.

In my own case, I suppose the mountain's influence manifested in an over-amped pursuit of seeking inner harmony thru nakedness and nature. But I felt that only by fully attuning to my senses could I ever hope to get beyond my senses and cultivate a more transcendent self.

At least, to my credit, I didn't go about claiming Mother Mary told me to tell the world it was time to go nudist.

During early days on the land, I simply wanted to *be*. I forgot about all else as I dialed into my sanctuary amid the junipers, with nearby Mount Shasta standing protective guard.

At first the quiet was deafening. To my road-jangled nerves the stillness was eerie, like being on some abandoned stage set and wondering where the stage crew and actors were. I recalled reading how a man from New York City, on vacation in the mountains, couldn't sleep, the quiet was so unnerving; he had a friend send him a recording of the city's traffic droning and blaring horns, and then he slept like a baby. I adapted too, but naturally, over time, soon learning to revel in the land's solid-state silence. At times the calm felt as magical and absolute as the brilliant luminous silence enjoyed swimming underwater.

The silence was punctuated by local residents. A feathered mini-jack hammer of a woodpecker loved drilling into an upper-sundeck post every morning in summer; scrub jays squawked a storm at appointed feeding times; squirrels skirled out their Morse code; chipmunks chittered the latest woodland gossip. I felt like a kid in a wildlife sanctuary: hummingbirds, Oregon juncos, robins, jackrabbits, polecats, deer, and, on rare occasions, mountain

lions—all had called the region home for time untold.
I discovered could still coax chipmunks to eat out of my hand.
They were cage-free now.

※

And I was clothesfree.

The nearest neighbor, an old sawmill retiree on disability, was two hollers away, and he drove out another way. The area was secluded, two blissful kilometers from the blacktop; most of the time I couldn't hear the sparse traffic. It felt like the area was not only the land time forgot, but the land it never *knew*: thirty kilometers from town, I was a world away.

I savored the freedom to be naked in nature again—like a gourmand once reduced to eating beans and rice after falling on hard times who then got a windfall and began dining in five-star restaurants every day.

The mountain's enormous mass created its own weather patterns, making the region about Mount Shasta a crazy-quilt of micro-climates. My own patch of high desert woodlands was the local banana belt: it had the least precipitation and most sunshine in the entire area. But people resisted moving there for its distance from town, its occasional healthy winds, the deep water table and lack of tall trees gracing more prestigious environs. More room for desert rats like me. "Go where there's no water; that's the only place the white man will leave you alone," was old Indian wisdom this white man took to heart.

I counted my blessings.

※

I spent a leisurely three years building a sturdy snug cabin. I built slowly. I could only afford so many building materials at a time from the odd jobs I landed, and it took time for know-how to seep in. (I was building to code.) Besides, I wanted to savor the experience, not scramble like a mad ant, worrying the world would end if I didn't complete by a given date.

During the drawn-out construction I lived in my earth-sheltered dwelling. It was compact and short on refined amenities, but had a warm bed, wood stove, cooking range, and kerosene lamp. And I was snug as a bug in a rug whenever big wind storms ripped over the land. I happily made do in the knowledge I was manifesting my dream house six meters away. I pinned a Shakespeare quote—from *King Lear*, I think—to my Z-braced plank door that went something like, "Though I be bounded by a walnut shell, I shall deem myself king of infinite space."

My diet, alas, was abysmal. (This was decades before turning vegan.) While priding myself in not eating animal flesh, like I said, I'd lost track of why I'd become vegetarian in the first place. I went thru powdered milk by the case and gobbled pasta smothered in melted cheddar; I had whole wheat pancakes, but they were swimming in honey and margarine, and ate "natural" peanut butter out the ears. I found I scrimped on food to have more money for building. Lacking refrigeration, I rarely ate any vegetables but potatoes. I knew so little about conscious diet beyond not eating flesh and avoiding the most over-processed foods that I got pretty anemic-looking; I could have been the meat industry's poster boy for what happened when you didn't eat your daily animal.

Years later, when my cabin was a fait accompli, people said I was lucky to have such a place. I did feel fortunate but luck implied it just fell into my lap. I'd placed building a home in the country the absolute top priority in my life ten years before (although my

144

determination got seriously derailed during the homeless years). I made whatever sacrifices were needed to manifest it, never eating out, delaying town trips until enuf things needed doing to justify the gas.

People claiming they could never save enuf to buy a parcel and build their own home were sometimes only caught in a convenience trap of their own making. They told themselves they couldn't go without their creature comforts—flush toilet, hot showers, infinite electricity and rivers of water on tap—even for a season, if that's what it took. So they forked over the lion's share of their month's earnings to a landlord to keep their central heat, dishwasher, and big-screen TV going strong and their wallets thin. Country living remained a wistful fantasy.

Perhaps it was only my Spartan streak, cultivated by the threadbare years—"worshipping in the temple of poverty," someone put it—that let me go without accustomed niceties long enuf to manifest my country homestead. And I was young, resilient, energy to burn. But it struck me that inertia prevailed for too many, especially as they got older and accustomed to their comforts. It was too daunting a prospect to go from furnished apartment, a block or two from Sid's Super and Debbie's Diner, to hunkering down in a trailer in the middle of nowhere while scrambling to carve out a homestead from raw land.

❄

I picked a tree-ringed site for my house, open on the south to the sun and spectacular view of Mount Shasta's twin northern flanks. Wanting to be self-sufficient, I built the place under my own steam. I needed to saw boards without having ears assaulted by the whine of power tools and growl of generator. And I didn't want to be beholden to some metered, distant power source, never knowing how the electricity was generated: damming rivers and making life tough on fish, burning coal or natural gas and adding to the greenhouse effect, or splitting atoms and creating ten thousand years of toxic waste.

I built the entire cabin with hand tools only.

Working nude when weather permitted—from digging the cinder-block foundation footings to screwing down the green-enameled steel sections on the 5:12 pitch roof—I was extra-cautious for the nails and splinters and sharp tools strewn about. It's amazing how much more mindful of surroundings one is when naked—conscious of every movement. In working by hand, I felt closer to the wood. The heady aroma given off from the 1 x 4 interior-wall cedar boards was like perfume as I sawed thru them with trusty 10-point Stanley crosscut. The wood pieces' swirling grain patterns spoke of trees' vibrant lives before the woodman's axe froze them in time to grace my walls. I prayed the pine, Douglas fir and cedar the lumber came from weren't old growth trees, and had been harvested on a sustainable-yield basis, that no ancient tree was sacrificed so the likes of me could have a home. This was before environmentally-conscious consumers convinced lumber companies it was good business to certify their wood.

Always curious where things come from, I wondered where the former trees—becoming my floor, walls, and ceiling—had lived, what birds had perched in them, what storms they'd weathered, how old they were at harvest, how much it hurt them to have their lives taken, what kind of mood the logging truck driver was in as he hauled their segmented remains to the mill, what plant workers felt towards the wood—admiration, indifference, resentment?—as they pulled the boards off the green chain to stack. Stories were encoded in the grain, if only I knew how to decipher them: Indians said the history of the planet vibrates within every rock.

Trying to minimize being part of the problem and depleting rapidly-dwindling forests, I used salvaged lumber whenever I could. When more conventional-thinking visitors admired my massive front steps and timber posts, I delighted in telling them I

146

got them at the Weed dump; I'd watch for their reaction. Some people refused to buy anything used other than houses and cars; perish the thought of salvaging anything from the *dump*. Items deposited there were instantly stigmatized, given the mark of Cain, relegated by someone to trash status; better to bury them together and be done with it than resurrect the tainted from the dead; never mind if valuable resources went wasted. Cover the crime.

My cabin was compact but had a natural earthiness. A soaring open-beam ceiling graced it, providing a spacious feel. It suited me better than any ticky-tack city dwelling ten times its size ever could.

Having designed and crafted it myself filled me with an abiding sense of accomplishment. On its completion, I gained an awareness of *place*, of belonging to the land. This, in turn, helped me feel more anchored in myself, even gave me the inner strength, supported by a low-stress lifestyle, to quit smoking and drinking (which sorry habits I'd picked up living on the streets).

Psychologist Carl Jung, who also fashioned his own home, came to see the owner-built house as spiritually embodying the person and representing self-knowledge. A custom-tailored habitat built by my own sweat did wonders for helping me tune into the elusive me I'd lost track of somewhere along the way. After eight years blowing like a leaf in the wind, I was establishing myself in the world. I'd made inevitable building mistakes—one owner-builder jokingly referred to his house as "my temple of accumulated error"—but it was home, sweet home.

I installed a generous bank of morning-sun-facing windows and captured the day's earliest radiant sunshine. This supplemented wood-stove heat in colder weather and provided morning cheer year round every sunny day. Some winter mornings when I slept in it might be below freezing outside, a thick white blanket of snow on the ground, and I wouldn't even have to start a fire on getting up for the sunshine streaming in and flooding the place with its cheer. Granted, it might have only warmed the cabin to 12°C., but it was generally a dry climate, with no cold moisture stealing warmth from the bones. I'd feel toasty just wearing a cotton nite-shirt while soaking in the sun's penetrating heat at my window table and sipping a steaming mug of fresh-ground Columbian.

❋

I wondered why more people didn't orient their homes to the sun and take easy advantage of its gift. Instead, we depended on bottled-up-in-time solar energy in the form of coal, gas, and oil. It was crazy: for a while, it cost more to buy a quart of milk produced by a local dairy than it did a quart of gas extracted from the depths of the earth, somewhere on the other side of the world, imported across the ocean, refined at huge bother and expense— all at ruinous environmental cost—and finally transported to the local gas pump. (I imagine this must seem as far removed from the reader's reality as me trying to imagine the realities of heating with coal before *my* day.)

I expected I knew the answer: no money in sunshine for utility companies, plus wanting to avoid the annoyance of having to scrap cookie-cutter blueprint designs and work with the sun at each site and create some actual environmental integrity.

Wanting to go with renewable energy later, I'd intentionally picked a parcel far from power lines. Essentially I'd an entire half section of land to myself. Power lines were concentrated in the other half, a kilometer away, where a handful of neighbors hunkered alongside them, content to pull on the centralized-power teat that never ran dry—except during power outages, when electrically-fed pellet stoves and electric-blower kerosene and diesel heaters were rendered worthless when needed most.

At first, conventionally-minded neighbors looked on me as sadly deprived for not having power. For a decade I met my illumination needs with kerosene lamps and candles. When I finally installed a solar-electric panel and battery-storage system, they were amused. When electricity rates skyrocketed and power outages became more frequent, they were envious. I joked how the only way I knew if we had a local power outage was by catching the local news on TV.

I remember the sense of wonder I felt hooking up the solar-electric panel to batteries and turning on a radio. A nameless joy coursed thru me knowing it was our star, some hundred-and-fifty million kilometers away, enabling Ike & Tina's "Proud Mary" to paddlewheel thru my cabin. They could as well been singing:

> Big sun keep on shinin'
> Oilman keep malignin'…

I read somewhere how each square meter of Earth's surface received on average a full horsepower of energy every day, free for the tapping.

Water came from the heavens, by way of my cabin roof and gutters transporting rain offerings into a large cistern. An in-line water filter rendered the harvest fit for drinking. I solar-heated water in warm weather and stove-heated it in cold. I didn't mind the latter being labor-intensive. The way I looked at it, it saved the cost of joining a gym. And I didn't even have to leave home for a workout.

Whenever I heard about some disaster leaving townspeople without running water or electricity—hallmark of deprivation in affluent nations—it made me muse over the relativity of lifestyles: To conventional ways of thinking, this was how I lived year-round. People were slow to give credence to electricity generated on site—as if because it wasn't generated far away, from a centralized source, it wasn't real electricity—and considered catching rain too okie-finokie (unless renting a fancy country house in Hawaii, away from water lines, in which case such a system became "quaint"). Industrialized nations learned to take centrally-supplied creature comforts for granted with amazing speed, considering a century or two earlier no one had either. Even in my day, millions of earth dwellers hauled their water and got by okay with limited or no electricity. I doubt most consider themselves in dire straits, and neither did I.

I fashioned a solar oven from plans found in an old *Mother Earth News* magazine, made by nesting cardboard boxes together and attaching a glass door and adding reflective aluminum foil to the attached cardboard solar concentrator. Costing almost nothing, it served admirably out on the porch for most of my cooking and baking on the frequent sunny days. On overcast days and at nite I fired up my propane gas kitchen range. I'd have preferred being independent of gas, but didn't fancy building a fire in a wood range every time I wanted to cook, and I wasn't ready for a raw-food regimen.

It was heart-wrenching, the way millions of us druthered living free of fossil fuels in our lives for heating, cooking and transportation—but weren't. We gagged on the fumes and prices and bemoaned the steep environmental havoc they caused at both ends. But either the technology wasn't there, or it was there but still too expensive for many, or too impractical for the breakneck way we lived: A purely electric car, for instance, humming along on the highway at a leisurely clip, just wouldn't cut it among others roaring by in their mini-tanks like so many White Rabbits, late for the Red Queen's tea party and afraid of loosing their heads.

TEN

The body seems to feel beauty when exposed to it as it feels
the campfire or sunshine, entering not by the eyes alone but equally
through all one's flesh like radiant heat, making a passionate
ecstatic pleasure glow not explainable.
—**John Muir**

BETWEEN BURSTS OF building efforts I freehiked thru the adjoining national forest, lost in a wonderland. I savored the solitude as I soaked in the wilderness, relishing my new-found body freedom.

Knowing the place was a naked oasis amid a desert of mandatory dress made it even more delicious. In a bent world, imposing piddly limits at every turn, there existed veritable *orchards* of forbidden fruit to enjoy.

One crimp in my naked reverie while off exploring: knowing I could be spied on from the fire lookout atop a hill peak across the valley. An old neighbor who knew about such things told me Forestry had a telescope up there, powerful enuf to zoom in on a person reading a newspaper on their deck three kilometers away and catch the day's headline. This knowledge sometimes induced stage fright while out freehiking: Big Brother was watching—maybe. For a while I imag-

153

ined it might be some college co-ed on her first summer job at the look-out, wishing she could be out enjoying the glories of nature too. More likely, I'd think, it would be some hardass just transferred from out of South Dakota, snorting in confirmation his suspicions California was indeed the Granola State, filled with fruits, nuts and flakes who liked to prance around naked in the woods.

Finally, it got to where I didn't know if anyone was watching and I didn't care.

✳

As soon as the building inspector signed off the final inspection—leaving me the impression he *knew* I was up to no good—I moved in the cabin. I'd bought an old upright piano, which I now rolled it out onto the deck to celebrate and serenaded the chipmunks. They chittered away when I galloped thru Joplin's "The Entertainer," whether in protest or enjoyment or something unrelated I couldn't tell.

Life was good. I'd built my bower in the wilderness and found sweet solace from "the slings and arrows of outrageous fortune." Life on the road had been so rough that more than once people mistook me for a Nam vet; I'd never take having a roof over my head and food on the table for granted again.

I'd become the nature boy I'd longed to be all along, going from living in the most densely populated area of California to one of the sparsest, from a place I couldn't go out your front door without involuntarily contracting the sphincter to walking out the door naked and hiking for hours.

At first, being naked around my place had felt so illegal I might as well have been growing a thousand pot plants on an open hill-

154

top during anti-marijuana aerial surveillance sweeps. But gradually I realized the place was a safe haven in which I could be my naked self whenever I wanted. Over time, deliciously forbidden feelings would transform into delectably allowed ones.

The wildlife served to assure me it was okay: Chipmunks didn't feel guilty scampering about without any little chipmunk clothes on; why should I?

I mellowed slowly—patterns of a lifetime couldn't change overnite. Or in a year—even ten. But eventually, it felt like my birthright to be naked the whole day long, not feeling the least bit indecent—at least not while *alone*. I'd duck in the brush the times I freehiked along the cinder roads around home and heard the infrequent car approaching. I didn't want to risk visiting negative attention on my lifestyle for being "some weird naked man hiking down the middle of the road." I wished things were mellower and we could've just waved at each other and continued our merry ways, maybe stopped and chatted if I knew the person.

While out rambling on a trail one near-tropical day, I marveled how much more alive—deliriously happy, even—I felt being free of clothes: sunshine kissing skin, gentle breeze enveloping, supple earth massaging the feet. I found myself wishing everyone could experience the same supernatural delight. A snatch of parody lyrics percolated thru my mind, sung to the Beach Boys' "Wouldn't It Be Nice?"

> Wouldn't it be nice if we could be naked
> Anywhere that we might chose to go?
> And wouldn't it be nice if we didn't ever
> Have to-oo-oo-oo wear any clothes?
> Wouldn't it be nice?

For three or four months—some years, five or six—skin was the only cover I needed around home. Spending entire days naked while going about everyday chores—gathering firewood, pulling dead brush, fixing dinner—took nudity out of the box, integrated it into my being.

Were it not for going to town or receiving visitors, I could've stashed my clothes and forgotten all about them for the season like so many snow chains or storm windows. During the rest of the year, the days I couldn't harvest at least an hour of sunshine in the buff were more the exception than the rule. Incredibly, on some winter days I could be soaking in the rays on the front deck, when just thirty kilometers away others were bundled up, shoveling two feet of snow and longing for spring.

Solid warm weather came early sometimes, making for bare-able weather from March or April on. It was always a special event the first day I could climb from bed after a naked sleep without having to throw anything on to ward off the morning chill and walk out the front door into the sunshine. I felt like a sail boater daring to venture beyond the sheltered bay and out onto the wide-open sea. And during hottest weather, when the sun's ultraviolet rays were too intense to enjoy bare *or* clothed much of the day, I'd ride out the heat wave in relative comfort, keeping naked indoors or out on shady porch, harvesting cool breezes as I sipped a tall glass of cold water.

You might say I became a nudaholic. Clothes and I were bare-ly on speaking terms half the year, at least while on the land.

❈

It got to the point I dreaded putting clothes on when readying for a town trip. What reason to? *"Because"* wasn't enuf. A sinking feeling, like summer's-over-and-I've-got-to-go-back-to-school swept thru me. I'd tell myself: "Time to deal with the *real world"*—*reel* world, I'd amend. For what passed as reality then often struck me as some lamely scripted movie *reeling* thru a master projector we were all extras in, a movie at once rated G for its

puerile asininity and XXX for its wholesale destruction of innocent pleasure and human dignity.

Anyhow, on warmest days, I'd eventually put off dressing at all
until reaching town.

Driving nude was perhaps the closest you could get to being
naked in public without being naked in public. As I tooled down
the rural highway in my little Geo Metro, not wearing a stitch and
enjoying the gentle sunshine, other motorists *assumed* I was only
shirtless. To be more uncovered was unthinkable, uncivilized,
indecent, beyond the pale of accepted social behavior. So of
course I had pants on.

I was amazed how easy it was to get away with it.

I felt like a naked drop amid an ocean of dress.

One May, after a discouragingly cold wet spring, a nude-worthy day manifested out of nowhere like an exquisitely rare flower.
Driving naked to town on my rural highway and feeling euphoric
over nice weather returning, I spun off new lyrics to the 1929 tune,
"Happy Days are Here Again":

> Naked days are here again
> It's time to lose your clothes again
> Stash them all inside some storage bin
> Naked days are here again!

I was vigilant driving nude, prepared to cover in a flash if need
be. Even so, friends I'd confided in asked me why I'd even risk it,
knowing the unpleasant consequences if caught. "Because it helps
me feel free," I'd say. Citizens of formerly repressive eastern
European countries, like the former Czechoslovakia, learned the
therapeutic value of being naked for unwinding from hard times.
Things weren't nearly so bad in the United States—tho some
claimed they were *worse* for being a velvet hammer system, one
that appeared to champion freedom...*until* you crossed the line over
some little thing like not wearing a seat beat, and then look out.

It was as much about getting freed from my own internalized negative mindset as it was feeling trapped in burdensome clothes. Being naked helped me feel good about me. My self-esteem, ridiculously fragile at times, derailed easily; I needed to feel good about myself any way I could; being naked worked wonders. It was phenomenal how the mere shedding of clothes could lift my spirits.

On mornings that warmed up slowly, I'd start the day semi-dressed and settle into one level of sensory awareness. It always came as a surprise later when as the day turned golden I removed my last bit of apparel—be it shirt, shorts or shoes—and reached 100 percent freebody homeostasis, feeling a renewed sense of oneness with the elements. I realized then that—at least for me—the degree of body attunement and total body comfort were inversely proportional to how much my sensory receptors were blocked by clothes.

Some days, after spending gentle naked mornings, I'd ready for town to shop or visit friends. As I locked my front door barefoot-naked, a rush of sweet liberation surging thru me, I'd smile inwardly, a variation on an old credit card company's ad slogan growling in my mind: *"Clothes: Don't leave home without them."* I walked across the wild grass to my car and drove off nude—*with* clothes, just not on me. It felt so natural I could almost imagine the whole world had gone clothing optional.

"Careful, Zet, or you'll get arrested for indecent exposure," a clothes-resigned acquaintance warned me.

Once I did get pulled over—for speeding. I had just enuf time to slip my shorts on. I wondered how the highway patrolman would've dealt with me if I hadn't:

"Do you know how fast you were...okay, sir, step out of the car—no, don't. Put your hands on the wheel... Dispatch, I've got a naked driver here on highway 7. ... Forget to do something

before heading out, did we, sport? ... No, the guy was driving butt-naked. ... Doesn't seem drunk or high, no. ... Ask him? ... Okay, flash, suppose you tell me why you're driving naked?

"Well, it's such nice weather; I didn't really see any reason to get dressed."

"Oh, a funny guy, huh? Hear that, dispatch? Got us a real comedian here. ... Bring him in? Okay, but I don't have anything to cover him with, and I don't mind telling you, I really don't want a naked man in my car again. Remember the last clown mooned everyone on the way to the station ... Yeah, right, that's why I earn the big bucks. Just wait, I'll get you."

☀

Dad died at a ripe old age late one April afternoon. Old for the times, anyhow: 79; I know, that would be considered too young to go now—like age 50 was in those times. He was buried, as per request, in his newest top-of-the-line suit, wanting to look dapper even in death, I suppose. We wrapped his favorite G# Hohner harmonica in a red silk handkerchief and slid it into his breast pockets remembering how he'd played "When the Saints Go Marching In" around the campfire like a house afire. I wished him a clothed heaven, if that's what he wanted; tho, for all I knew, he looked forward to being naked in paradise after dealing in clothes his whole life.

As it turned out, his earthly clothing empire wasn't overthrown by hordes of nudeniks, rejecting his and his industry colleagues' body coverings and sending the company's stock into the ground.

He left each of us a tidy fortune.

My brothers promptly bought new homes and sporty cars. My sister gave away most of her share to a multitude of social and environmental causes, leaving just enuf to live on in Brazil, where she'd moved on wild impulse.

Mom, who had loved Anatole despite his controlling ways, became a merry widow in short order. She traveled the world, visited family and pursued her life's passion, watercolor painting, which she'd put on hold to raise us. She visited her sister's nudist park in Florida and briefly gave the naturist lifestyle another try at 75. "It was all right, but, given my druthers, I still prefer clothes. I'm funny that way," she wrote me. "But I'm glad if you're finding happiness carrying on the family tradition. Just be careful."

I'd loved dad too, but it took decades of letting go and accepting he'd had his reasons for being the way he was. He was the product of a smothering Victorian society. His own generation no doubt staged its own rebellion against *their* parents' outmoded ways, but only gained so much yardage—not unlike Noah Webster's managing to Americanize a few of the British spellings of English words—before running out of steam, integrating the rest back into their mindset by default, the same as with every generation, I suppose.

I sold my shares of the company stock. I could only imagine the conflicted feelings I'd have had otherwise, rooting for his clothing chain to do well: *"Come on people, buy more fancy suits; Junior needs a new nudist time-share on the Riviera."*

The inheritance freed me from the necessity of working for a living, a reality I'd only toyed with all along, truth be told. My Spartan lifestyle needed little once I got the cabin built. Before the inheritance, I'd dug up odd jobs—tree planting, fire-crew kitchen, polka band roadie—anything to pay the bills that wasn't too pressing or long term.

One year I landed a part-time gig playing piano for a local Irish bar-restaurant. The owner might float by and ask me in his rich brogue, "Fancy playing a little 'Danny Boy,' Zet?" I enjoyed flirting with being a professional musician—"If they pay you, you're a professional," someone told me—but I wasn't wild about having to spring for shoes, slacks, dress shirt and clip-on tie to play in. "Beware of all enterprises that require new clothes," Thoreau had warned. I sailed thru "Cast Your Fate to the Winds" and "Wooden Ships"—hoping the feeling I invested into my playing mitigated the compromised integrity I felt wearing a monkey suit.

I now had worlds of time to pursue my old passions, music and writing, and develop new interests—like collecting pre-1920 sheet music. Before radio, TV and movies, artists poured everything they had into creating visually arresting covers, with hopes of making each the latest must-have in America's music parlors. At the peak of my collecting mania, I went on road trips and scoured antique and collectible shops thru a ten-state region in search for covers that struck my fancy. To me, they were like so many little time machines visiting from bygone eras. Or photography: I hoped to capture Mount Shasta in its every nuanced lighting and snow cover and went nuts whenever the mountain gave birth to a huge symmetrical lenticular cloud. One time a gargantuan double-decker spun off the mountain, all but filling the sky; it was as if the skies were singing the Hallelujah Chorus.

After the windfall I still wanted to feel productive. I started a cottage industry harvesting the pungent sagebrush growing about me in wild profusion. Using colorful cotton floss, I wrapped up handfuls into double-helix-patterned smudge sticks, with bulging boles tapering to the top, and then let them air dry. People lit the tip of the dried smudges and then blew out the flame for the smoke's purifying properties, as Indians had long done. Now conscious people of all cultures knew our world needed *lots* of purification. I sold all I could make. I usually gathered in the nude, discovering that in so doing I felt an almost supernatural oneness with the plants. I wholesaled the sticks—*wands* to the la-di-dah new age industry aiming at the spiritually-challenged-but-affluent market—mostly to the more down-home natural food stores and body shops and select bookstores around the north state.

I'd found myself with a thriving concern, but a decade and

14,000 sticks later I folded my tent. My tolerance for blazing summer heat had declined, linked, I'm sure, to the ozone layer thinning out, and the repetitive motion of wrapping threatened to give me car pool tunnel syndrome.

And, as mentioned, my diet was often far from the best. When younger, I could neglect my health and get away with it. The older I got, the more important eating well became and I suffered when I didn't. Without a refrigerator my choices of foods that kept were limited. I'd been a de facto "grainarian" for years, with dairy thrown in during colder weather when my back porch doubled as an ice box.

I was still decades away from the gut realization that not only were dairy and eggs almost as harmful to the body as meat, but eating them perpetuated the abuse and death of animals. Refrigerator or no, it was my ignorance about food more than anything that kept my body less than thriving; Even as I stressed my body with dairy and junk food and gallons of honey-laced coffee, I thought I was cool because I didn't eat meat. *"Triple cheese in that sub, please. Do I look like I'm worried about high cholesterol?"*

I wanted to make my mark in life, but didn't want to be part of any *rat race*, as we called the workaday world (to the insult of industrious rats everywhere, who we forced to scramble thru mazes in behavioral experiments). I didn't want to bust a gut scrambling about, doing unfulfilling work for insulting pay. As U. S. President Reagan once quipped, "It's true hard work never killed anybody, but I figure why take the chance?" I *liked* work; I wasn't like the idle rich, shocked at the thought of getting dirt under their fingernails. But work had to feel relevant, have a civilized pace, allow a modicum of human dignity. My creative spirit needed to be nourished or I quit before I started.

Eventually, I concluded I was basically useless to the workforce except as an artist.

Money was funny: you could have it and still feel poor or not have it and feel rich. I'd felt rich before, even while living below the official poverty line—that level below which people weren't living *nearly* so much beyond their means. I had my own land, free and clear—as long as I kept feeding the county property tax meter to keep from being towed away—and tho I lived in a temporary hovel while building the cabin, it was *my* hovel. No landlord giving me 30 day notice to hit the road because he wants to move his mistress into it and decides to keep the damage deposit because there were thumbtack holes in the wall from putting up art posters to brighten up the soulless ticky-tack.

I was surrounded with the myriad riches of nature, drinking in the land's tidings and inhaling the pure air as gratefully as any smog-choked Tokyo traveler bellying up to an oxygen bar. The Beatles' "Baby, You're a Rich Man" chorused thru my mind. I counted the number of blue-winged stellar jays swooping in to feast on the daily-scattered birdseed like a miser counting silver. When a family of three big wildcats honored my land with a visit, attracted by the dish of water under a shady juniper I kept full thru the soaring heat of summer, I felt I'd won the wildlife lottery; as they lingered and lolled on the ground, the land transformed into the Serengeti Plain.

Let others slave doing work they disliked to make the rent on overpriced digs amid noisy, crowded environments, I'd think. I'd work a little and be happy with my cracker-box palace nestled in the serenity of nature. Quotable Thoreau again: "I would rather sit on a pumpkin, and have it all to myself, than be crowded on a velvet cushion."

I couldn't begin to put a price on my freedom to go naked. While some fellow nude enthusiasts blew a half-month's pay to fly to exotic nudist resorts and get naked a while amid the elements, often schnockered out of their gourds; I lived soberly in clothes-free simplicity half the year for free. While the scenery may have not been as exotic, I didn't even have to leave home.

When my ship came in, I didn't feel all that different. I'd long cultivated a minimalist lifestyle by then, and didn't want to change. Oh, sure, I'd indulge in travel some, and make little splurges here and there—finally got a propane refrigerator, and paid a pretty penny for a near-mint copy of forgetably-tuned piece of 1912 sheetmusic; the cover illustration depicting the sinking of Titanic (cranked out the day after the tragedy, no doubt), complete with an oval insert photo of Captain Smith. But my lifestyle stayed much the same. I laughed on reading about a French peasant who'd won the lottery but didn't change his accustomed way of living at all, to the bafflement of neighbors. When he died, they found all the money gathering serious dust bunnies under his bed.

Perhaps I was living a variation of dad's Depression years movie, in which he felt the wolf at the door no matter how rich he became: With me, having lived on the streets and sometimes going nearly a week without eating gave me a poverty consciousness I had to shake off. I didn't want to be telling younger generations what fun it was to be homeless.

That said, tho, there *is* one story I like to share. I was hunting an unlocked car below Pike Street Market in Seattle late one nite for a place to sleep out of the cold (figuring their owners had left them overnite). Earlier in the day I'd made a meal of the wild blackberries growing nearby. I tried a dozen doors—all locked. Then I approached a two-door coupe with a bumper sticker reading:

Prevent Theft - Lock Your Vehicle

I thought, *why even bother?* but checked anyway. Unlocked! I chuckled at life's little ironies as I climbed into the back seat and curled up. I was drifting off to sleep when pulled back to wakefulness by the sound of jangling keys and male voices right outside the car. Hoping to minimize an awkward moment, I opened the door before its owner inserted his key and announced my presence with some sleepy mumble. The owner stood back and silently held the door open wide like a doorman at the Ritz, letting me climb out and melt into the nite, a few remaining shreds of my dignity thus spared. He could've detained me and called the cops. But he didn't. He wouldn't've had to. He *was* a cop.

Those years were long gone, yet memories of the more soul-trying experiences lingered, coloring my outlook on life, even tho the sun of good fortune had since shone on me.

I seldom felt lonely—lonesome, yes; but not lonely. I obviously had a greater need for solitude than most. Living a solitary life might've left me feeling a bit empty at times—*that* was lonesome. Loneliness, on the other hand, was a constant gnawing ache to be with others, a depression for feeling too disconnected from others, and life in general, and this I rarely felt. Surrounded by a natural, oftentimes zero-stress environment, I'd learned to keep myself pleasant company, having worked past self-alienation and nurtured an inner life, while still feeling more or less connected to life at large—often thru the magic carpet ride books offered.

I was an omnivorous reader. I packed my copious built-in bookcases with books—novels, how-to, history, pictorials—and still had stacks double parked on the piano and boxfuls unceremoniously stashed under the bed and in the basement, all patiently awaiting more worthy placement. Some books I splurged on, buying new, but most were prized from the dingy coalmine-recesses of local thrift shops, for a pittance. Every book, no matter its pedigree, warmed my spirit, activated my brain cells, ignited my imagination, fused me thru time and space with others and the planet at large. I especially became a bookworm during rainy falls and snowy winters, when it was easier going within. Zet's Reading

Room in the Wilderness. I galloped thru suspense and adventure stories, but enjoyed leisurely savoring other writers' finer-wrought passages, re-reading them, building images, turning over delicious phrases: colorful seashells cast ashore in my mind.

Unread, partially read and someday-maybe-to-be-re-read books piled up throughout the cabin, yet I continued bringing home bag-fuls of fresh-caught books with each new foray to thrift shops, ongoing library sales, and new and used book stores. I soon discovered there was a fine line between a bibliophile and a biblio-maniac; I wore a well-trod path between the two.

Once, in efforts to gain perspective after threatening to have my cabin so overtaken by books they kicked me out, I did a medita-tion. Ever notice how the blanks between words on a page some-times lined up to form distinct, intriguing rivulets of air space? I imagined them as fractures in the book, fractures that in time would start the book on its biodegradable journey back to dust. Then I'd think there were other things in life worth savoring before *I* returned to dust. (It didn't help, but I liked the image.)

Once my vision started slipping in my early forties, I stocked up on dollar-store reading glasses like people living over the San Andreas Fault stocked up on earthquake-readiness supplies; I was forever misplacing, scratching and breaking them. I'd up the mag-nification power of the stash every few years to match declining vision. Always in the back of my mind was the classic "Twilight Zone" episode in which a myopic bookworm, whose nagging wife and teller job kept him from reading, finally got all the time in the world to read after becoming the sole survivor of a nuclear blast—and in a clumsy instant let his only pair of prescription glasses shatter into smithereens. Reading glasses littered every perch in my cabin like long-legged, giant-eyed bugs—atop shelves, tables, on the piano—ready to hop into service on my nose. (Why not just wear a pair around my neck? Too easy; part of me liked making life complicated.)

I wasn't a total hermit; I got out. I attended the local junior college, where I learned the rudiments of pottery and pursued stagecraft again, helping put on productions of *My Fair Lady* and *The Crucible*. A home phone further connected me to the world at large, and I could always drive to visit friends or invite them over. Besides, I was never really alone, what with all the wildlife teaming around the cabin—and, if I left the door open too long, *in* the cabin.

Maybe I didn't have much of a life, but I had a *great* half-life.

There were the times, tho, when all my books and friends and pottery and nature hikes and wildlife weren't enuf. I'd find myself yearning for some constant companion, a helpmate, a lover, to share my rustic paradise with. Tho most family members from both sides of my parent's lines married and had herds of kids, every now and then our family trees sprouted life-long bachelors. I feared I'd become my generation's designated loner, my nephews' and nieces' oddball uncle living alone in the woods.

I'd been unlucky in matters of the heart. Not for lack of prospects. I'd feel wild bursts of attraction in the first flushes of each possible new relationship, but commingled with a guilt-laden lust and feeling of hopeless ineptitude that doomed any chance for a new romance to blossom right out the gate.

My hopelessly romantic imagination soared like an eagle, but if my latest attraction didn't respond in kind to my chimerical fascination—which she'd have to be psychic to catch I hid my feelings so well—the thrill vanished, aborted before birth. Without confirmation she'd felt something too, by word or touch, I couldn't sustain my fickle infatuation long enuf for her to respond: I'd be dressed in black and mourning what might have been and walking away from the latest shallow grave littering my heartscape by the time she'd think to maybe give the poor boy a try.

My relative inexperience could leave me feeling like a callow teen trapped in an older body. I flip-flopped between acting my age and wanting to let my feelings out—let the chips fall where they may. Perhaps I had a touch of the *Lolita* syndrome in me, the boy torn away from first tender teen love-lust and forever trying to recapture the feeling. While I didn't lust after young girls like Humbert Humbert, I suppose some part of me *was* futilely seeking another Dawn of my teen years, when life was simpler and there existed a shared mystery of self-discovery; not my current life in which most of my more mature peers were already grandparents, with one or two marriages under their belt and regular sex a given.

Result: I had long droughts between plentiful rains. The few women who'd graced my life gave me hope each time I was maybe at last becoming couples material. But I was never able to establish a solid foundation of understanding to make it last. Six months together with someone was to me what six years was to others.

Long story short: By the time I hit fifty I'd all but resigned myself to perennial bachelorhood—until I met Nuela at a rainbow gathering, and my whole life changed.

ELEVEN

The supreme happiness in life is the conviction that we are loved.
—**Victor Hugo**

I WAS STANDING IN LINE at the Jah Man Camp, one of the national rainbow gathering's more popular free open-air camp kitchens. Each had its own specialties, makeshift ambiance and personality. A milling crowd of tie dyes, long hair and bare feet might've led the uninitiated to think the 60s Haight-Ashbury had somehow been zapped thru time and space to the Idaho wilderness.

Not knowing why—maybe an intoxicating whiff of gardenia in the air—I turned around...and fell headlong into the dancing violet eyes of a woman with a face like a flower.

My heart stopped—and then started racing so fast it threatened to break a rib. Long raven hair spilled down her head like a waterfall. Full bangs splashed over her forehead, enticingly concealing her third eye. Her mellow vibe and lithe figure, all but revealed by her golden half-sarong and abbreviated purple tank top, combined to leave me gasping for air. I almost dissolved on the spot. They'd have placed a memorial marker: "Here lies Zet, reduced to a molten glob by unbearable beauty."

Remarkably, I managed to exchange a few tongue-tied words

with her while we waited our turn to be served, after my heartbeat slowed to an easy gallop—words like "hi." She was gracious, all charm and radiant smiles, with the open-circuit energy I aspired to. We introduced ourselves. While people at gatherings could hang for hours—days—and have a grand time without feeling the need to learn each other's nametags, I reached for the obvious conversational ice breaker.

"I'm Nuela." The name fit her somehow; the way she said it evoked an image of gentle ripples in a snow-melt stream. I told her mine.

"Zet? I've never met a 'Zet' before," she said. "Intriguing name; it's got a subtle kind of pizzazz." She buzzed like a bee on pronouncing the last word.

My name had always bothered me before for sounding too abstract or foreign. I'd envied people with common names like Bill and Jim and Bob. Suddenly I was happy with my moniker.

***

Rainbow gatherings happened every summer. The high flying alternative-culture get-togethers were launched in 1972 by hippie-types holding a far-minded vision of forging a year-round Peace Village, an intentional rural community of grand scale and high ideals. The goal: like the Joni Mitchell song, "to get ourselves back to the Garden."

Such dreams never panned out on any substantial level then, besides rare places like The Farm. Group energies were too scattered, money too scarce, and oppressive forces too great to manifest our current way of living then. What was meant to be a summer workshop of combined talents and resources to brainstorm for the creation of a permanent alternative community instead morphed into an annual summer rendezvous, a place so-minded people came to nurture the hippie-rainbow dream of living together harmoniously on the land—at least for a few weeks each year. Those of us that saw the handwriting on the wall (and could read it) saw the old world dying and wanted to be part of a new one striving to be born. The gatherings, at their best, gave people a chance to help make the vision a reality. They gave guidelines for what was possible when people truly worked together.

Participants from all walks of life came together on remote national forest lands, far from *Babylon*—what we called the crazy "normal" world, marching lock-step into the tar pits of certain self-destruction. Open to all and bursting with a non-denominational, earth-religion flavor, the gatherings—while attracting the adventurous outdoors type and those resonating with countercultural values—were otherwise made up of your basic cross-section of human consciousness. There were sailors and pirates, dolphins and sharks, builders and destroyers, and hybrids of each, not uncommon in those trying times. (One could put on a holy rag one moment and fly off the handle the next.) As a gent I met there named Starvin' Marvin put it, "At every gathering you have people who *make* it happen, people who *watch* it happen, and people who stand around asking, *"what's happening?"*

Held for decades the first week of July, each year in a different state, rainbows could number over 30,000 celebrants. All-volunteer organizers prided themselves in living light on the land and leaving the place cleaner than they found it. Free camp kitchens (most offering tasty veggie camp-cuisine), medical tents, child care and spontaneous live music, all donated by participants and angel backers, transformed the wilderness into an instant, albeit ephemeral, village in the wilderness.

Individuals felt safe going about naked or in abbreviated glad rags for hours, days at a time. Droves of people, including me, ventured further out of their nudist closet. At times there were mishaps for going naked too long. Persons descended on the first-aid center with painful all-over sunburns after being naked all day in the high elevation; and with cut and bruised feet for going bare-

171

foot over sharp, rocky ground.

The gatherings also served to help people deal with body shame, perforce, thru public privies. Doing your business squatting amid scores of people in mutual view, while daunting at first, was a liberating experience, every bit as much as growing to feel at ease naked in public. Some speculated maybe it was our eliminative process that made our bodies feel "dirty" in the first place—disgust by association—for our sexual organs, which did double-duty for peeing, shared proximity with our butt holes. Whatever the causes, we further came to terms with our bodies and their functions.

At first I'd only skinnydip in the river or sit naked on a rock by the water, feeling too self-conscious to go nude beyond the bathing area, even if the day was baking. There's some hardwired primordial connection between our mostly-water bodies and bodies of water, making being naked near liquid feel more natural somehow. At clothing-optional beaches, if you walked away from the water naked—say to go across the road to a grocery store—you'd get busted in a heartbeat. Established naked zones were etched in stone, and woe to the one who crossed the line.

At the gatherings, bolder souls went about or hung out at camp with few or no clothes: Whether out hiking, sitting about a kitchen campfire, dancing to drums by the bonfire at nite, or dancing at noon to troubadour musicians galloping thru faithful renderings of "Uncle John's Band," more than a few shucked their rags and said howdy to their natural selves.

At first I didn't know how to muster anything approaching the aplomb and easy confidence others displayed being naked in public, happy grins on their faces. (I was convinced every last one of them had just gotten laid, or expected to momentarily.) They set the example, tho, and I'd finally get the courage to leave the river area naked and timidly walk a ways about the far-flung site. I'd still feel painfully self-conscious; my old headspace lingered. Thoughts segued from *I guess no one's going to arrest me,* to *I feel like I'm on stage,* to *everyone knows I've never done this before,* to *no big deal.*

I trekked to two gatherings all told, after being encouraged to by Cousin Zor. "It'll do you good, Zet," he said. "I promise. I think you're ready for the rainbow experience. And I bet you'll meet someone you'll hit it off with, you old dog."

The first one, in Nevada, rosy predictions notwithstanding, was a bust. I'd been between girlfriends too long. Horny toad that I was, being amid scores of beautiful, free-spirited, often naked and topfree women, blithely enjoying nature, was one tough acid test; I flunked miserably. I couldn't get my head, heart and loins on the same page to save my life. I felt like a penniless urchin with a raging sweet tooth, looking thru the plate glass window of a candy store loaded with every sweet treat on earth.

I was too much a stick-in-the-mud, too much yet a stranger to myself, to gear up into the fast-swirling gypsy currents surging thru the site. The divergent group energies were rough at first— like the Oklahoma Land Rush, everyone scrambling to find a nice spot, set up, and settle in—but coalesced by the third or fourth day into a palpable force, an increasingly unified field of energy, each person a synapse in a group nervous system. One was either open, allowing the high-voltage energy to flow thru and energize; or closed, in fear of getting over-amped and loosing oneself.

I snapped shut. For me, the scene was a perfect example of heaven and hell alloyed in equal portion, creating an unimaginable purgatory. John Fogerty's plaintive wail, "Have You Ever Seen the Rain?" played on the jukebox in my head as I walked amid the sunshine-splashed paradise a walking cloudburst.

People always told me everything works for the best. That lamentable experience forced me to face myself on yet deeper levels,

173

ones I never knew existed. I confronted unreal expectations over how my life *was supposed* to be and irrational behavior patterns forever sabotaging my life. I scraped some more barnacles off my hull.

By the time I headed to my second national gathering, in Idaho, a few years later, I was still exorcizing demons, but I'd come to know myself better, was more friend than foe to myself. I was actually beginning to feel like a real human being.

I was primed to meet life on a new level, even if I could still be painfully shy around women I felt attracted to.

☀

Our turn came in Jah-Man's outdoor food line.

The volunteer crew served us tempeh burgers with grilled portabella mushrooms, mashed potatoes, and corn on the cob. Such quality offerings were a rarity at gatherings and supplies were limited, so gourmet-minded veggies had cued up hours before.

"Irie," said the stout worker, with dreads down his back, in open admiration to Nuela as he took her bowl to fill. (One brought their own bowls and cups or didn't eat.) I wasn't up on my Rastafarian, but the way he said it sounded somewhere between "positively righteous, woman" and "I want to be your love slave"—or was that what was I was thinking?

We shared our little feast sitting on a big flat rock nearby. A wandering troubadour serenaded the dinner camp with reggae tunes and world beat songs. Most, but not all, were dressed. I was amazed how much keener my appetite was, eating outdoors and being in such bewitching company as Nuela. As I munched on the cob, kernels burst into a symphony of sweetness in my mouth. The tempeh burger fired up so many feel-good endorphins I felt giddy. And the mashed potatoes—real mashed potatoes, not the cardboard concoction 98 percent of places palmed off—drizzled in olive oil and sprinkled with nutritional yeast flakes and raw garlic from my personal stash, anchored in my belly like a ship taking ballast.

After we finished, Nuela playfully took my hand and suggested we go off on a hike to work off our meal. Feeling a force pulling us together like a tractor beam, I offered little resistance.

I rarely felt comfortable playing the bold initiator in any new relationship. I loved assertive women—as long as they were sweet in their forthrightness and didn't trounce on fragile male pride in the process. Admittedly, it was a fine trick, one few women ever learned—or were wont to try to, for the way it could pull them out of their comfort zone by appearing fast.

"Promise me you won't get too excited, okay?" she said offhandedly after we'd hiked and chatted a while. She was out of her clothes and sandals as fast and effortlessly as another might remove her hat.

"The day's really too nice for clothes. That sun just feels so awesome." She stood still a moment, closing her eyes and facing up towards the sun, smiling, stretched out her arms, as if silently acknowledging an old friend. She was such a vision standing there blissfully naked, it pained me; made me wish I was the sun she was reaching out towards.

Sensuous beauty always had that affect on me. Whether it be the pure rich wash of aquamarine of a baby spot flooding the stage, an intricately-convoluted Bach fugue, or the exquisite curves and glow of a woman's body, beauty could often inspire feelings of unbearable agony in me. The female form was interactive artwork I wanted to gaze on in a thousand different lightings; a virgin continent, brimming with mystery, I wanted to explore with infinite leisure.

"Feel free to join me," she said gently, possibly the faintest shadow of a smirk on her face, as if she knew the effect she was having on me.

I knew what she meant: I'd've been amused by me too, if I weren't so preoccupied feeling stuck wishing I was where I thought I ought to be that I could never get there.

I was flustered by how fast our relationship was progressing, not that I was complaining. I suspected getting naked might only make me hornier, and I wasn't sure that would be a good thing.

"Don't mind if I do," I said, loosing tank top, elastic-waist shorts and flip-flops in four seconds flat.

Ambivalent feelings aside, I never needed encouragement to escape my cloth cage, except maybe at a doctor's exam room or airport strip-search. Strolling naked thru the woods with a new-found maybe-sweetie on a sunny day was my idea of paradise. I stashed both our outfits and footwear in my day pack and we continued strolling au naturel.

I called on supreme will power. The reality of walking thru the woods with a naked goddess nearly overwhelmed me. (To my credit, I didn't salute her divinity.) Something good was definitely-maybe in the offing. I knew I'd bungle it in my puppy-dog eagerness to ravish her on the spot if I wasn't patient and follow her lead.

"I spend a lot of time naked around home," I admitted to her. This wasn't a revelation you let drop to just anyone, lest you engender "way more than I wanted to know" responses.

"I'm not surprised," she said as we walked on, as if I'd said my favorite color was teal. We were strolling slower now, in our bare feet, mindful of each step, attuned to the wilderness. "I noticed your tan right away. I bet you spend a lot of time naked out in nature, don't you?"

I looked over before answering.

Damn! Just when I was doing so well. I noticed how her breasts quivered enticingly with each step, exciting instant frenzy in me. She was a peach tree, laden with fruit, swaying in the breeze; I was a harvester, trying to remember what I did with my ladder. I was glad for a subject to distract me. "Sure," I said, voice thick. "I live out in the high desert; I pretty much go bare whenever the weather's nice."

"A*ha*!" she said, like she was putting a board puzzle's blue sky piece in place, oblivious to the effect she was having on me. She stopped and faced me. "I *knew* there was something about you felt simpatico. Were you raised a nudist too?"

"No, I—*you* were?"

"Well, yes... No biggie, really; most of my friends growing up were too."

"Maybe no biggie to *you*." I looked at her in wonder, incipient lust replaced by awe and not a little envy. For a second I wondered if maybe she was the girl in the nudist magazine with WE LOVE ELVIS painted on her backside. We started walking again. "I come from a long line of nudists, supposedly," I said, "but I've never been to a nudist resort in my life and never knowingly met anyone *raised* nudist my whole life...well, other than my aunt—and my mom, but she only visited nudist camps in summer and didn't like them at all. I wished I could've gone to them growing up. Then I could've gotten all-over burns instead of those funny ones, like a red apple chomped white around the middle."

Nuela giggled.

"Your parents were obviously nudists, then," I said.

"Big time. They believed nudism was part of a wholesome way of life: fresh air and sunshine, natural food—you know...living close to nature. Like this!" She stepped out and twirled around, arms over head, in a little dance of joy. "My sisters and I grew up in Florida, in one nudist community or another. We spent so much time naked getting dressed was a treat. Within reasonable limits, mom and pop never forced us to go dressed *or* nude. They tried to let us make our own choice in the matter. They were vegetarians; no double-cheese murder burgers for us. While other kids in school had their tuna fish or ham on white bread, I had tofu on home baked sprouted whole wheat, fresh fruit and nuts. Pop was a professional massage therapist and mom an herbal practitioner."

177

The reality of her naturist pedigree, plus coming from the same state and lifestyle circles as my mom's family, sank in as we hiked thru the wilderness and traded further histories.

We held hands to help each other over rocky terrain and at some point kept them nested. I felt one with her entire body just holding her hand. As awesome a feeling as that was, somehow our minds—even our spirits—were melding too. I knew we had soul receptors in our palms—along with our tongue tips and soles of our feet—but I'd never before felt such an powerful connection just by holding hands. She felt it too, I was sure.

She told me more about herself. Nuela was seven years younger. She was a yoga instructor, a newly-published writer, and played the flute and glockenspiel ("xylophone to most").

She said she hadn't been involved with anyone in a half-year (music to my ears). She'd left her last boyfriend, a self-proclaimed spiritual teacher who predicted the rise of Atlantis on a specific date. "I'd liked him a lot, despite his eccentric notion." But he was never the same after the day came and went without a rise from the ocean floor. "Last I heard, he was trying to channel Charlie McCarthy." She'd just moved from Florida, having driven cross-country, sleeping in her Chevy 20 camper van en route. She was intent on putting a down payment on some country land from savings and what was left of a modest royalty advance for her second novel, *Life on Planet Earth*, which (I later read) was about quirky characters abandoning a worn-out big city lifestyle and making a fresh start in Telluride, Colorado. Now that she'd given her fictional characters new life, she figured it was time to follow suit. She wanted to make her own fresh start by building a little house on the land and living the good life, somewhere in the Northwest.

Her eyes lit up when I told her that was precisely what I'd done. I showed her a wallet-size snapshot of my place I carried in my medicine bag like a proud papa, along with loose sage, citrine, rose quartz and hematite.

"It looks wonderful. You built this yourself?"

"I did, indeed. And without power tools," I added, like a parent whose child was enrolled in a class for the exceptional.

"Well, *I'm* impressed," she said and laughed a laugh of tinkling silver bells my ears lapped up as music. "I'd love to visit you sometime. I want to get more ideas on how to build my place. You open to visitors in your hermit kingdom?" She gave my hand a squeeze as she asked that sent an extra current of indescribable energy coursing thru my being. I wanted her so much I had trouble thinking of anything else.

"I am," I said, the words catching in my throat. Embarrassed for my voice betraying my feelings and afraid to say anything more, I looked away. I happened to spot the glimmer of water off to the right. "Look, just what the doctor ordered, a swimming hole."

"I'll race you," she said, and grinned. If my heart was on my sleeve, she didn't seem to mind.

We sprinted over and cooled off in a small pond fringed with watercress, in the process startling some tadpoles and a flotilla of water striders. She shrieked over the water's icy coldness. I screamed silently and worked to get my breath back. I'd needed a good cooling down in more ways than one. After a brief splashing fight, we jumped out and made like frozen food popped in the microwave, sunning ourselves warm on the pond's wild-grass shore. We munched on some 'cress and shared my last Fuji apple I'd been carrying since morning.

A pregnant moment came when it felt only right to lean over and kiss her, so I did. She met my kiss and responded in kind. Then, as if by silent understanding, we restrained from going further.

That nite we didn't.

By morning, I felt I'd died and gone to Heaven and returned to Earth to proclaim the wonders.

✳

Nuela and I became inseparable. Ours became a decade-long union.

Later, we'd agree our meeting had been predestined, the logical outcome of our individual life-flows coming together at precisely the right moment. We were both open to fast-tracking a new relationship, and she was able to guide it.

I gave her a sense of anchor, the feeling she could share anything with me, and an appreciation for the depth of her feeling and the span of what I discovered was a considerable intellect. She gave me a sense of anchor as well, made me feel it was okay being me, saw beyond my low-key exterior hiding a volcano of passion, gleaned my potential to become a fuller human bean. Not that she was the kind of woman who thrilled at the prospect of changing a man over—I avoided those like telemarketer calls at dinnertime, offering genuine knock-off whatchadiggies "...*below* cost; how can you refuse?" This woman just made me want to *do* things: be more, see more—everything but snore more.

A new-fledged couple, we caravanned from the rainbow gathering—after it wound down four days later—to my homestead. She loved the place to a fault, and the placing, too. She decided Shasta would do just fine. "I can't believe the view you have," she enthused, looking out the upper windows at the mountain, mantled in snow. But my cabin was small. Each of us treasured our alone time almost as much as our together time; plus, she needed a quiet inviolate space for her writing and yoga, as she'd originally planned. Serendipitously, the first day we looked we found a nice parcel for sale, cheap, a five-minute walk thru the junipers from me.

✳

She claimed it was no biggie, but, to me, Nuela's having been raised nudist was a rarity beyond imagining in our perennially-dressed world. I made a wild guess not one in a thousand Americans knew anyone who'd been raised nudist, and maybe only one in a fifty thousand—if that—who were themselves raised nudist.

Nuela became a super role model for me to continue straightening out my skewered physicality and repressed feelings. At once I got more into my body and beyond it, and thus learned to more fully embrace my greater self (as she called it). Keeping a grand perspective on things, she pointed out how our narrow-minded world, with its dead food and body-unfriendly environments, had not only denied us the freedom to enjoy our physical selves unwrapped, but a godless materialistic world had equally made difficult becoming aware we even *had* transcendent selves to get to know.

"We know God—Supreme Being, Divine Mother, Great Spirit, whatever you want to call it—is infinite," she said one day when were off on one of our freehikes from home. She was waxing spiritual. "Made in the Creator's image, we're infinite too, even while inhabiting these finite forms called bodies we often over-identify with." Her face clouded. "Letting people nurture this awareness and become self-empowered threatens those in control who—ignorant or rebellious of the Universe's plan—want to keep the little people in their place, to preserve their twisted little power base on this rock in space."

Her face brightened. "Sometimes, I see them like so many Wizards of Oz, hoping to maintain the grand illusion for us simple-minded Munchkins that *they're* the wise, all-knowing ones who are always looking out for our best interests. And we, too helpless to help ourselves, should trust them implicitly. But as we embrace our greater selves, Totos everywhere are pulling back the curtains on their grand deception, exposing them for the rank

181

frauds they are, in dire need of hotfooting it to Power Freaks Anonymous." She laughed at the image.

We paused to admire the sunset splashing the sky with rich lavenders and exquisite pinks. Gazing on the sight, I couldn't help but think the universe was unfolding according to plan.

We started back and she finished her thoughts. "The thing that gets me is how becoming enlightened can be as simple as enjoying sunsets, really enjoying them, like we just did—oh, check that funny pinecone—and learning to recognize the illusionary obstacles put in our way we'd come to accept as realities. It's like Emerson said, 'we are wiser than we know.' Lots of people are already enlightened but don't even realize it. Until we learn, we'll refuse to make that leap past the deceptions we've bought into and tune into the higher realities of life's bounty. We'll cling to the memory of a nitemare even while walking thru paradise."

It took me a while to digest that one. I'd always thought of myself as more or less enlightened. I suddenly realized I'd been holding onto a slew of nameless fears that kept me from being more in the here and now.

Nuela displayed such laser-like perceptions and perspectives, at times it made me wonder who she was—really. Add the way she possessed such an extraordinary unselfconscious acceptance of her body and those of others, and it was like she'd beamed here from another world: *Greetings, people of Planet Earth. I am Nuela. Be not alarmed, I come to you in naked peace.*

Once leaving home—"I never got used to the humidity"—it had taken her a while to learn how to coexist in our over-packaged world without it crimping her style. In time, she adapted and could be dressed or nude with fairly equal ease, always choosing clothes the most body-friendly and weather-matched, but at the same time managing to look spiffy.

We fixed dinner together later that evening. Needless to say, being the daughter of veggie parents, she knew worlds of culinary tricks. She helped get my diet back on track. She had ways of fixing grains and vegetables together with tofu and mushrooms and nut butter sauces that kept my taste buds eager for more, and showed me how to make them myself, enabling me to return the favor other evenings.

"I thought of starting a restaurant once, but decided I didn't want to spend *that* much time in the kitchen," she said. "I don't believe in recipes per se; I run on intuition in food combining, like any good cook. I love improvising on the spot, using whatever's on hand.

The next day, we were both looking spiffy in nothing, off on another nature stroll, wending our way along one of the parallel-stick-defined trails I'd etched thru the adjoining national forest as a low-key amusement ride for meditative hikers. We'd been talking about body awareness.

"You grow up nudist and you have a whole different attitude towards clothes," she said. We were passing a bleached cow skull I'd found hiking cross-country and placed beside the trail as a curiosity. She saw it and laughed, diverted. "I'd only put clothes on when I felt like it—except when we went on the road, of course, and then my parents explained how things were beyond our gates, how most people were uncomfortable with their bare bodies and in seeing others'."

She became so intent on her subject she walked right by another item I'd found in the forest: a coffee mug, ceramic handle gone, reading: "Mutants for Nuclear Power." It sported a Cyclops happy face.

"How could people reject their own bodies?" she asked.

"It's a bafflement."

"It struck me as totally weird. I mean, how weird is that? When I was small, I naturally assumed the whole world was clothing-optional. I'll always remember the day I was disabused of that notion.

"I was in town one day with my parents. Even tho I must have been wearing something myself, I remember thinking how odd it was how all the people around us looked like they were wrapped up like cocoons. *Who are all these cocoon people*, I thought. What was *that* all about? It took me years to understand. It saddened me to realize nudists were only a tiny minority in a body-phobic world, publicly wed to dress.

"But, strange to say, I rarely felt 'imprisoned' in clothes—as you put it—when I got older. Only when we were away from home too long in the textile world and I longed to pull off my clothes on a hot day but couldn't, and so started overheating—*then* I felt trapped. My parents always tried to get us the thinnest, most breathable cloth for such excursions to minimize discomfort."

"Lucky you, growing up with such thoughtful parents," I said. "My dad was the Cocoon Master."

She laughed, then grew thoughtful. "I suppose I was at that," she mused. "It's so easy to take for granted the way we're raised until you compare notes with others later and start to appreciate what each of our parents did for us. For instance, I envy how you got to grow up all in one place, not having to move to other towns and leave old friends behind. *That's* a rare thing, too. But it's too bad your mom felt forced to be naked at that summer camp as a child, like you told me. That could turn anyone off to the nudist lifestyle. I understand now how tortured you must have felt growing up the way you did. Poor thing."

She stopped and turned and gave me a hug; her pointed breasts, twin heat-seeking orbs, burned into my lower ribcage.

"Why'd you leave?" I asked, suddenly feeling better, a flood of endorphins having magically transferred into me as if by osmosis. "I don't think I'd ever want to, or could, even."

"Well...free as it was in some ways, I found the main focus on nudity limiting, finally. I understood the need for such focus to defend and nurture a lifestyle that went so radically against textile consciousness, but such a constant focus began to cramp my style.

People had moved in—the manager lowered the bar to keep afloat—who were basically unfamiliar or uninterested with naturism. 'Yahoo nudists,' I called them. You know, people thinking and behaving just like mainstream society: drinking, smoking, meat-eating, loud music, fixated on speed and engines—everything but preferring to go naked a lot. They were a minority, but all it took was a few. They just couldn't connect the dots between being naked and living in harmony. I wondered: Were we naked to live, or living to be naked?

I was too dyslexic to want to even try grasping that one, knowing it would drive me nuts, but I thought I knew what she meant.

"Anyhow, those yahoos made me realize it was time to move on; the universe was giving me a hotfoot. I figured I was willing to trade the body freedom a nudist community offered for the chance to explore other cultures, climates and lifestyles—*hoping* to live without clothes when I wanted, but having it be only a part of my lifestyle, not the single defining one. And here I am, having a micro naturist community with you, fellow nature nut." She turned and gave me another hug and added a smooch.

The juke box in my head retrieved "Afternoon Delight" from its song bank, cued it up, and commenced playing.

☀

Nuela resonated with my neck of the woods. Other properties, closer to town, with tall trees, easy water and utilities stubbed in—costing up to fifty times more for a fraction the size—were more popular among those who could afford it and liked living close in. But everyone's house was in sight of everyone else's, or nearly so—too close for naked comfort anywhere but in a nudist community. Why'd people feel pulled to crowd themselves so close together? I supposed having shopping conveniences, cultural amenities and proximity to jobs and schools were more important than the peace and quiet and freedom of lifestyle deep country living provided. I'd once pinned a quote from Isaiah:5:8 by my cabin door that captured my sentiments exactly: "Woe to those who join house to house, who add field to field, until there is no more room, and you are made to dwell alone in the midst of the land."

She stayed in my cabin while we built hers. Since I'd built a generous south porch, we lived around the place as much as in it and learned how not to cramp each other. My former bachelor ways, with their sometimes lax housekeeping standards, had a rude awakening living with a woman having thresholds of neatness and cleanliness higher than mine, but I bowed before the inevitable and made concessions. I gave the wood floor planks the first honest scrubbing they'd had in years, started putting dirty clothes in a wicker hamper she scored from a thrift shop for a dollar, and switched over to real dinner plates after a long existence using paper to save on water and time spent washing. I figured I got off easy. She didn't freak over the occasional spider wanting to share the place, or unduly mind the windows not always being kept spotless—not even that the kitchen table was fashioned of floor plank remnants.

Nuela knew how to swing a hammer. We fashioned her new home the next spring and summer on a tucked-away parcel of juniper and sage with the same fabulous mountain view. We constructed it almost entirely out of recycled lumber, bought cheap from a local disassembled sawmill.

We built without the blessings of the local building department. Over-rigid building regulations could make you feel your determination to live the simple life—free of conforming to maddening specs for room size, ceiling height, stairway width, nail spacing, every last solitary piece of building material—was an unreasonable intrusion on one's pursuit of domestic tranquility. It could leave you with the feeling you were building for the State rather than yourself. I'd told her how I'd felt so much under their gun I turned alcoholic for a year to cope; I brewed five gallons of indus-

186

trial-strength beer every week to fuel my thirst to escape bureau-
cratic intrusions (and, in fairness, to unwind from the brain-numbing strain of homeless living).

She decided she wanted none of that. Part of her Goddess Prayer
went "…and deliver us from Babylon…" She could live in an
unofficial dwelling quite nicely, thank you, safely out of sight of
vagrant whistle blowers; the building department had bigger fish
to fry, anyway. Between them and the health department, our
parcels were too small to qualify for setting up a composting toilet, but we installed one anyway—non-electric.

She planted rose bushes around her doorway and built planter
boxes underneath her two south windows for finishing touches,
soon giving her cottage an enchanted storybook air. Later, she'd
start up a vegetable garden after mulching lots of hay and compost
into the sandy soil, heavy on the tomatoes and corn. She'd gotten
a rain cistern in place and it had rained enuf to have water to play
with. She couldn't believe I'd never done a garden; neither could
I. After I learned the joy of organic gardening thru her, of producing food from your own labor, I started my first one: garlic and
potatoes; I liked underground food. I also planted a sapling apple
tree and hoped for a miracle.

Nuela again indulged in being naked to her heart's content, at her
place, at mine, and in between, weather allowing. We were forever visiting each other's place on foot, strolling along the intercon-
necting path on forest land we'd marked—not visible from the seldom used cinder road. We removed any sharp rocks and twigs to
make the link barefoot-friendly. We came to think of our two
dwellings as one home with an extra-long connecting breezeway.
Over time, we developed favorite spots in between to linger at
should we meet on the way over to the others'. Sometimes, if one
was bringing food to the other, we had an ad hoc picnic on the spot
we met and left something for the wildlife to feast on. There was

nothing like naked lunches in woods with congenial company to stimulate the appetite.

She had certain hours earmarked for her writing—freelance magazine articles, researching her next novel, journaling—and she drove to town twice a week to teach yoga classes. During such times I enjoyed tinkering at my upright piano, toying with writing of my own, or puttering around the place: gathering firewood, getting mistletoe out of the trees, re-filling the hummer feeder, trying to remember where I buried three silver dollars twenty years before and why. Sometimes I'd brainstorm home and land improvements that stood a one in ten chance of advancing beyond the fantasy stage, but that was all right, or what was an imagination for?

Sometimes, together at my place, we enjoyed playing duets at the piano: "Scarborough Faire" was one of our favorites; she alternated between flute and glockenspiel. (She'd learned the latter in high school marching band and still enjoyed its shimmering sound, but you didn't ever ask her to play "Louie, Louie.") We'd segue from that tune into "Greensleeves," which shared similar chord patterns, and then back again. "We'd tackle Three Dog Night's "Joy to the World" in our wilder moods, and she cut a mean flute on "California Dreamin.'"

Nuela was just what the doctor ordered: a cheerful companion and helpmate, a fellow artistic spirit, a friend who resonated with my quirky nature—and a beautiful woman with healthy appetites and a clear-water perspective on life.

Among other things, she taught me how nudity and sex could be the same or different, depending on how we chose to direct and focus our energies.

"Keeping your sexual energy balanced and integrated is the main thing, Zet," she told me one day in her soothing voice. (It was like smoke curling up out of a chimney—one of the things that endeared her to me from the start—along with her bright laugh. Some people I was otherwise fond of could have voices like clogged gutter pipes or squealing door hinges.) "Keep your energy on even keel," she said, "and then you don't go overboard trying to catch up, driving yourself nuts with sex on the brain for feeling you're missing. Keeping balanced is the key: It's that simple. Then your body isn't sexual and it isn't *not* sexual; it just *is*."

It took me a few years to understand that. I could be a slow learner, but she was a patient teacher.

✳

If I hadn't met Nuela, I doubt I'd be penning this rambling narrative now. Besides getting me on track to rediscovering and accepting my natural self, she inspired me to take up my pen again. And once she convinced me it was time to join the twenty-first century, the blank computer screen now became my friend, waiting patiently to be filled by whatever I wanted to say.

I despaired at first of ever learning the critter—I all but lost it for a while, feeling like a Ludite—but once I got it down, it liberated the writing process for me. I could capture elusive thoughts fluttering thru my mind two to three times faster than any desktop manual typewriter ever let me and with a fraction of the exertion. At first I missed the resounding key action on the typewriter that had felt so satisfying, like giving the piano a percussive workout; I'd found the resounding clatter of the striking keys aided the thought process. The action of the computer keyboard was percussive too, I learned; just a little subtler, like an electric piano's. I didn't appreciate there was no going back until I had to unearth my manual Underwood typewriter once in winter after I ran out of stored solar juice for the laptop. Its primitive action and clatter and constant carriage returns after the Pavlovian bell cue were now unacceptable—the difference between driving a sputtering relic of a Studebaker and a purring Mercedes fresh off the show-room floor.

Thanks to Nuela's encouragement, I'd gain a depth of creative fulfillment from writing I hadn't felt since my construction days. She wrote a nugget of writing advice I managed to keep a copy of over the years. Even now, it's over my desk, encouraging me with this project:

Dare to write what you *really* think and feel and imagine. Get it down—you can switch hats later and be editor. Play with it, shape it, mold it into a story and you fashion something unique that didn't exist before. Polish it to a fare-thee-well and it's possible you'll have something others will enjoy reading.

To the mind and spirit, writing is as real, as solid, as lumber; as penetrating as nails. With a completed work you've fashioned a veritable structure of words, a storied dwelling—one among the myriad populating bookshelf villages around the world.

Possibly few people will ever see it; most that do will only absently glance at the cover; some poke their heads in distractedly, half-hoping the words will leap out and embrace them like a long-lost lover. A select few, though, will feel led to it and come to explore it at leisure. They'll admire the architecture, the furnishings, the paintings on the wall—glad for their imaginations having found sweet haven for a while.

I hadn't her patience for revision work—"Oftentimes, 90 per-cent of writing is *re*-writing," she told me once—but I did the best I could, along with interminable proofreading, without driving myself mad. Far be it be for me, tho, to deprive certain readers of the satisfaction of pouncing on an occasional mispelt word or mis-placed, comma.

TWELVE

By walking naked you gain much more than coolness. You feel an unexpected sense of freedom from restraint, an uplifting and almost delirious sense of simplicity.
—**Colin Fletcher**

EVEN AS I'D changed my tune and pursued domestic happiness, growth-oriented people everywhere pulled themselves together, discovering more positive paths in their lives. Some, echoing Nuela's view, believed it wasn't so much our evolving as it was the remedial excising of internal obstacles—mindsets keeping us from being our natural selves, programmed into us by reality manipulators. Their attempts to control the planet's consciousness for their own demon-god amusement, wonky gratification and spooky notions of noblesse oblige, once understood, lost sway over us.

Of course, there were plenty of external material challenges to overcome too. Like the countless environmental poisons then part of conventional lifestyles.

Sixty percent of processed food in supermarkets was genetically-modified (*Frankenfood,* one wit called it: "It's a*live!"*—or is

191

it?"); we nuked meat products with the radiation equivalent of 2.5 million chest X-rays—destroying vitamins and possibly creating mutant bacteria and viruses; toxic aluminum in underarm antiperspirants worked to compromise the body's immune system; cheerful-looking but harmful chemical food colorings shot thru our over-processed food products in efforts to make them look palatable after being eviscerated; toxic chemicals in toothpaste included directions for calling poison control in the unlikely event children ever swallowed any; tasty chlorine was dumped into our drinking water to kill the pathogens lurking in our over-centralized water supply reservoirs; and deadly mercury amalgams in our dental fillings poisoned the bloodstream whenever one worked loose.

Our environment was a toxic minefield we navigated constantly. We learned to dodge laundry detergents reeking of cheap perfume and that irritated the skin; fumes from women's hair spray, peroxide tints, nail polish and nail remover could make a strong man gag; and new homes outgassed such witches' brews of formaldehyde and other deadly substances—in the plywood, carpeting, insulation and paint—that happy new home owners' celebrations might be interrupted by going into toxic shock.

Environmental physicians believed certain, more sensitive people could only absorb only so many such toxins before triggering a tipping point and their bodies screamed "Enuf!"—becoming so ultra-sensitive even the smallest pollutant could set off a crippling reaction. For one such, a dedicated reader, the paper-processing and binding chemicals used in book manufacturing were triggers. She couldn't read safely without first airing the book out in the sun for days and then putting the book inside a transparent box, with an open side for gloved page-turning.

The ubiquitous products of a ridiculously powerful global cartel of mad-chemist pharmaceutical corporations were the bane of our lives. They invaded our lives at every turn with patent medicines, most of which, if lucky, would do no more than drain your wallet and teach you to know better; and, if unlucky, might kill you. Such over-prescribed wonder drugs, too often randomly con-cocted by Mad Hatter lab scientists who then said, "let's see if we can market *this* for something," came with reassuring warnings like "possible side effects may include dizziness, heart seizure and death. See your doctor." (And these were drugs that, even when used "properly," killed over 100,000 a year in the U.S. alone; and, idiotically, were touted by the same system campaigning for "a drug-free America.") It's not that there weren't many real life-sav-ing drugs mixed in, but people might lose their lives trying to find them.

As we got a handle on such material obstacles and learned to live more naturally, we began waking up to the illusion-based mindset we'd formerly bought into, holding us back from being empowered and healthy beings. We adopted natural medicines and preventive healthcare and cruelty-free diets, avoided toxic prod-ucts, quit using products exploiting the animal kingdom, became super-select what television programming, if any, we watched (turning off commercials to avoid brain rot); moved to more peaceful environs, worked to preserve and restore wild habitats, got fit, recycled, pre-cycled, adopted renewable energy sources...whatever it took to reclaim our lives.

The more we left a guilt-ridden, body-alienated past behind, the more mindful a role nudity played.

✸

Among the innovative methods to help people re-attune to their bodies—especially in the late 1960s—were sensory awareness workshops. These experimental classes, often employing nudity as a healing aid, drew in numbed-down city dwellers like magnets, as people felt a dire need to re-sensitize to their bodies after a life-time of abuse. Held in supportive atmospheres and often guided by professional therapists, such nude workshops helped strip away any influence clothes might have had in blocking growth and awareness of self and others.

My cousin Allen had a breakthru at one. After an intensive five-day workshop at Big Sur's Esalen Institute in California, he walked away seven hundred dollars lighter, but feeling richer for the new positive body attitude he'd achieved. It inspired him to go on and become a therapist—which work would soon enuf net him seven hundred dollars a *day,* and then he'd go to his own therapist to deal with that.

People from all walks of life discovered a new serenity and heightened sense of self that came with going mindfully bare. We felt more open and honest.

Of course, we felt more sunburn, too, caught more poison oak, got sampled by more mosquitoes, and got more sand in more ticklish places—every plus had its minus. But we found being free of their clothes so exhilarating any downside was worth it.

A nudist lifestyle wasn't for everyone. Many considered walking about naked as something we'd evolved beyond along with hanging in the trees and munching grubs. They seemed genuinely happy, or at least duly resigned, to always wearing clothes, regardless of weather. (And they were always startled to learn not everyone else was.)

The most clothes-happy were hooked on the fit, the feel, the color of clothes. Also, the creativity in forging an ensemble allowed them to make their own personal statement, reflecting the way they felt: "This is *me* (or at least this *was* me three hours ago, and now I'm stuck in this persona until I can change again)." Such ensemble artists preferred to keep their naked states private between costume changes, like actors changing backstage between scenes, out of sight of their audience: "I'm not dressed!" they'd yell when someone knocked on the door. Like salad and roasted turkey, they were incomplete without dressing.

Others gave the impression they'd *like* to be naked more often, but treated the idea as so much wishful thinking, a forbidden fantasy that could never happen. Such would-be nudists settled for getting pretend-naked, clinging to bits of cloth in token allegiance to the clothed order. Altho coming closer to a freebody mindset, they stalled at the last, letting prevailing body shame and group censorship triumph over the persistent yearning for full body freedom. Beachfuls of people wore the least they possibly could get away with. They forever adjusted uncooperative swimsuits, wrestling the constant wedgies and ridings about, worried how fashionable their outfits were, and thought about juggling their budget to schedule visits to tanning salons to even out unsightly tan lines.

While much of mainstream society settled for getting *almost* naked, bolder souls took the plunge and discovered the liberation in being utterly, simply *nude*. Free beaches, hot springs and nude resorts multiplied merrily like tropical naked isles amid textile oceans. People drove and flew hundreds—thousands—of kilometers for the opportunity to experience the simple joy of being naked amid pleasant, healing surroundings with like-minded people.

One Mark Cornick summed up the emerging freebody trend and its deeper implications: "Many of us are quite happy to be nude by ourselves; naturism challenges us to share that happiness with others…"

Some mineral spring resorts once requiring public-zone cover-up embraced changing body attitudes: We witnessed the advent of open-minded policies once unheard of: coed dressing rooms and clothing-optional, mixed-gender pools, saunas and sundecks.

Others still required swimsuits by day but allowed nudity at nite.

Some had a special women's nite to let women socialize freely without having to deal with naked men sitting next to them perhaps more interested in the rosy complexion of their areolas than hearing about their kids' latest caper during a field trip to the zoo.

Some places became veritable checkerboards of clothing-optional and cover-up zones. The hope was to accommodate both those still preferring to keep wrapped in public areas and those wanting to get naked and *stay* naked. In such places people per force became adept quick-change artists: cool here, not cool there, cool here...

You might have been pleasantly soaking in a private tub room, naked of course, but then had to cover up to go as little as two meters down the hall to the sauna, where you could be naked again; *then* had to cover up from the sauna to the sundeck or cold-plunge, where you could be naked again—before covering up *again* to go back to your tub room... All the energy flow disconnects by stopping to wrap and unwrap could make a person feel like a human 8-track cassette recording (obsolete technology with interrupting pauses—like this parenthetical aside—as the flow-challenged tape system awkwardly switched tracks). It was all very schitzy, but it reflected the times perfectly: Was it or was it not okay to be naked in public?

As I've indicated, part of the problem hampering a smoother acceptance of our naked selves stemmed from the cards being stacked against us at every turn. It wasn't only church and state, but business and media as well: Those with the gold made the rules. Business and media had vested interests in perpetuating a dumbed-down consciousness, along with wares and sales slants built around a mandatory-dress world. Strange to say, it was as if they *wanted* to keep us flustered and uncomfortable, disempowered, insecure about our bodies and our lives in general. They determined our being wrapped up and thrown off-center generated greater mass sales from "consumer units"—as we shoppers were endearingly called.

By continual body objectification, drop-forged linkage of nudity to sex, compulsive dress; and alienated body-imaging, businesses built a lucrative industry systematically exploiting suppressed sexuality and the perpetual longing for a sense of natural being. If we couldn't find inner happiness, we'd more likely throw money at things outside ourselves in that elusive search for inner fulfillment.

They were shameless—doubly so for trying to shame freebodies to feel ashamed for feeling shameless. It was *all* a shame.

✳

In my more benighted days, I sometimes slinked into San Francisco *strip bars*. These were places where women took off their clothes on stage in slow, teasing installments during barebones stage skits set to music, while other girls, naked to the waist or bare-bottomed, served overpriced drinks to horny, half-drunk patrons, mostly men. Baring performers wiggled close to those bearing money, who tucked folding money into the dancers' G-strings in appreciation and the chance to get close and briefly touch them. In those days of perpetual horniness and a drought of meaningful relationships in my life, I drooled with the worst of them in those alcohol-soaked dens.

Not long after I changed my tune, I visited a strip club again—Tinkled Pink, in the tenderloin. This time, tho, I had a vague, misguided hope of trying to redeem myself by helping others see the light, how such places were degrading to both women and men alike.

I know; I was naïve.

"Is she hot or *what?*" a pudgy, polyester-shirted man, chomping an unlit cigar, asked me after I sat nearby and ordered a lime sparkling water.

I looked. The woman then on stage was indeed pretty, if slightly jaded looking, a young short redhead with perky breasts. She was cavorting to "Take Five," which, with its complex, 5:4 time signature, made it a challenge to dance to, but somehow she pulled it off. If one didn't examine her face too closely, she looked to be having the time of her life strutting around on the stage, eventually 98 percent naked, for a bunch of salivating, soused men. I read her face tho, and, judging from the thinly-disguised boredom, suspected she might've been happier vacuuming the apartment, scrubbing tile grout or routing thru junk mail.

"Yeah, I suppose," I said, stalling, trying to think up a way to segue into launching my crusade. His obnoxious, frenzied mind state sabotaged my ability to function at all.

"Whadaya mean, 'you *suppose*'?" He took a gulp of his latest whiskey sour and gave me a once over, as if trying to determine if I was blind, gay, or a detective hunting him down for back child support. "You don't know good horseflesh when you see—yeah, baby, *that's* it!" The woman—working to earn money for a degree in astrophysics, for all I knew—was bent over, face under her legs, wearing a wan smile and wiggling her butt. "You shake it, sweet cheeks!"

I abandoned all hope for an opening to launch my proselytizing effort, but I often got locked into a course of action, doggedly refusing to let changing realities interfere.

I just blurt it out. "What I mean is if we were all of us naked more often in everyday life, would she be turning you on so much now?"

He stared at me again, finally pegging me for a Martian. "Why, that's the sickest thing I ever heard: '*All of us naked.*' What are you, some kind of *pervert?*" Turning back to the naked girl, he waived a twenty-spot. "Come to Daddy, sweet thing!" Her money-radar on automatic pilot, she half-squatted and gyrated in front of him, pausing just long enuf to allow his sweaty hands to tuck the used-paper offering into the cloth patch barely covering her shaved pudendum, then thrust her pelvis twice by way of a thank you, as she did rolling her eyes, as if to say, *the crazy things I do for a living.*

"Oww-w, baby. You *know-w* what I like!" the man roared, spilling his drink and nearly destroying my fondness for a rock 'n' roll classic. "You see—" he started, turning to my now-empty seat.

I'd seen enuf. I aborted the mission, realizing I stood a better chance convincing a Nebraska cattle rancher of the merits of tofu.

❋

Movies depicting any kind of positive, non-sexual nudity were scarce in America. While notable exceptions, like *Emerald Forest*, showed how natural and unselfconscious nakedness could be, the overwhelming majority made the hardwired connection between nudity and sex every time; or nudity and violence; anything but casual, healthy, non-sexual nudity.

It fascinated me—not unlike one's rapt attention over a train wreck—how our frustrated yearning for body freedom was so shamelessly manipulated by body product makers. Their spoken message: "Buy this, buy that and you'll finally feel good about yourself and be accepted by others." The stark truth: "We're pandering to your every raging body insecurity, your every petty body obsession, your *futile* longing to lose your body alienation, re-enforcing them at every turn while offering you illusory crumbs of salvation thru our lovely products." They were drug dealers in three-piece suits, hoping to get us hooked on things not needed or outright bad for us, products good only for draining our pocket and re-enforcing the disconnect from our real selves: *first one's free with handy coupon; void where prohibited; certain restrictions may apply...*

The biggest dealers, of course, were the multi-billion dollar clothing and textile concerns. They were like comedians, the way they tried to keep us in stitches. They made us feel it our patriotic duty to go out and buy ever more of their endless textile offerings to stimulate the economy. *This Saturday only: 40% off our regularly 50%-overpriced offerings. Doors open at 3 a.m. Free deluxe Q-tips to first fifty customers. Don't miss it!* Clothes-junkies that we were, we'd gladly succumb, going out hunting new threads to drape over our bodies, tho our closets be jam-packed. No problem. We'd go thru them later and hold yard sales or donate no longer wanted clothing to charity to make room for our latest trophies.

The United States may have known poverty and malnutrition, but the poorest of the poor almost always had access to rivers of free and cheap clothing—castoffs in a swelling sea of surplus apparel from a nation oversupplied by the legion of overseas textile mill workers, running amok like silkworms on speed.

In the 1980s I'd sometimes salvage select discards at my local town dump, hoping to recycle them. The thrifty New Englander in my genes was dumbfounded and infuriated by the sight of the mountains of still-serviceable things we routinely threw out. It was like we were sacrificing virgins to try to appease the angry volcano gods or something. Among the mountains: tons of clothes. Our clothing addiction, combined with a capricious buying and discarding habit, perpetuated an inconceivable waste of resources, both human and material, and a sorry degradation of our environment—and guaranteed renewed business with the textile pushers.

I don't know; maybe we went thru them so quickly because we were initially attracted by their sight and feel and didn't pay attention to how they felt *on* us, or how the chemical dyes irritated our bodies, or how flimsy their construction was, or how one wash and it lost its charm. (Not unlike how we got a visual fix on some food item, telling ourselves how much we enjoyed the taste and

200

texture, disregarding whether or not our *body* would enjoy it past those hypnotized taste buds.)

Occasionally I'd come across maybe a dozen fresh-tossed garbage sacks, tied off, each brimming with laundered and neatly folded clothes—some bedraggled, sure, but most with plenty of mileage left. *Yard sales rejects*, I thought. But then I tried to recycle them at the local thrift shop…and learned they *came* from the local thrift shop: These were donated clothes the shop had maybe tried moving in their Free Box in front of the store and couldn't, or had rejected outright, to keep from getting buried under the constant donation avalanches.

All but the most destitute had more clothes than they knew what to do with. We were *drowning* in clothes.

The clothing industry worked our body freedom yearning to the nth degree. The voice-over in a bra ad cooed: "It's like wearing *nothing*." *Why not wear nothing instead*, I thought as I tackled another week's laundry. *It's a lot easier and cheaper, too.* Seemingly implicit in the clothing industry's message: the understanding that real, clothing-optional body freedom would never happen—*and why would anyone want it to, really?* But, hey—here's something even *better*, only $9.95, available in a rainbow of colors. Hurry, while supplies last.

Was it any wonder it took us so long to see thru the relentless brainwashing keeping us from gaining a semblance of positive body acceptance?

Mainstream media gladly did their part perpetuating the negative mindset. They trivialized and marginalized whatever freebody happenings made it past the usual reporting blackout. They were spun into bon mot in print and on the internet under headings of "Weird," "Odd," and "Strange;" and smirking, closing sound-bites on radio and television:

"And, finally, in the news tonite: Ten people were arrested today in downtown Atlanta after staging a nude protest for more humane treatment of homeless cats and dogs."

"I love my dog, Jim, but you wouldn't catch me doing *that* if his life depended on it," the co-anchor deadpanned from the teleprompter's prepared script.

"I can't believe that, Bob, not even to save his life?"

"I'd die of embarrassment first. What good would the mangy mutt be to me·then?"

"Ow-w, he doesn't mean that, folks," the anchor assured viewers with a wink. "Please, don't write in. And that wraps it up for the late edition. Stay tuned for tonite's goldie-oldie movie offering: *Naked Obsession,* with William Katt and Maria Ford. Parental discretion advised."

❀

By now, people began to wonder if maybe the weirdest, oddest, strangest thing of all wasn't media's attitude on the subject.

Tenuous breakthrus were made in the U.S.: New York, Ohio, North Carolina and Washington D.C. made it kinda, sorta okay for women to go responsibly topfree anywhere a man could—if they dared weather the storm of stares and hoots and possibly policemen acting in ignorance or contempt of the new, untested law. Parts of Canada allowed women to swim topfree in public pools, sometimes. Mothers could nurse their babies in public, in twenty U.S. states, anyhow. Naked street theatre was tolerated in Berkeley, off and on. Clothing-optional beaches flourished, unless shut down amid rallying cries of family values.

It often appeared to be three steps forward and two steps back.

I witnessed the advent of the thong-bottomed swimsuit. More daring women could at last sun their buns freely (except some felt

202

they now had a string up their butt). That is, unless they picked the wrong place and got hassled—like my twin nieces Zena and Zoey.

They were college co-eds, enjoying spring weather at Rockingham, a private Vermont college. Since the 60s the school had had a liberal tradition of allowing students to be discretely naked on campus. Then a new college dean decided to fly in the face of tradition of the college's flying in the face of tradition and clamped down on college nudity, proclaiming, "In case no one noticed, we are not a clothing-optional society."

Zena and Zoey, in concession to the dean's new cloak-thy-bod policy, now sunned in their thong suits, matched in style, differing in colors—one a neon purple, the other, electric chartreuse. [No way I'd've remembered *that,* but they described the outfits in a saved letter.] They'd bought the scant swimsuits more for visiting the region's textile waterfronts, not really needing them at school—until then. But even tho they felt over-dressed by dutifully wearing tops and thong bottoms in the former freebody zone, the dean *still* busted them for not covering their butts.

"That was the last straw," Zena, a poly sci major, fumed. "We weren't going to take that lying down."

They organized a grievance committee at the peak of a heat wave socking the region. "Our neighbor state has a motto 'Live Free or Die'; we changed it for our rallying cry to 'Go Bare or Fry.'" They strengthened their case with solid arguments and gained support from both students and parents. ("My daughter is in *liberal* arts: what are you going to do next, dean, cover up nude models in Life Drawing? Perhaps we should find another school.") The dean backed down with a compromise plan that allowed him to cover his own butt: "You can be naked on the *West* Lawn and the pond area *only,*" he told students. "I catch you naked, or even topless, on the *East* Lawn or anywhere else, your ass is grass and I'm the lawnmower."

Meanwhile, Europe was light years ahead of America in accepting public nudity. In my research I unearthed a revealing book of the time, *Naked Europe*, by Daphne Dancer, which gave an idea of the then-advanced body attitudes in Europe, worth sharing here. She noted that:

- All but two beaches of Denmark's thousands of kilometers of coastline were clothing-optional.
- Swedish coastlines were almost as tolerant.
- Beach nudity was the fashion in Romania.
- Zurich, Switzerland officially accepted nudity in municipal pools in 1989, after finding there was only eighteen percent opposition.
- In Munich, Germany, office workers on lunch could sunbathe and picnic in the buff in parks right in the middle of town. One in eight, or 10 million, Germans felt totally relaxed stripping off clothes at parks and beaches.
- In Greece, a 1983 poll showed two-thirds of citizens favored establishing official nudist facilities.
- During a heat wave in 2002, German workers opted to work nude in the non-air-conditioned office to beat the heat and it was no big deal.
- In many German saunas, people were asked to leave if they tried leaving on towels, swimsuits or sandals; the sauna was deemed a pure, healing freebody zone, clothing *verboten*.
- In France a 1995 poll found only seven percent were shocked by the sight of naked breasts on the beach; an earlier 1982 Harris poll found eighty-six percent of French favored nudity on public beaches.
- One French nudist resort on the Mediterranean, Cap d'Agde, was a full-fledged nudist resort town, attracting 300,000 visitors each summer. It boasted 120 businesses; residents went about their daily life, doing banking, post office runs, shopping, recreation, dining out and dancing, all in the nude or varied states of

dishabille (thus being a primitive forerunner to our current society).

• In Holland, one in 422 citizens was a dues-paying nudist (vs. one in 6,856 in the U.S).

• In sauna-happy Finland, with one for every 3.5 people, saunas were almost always enjoyed nude and traditionally in mixed-gender company.

It appeared everywhere in Europe—Britain, Spain, Belgium, Greece—had greater mainstream acceptance of public nudity than our land of the fee—er, *free.*

An example of how our bodies had been co-opted as commercial goods: During my travels thru Idaho I asked an outgoing man standing in front of bar in Boise where the nearest clothesfree resort might be.

"Wanna get naked, huh?" he said, smirking. "Think the nearest place is 200 miles across the state line, twenty bucks to get in, I hear—but, hey, you wanna *see* naked, come on in. No cover, two-drink minimum, whadaya say, sport?"

In the year 2000 a national Roper Survey, commissioned by the educational branch of The Naturist Society, revealed 80 percent of Americans were okay with the idea of having designated free beaches and 25 percent admitted to skinnydipping and/or nude sunbathing in mixed-gender social settings.

The clothed world running government, pressured by a religious right busy raising intolerance to an art form, was alarmed by this dismal trend. Some of the loopier stalwarts busied themselves with throwing clothes on venerable public nude statuary—like my Uncle Felix: He was upset by the life-size reproduction of Rodin's "The Kiss," of two seated naked lovers embracing disgracing Dubuque, Ohio's fine arts museum foyer. He and a friend went to work and soon she was sensibly dressed in red gingham while he looked dashing in kakis. Security removed them *and* the couple's new wardrobe before many could laud their efforts.

Beyond such idiocy, extremists tried enacting new oppressive laws and dredging up old ones, equating any and all public nudity with indecent exposure, disturbing the peace and obscene behavior.

Not being suited was *clearly* unsuitable, grounds for legal suits to address, thru briefs, a means to cover the body of evidence.

One state, perhaps noting the gender inequality, tried to remedy the situation by proposing a bill that would again forbid men from going topfree, but it didn't pass. In 2000, Indiana *did* pass a law in which persons found skinnydipping or nude sunbathing on public land, no matter how remote, could not only be arrested but *made to register as sex offenders*. The jaws of every free-minded person who heard about it dropped over that one. Other states tried to follow suit. Kansas tried passing a law that would have made the penalty for skinnydipping the same as a violent sexual crime: If Great-Uncle Zep had tried starting his nudist camp there instead of Missouri I suspect they might have run him out of town on a splintery rail instead of just closing him down. Such repressive bills were defeated in legislature only after The Naturist Society's vigilant political action committee rallied forces and offered the voice of reason.

Always-clothed people, especially those Nuela liked to call the frightful right, felt smugly superior, in their stylish-yet-sensible cover-ups, over the shameless naked apes nudists were perceived as being. In a world of clothing chauvinists, those refusing to drape their bodies were thought primitive, uncivilized, inferior— we lived on the *Planet of the Drapes*.

Because of enforced dress codes, freebody enthusiasts might sometimes have felt like unpaid extras in a life-long, cheesy flick: *Invasion of the Body Thatchers*. A suspense writer might've written a novel about the perplexiating riddle of a world full of people forever wrapped in cloth—*Mystery of the Cocoon People*—but most people wouldn't have thought it baffling at all.

It was as tho we had fallen under the wicked spell of some dark magician: With mandatory clothes his illusory device, he'd hypnotized us into suspending our disbelief of what was unnatural and illogical, hoodwinking us into disavowing the integrity of our own biologic beings.

Abracadabra, it's gone.

THIRTEEN

*The vulnerability of the nude body
is a peace sign, in and of itself.*
—**Toni Anne Wyner**
activist naturist, once arrested
on a Florida beach after wrapping herself
solely in an oversized copy of the Bill of Rights

It WAS TOUGH going, those days. People trying to enjoy going clothesfree beyond the confines of home and the few designated free beaches and private lands risked extreme discomfort, ridicule, and shunning—even job loss and arrest. It was as frustrating as vegetarians seeking nourishment at any eatery called Chester's Charnel Chuckwagon.

People refusing to cow-tow to the system's irrational body-shame bluff became thorny problems for the clothes-minded. The notion of being unabashed about their own nakedness was incomprehensible: *"Why, they're shameless!"*

A prudish vocal minority, leveraging media to appear a majority, mounted a frenzy when a "wardrobe malfunction" revealed a female performer's breasts for 7.3 nanoseconds during a live TV special, claiming viewing children were traumatized for life.

Americans' championing of freedom rights often appeared limited and selective. We sent our young around the globe to fight for political freedom, but at home we were denied one of life's most personal and basic freedoms: the freedom to be our natural selves, stripped free of man-made materials, which on every warm day only served to reflect a wrong-headed, perverse judgment against the decency of our own earthly temples.

Law-makers, reflecting the ingrained body-denial of the populace, turned a blind eye to our constitutional protections, guaranteeing an inalienable right to the pursuit of happiness: our pursuit was definitely being alienated. The freebody community was subjected to a litany of shame and denial. Too bad if it made you feel more alive and happy, authentic, that it fostered a *joie de vivre.* Tough patootie, they told us, if it brought you peace of mind. Can't allow it. Can't do it. Buncha nuts. No decent person. Why, the very *idea*. Ad infinitum.

It was as if body phobics' aversion to others' naked selves mirrored some intractable alienation they felt about their own bodies. "We become what we behold," Marshall McLuhan said. Freebodies were essentially storming the walls of denial of body phobes, threatening their dully accepted belief that wearing clothes made one decent. Reality crowded the illusion, triggering a red alert. Wearing clothes was a no-brainer and the alternative unthinkable—except while fantasizing in risqué novels and sex-drenched movies, which people consumed like locusts in titilated frenzies.

I'll illustrate. In early 1985, I was living in a tent at a public beach on Hawaii's Big Island, north of Kona-Kailua, with my girlfriend of the time, Wendi. Like Nuela, Wendi was worlds further along in body acceptance than I. We liked strolling over to a nearby large sun-warmed tide pool to skinnydip. On one such visit with another camp couple, we found, much to my dismay, two older, well-heeled tourist couples set up—replete with shade-tent and lounge chairs—not twenty meters from us, on the opposite side of the tide pool. The women both looked up from bright-covered paperbacks—which may or may not have been novels laced with juicy bodice-ripping scenes—no doubt wondering what these hippie-looking people were up to. They had cause for concern: Wendi, who was a looker, was also an unabashed nudist: She blithely removed her sarong and waded nude into the water, face aglow with pleasure. The men stared, transfixed—until their wives' less rhapsodized reaction broke the spell. The way they broke camp and departed post-haste was both comical and sad. Daring, that girl. We all joined in after she'd liberated the spot with one pull of her sarong.

☀

In the 90s and double-aughts, I felt pulled to Wayward Mineral Springs, a rural resort an hour-and-a-half drive from home, in the next county down. Nestled amid thick stands of spruce and quaking aspen—with rushing creek threading its way thru—the place felt like another world. A shingle-sided, slate-roofed bathhouse provided seven mineral-water tub rooms (each decorated with a different theme), a wood-fired sauna, and a generous sundeck. The creek beside it served as a cold plunge for anyone willing to brave the icy snow-melt waters.

People came from near and far to soak in Wayward's lithium-rich waters, relax in the saunas and unwind in the serenity of nature. Situated in a conservative mining community, tho, the place's standard policy had long been to always cover up beyond the private tub rooms and brief creek plunge. While he place had joined the wave of body liberation of the late 60s and early 70s, becoming very clothing-optional indeed, it later fell on clothed times again.

By the time I stumbled onto the place, a plaque on the office counter read:

No Nudity in Bathhouse

The sign—part serious, part zen riddle and part management's warped sense of humor—led more than one person, taking it literally, to ask if it was okay to be naked in their private tub rooms. Another sign, on the sauna door, warned one and all:

NO NUDITY
IN SAUNA

In my first year or two visiting (long before Nuela), I was still too self-conscious to be comfortably naked around others. The sauna sign didn't outrage me much for its body-repressive message. I was still a slave to body shame, even if I had by then learned to feel all right as a private nudist. Oh, I'd grumble and titter, "you believe that?" like one slave complaining to another about how tight our manacles were.

Even tho I'd eventually rebel and get naked among other scofflaws in the dim, fire-lit room—once safely seated and still on a bench—I'd be made to feel uncomfortable whenever the eyes of certain dutifully-wrapped sauna-goers bored into me for breaking the house rule. I'd feel indecent. But the discomfort I experienced being psychically hassled by others for not hiding my body was outweighed by the discomfort I felt keeping a clammy towel on in a dim, super-heated room. I slowly began nurturing a growing conviction the whole place should be clothing-optional. If not in a bathhouse, where?

But even tho I rebelled; I still thoroughly objectified myself and others; still felt a numb disconnect between my body, mind and spirit.

Then the day came one winter that marked a turning point in

my life, destined to reverse my self-alienated mindset. For some reason I was standing in the middle of a packed room, lit by the glowing fire-view stove in front of me. Maybe I was letting my eyes adjust to the dark before seeking an open perch. Anyhow, suddenly my small towel, with a mind of its own, slipped to the floor.

Once, in second grade, I'd gone to school wearing a short-sleeve shirt under my jacket. I hadn't picked it out to wear. I preferred keeping sheathed in long-sleeved shirts, gangly pipe-cleaner arms safe from scrutiny. But my mom, maybe sensing my extreme body hang-ups, suggested I wear it. Taking off my jacket for class and exposing my limbs unaccountably left me feeling semi-naked, even tho many in the class were also in short sleeves. The girl next to me—who I had a mad crush on—teased me, maybe sensing my vulnerability, looking up my arm in mock-excitement and saying "Ooh, naked armpit!" I turned scarlet.

Now I was on center stage, completely naked before a roomful of people, without a shred of modesty-preserving cloth. It didn't matter that a few others in the sauna were naked too; they were safely perched around the chamber's dark recesses and still as statues. The spotlight was on me: *And now, ladies and gentlemen, for your delectation and amusement, Zet will reveal his undisguised nakedness to you...*

I wanted to die, to melt into the floor ducking and join the cricket that took up residence there and see if he'd teach me how to chirp like him. I hastily retrieved my towel and re-wrapped my trunk and sat down, feeling dizzy with mortification and shame. It was a moment of reckoning, as if all the sins of my objectifying others' bodies over the years had come home to roost.

No one said anything. I didn't know what I expected to happen. No nude police came for me, no inquisition down in a dungeon for the nefarious naked; not even a snicker.

I soon got over the shock. The incident served to help bridge the yawning gap within me that kept me from feeling more integrated. It carried me beyond feeling like a turtle without a shell when publicly nude—at least while in relaxed environs. New tendrils of body acceptance grew in me from that day forth. I'm sure most of those sitting around in the sauna group had been more accepting of my body than I was, maybe sensed my distress when the towel fell and silently assured me it was okay. Altho still time away from fully overcoming the idle urge to objectify others' bodies—so deeply had I absorbed the dominant male chauvanistic mindset of the 50s growing up—the episode at least put me on the road to mending my errant ways.

Over the years of my visits to the place—always a splurge for the taxing hour-and-a-half drive each way and soaring price of gas— I became gradually more relaxed naked around others. Getting socially naked was great therapy for counteracting the effects of my body-phobic upbringing.

Countless others found it good therapy too. Wayward Springs was poised for a naked comeback, the way grocery stores were poised for a return to organic foods, city dwellers for an exodus from cities, and Harry Potter producers for another movie.

What was to unfold there reflected a surge in positive body acceptance among more freethinking people at large: Individuals wanted the freedom to shuck their wraps. We'd long enjoyed being naked in private—alone, as couples, family—and it dawned on us that limiting it to that didn't seem right. Especially while in peaceful, natural environs that got us back in touch with ourselves.

We were caterpillars, slowly unraveling from our cocoons on the installment plan. As we transformed—graceful, colorful selves unfurling and taking wing—we'd yearn to leave the dross of dress of the caterpillar's world behind, if only for a while.

The dim lit sauna afforded a perfect healing atmosphere; the room was womb-like. The wood stove's mellow heat filled the chamber with a magical radiance that enveloped and suffused us, while the ruddy golden glow of the stove's glass door fairly transfigured people's bodies—no matter what shape—into burnished living gods and goddesses.

Over time, grumblings grew over the restrictive cover-up policy putting a damper on things. Traditionally, the sauna was where one got free of restrictive cloth, sweated out toxins, relaxed, wound down. Yet there we were, expected to keep wrapped in sweat-soaked, bacteria-infested cloth, in a room hot enuf to slow-cook dinner.

As I said, the rebels among us felt like outlaws for ignoring the sign and getting naked inside. Whenever the door opened, we scrambled to wrap up in a flurry of slapped wet towels and sheets, fearful it might be the attendant who'd report us to the manager. The times it was only a fellow rebel entering, we chorused, "Oh, it's only *you*," in mock disgust and uncovered again.

But few if any of us complained to management about the comfort-crimping restriction. Either we felt funny admitting we wanted to be naked or we didn't want to rock the boat by complaining and risking the hot-headed manager's displeasure by suggesting we didn't care for the way he ran things. As a result, the only complaints he received were about the shameless naked people flouting the admonishment to keep their frames covered—which in turn served to reinforce the perceived need to keep the policy.

Yet another sign, out on the sundeck, pleaded:

PLEASE
NO NUDITY
ON DECK

If it felt great naked in the sauna, it felt divine in the sunshine. It could be glorious weather, sun pouring down like necter, drenching the skin with its radiance, the white-noise rushing of the creek fostering total relaxation, and patrons were expected to keep their clammy wet sheets, towels and swimsuits on.

More regular guests grumbled among themselves about this situation too.

And while you could cold-plunge naked in the creek, you were expected to cover up *immediately* out of the water; no shilly-shally, no dilly-dally. One day I witnessed a scene involving a female acquaintance who'd known the place in more bohemian days, perhaps unaware how restrictive things had become. She was peaceably sunning and meditating, naked, on an island rock near the creek's edge after her dip; mermaid on a rock.

"Cover up! You've got to cover up!" the dutiful bath attendant was screeching at her from the deck above, arms flailing like a mother hawk trying to frighten off predators from her nest. Some sourpuss no doubt complained about my friend's wanton display and the attendant had to play enforcer.

My friend turned and looked blankly, first at her and then at me, with a *you gotta be kidding?* look. I could only offer a Gallic shrug of sympathy; I was dutifully wrapped in a towel at the moment. She complied, not wanting to make a scene, but the incident only deepened her suspicions management was quite possibly nuts.

In the sauna one day, some of us entertained wishful thinking on the subject.

"They should allow nudity here in the sauna," one man, naked, ventured, crumpling dried white sage leaves on the wood stove.

"I'd rather have it be okay on the deck," said another on the far bench, doing a yoga stretch as best she could with a sheet on.

"If I had to choose, I'd say we should be able to sun naked by the creek after dipping," said a third, a sheet-wrapped man prone on a high bench, coming out of a mini-meditation.

I'd never been a body-freedom advocate before, but something stirred in me that day. "Why not all three?" I asked extravagantly, suddenly inspired. (I was naked.)

"Oh, no," said the third. "You don't want to rock the boat asking too much or they won't allow it anywhere."

"Yeah, that'll never happen," said the second. "The place is just too conservative.

"I agree," said the first. "I don't want to have to see too much skin myself; the dim lighting in here is perfect."

"If we had to settle on one, then I say the deck should be the place, where you can catch some sun."

"No, the creek's the logical spot; you're naked from plunging anyhow."

"No, the sauna; it gets too uncomfortable in here otherwise."

Around it went; I grew dizzy.

*

As penny-ante as the discussion was, we'd at least brought matters out into the open, past the unspoken, personal thoughts of private nudists.

It appeared everyone and their uncle was a secret card-carrying nudist. Society's cover-up mindset was so draconian, most took keen conspiratorial delight in being naked in places we shouldn't be, or *thought* we shouldn't be. Altho we might feel bold and daring, proud of ourselves rebelling against enforced dress—on however small a level—for the lame restriction it was, we were usually content to keep our personal rebellion just that: a private little victory. No matter how much we savored the experience, feeling it natural and right, few thought to do anything to try to get the rules changed.

At least not in my neck of the woods.

Maybe it was because forbidden fruit tasted so much sweeter the way things were we didn't feel the need to change policies. It was perhaps a little like the pleasure some women felt wearing a tight sweater or tighter spandex bodysuits: the male attention they got accenting their curves outweighed any constrictive body discomfort they might have felt. Similarly, the normal, compulsory dress condition of our lives was made bearable for the condition creating the rush of pleasure we felt when we *did* get naked.

We'd tweaked ourselves into accepting things the way they were. For most people, the always-clothed habit was so deeply etched in the brain they accepted clothes as a permanent extension of the body—at least while in public—and, much like the meat-and-dairy habit, it was absurd to think things would ever change.

I'd never really gotten involved in politics or social protest before—not even during the Viet Nam War, beyond wearing a little peace sign my college girl friend gave me. (Not knowing any better, I'd pinned it on upside-down; it took an arch-conservative classmate to drolly point out my faus pax.) But a growing awareness of how peoples' personal body freedom, not the least of which my own, was being systematically suppressed at last pushed me out of my bland acquiescence to the status quo.

I'd been reading naturist literature a while by then and was gaining a whole new perspective. I knew a viable body liberation movement was afoot and the possibilities excited me as much as when I first turned on to natural foods—probably more: if good organic food made me feel great, the freedom to be naked made me near-ecstatic.

One day, steeling my nerve, I approached Frank, the springs manager, in his backroom office. A short, acid-tongued, devil-may-care man, he gave the impression he'd be more at home coaching a football team or riding the rodeo circuit than running a bathhouse. He knew me for a nudenik and mostly tolerated me, if warily. He wasn't rigorous about enforcing the no-nudity policy unless someone complained, but wasn't about to take down the signs either. Confusion reigned supreme.

I said, "You know, Frank, I understand how you try to make guests feel comfortable here. Maybe there once was a time when most people preferred keeping covered, but those days are fading fast. You've got to change with the times. It's just a vocal minority raising a fuss now over nudity here. More people than not want to get naked—or at least have the *option*. If you don't offer them that they'll start going elsewhere."

"Ya think?" he fixed me with his trademark gremlin grin, leading me to conclude I was wasting my breath.

Then, to my surprise, he told me he agreed. It turned out he'd only been keeping the policy in deference to the older woman running the front office. A kinder lady you'd never meet, but she was uncomfortable with public nudity. She and Frank talked things thru, concessions were made, and before long a new sign graced the sauna door:

Clothing Optional Sauna

Victory. Guests and day-visitors could once again be naked as jays there. Not long after that policy change met with increased business and happier customers, the outer sundeck and creek area became freebody zones as well.

Covering in the bathhouse hallways remained the policy for a while longer, a lingering reminder of the buttoned-down past. Then, predictably, a trickle of people chose to ignore this last restriction, going topfree or naked there too, toddlers and their parents leading the way. The trickle became a torrent; until the bathhouse became more like...a *bathhouse*.

☀

Not surprisingly, I found it easier being comfortably naked at the springs if I was either sexually fulfilled or happily celibate. Before Nuela, I hadn't been sexually fulfilled in a month of Sundays, and, since puberty hit, I didn't think I'd been happily celibate a day in my life. When I learned Judaism considered celibacy a sin, I thought of converting. Sex was the feel-good elixir, the grand tension releaser. But sex wasn't always enuf by itself, I'd discovered. If an earnest heart connection was missing, instead of a celebration of love the sex could act like an addictive drug, needed in bigger and more frequent doses to keep the temporary high in force, or all that was left was a hollow feeling. So until I got myself together enuf to foster a healthy relationship, I'd learned to favor celibacy over bandit sex—even if repressed desires could drive me nuts.

After Nuela brightened my life; with her sincerity and forthrightness, her healthy libido and practical sexual perspective, a miracle was wrought in my life: Not only did my body shame and sexual guilt fairly vanish, at times we'd go celibate a month or two in order to work on dissolving old energy patterns and integrating new ones. And I was all right with it. I learned how a quality coat of paint could be surprisingly durable.

Early freebodies emphasized socialized nudity wasn't sexual. Understandably, they made every effort to distance nudism from hedonistic behavior, due to the automatic, exclusive linkage in most people's minds between nudity and sex. One would almost think nudists *had* no sexual urges, the way things were downplayed. Airbrushing out genitals in early magazine photos worked to reinforce that impression.

I concluded social nudity both was and wasn't sexual. I reached this contradictory perspective after ending a sorry sexual dry spell so long I'd completed half the paperwork for disaster relief funds. I bought condoms with an encouragingly distant use-by date, only to check them later and find they'd expired ages ago. Result: oftentimes I couldn't help but emanate a randy vibe while naked among naked women, despite my best intentions not to. Maybe others, who were either sexually fulfilled or had milder libidos, could; I couldn't.

Once, my excessive admiration of the female form led a woman to complain to the office that a man looking suspiciously like me was staring at her in the sauna and making her uncomfortable. Frank took me aside later and strongly advised me to behave myself. I'd try, but it wasn't easy. I felt like the hooligan in *West Side Story,* explaining to Officer Krupke why he was no good: "I'm depraved 'cause I'm deprived."

I knew the love of a good woman was all I needed. Sure enuf, after Nuela came in my life (a Scorpio, by the way, who mysteriously possess the power to resurrect the dead), my long-term frustrated pattern of idly lugging and revving sexual energies in lust-fueled fantasies evaporated overnite.

In due time, under her guidance I moved beyond simple physical urges and sought more complex, more social ones—like coming together energetically as a group. In the buff at the springs, I shared a new-found sense of well-being and fulfillment with others, most of whom were more or less happy in their skins too. Our being out of clothes together wasn't sexual *per se*, but it was our being energetically grounded, primarily thru sex, that served as a springboard to our richer, more complex, sex-transcendent coming together.

That's how I saw it, anyhow.

We lost some loyal visitors at the springs after the policy liberalized—a sketchy acquaintance of mine, Filbert, among them. He'd joined one of the region's many local, exotic spiritual disciplines, down on the body as something to be subdued while trying to hasten one's spiritual ascension to higher realms and forever leaving this sorry-ass world behind. They viewed the body akin to an alba-tross around the soul. Wayward Springs was rigorously con-demned henceforth by his group for having strayed from being a sanctuary from the flesh world. Some people concluded they were *all* nuts.

☀

Nudity at the springs became more accepted—and could even become *expected*: Once I got busted for not being naked.

A visiting nude-resort owner from the Southwest, Bob Everbare, seeing the freshly-posted "Clothing Optional on Deck" sign, promptly stripped. Until the day before, the deck had been off-limits to nudity for decades. I introduced myself to him there while wrapped in a small towel out of long-accustomed habit. Bob and I soon got to talking about body freedom; the irony of my talking about nudity while wearing a towel wasn't lost on him.

During our talk he paused, gazed at my towel and asked point-edly, "Why are you wearing a towel?" It was asked in roughly the same tone one might have asked, "Why are you naked?" at a Rotary Club meeting. I sheepishly explained how the policy had just changed, old habits died hard, and so on.

He wasn't buying it.

"The sign says 'Clothing optional on deck,' doesn't it?"

"Yeah, but…"

"Then I don't understand why you're wearing a towel."

Busted.

The episode, surreal at it was, helped me understand how others resisted the notion of getting naked more if they felt it was being forced on them. It was like *Thou Shall be Naked* (as happened with my mom), rather than having a no-pressure option to be wrapped or not, according to one's mood and comfort level in the moment.

Long established habits could be really, *really* slow to change. Even if one even wanted to change, the mountain of inertia to overcome was daunting—doable, but daunting.

And droves of people didn't want to; not at all. The prospect of people having the option to be naked in public was scarier to most than a meat-lovers' convention running out of prime rib.

I naturally suspected a rabid but influential vocal minority had something to do with it:

"Officer, I'm making a complaint. There are naked *people over there on the park lawn. ... What do I want you to do about it? Why, arrest them, of course .... Doing? Well, they're eating lunch, braiding each others' hair, playing Frisbee—dammit, man, they're being naked is what they're doing! My God, isn't that enuf? Listen, I supported your chief for re-election despite allegations of illegal campaign contributions, and now we want our money's wor—I want you to do your job. Do you follow? ... Well, all right then."*

✺

My own fitful transformation to freebody awareness reflected other lifestyle changes I made with Nuela: getting rid of idle belongings, going vegan, learning to enjoy little things in life more—gazing on dragonflies in flight, listening to the woodpecker's cry piercing the woodlands, leisurely drinking in sunsets and watching the sky sequence thru a hundred nuanced shades of color and light.

And, like I said, my changes only reflected the dramatic changes countless others were effecting in their lives: regaining finer-tuned sensitivities to how we lived and where we lived, what we ate, the way we earned a living and our perspective towards work and service, nurturing an inner life, and distinguishing what was rational from what was not.

Threads of mega-change in people's lives were weaving a rich new tapestry.

The more we left the body-unfriendly industrial age behind— getting in tune with ourselves and each other, evolving deeper relationships with nature and each other—the more we longed to be one with Earth. Pure and simple: clothes interfered. Some felt it a foregone conclusion we'd eventually rebel, concluding that being forced.to wear apparel on nice days was just too weird.

Those living in more open-minded regions opted to wear less and less during fine weather. They discarded clothes outright whenever in relaxed natural surroundings, and derring-do and lighthearted vibes allowed.

Some even took it to the streets.

FOURTEEN

It is an interesting question how far people woud retain their relative rank if they were divested of their clothes.
—**Thoreau**

THE MORE WE FREED ourselves from oppressive forces in our lives, the more some of us expressed our new sense of liberation by daring to go naked. All across the nation and around the world, people were increasingly flirting with the idea we didn't really need to wear clothes in nice weather. And being publicly nude served both as an effective method of protest over injustices in the world as well as a personal expression of the freedom to be comfortable. "The Beverly Hillbillies" television show had invited viewers to "take your shoes off, set a spell." People began going that one better.

Berkeley, California was often the crucible for radical breakthrus in America. "The eye of the hurricane of social change," someone dubbed it. In the early 1990s, UC Berkeley student Andrew Martinez, a.k.a. "the Naked Guy," became a popular-culture leg-

225

end. While I was still learning to feel comfortable naked alone in nature, he was boldly walking around campus and attending classes wearing only sandals, a peace symbol pendant and daypack. He did it so naturally and inoffensively, no one complained for a long while. (Eventually, a female student protested she felt sexually harassed by his bare presence.)

Low-key, calm, and natural about it, Martinez, a rhetoric major, argued for the right to not wear clothes: "Clothes are totally a creation of need and of capitalistic society," he said. "I don't want to facilitate the power structure with my conformity." At a Nude-in at the campus's Sproul Plaza, twenty-five people joined Martinez in getting naked after he sang The Doors' "Break on Through to the Other Side"—including my cousin Zor. He wrote of the episode: "God, there's no place like Berkeley. After the rally some of us kept naked and strolled down the streets, digging the day; some people looked at us in disbelief; other studiously ignored us, like we were part of another dumb fraternity/sorority initiation; but some faces lit up in conspiratorial grins."

Martinez had told the crowd of 400, "The shame needs to be eradicated. It would be nice if everybody, around the world, would rise up their arms and take off their clothes." A growing wave of freebody proponents around the world no doubt agreed. From Sunday strollers thru London's Coventry Gardens, sunning tourists in Miami Beach, and surfers on Australia's west coast, to bicyclists in Madrid, bathers on the African shore, and Rasta dancers on the Miami shore, a far-flung group of humanity leaned towards wanting more body freedom in their lives

Youth in particular had a more casual, body-positive attitude—with the odd exception of some drag-bottomed teen males, including my nephew, Todd: "No offense, Uncle Zet, but the thought of being naked in public grosses me out." (This from a boy who wore his pants so low it revealed half his Mickey-and-Minnie boxer shorts.) Many youth, during warmest weather and in free-thinking regions, opted to dress in minimal apparel that seemed to say,

"Having to keep our bodies concealed is so ridiculous; but here's a few token threads to appease any lurking rag police, ha-ha. Get over it, people!" Girls sported bare midriffs; semi-transparent and gauzy, diaphanous clothes gained a bit of popularity in some circles; and it became trendy, around 2003, to wear pants so low on the hips it looked like they were sliding off—surely a sign the end was almost in sight (of mandatory clothes, that is).

Easy-on, easy-off sandals and flip-flops regained popularity, making for happier feet, too long imprisoned in binding shoes and sweltering socks. Going barefoot found favor again, as in the old sixties; people rediscovered the comfort of having a grounded, bare connection with Planet Earth.

And one could feel twice as fine naked *and* barefoot as when wearing only footwear. At times, I'd still feel half-dressed if I had just shoes or sandals on. Something about a reflexological activation of the entire body by receptive earth thru the soles of the feet fostered a sense of super-integration of body, mind and spirit we fairly take for granted now. After a lifetime of body oppression the feeling was a rush, like the entire body was being massaged by the earth, a feeling everyone knows who's ever strolled barefoot on a warm sandy beach or walked over supple ground. Millennia of wearing footwear to protect our feet and cushion our skeletal structure from hard pavements had softened our soles; we had to work to toughen them back if we hoped to walk barefoot more.

☀

Group streaking by free-minded friends and various sport aficionados gained popularity in certain circles.

An in-line skating group, led by one Sandy Snakenberg, enjoyed making periodic nude skates in and around San Francisco. As many as forty people made quick glides thru Golden Gate Park without a stitch on. "The whole point is getting a lot of like-minded souls together to go out and play," he said. A dozen of them bare-skated across part of the Golden Gate Bridge; they waved cheerfully to passing motorists.

In Seattle, nude bicyclists became an ad hoc part of the Freemont Arts Council's annual Summer Solstice Parade. In 2003, eighty participants, festively body-painted and psyched with naked camaraderie and easy self-acceptance, wheeled thru the parade, some performing prankster street theater, to the amusement of spectators, young and old alike. One skit had mock policemen chasing mock nudists dressed in flesh-tone body suits.

In Wisconsin, up to 1,000 college students regularly celebrated school's end with a nite-time run in the buff; other colleges held similar rites every year. And neo-pagans rallied for their right under religious freedom to be sky-clad (clothesfree) for their coven ceremonies on public lands.

Streaking inevitably went commercial. Professional streakers, running naked at events to startle and draw attention to brand names, slogans, or events plastered on their hides, earned a fee per streak from marketing companies. If it was about corporations making money, okay; if it was for personal freedom, no way.

I was taken by the daring stand one woman made in Eugene, Oregon, not far from where I lived. On a gentle summer day in 2001, one Terri Sue Webb chose to bicycle nude thru town. She believed it her right to set her own dress code. She biked calmly and inoffensively, yet was promptly arrested for disorderly conduct. Appearing nude at her court date, she was arrested again, for contempt, and required to undergo psychiatric evaluation. She then challenged the court's presumption that preferring nudity was a sign of mental disorder. Body freedom activists rallied to her defense. She said, "To be offended by the visual appearance of another person is prejudice, akin to racism. The right to exist, uncovered, should hold precedence over the right not to view this, for the objection is irrational." I never learned the case's outcome but whatever happened she'd broken new ground and stirred up people's thinking.

✺

Nude protests for various causes became more frequent around the world—a sure way to get press both for their cause and also for the cause of body freedom.

A popular ad campaign by animal rights supporters PETA (People for the Ethical Treatment of Animals) had celebrities posing nude with a caption saying, "**I'D RATHER GO NAKED**...than wear animal furs." Later, some of their proactive members ran naked in Pamplona, Spain to protest against bulls being mentally tortured during the annual Bull Run and then slaughtered for sport in the ring.

In November 2002, people staged a nude protest over the approaching war in Iraq. The Baring Peace project was launched by forty-five anti-war women in Marin County, California. They'd bared for the camera at Love Field, forming a living peace symbol, hoping the gesture might help diffuse the growing war fever. It was such a bold statement, in time thousands of peace-loving, clothesfree people around the world followed their example. Men and women of all ages stood up and lay down in natural settings— sand, grass, even snow—forming peace signs and spelling out anti-war, and pro-peace messages with their bare bodies. It didn't stop the war but it helped revive the peace movement.

My cousin Zori joined sixty-five other women on a rocky bluff overlooking the ocean, near Arcata, California, to form a nude peace sign. "Greatest experience of my life so far," she wrote. "We felt like we were a living, breathing prayer for peace on earth." In Australia, 750 clothesfree women formed a giant heart on a hillside with **NO WAR** spelled inside in lettering two bodies thick. Efforts to block one such nude protest in Florida were defeated when U.S. District Judge Donald Middlebrooks ruled "nude overtly political speech in the form of a 'living nude peace symbol' is expressive conduct well within the ambit of the First Amendment."

In England, TFTBY—The Freedom to Be Yourself—was spearheaded by one Vincent Bethell, who early on spent six months in jail naked for his beliefs. I learned about this movement thru my oldest brother Jason who'd called Manchester home for ages. While he wasn't a nudist per se, he admitted he found it all "jolly interesting."

Bethell and fellow naked freedom supporters protested nude in public...*for the right to be nude in public.* "Legalize your physical identity," Bethell urged. "...you should not be persecuted or victimized for being born human, with a human body - NAKED!" Explaining further, he said, "...I just think you should have the right to walk down the street naked. I firmly believe that naked people should have equal rights with clothed people." Their campaign pointed out the absurdity of hiding our human identity. The group forcefully summed up their case on a website:

HUMANITY AT PRESENT IS ILLEGAL. YOUR HUMAN BODY IS NOT ALLOWED. IT IS SUPPRESSED BECAUSE YOU ARE ILLEGAL. STOP THE OPPRESSION AND LEGALIZE YOURSELF. IN REALITY, BEING HUMAN IS NOT A CRIME.

Jason, knowing of my interest in all things clothesfree, alerted me to another British happening. In the summer of 2003, Steve Gough, a.k.a. "The Naked Rambler," dared to hike the entire length of Britain nude—over 1,500 kilometers—from southern England to northernmost Scotland. He ignored what he saw as antiquated attitudes towards the naked body. "I am celebrating myself as a human being," he said. "We have been brought up and conditioned to think our body is something to be ashamed of. We are made to feel bad about ourselves and that is damaging society."

He was arrested over a dozen times along the way, beat up by town hooligans, and considered a shameless exhibitionist to some, a hero to others. He claimed he wasn't even a nudist but wanted to "...enlighten the public, as well as the authorities that govern us, that the freedom to go naked in public is a basic human right." On his website a woman emailed during his trek: "Hope you make it. My husband said you should be arrested." He repeated his journey two years later, along with his girlfriend.

His bold example made me feel more open to the idea of being naked in public without feeling weird about it. It dawned on me there was a growing trend of body freedom advocates who, while they didn't consider themselves nudists or naturists—or any other kind of –ist—felt the right to be nude was a basic civil liberty, one being systematically suppressed.

Three more examples of those changing times:

Citizens of all ages in many countries posed tastefully starkers for calendars to raise funds for worthy causes. Organizers were startled how many volunteers agreed to pose in the buff. Sales were brisk, and soon scores of different calendars came out. A movie, *Calendar Girls*, was made about the wild success of one in England.

On August 4, 2002, 1,130 moms and their babies gathered in Berkeley for an intercontinental nurse-in competition, beating out Australia, reminding everyone of the functionality of breasts. In effect, they demonstrated for the right of mothers everywhere to nurse in public. The event underscored the fact breast-feeding was regaining popularity.

The annual Burning Man festival on an ancient lake bed in Nevada was a week-long surreal community of 30,000 or so. Participants were playfully challenged to express themselves in ways far beyond what was normal in everyday life. People often employed nudity to help achieve this, sometimes with bright body paint overlay or wild abbreviated clothing. I participated in it once and spent most of the time just wearing a sombrero—and flip-flops when the ground heated up; I helped new-found friends run a twin giant mist-sprayer setup for refreshing heat relief.

✹

How gladly we greeted the prospect of being naked was usually tied to the degree of body-friendliness of our environments. Our steep dependency on the roaring missiles of gas-guzzling vehicles, and devotion of precious public space to run them on, radically reduced any such friendliness.

Things had been bad enough. Then vehicle makers came up with a way to circumvent U.S. government's fuel efficiency guidelines. Trucks were exempt from such guidelines, so makers put modified car bodies on *truck* platforms. The makers catered to drivers' competitive king-of-the-road fantasies thru beefy, take-no-prisoners vehicles; fuel efficiency wasn't a concern. Who cared, if you had money to burn and felt surges of power driving them? People were on their high horses—a phrase, incidentally, that originated in days of yore when knights rode the biggest, sturdiest horses they could afford to support the weight of their armor and give them a high-vantage edge over rivals.

These thirsty, heavyweight mini-tanks—prosaically called Sport Utility Vehicles, or SUVs—sold like crazy for years. When our oil supply began dwindling and the price of gasoline soared, most scrambled towards leaner-running rigs and developed more Earth-friendly technology.

Car commercials showed such stalwarts blithely plowing thru snow drifts and scaling rocky summits—all but leaping from peak to peak—but *99 percent of owners never drove their rugged beasts off the pavement.* My own conclusion: with names like

Expedition, Mountain King and Earth Bounder, they provided the *semblance* of a nature connection, the wild freedom of creation beyond man's artificial world. Like so many Walter Mittys, owners wistfully imagined galloping their trusty steeds thru pristine wilderness, gloriously despoiling it, even while stuck like giant metallic bugs in gridlock traffic.

SUV-happy industrialized nations, especially the U.S., sucked the precious oil from the rest of planet to fuel these millions of hell-for-leather high-tech chariots. The woeful fuel-inefficiency of such behemoths stepped up our already-extreme dependency on oil, adding that much more to the greenhouse effect destabilizing global weather. The United States guzzled hundred-million year old fuel like hop-headed frat students at keggers seeing who could down the most the fastest: We went thru a quarter-million gallons a minute, four billion gallons each eleven days.

It puzzled me how inordinately fond owners became of these overweight beasts. I could maybe understand gaining peace of mind for the extra traction they supplied in rain and snow, the extra crash protection, the desire to feel cocooned in them and garner a greater sense of security in our fast-paced, unsettling world. But was twice the bill at the gas pump and increased air pollution and environmental degradation worth it?

Reducing yet another complex situation to sophomoric rhyme, I penned in my journal:

> We'd implore Igor to explore more, shore-bore more, so we could pour more, store more, roar more, peddle to the floor more—hardcore!—in the top-drawer, four-door 4X4 we did so adore, senior.

Others, not so enamored by the pretty beasts, drove more fuel-efficient cars, sought hybrid gas-electric vehicles, drove motorcycles, got around by public transport, ride-shared, biked, walked, skated—even skate-boarded.

❋

Cavalier attitudes towards our environment-eroding vehicles—like a plague of locusts consuming the earth—inspired naked rebellion, of sorts.

The summer of 2004 saw the advent of an annual global event dubbed World Naked Bike Ride. On that day, participants in thirty cities around the globe bicycled thru town in packs—some clothed, some half-naked, some totally naked but for footwear to protect feet. It was part protest over oil-dependent vehicles—SUVs in particular—and the danger they posed to everyone not hurtling about in the two-ton juggernauts, smaller-car drivers included; part championing bike riding as an Earth- and people-friendly alternative to our over-dependence on steel beasts; and part celebration of the power, beauty and individuality of our bodies. As one organizer, Conrad Schmidt, put it, "A bicycle represents something simple and so much fun (and) being naked is like saying 'To hell with all these silly norms and rules...'"

Some cities, like L.A., many of whose denizens had practically morphed into human-auto-cyborgs, were a near-bust; others, like San Francisco and Seattle, were freebody successes. In Seattle there was good-natured public acceptance of the nearly fifty naked and half-naked bicyclists cheerfully peddling across town and splashing around the International Fountain afterwards. Hundreds of intrigued spectators watched, and some joined in.

A Seattle friend of mine, Gulliver, participated and emailed me later: "Zet, you should've seen us. At first I said *no way*, then I said, *what the hey*. I gave some real attention to peddling position to avoid hurting my nuts. It was a rush once I overcame feeling scared silly being naked on a moving mechanical device in front of God and everyone. For a while there I felt like a Chippendale [male strippers of the time]. I didn't run into any negative reaction, and we biked kilometers thru town. People *cheered* us! (Of

234

course, I think many simply stared at us in stunned disbelief; the sight of naked people biking thru town shorted out their brains.)"

By 2005, over fifty cities participated in World Naked Bike Ride. Peoples' awareness grew over the steep price we paid for our oil dependency in our love affair with cars, especially in the body-unfriendly habitats we created to accommodate the machines.

The event's coordinating website stated: "We face automobile traffic with our naked bodies as the best way of defending our dignity and exposing the unique danger faced by bicyclists and pedestrians, as well as the negative consequences we all face due to dependence on oil and other forms of non-renewable energy." Participants were not always your avid nudists, either: Rider Melissa of the 2005 London ride, for instance, said, "Like many people, I'm afraid of showing my body in public, but I'm more afraid of relying on environmentally-destructive fuels."

What struck many, including me, as unrelated things at first—nudity, bicycling, oil, and car dependency—revealed, as we connected the dots, how much our lack of body freedom was tied, part and parcel, to how we lived. Who wanted to be *clothed* amid a roaring, fuming sea of such juggernauts, let alone naked? But by going that extreme, naked bicyclers reminded people how nice things *could* be—*"lovely day for a naked bike ride"*—once we changed body attitudes and the way we lived.

Conservative hobby nudists, not at all attracted to the idea of mustering body freedom into everyday living, were turned off by such protests, thinking such confrontational nudity would only create an anti-nudity backlash, with fears of participants being perceived as little more than unruly exhibitionists. But the more progressive-minded saw how people were integrating things together on a higher level; saw the grand interconnectedness of it all. You suspected that many among the cheering crowds lining the streets rode vicariously with the bicyclists, more than a few vowing to join their number next year. The more such public nudity became a light-hearted participatory thing for *everyone*, rather than spectator entertainment provided by the bold, beautiful and bonkers, the more everyday people felt like joining in.

I almost joined in one year, when a merry contingent biked naked thru Ashland, 60 miles north, over Siskiyou Summit. I bought a bike for it and practiced biking in traffic even, but then came down sick. (I probably would've gagged on traffic fumes anyhow.)

❀

On other fronts, international nude-group photographer Spencer Tunick gained controversial renown. He assembled up to 6,000 naked volunteers at a time in public places around the world and orchestrated artistic poses for the camera. "I want people to feel uncomfortable that they've demonized the body," he said. "These grouped masses which do not underscore sexuality become abstractions that challenge or reconfigure one's view of nudity and privacy." He was often arrested early on in New York City, welcomed in later years in such countries as Australia, Chile and Spain.

Enthused one first-time poser in Texas: "It was like I'm freed to be me."

In June 2004, he did what he called a nude installation in Cleveland, Ohio. Cousin Zane, often in the thick of things, flew there to join in. As it happened, a television reporter, Sharon Reed, covered the event in the nude. She held it was an important story about art, and wearing clothes would have been inappropriate. She took heat for her naked stance. As Zane later quipped, "While her station prided itself on covering events for viewers with eye-witness reporting, it drew the line on viewers witnessing its reporting eye uncovered."

Another nude photographer, Harvey Droulliard, prophetically captured something of our current freebody world, in which the nude and clothed intermingle casually. In his 2002 pictorial book, *The Spirit of Lady Godiva,* he set up photo shoots around the United States with naked volunteers in public city scenes filled with random, non-involved clothed people. The photos were shot quickly, after careful setup for quick disrobing and cover-up; many times people weren't even aware of freebodies in their midst until afterwards, and sometimes not even then. Being an amateur photographer, I was in awe how he accomplished it, sometimes staging over a dozen naked people in busy city scenes.

He got arrested for his efforts, like Tunick, but kept shooting his vision—including a photo of two women casually strolling nude past Ann Arbor, Michigan's City Hall and Police Department. These then-daring photos, filled with body-positive energy and *apparent* nude tolerance (sometimes actual, as a few people realized it was a shoot) stretched people's imaginations to new realms of the possible, letting us visualize the body-friendly world we now take for granted.

It appeared there mightn't be the need for people like me and Nuela to be out in the middle of nowhere much longer, if only to live clothesfree. Maybe the days of nudist mobile-home and condo park-resorts—places in which nudists flocked together in isolated or enclosed compounds, per force, to keep the clouds of textile world disapproval from blocking their sun—were on the wane.

To the astonishment of clothed people and freebody advocates alike, the world, or at least parts of it, appeared to be getting amazingly body-friendly.

Six thousand naked people out on a public boulevard of a major city in broad daylight struck many as an encouraging sign.

237

FIFTEEN

The human body can remain nude and uncovered
and preserve its splendor and its beauty.
—Pope John Paul II

FORCES WERE POLARIZING on myriad levels. Our collective body acceptance—or lack thereof—reflected the degree of respect we held not only for ourselves but for the planet and all living things.

It struck observers like me that things were getting better and worse at the same time. With everything: transportation, environment, diet, housing, cost of living, education, entertainment, literature... At times it felt as tho human consciousness was at a great divide, and we came down on one side or the other with every choice we made in our lives. I held a metaphysical image of humanity's diverse energies moving at once in two diverging spirals: one positive, rising upward in a flood of expanding awareness and compassion; one negative, plunging downward to new depths of madness and depravity.

While many continued on with strange and cruel diets, blindly unaware or unmindful how they were slowly killing themselves—

let alone billions of sentient beings—a surge of positive-thinking people underwent radical diet changes. Select colleges began offering a vegan entrée in their cafeterias. Baseball game vendors introduced veggie hotdogs. A blizzard of books, radio talk shows, and magazines, focusing on conscious nutrition, alerted people to sobering realities: The animal-skewed, over-processed, pesticide-laden offerings of mainstream culture were ruining our health and perpetuating an unkind world. Now a gradual convergence of science and spirituality, reflecting the surge towards interconnectivity awareness, shook up the life priorities and value systems of everyone not hopelessly hypnotized by dying cultures' siren songs.

As John Robbins put so clearly in his landmark book, *Diet for a New America*, we'd been "...held prisoner by a point of view beneath the threshold of our awareness." Now more and more grocery shoppers awakened to the reality of having essentially been members of an institutionalized flesh-eating cult. The average American consumed 2,500 animals in his life. We'd needlessly inflicted mortal pain on fellow sentient beings to satisfy a primitive food addiction, disguised as necessary or prestigious but essentially the key for resonating with and partaking in the corrupt and misery-based bounty of Babylon.

Among other things, people now realized meat diets tied up fertile land for grazing and growing animal feed that could far more efficiently be used for feeding the millions of the planet's starving. Land given over to growing food directly for humans fed twenty times more people, with a fraction of valuable water used, (and without the mountains of excrement and viscera to deal with). The same acre of land that produced 165 pounds of beef could produce *20,000 pounds* of potatoes. And people learned how inefficient meat was: by feeding our grains to livestock (which we then ate), we not only wasted 90 percent of grain's protein; but also 96 percent of its calories, 100 percent of its fiber, and 100 percent of its carbohydrates. As more rational-thinking people realized these things, plant-based diets gained in popularity.

Now restaurants begun by true believers, catered to the gourmet vegetarian and vegan palette, providing mouth-watering meals and making enthusiastic new converts. And agri-biz and food processors, alert to the latest money-making trends, knew the glory days of confusing food shoppers were perhaps winding down. (*"I'm surprised the idiots didn't catch on sooner,"* I could imagine them saying.) They either started delivering the goods—organic, whole plant foods (and ostensibly free-range and cage-free animal products)—or provided the *illusion* they were, with watered-down organic certification legislation and unending choruses of "All Natural!" plastered across their same old products. (*"Now with one percent wholegrain goodness!"*)

More discerning consumers, leading the exodus from the land of fuzzy half-truths and intentional deceptions, knew the real deal when they saw it. Responding to the demand for organic foods, where once there was only the little hole-in-the-wall natural food store there were now entire chains of whole-food supermarkets. Some cities offered a scattering of hybrid supermarkets as well.

It amazed me how the small towns around my basically conservative home region, while sporting a few whole food stores, had a paucity of organic produce in its regular supermarkets; but if I drove an hour to more progressive Ashland, with its thriving food coop, some of the town's once-conventional supers had morphed into hybrids, bursting with organic produce, organic teas and coffees, recycled-paper products—things once never found outside modest natural food stores. By 2006, the huge Safeway supermarket chain introduced small lines of organic products in their stores. Such mongrel offerings struck me as too weird for words at first blush—like organic cotton lining acrylic outfits, or plastic radio stations playing cool music. To offer organic foods right next to conventional, sprayed, devitalized and genetically-mangled staples seemed madness—the Mad Hatter willy-nilly offering pots of premium organic green teas and artificially-flavored mystery blends. But I realized such hybrids were probably needed: They were the wave of the future, as humanity's appetite for real food, produced with a modicum of integrity, awakened after the long nightmare of quasi-food. Natural food stores alone could no longer meet skyrocketing demand in certain regions.

Organic wasn't enuf, tho. That was just getting us back to Square One, before we'd begun pesticiding, insecticiding, and chemically fertilizing ourselves sick. The personal care and more civilized pace that came with shopping in stores infused with down-home interconnectedness—typical of the first natural food stores and co-ops that made shopping a pleasant and refreshing experience—was now in danger of getting lost in the shuffle. The same with the family farms and small processors who supplied them: The caring quality once mustered into the foods by smaller scale, down home operations was sacrificed as such concerns were bought up by diversifying corporations—like General Mills buying Cascadian Farms in 1999 and Phillip Morris snapping up Boca Foods in 2000—and geared up to produce enormous product volume. The food might be organic, but the energy behind it could be as indifferent as ever.

On the subtle level, the degree of harmonious energy in foods affected our eating pleasure, as well as our spiritual nourishment. As a friend once told me, the best insurance to eating well was to focus on energetically purifying the food first, neutralizing any discordant or toxic energies attached to it. It could be more important than whether the food was organic or not. The more our groceries came from mechanized, hyper-driven corporations, the more important this was, ensuring the food we took in resonated with us, rather than becoming edible trojan horses invading our bodies.

Local organic farmers' markets, as if compensating for the bigger-is-better trend, cropped up like mushrooms after a rain. People became aware how foods locally grown harmonized with a body's attunement to a given climate and that the average supermarket item was brought from 2,000 kilometers away. They realized the hidden energy and pollution costs in food transported such distances. Food shoppers liked to know where things grew and getting to talk the people who grew them.

A budding awareness of the innate spirituality of food emerged as people attuned to more integrated living. At times it appeared maybe the whole world was going natural (especially if living in a progressive region). That is, until you saw people in front of a restaurant chain peaceably assembled to protest the unethical treatment of cattle and the clear-cutting of Amazon rainforest for grazing land being arrested as terrorists. Or remembered that even the mellowest natural food store often carried flesh products and byproducts. (They wanted to offer free-range meats and cage-free eggs to shoppers still hooked on such foods, sometimes including themselves.) It was a slow road back to Wellville, but a major cultural shift in dietary awareness was definitely underway.

☀

In contrast, the road back to Freebody was barely on the map. It was easier changing diet and putting up with meat-loving friends' ribbings and suspicious waitress looks when asking if the soup had an animal base than it was spending Saturday at your local beachfront naked and risking arrest.

Many, if not most, thought it frivolous (if not absurd beyond words) to give *any* attention to the right to be naked in public—especially during those perilous times. Besides, the subject had such a high giggle factor, few took the subject seriously.

But those were rarified times as well; a time of quickening when *all* things—many hidden for ages—were coming to light and examined with laser-like objectivity. The level of body freedom and mutual acceptance for one another's biological self were no more and no less parts of the vast healing process underway during those meltdown times. The more we achieved greater wellbeing *in*side our bodies—thru conscious diet, exercise, yoga and such—the more we wanted to extend the sense of wellbeing to our *outer* bodies as well.

As within, so without.

Even as pockets of more enlightened humanity made breakthrus in garnering body freedom rights, repressive forces went on full attack. One state tried slipping thru legislation to make nudity in one's home punishable by up to ten years in prison if children were present.

The same retail stores openly selling R-rated movies, depicting mind-numbing brutality and dehumanizing nudity, made photolab customers feel like criminals if their rolls contained any nakedness, refusing to print copies, no matter how innocent or tasteful they were. Caving to body-phobic shareholders and frightful right shoppers, they demonized the subjects in real-life photos (or, in the case of one bare-waisted three-year-old in her wading pool, her parents), that affirmed the sweetness and beauty of life.

Some bookstores, for similar reasons, stopped carrying naturist periodicals on their long magazine racks. Copies *had* been antiseptically sealed in opaque wrappers, as if wanting to save respectable prurient browsers from mistakenly thinking they'd picked up a skin mag, which had somehow escaped similar containment, in their search of gratuitous crotch-shots, and have their fantasyland sensibilities shocked by photos of everyday naked people. Apparently that measure wasn't enuf, tho; to protect the public from subversive notions of body integrity, naturist magazines were pulled altogether. Respectable porn magazines, no doubt having eyed the upstarts on the shelf uneasily, sighed in relief.

To the muckety-mucks and their minions, living in a warped-out anti-universe cleverly disguised as God-fearing conservative

Christianity, anything promising to let the masses reclaim a modicum of self-respect and personal empowerment constituted a threat to their controlling agenda. That's why they were up in arms to censor the Internet, and why, centuries before, they loathed Gutenberg's insidious new invention: both held the power to make end-runs around their communication blocking.

Someone called such wonky reactions "the madness of The Beast," which had much of the world in its grip; at times there was no making sense of it—short of buying into the belief master races had invaded Earth eons ago and had been holding its inhabitants ransom ever since to serve their selfish needs. In this school of thought, these "Masters of the Universe" had somehow managed to get themselves stranded here while planet exploring, perhaps loosing their superman powers to planet-hop after over-indilging in the kryptonite lures of earthly pleasures; they become so embittered over their plight they amused themselves by stirring up strife, watching humans kill each other and destroy the planet-now-prison they held zero affection for. As internationalist billionaires, with different homes around the world, they held no allegiance to any one country and thought nothing of destroying a country's economy if it served their purposes or gratified their sadistic humor.

In any event, for whatever reasons, the naked human body had been deemed indecent, publicly acceptable only as a lure for commerce. But nudists were having none of it. Dan Speers, president of Tri-State Metro Nudists, summed up the pity of it all: "For someone to tell me—especially the government authority—that I have to wear clothes...they're telling me that I have to be ashamed of myself: government is mandating that people shame themselves." Such voices in the wilderness made me seriously re-think the subject.

※

With the phenomenal advent of Internet use, word about body freedom disseminated far and wide. Budding nudaholics like me surfed web sites like clothesfree.com and naturistsociety.com and joined bulletin board discussions, gaining awareness of the growing movement and related events and happenings around the world.

Thru one website, I connected with a naturist travel agency that booked Nuela and me on a week-long clothing-optional cruise thru the sun-drenched Mediterranean.

My first cruise ever, we boarded the older ship with 300 other passengers, mostly Spanish, in Barcelona. We sailed out in balmy June weather, over the week visiting Ibiza, Corsica, Rome and Nice. Way under-booked; the ship bristled with as many crew and workers as there were passengers; you couldn't take two sips of coffee without an attentive waiter, geared up for serving twice the people and feeling idle, asking if you wanted a re-fill.

Not having to dress for dinner was fun. Altho ho-hum now, then it was a waking dream: We left our stateroom fully naked—no footwear even, thank you—walked the carpeted length of the ship, up three stair flights and across the open deck to reach the busy buffet room. We selected our food from the serving line's bountiful choices. (We were both still lacto-ovo then, or we might have been skeletons at the feast.) We sat at round ocean-view tables, after first spreading obligatory towel on the chair, and enjoyed our meal among other passengers—naked and clothed together, no one blinking an eye.

Getting to play a lounge's ebony grand piano naked between scheduled room use was another treat. One day a Spanish woman with her Niño, both naked, came over; she sang along as I ventured thru "Morning Has Broken." It began to feel that maybe it really had.

Nuela was amused—and a bit concerned—how enthusiastic I

got over the opportunity to be as naked as I wanted to be—while on board, that is. When in Rome, we did as Romans did and wore clothes, tho the heroic nude statuary at Trevi Fountain reminded us what Romans *used* to do. I tried keeping clothesfree around the clock on board, even when we sailed away from our last port-of-call, Nice, towards sunset. Cold gusts buffeted everyone who came to the stern deck to bid the French coast adieu—mostly nude.

"Put some clothes on, sweetie; that wind must be cutting you to the bone," Nuela said, hugging herself to keep warm.

"Nah, it feels good," I lied, gritting my teeth and clinching my muscles like crazy to stave off the icy blasts of the legendary mistral winds. I was among a dozen diehards who knew it was our last chance for outdoor nudity and sun rays on the voyage. As the French Riviera with its impossibly-rich blue waters receded in the distance, we weathered the buffeting gladly, feeling galvanized for being near a land of historically greater body freedom.

☀

Next year, on a decadent whim of mine, we went on a "Happy Cruise" with the Carousel line. I know, I should have known better, and Nuela had her doubts, but went along because I was so curious about them. Of course, I'd gotten spoiled silly my first cruise, where one could be naked, anytime, anywhere, except the formal dining room; now I'd have to stay wrapped everywhere, all the time, except in our cabin and the sauna. Maybe, like Hesse's Steppenwolf character, I felt a wayward fascination revisiting the bourgeoisie lifestyle of my past—sort of a weird sentimental journey—maybe only to remind me why I'd forsaken such a somnambulistic lifestyle in the first place.

We sailed out of New Orleans a half year before that fabled musical gem of a town was devastated by Hurricane Katrina. Our destination was Jamaica. *Golden Unicorn* was a brand-new, 3,200 passenger-capacity, half-billion-dollar floating resort, averaging twenty-five *meters* to the gallon of diesel. The ship bristled with dazzling décor and offered luxurious, if sometimes tacky, features at every turn.

We especially loved the generous-sized wet and dry saunas in the separate gyms, even if they weren't co-ed. Most users, hewing to the textile mindset, kept wrapped in thick white towels in the sweltering chambers; we didn't. As I sweated away, I'd gaze out over the blue Caribbean Sea thru the dramatic all-glass end wall of the men's sauna, catching for the first time a setting sun's last light flashing green a second before dipping below the horizon. It turned out Nuela had caught it too, next door. (We could've tapped out Morse-code on the common wall but neither of us knew any— dash it all.)

Naturally, it struck us as absurd couples couldn't experience a sauna together and share such natural wonders during their adventure-of-a-lifetime vacation. In other ways, the ship experience was not as carefree as advertised. Flocks of people got pretend naked on the Lido deck in their skimpy swim suits to soak up the subtropical sun; to go further and remove the tiny, strategically placed pieces of cloth would've made many passengers happy indeed— were it not for the certain knowledge ship's officers would swoop down on them for their effrontery.

Of course, the only people on board who could bare their bottoms were the revue dancers in the nitely Las Vegas-style floor shows. Seated passengers got pleasantly toasted while watching them cavort thru schmaltzy if spirited singing, flashing their flesh, turning systemic body suppression into risqué spectacle. We were effectually being told: "We hope you enjoy our tastefully naughty productions, but please don't try this on board or you will be left at the next port-of-call. We thank you for your cooperation; and enjoy the cruise. Blackout bingo at ten in the Purple Pony lounge."

Unbeknownst to most Carousel fans, the same line leased out

one of their ships, *Platinum Peacock,* to a nude vacation travel agency once a year. In a hundred-and-eighty-degree reversal of the ship's normal policy, the only place then *not* clothing-optional on the *Peacock* was the formal dining hall. We might've gone on that instead, but you had to book a year ahead, and neither of us could lock into plans that far. When we wanted to travel, we wanted to go *then*, not twiddle our thumbs forever.

Dining faire was generous and unending, same as before. But again, if we'd been vegan then we might have gone on the hungry side and had non-organic iceberg lettuce salads, celery and carrot sticks out our ears. The main offerings were all animal based: scrambled eggs, pasta au gratin, butter-drenched potatoes, cereal with cow's milk, seven varieties of cheesy pizzas, dairy-loaded deserts… It would have been all-you-can-eat and nothing to eat.

One exception, to their eternal credit, was their soy burger offering at the grill, which we visited often. I estimated 98 out of a 100 takers opted for the dead-critter variety. Once, when I gave my order over the counter, I threw off the server's rhythm. He'd been on a lightning-fast roll serving the meat-loving masses. With me his work pattern came to a screeching halt. He had to go back to a freezer to pull out the soy patties that were going begging. I felt like such a bother.

Mandatory swimwear really put a crimp in things for me. But not Nuela. As I mentioned, she generally adapted graciously to the body-freedom restraints of general society, having learned to walk both worlds with fairly equal ease; she hadn't experienced a mandatory-clothes upbringing like me and 99.99 percent of the rest of us. Obviously, I was still rebelling from having been chained to cloth too long; I resented having to even *own* swim trunks.

"Hey, at least our *stateroom* is clothesfree, Zet," she said as we came back from the Lido deck's outdoor area and stripped almost

249

before the door closed.

"Yeah, but I really wanted to do that waterslide bare-butt. I mean, it was still a rush—*whoosh!*—then my trunks got so damn clammy I felt like I'd gotten drenched in a rainstorm and couldn't change out of my street clothes. I should've—"

"Yeah, yeah. I know, it's terrible, sweetie, you oughta sue. You know *shoulda-woulda-coulda* don't pay the reality bill. You knew what we were signing on for here. 'It'll be like a Disneyland afloat,' you said. Well, you can't very well get naked in Disneyland now, can you? Last I checked there wasn't any "It's a Bare, Bare World" attraction opening. I mean, what would Snow White think? And Minnie; why, she'd *freak out*: 'Eek! A naked human!' Remember, a clothing-optional world can't be built in a day."

I knew she was right and I really had no right to complain. That didn't stop me. I kept grumbling how nuts things were. I knew better, but at times I swore Nuela was an apologist for the textile order the way she adapted so easily to covering up, like some cultural contortionist who could bend herself into whatever shape society expected at the moment and keep on smiling.

It was frustrating being me: I wanted change *now*, not tomorrow. The rest of the world was guilty, on all counts, for not hastening the day. A waterslide was *made* to be enjoyed naked, the way I saw it—a tushie treat if ever there was one. I remembered how the International Nudist Association had signed to lease the use of a Central California water park for a day from its open-minded owner. Conservative forces got wind of the plan and threatened a boycott and certain financial ruin if he didn't cancel the agreement. The owner apologized to the nudists, but had no choice but to cow-tow to the clothed order if he hoped to stay afloat.

Nuela and I showered off and spread towels on the carpet and sat naked in the sunshine streaming thru our own all-glass wall. We were plowing over wind-capped waters on the way back to port, after a too-brief visit to Rasta-land that left me wondering if

I'd really been there. The reggae-colored headband I'd bought from a phenomenally pushy vendor—it was easier than resisting once I made the fatal error of evincing casual interest—did little to convince me otherwise.

Nuela and I, bored silly after five minutes of lounging in the sun at the private tourist beach we'd been shuttled to from Montego Bay, had asked attendants for litter bags so we could gather up some of the atrocious amounts of litter that had washed ashore nearby and were left for bizarre seashells.

"Oh, no, mon, I can't ask you to do that. You're here to relax, not work."

"But we *want* to. We like picking up litter in nature and, if you'll forgive our saying, parts of this beach *really* need it. We'll enjoy doing it."

"Oh, no, mon, you just relax, okay?"

It took a while to convince them we were in earnest. Paid guests volunteering to clean up the place wouldn't look good if the business head dropped by, but he indulged our strange request. We'd each filled a large trash bag in no time flat.

The exotic mini-solarium and pleasant company were mellowing me some. "I should've known that nude cruise would spoil me for anything else," I admitted ruefully.

"Sure, but remember how the ship just had that one stingy little porthole?" she asked. "And how cramped our quarters were on that rust bucket? This is *nice*," she said, stretching out in the Caribbean sun like a contented cat after a good meal.

"Yeh, but—"

"No 'yeh, buts,' you!" She sat up so suddenly I dropped my bag of trailmix from home. "C'mon and try to enjoy it the way it is. Check out that room towel the nice steward left us, origamied into a duck-billed platypus; isn't that wild? And there, a complementary bottle of champagne management brought up after you groused how the loud toilet flush upset your nerves. Honestly, sometimes I think you just *have* to have something to complain

251

about to feel you're earning your keep on the planet. You could be Andy Rooney and Molly Ivins' love child. Why not just hang a shingle out: 'Zet Quimby, Certified Critic. No topic too big or small to fault-find. Reasonable Rates,' and be done with it. Is that really your role in life?"

"Hey, it's hard work, but somebody's got to—"

"Not buying it, Darlin'. Here now, hush up and rub some skin cream on me." She handed me a bottle of vitamin-E-and-aloe lotion and lay back down. I soon forgot what I was so upset about. Working her supple skin made me feel like a kid in a sandbox on a sunny day.

SIXTEEN

*Challenging the validity of accepted societal norms
makes people uneasy. It brings up issues most people
never think about, let alone want to talk about.*
—**Joanne Stepaniack,**
The Vegan Sourcebook

BY 2010, A VIABLE freebody culture thriving between the cracks of the clothed world kicked into higher gear. A vibrant, free-thinking culture blossomed out of the decomposing old one. Larger mini-pockets of humanity, mostly in regions with nice weather and liberal traditions, became more accepting of themselves, naked bodies and all. As in the 60s, we were again in the midst of extreme social instability and disruption: wars, diseases, natural disasters, repressive governments, long-term marriages disintegrating, and more people without steady incomes or homes. But there also emerged fresh vision, new ways of thinking and doing and being—which extended to both our choice of diet and, explored here more, manner of dress.

One James Laver wrote of the beginning of the Renaissance in the fourteenth century, "...life was opening like a flower and clothes were responding with a symbolic gesture, as they always do." Now, in at least the most liberal-minded areas, blessed with freebody weather, clothes were responding with a radically new gesture—by clean disappearing.

An old paint company cleverly coined as their motto "Cover the Earth;" it could have doubled as the motto of the clothes-minded. The growing sentiment among body freedom proponents: "*Un*cover the Earth."

Many dedicated grassroots efforts to establish free beaches near metro area were at last bearing fruit. Freebody activists from Seattle and Chicago to Burlington and Virginia Beach had garnered enough public support to gain official clothing-optional public beaches—select handfuls of waterfronts where people could enjoy the naked beauty of nature while the same.

Such places pulled in record numbers to luxuriate in sun and water, free of textile restraint. More men than women went fully bare, as had often been the case in male-dominant societies. (More's the pity, as most women, generally better body-attuned than men, adored being unadorned when circumstances allowed.) The numbers began to even out some as we moved towards a more egalitarian culture. Women had empowered themselves to be more than beauty objects (and child bearers and housekeepers); and men, overcoming age-old male chauvinism, learned to quit objectifying them. Women who still clung to bits of textile increasingly wore thongs or G-strings, and men had their own brief variations, both of which could still get them arrested if they strayed too far from designated freebody zones. Many of both sexes felt the absurdity of keeping these on and eventually dispensed with them:

"I can't believe I paid $20 for this ridiculous piece of Lycra."
"I thought it was only $19.99."

254

"Careful, it'll still work as a slingshot."

With increased casual nudity and semi-nudity, the more open-minded people desensitized from being startled or shocked by public nakedness.

During my more sexually-inactive years, visiting various mineral springs and free beaches could be maddeningly arousing, more like an exotic wet dream than waking reality. Sudden increased skin exposure left nothing to prevent the pheromones from flying like sparks off a sparkler. Seeing long-hidden parts of women's bodies, accentuated by intriguing tan lines, sometimes made me feel like The Man with X-Ray Eyes. But I adapted in time, learning to keep any lustful thinking well in check, as did others. We gradually reprogrammed our mental circuits.

On the other hand, the most backward and genetically-challenged had a field day—one giant, ongoing ogling fest, replete with binoculars and cameras. Some would actually stand near groups of the naked, as if in catatonic trance and staring at a screen in some darkened porn theater. Worse, the more unstable sometimes went overboard and sexually harassed and assaulted unvigilant freebodies of both sexes who were only hoping to commune with nature.

To nip the possibility of such incidents in the bud, the more popular free beaches—like Maui's Little Beach and Haulover Beach in Florida—developed grassroots watchdog groups. Local volunteers, often wearing distinctive Day-Glo caps, worked to keep upbeat and safe atmospheres. They maintained litter patrol; banned boom boxes, alcohol and drug use; and responded with rapid intervention to untoward attentions paid any beachgoer. Free beaches not having such community involvement either reverted to textile beaches soon after the first unsavory incident and public outcry or learned to emulate the success stories.

If progressive-thinking governing administrators noticed how well community-involved beaches policed themselves, they especially noticed how places like Haulover Beach brought in an infusion of tourist dollars from its million-plus annual visitors. Authorities learned to work with nude enthusiasts, if tenuously, developing sites and policies that accommodated both freebody needs and modesty concerns of the textile-minded. Parts of the U.S., then, experienced a *joie de vivre,* embracing a body mindset similar to that which Europeans had cultivated, lavishing attention on body comfort and the enjoyment of innocent sensual pleasure.

No scientific surveys were taken about how many slept nude, but one I caught around 1998 revealed four percent of women and 18 percent of men regularly did. Now, as more people experimented with such nocturnal freedom—baby steps—a new survey revealed 14 percent of women and 36 percent of men did. Still cocoons by day, but now butterflies by nite.

After a warm-weather nite of enjoying being naked while protectively under covers, one got up and realized: *hey, I don't have to put anything on just because I'm out of bed. My sweetie (or Duke) won't mind if I don't cover up.* This realization led, in turn, to making morning tea or coffee naked, maybe taking it out on the back porch and savoring it along with the sun on the skin in the fresh morning air. Free time allowing, a person might indulge in nude sunbathing while reading or puttering around the back garden—even sally forth to the front lawn if that's where the morning sun was hitting, some no longer caring if others saw them unwrapped or not.

The growing mantra became "I'm nekkid. Big deal. Get over it."

Pleasant weather inspired barely-there wear for venturing further from home, token cover-ups for maximum body comfort and receptivity to the elements.

Thong underwear had caught on several years earlier among women, all but freeing derrieres from restrictive double-wrapping. The next logical step was *no* underwear, as in the days of old. In nicest weather, many people, duly hygiene-conscious, skipped wearing them entirely, something few "self-respecting person" would have done only years before. People felt any extra laundry work for dealing with any errant pee dribbles, body sweat and such on their single-layer cover, once contained by underpants, was worth it for the extra comfort not wearing them allowed. Besides, they discovered sweating was minimized with their bodies no longer getting so easily overheated. And, with the wholesome living-food diets many people adapted to, stools became firm and well defined—like large deer pellets—and buttholes were often no longer a tissue issue.

Many of us veered away from needlessly constrictive, chafing clothing. Simpler, warm-weather pant designs forewent dress-intensive zippers, buttons, snaps, belts and buckles in favor of gentle elastic waistbands and draw-strings. Relaxed-fit, knit-cotton and flannel pajama bottoms had gained currency among younger folks a few years earlier, much to my initial astonishment *Pajamas in public? How...daring.*

I discovered that the longer I spent naked the more sensitive I became to what I threw on for going to town. Accordingly, I stopped wearing conventional pants, which I found too constrictive and skin irritating. In warmer weather when I *had* to dress, I'd wear simple elastic-waist thin-cotton shorts, solid-color tank top and flip-flops. Being able to dress or undress in five seconds flat simplified life. When Nuela and I went together on expeditions she'd dress more elegantly, favoring fancy patterned tops and shorts, or sarong, along with stylish sandals.

I was astounded how others could walk around town in roasting weather without getting heatstroke, wearing long pants, shoes and socks, long-sleeves, top shirt-button done and tie knotted tight.

"How can they *do* that?" I asked her one day as we crossed the parking lot to one of our local organic-food stores, Peoples Food.

"Is the average person really that insensitive to their own body comfort?"

I'd learned the rudiments of designing clothes in my younger days, when dad tried grooming me to help carry on the business. Along with a purple tank-top, I was wearing a quasi-kilt I'd fashioned out of knit cotton with a Black Watch tartan pattern. I loved the semi-nude feeling it allowed, half hoping no errant wind revealed what I wasn't wearing under, half not caring. Nuela had on a periwinkle halter top with an ocean-theme half-sarong bottom, guaranteed to divert all attention away from me anyway.

"I don't think it's that," Nuela said. "Maybe they do numb down their body awareness a bit to cope, but remember how you said you got more sensitive to clothes the more you went without them? I've got some more ideas on that score. I—" She stopped suddenly, rummaging in her yellow Guatemalan bag. "Where's our shopping list?"

Usually neither of us could remember what we needed without writing it down. When we forgot our list we'd come home with everything but what we meant to get. Our food cupboards were all but bare that time. We were out of everything but stuff we'd probably never eat short of a teamster strike shutting off grocery store supplies. We'd run out of our current morning staples—Fujis and pears, raw almond butter and tahini—days ago. Between garden harvests, we were pretty much reduced to rapidly-wilting celery stalks; broccoli turning fascinating shades of yellow-orange; and a mysterious rutabaga neither of us remembered getting. I suspected we'd sooner fast.

I held up the grocery list in my hand.

"Good. What was I saying…oh, right. I think a *lot* of people subject their flesh to all that discomfort for a combination of reasons. But it all pretty much boils down to a few, like wanting to look spiffy; wanting a buffer from non-body-friendly environments, and wanting to armor themselves against people around them they don't know and aren't sure about—all because of the sorry lack of mutual acceptance of each other and respect for the planet."

God, I loved her mind, and told her so. She'd hit it on the head, I thought: As long as our world was unloving and un-body-friendly, we'd seek a sense of security wrapping ourselves like the industrial plastic packaging of electronic goods.

Her deft analysis left one less thing to mystify me. But my list was long. Like why was the song "Waltzing Matilda" in 4:4 time? And why were all but one of Round Table Pizza's tables square? And why did radio and TV hosts tell you not to go away just before *they* did? Reality was often a fuzzy concept. I needed to learn not to wrack my brain so much, trying to make sense of a nonsensical world. But so many things baffled me. Like, why didn't cars have a switch to turn off inside lights so you could leave doors open if you wanted to without draining your battery? And why'd we have hundreds of orchestral melody rings for cell phones, but for most land phones the only choices were between shrill, obnoxious and Baby Klaxon?

In colder weather, following the lead of youth I began wearing PJ bottoms, along with Chinese slippers, while bundling up good on top. I suffered no weird reactions that I could notice. I remembered how, as a bored teen, I once amused myself walking out the house wearing only PJs, bathrobe and slippers and catching a crowded #55 diesel bus downtown and back. Nobody blinked an eye; every day was Halloween in San Francisco. The first few weeks I wore PJ bottoms out I felt only half-dressed, but the pants police never came for me, and soon I would've felt overdressed in anything else. I chose conservative solid colors; no SpongeBob SquarePants for me, unlike what some PJers wore with an insouciance I could only admire. Nuela preferred yoga pants, just as relaxed a fit but of sturdier fare, and wore her stylish sandals without socks in all but coldest weather. ("My feet want to breathe.")

To both of us, most of the prevailing dress conventions were one big wedgie.

＊

By now I'd long enjoyed being naked around our home front. And I felt comfortable socially naked—at least in the safe havens of free beaches, nude resorts and mineral springs. (It was worlds easier being naked then if most others were too.) But, beyond my one leisurely Seattle streak and the nude cruise, I'd yet to venture into general public zones without the de facto regulation cover-up. I was still a freebody novice, only beginning to comprehend how much prevailing body-alienated energies cramped my druthers to be naked, or at least in some state of dishabille. Why couldn't we just wear a long tank-top without feeling weird about it? (*"Forget to finish dressing, did we?" Smirk, smirk.*)

My academic and political interest in the subject was sparked years earlier after getting the oddest phone call of my life. Out of the blue some publisher or other was asking me if I'd written a book on nudism. The question tickled me, as I'd often interject talks with friends on subjects I felt strongly about by saying "I could write a book about it." I told the caller "no, but I bet I could."

There'd been something eerie about the call. I felt like an actor in a movie whose destiny had just taken a significant turn. For one brief, dreamlike moment, I felt I *had* written a book.

The upshot of the incident: It spurred me to rethink the entire phenomenon of people wanting to get free of clothes more often. I began studying nudist literature in earnest. Pushing my attention past the pix of unabashed naked women—feeling I was maybe at last gaining a modicum of maturity—I'd read articles and glean the deeper social and political implications of a people wanting to live free of clothes in warmer weather, who strove to gain body freedom rights in our clothing-crazed world.

I sought to get a handle on what I soon realized was an incredibly convoluted, controversial and yet strangely neglected subject. Not unlike vegans and meat lovers, naked and clothed people could be like oil and water. A parody of Rodgers and Hammerstein's "The Cowman and the Farmer" sprang to mind:

> Oh, the nudist and the textile can be friends
> Oh, the nudist and the textile can be friends
> One of them likes to live in the buff
> The other one can't get dressed enuf
> But that's no reason why they can't be friends

Towards century's end, Reader's Digest and National Geographic, among others, put out exhaustive retrospective tomes on 20th century popular culture. All sorts of new and unusual fads, pastimes, and social developments were covered—everything from flag-pole sitting and miniature golf to mah-jongg mania and women mustering in the work force—but not *one* word about nudism. (Turner Publishing's *Illustrated History of the 20th Century* was a fount of knowledge in comparison with its one-line mention of nudist colonies under a **New in 1929** side-bar.) No matter if it was the advent of a new lifestyle destined over the decades to transform the lives of millions of people around the world, the subject was studiously ignored as if it never happened. Was it the cripple who hated dancers, or a well-oiled power structure enforcing mandatory dress to keep people's free spirits muffled?

Jokes and cartoons about nudist colonies, on the other hand, were rife. Writers used them stereotypically for settings of murder mysteries, and movie producers twisted their reality into escapist fodder for the too easily amused. But actual social nudity was all but ignored, the weird family secret nobody talked about.

Against such denial, the freebody movement strove to turn

around a body-alienated culture any way it could short of getting arrested, sometimes not stopping there.

SEVENTEEN

*I can see a future when people would hardly be able to believe the
ancient legend that once, before they knew better, human beings
sickened themselves by eating the corpses of animals...*
—**John Robbins**
Diet for a New America

FOR YEARS I'D SEEN naturism as only
about being socially naked. Being able to do that seemed miracle
enuf in our anti-life culture, bent on keeping everything wrapped
up, locked down, closed up and otherwise stashed out of sight. For
a while, I'd thrive on the feeling of utter liberation and joy of going
naked in sheltered public places and how it helped me overcome
nagging body shame and guilt complexes, how the people I met at
such places were generally amiable and upbeat.

Over time tho, after visiting a few California nudist resorts,
something felt missing, something not right. Finally it dawned on
me: Apart from enjoying being naked together in a semblance of
nature, the lifestyles of many fellow freebody enthusiasts
appeared abysmally conventional. To an eternal nonconformist
like me, I found this discouraging. Resort restaurants gave only
token attention to plant-based dishes beyond their perpetual iceberg salad, and the offerings that didn't have meat were over-

processed or loaded with dairy and eggs. Many guests smoked and drank and thought nothing incongruous about it. But now I thought, *Why would people rave about how natural and healthy it was to go without clothes, and yet continue to coat their lungs with tar, clog their arteries with animal fat and pickle their livers in alcohol?*

It didn't compute.

As mentioned, at the time of the original German nature-cure movement, nudism—at least among the minority hardcore branch—was seamlessly integrated into an overall natural, healthy lifestyle. Practitioners embraced plant-based diets; eliminated meat, alcohol and tobacco; and otherwise paid serious attention to nature and her ways—no less than pursued getting free of clothes.

I knew nothing about this.

My gut feeling something was amiss was finally confirmed after serendipitously stumbling across Gordon Kennedy's book *Children of the Sun*, about the original movement. It was a revelation: *Richard Ungewitter, "The Father of Nudism," was a dedicated vegetarian.* Having witnessed the many dissatisfactions with modern life around him, one day he had a brainstorm. He felt nudism could, as Cec Cinder pointed out in *The Nudist Idea*, "...serve as the central metaphor for the entire new belief system, not just an adjunct to it but the central motif and powering force, the flame...which gave light and heat and energy to the new natural, holistic approach to life!"

But what he saw as the integrating lynchpin had become isolated.

Then, as if I needed any more confirmation, I discovered that Ungewitter hadn't been alone in his diet beliefs. Dr. Heinrich Pudor—contender for the claim of starting nudism (who felt mandatory dress basically amounted to slavery)—*was also a dedicated vegetarian.* Pudor's larger belief system, as set forth in pamphlets like "Naked Mankind: A Leap into the Future," held that, in the process of learning to live in harmony with nature, it was just as important to rid ourselves of foreign invaders—in the guise of meat, alcohol, tobacco and other toxins—from *inside* the body as it was to lose artificial covering from the outside. One wouldn't break the outer shackles of forced clothing and declare body liberation while blindly ignoring remaining manacled inside by unhealthy and cruel diet, would they?

Or would they?

Maybe latter-day naturists couldn't be faulted if they did. As I said, diet wasn't part of the deal here. I couldn't learn if American nudism founder Kurt Barthel was a vegetarian or not. If so, he maybe realized he'd loose prospective nudist members if he tried tying veggie diet to nudism. In the land of bacon and eggs it would've flown like a tank with butterfly wings. (It hadn't always gone over big in the land of sausage either.) If not, it made his task that much easier.

It was one thing to flout the single entrenched convention of clothes-wearing, another to tackle the entire citadel of Mammon, with its sundry disconnects from nature influencing virtually every sector of society. I doubt an optimal natural lifestyle— vegan diet and avoidance of alcohol, tobacco, coffee—would've appealed to many modern, card-carrying naturists. Call me a cynic, but I think some would've sooner gone back to clothing's ball and chain than give up their tri-tip sirloins and lobster thermidor, or hamburgers and meatloaf.

Granted, surrendering a lifetime of mandatory clothes could be a lot more fun—and, for most, easier—than re-educating one's taste buds to go cold turkey on...well, cold turkey. Meat-eating had probably been locked into the cultural mindset longer than body covering and, being something intimately taken inside our bodies thru our mouths, was a more visceral, emotionally-loaded habit. Even so, the situation struck me as too weird for words: People touting getting free of clothes for health and wellbeing sooner went under the scalpel for catastrophic quadruple-bypass surgeries from arteries clogged with animal food residue than give up their dead cow dinners; sooner had a lung removed sooner than quit smoking; sooner went on a waiting list for a new liver after a lifetime of "social" drinking than give up their drinky-pooh.

Nudism had turned its back on its naturist parents.

Add on the dominant culture's addiction to gas-guzzling vehicles, polluting techno-toys, breakneck living pace and throwaway consumer mentality, and it struck me how various proponents were unwittingly helping make the planet less of a place one *wanted* to be naked in. It reminded me of how people bought foods with "all natural" on the labels of inorganic, highly-processed foods masquerading as whole, living foods and thought they were eating right.

While I continued supporting the efforts of the body freedom movement, in time I'd stop thinking of myself as a nudist or even a naturist; I was just me, wanting to live free.

❉

Along with the tobacco habit, addiction to animal-based diets was—more and more people came to realize—one of the deadliest habits on the face of the Earth. Altho the results of hundreds of objective studies over a half century had demonstrated growing mountains of evidence significantly linking animal-based diets to degenerative diseases, it didn't sink into many people's awareness.

Then a wave of fresh awareness crashed on the shores of human consciousness in the early 2000s. As if shaken out of a cultural delusion, millions became aware of the health benefits of vegan food diet over exploited-critter faire and how abominably we were treating animals and wrecking the environment. Nearly two decades after John Robbins' classic, *Diet for a New America*, first shook up the world, a new flood of incontrovertible scientific evidence linking conscious diet to more vibrant health came to light thru a slew of new book releases, one of the more noteworthy being Dr. T. Colin Campbell's *The China Study*.

Dr. Campbell was a rigorously trained nutritional scientist who'd dedicated his entire professional life to conducting peer-reviewed, taxpayer-funded studies on nutrition throughout the world. Raised on a dairy farm, Campbell used to put down plant-based diets along with everyone else; he'd bought the assumption we needed meat and dairy for good health and complete, balanced nutrition. Then, over decades of studies, he made increasingly startling discoveries: *irrefutable study results linked the consumption of animal-based diets to the onset of practically every degenerative disease under the sun.*

A staggering 60 to 70 percent of all heart disease, arthritis, adult diabetes, stroke, most every kind of cancer—*diseases people had always assumed were the unavoidable, natural products of ageing*—were positively linked to diets heavy in animal product consumption. In stark contrast, he found only about five percent of degenerative diseases linked to a genetic predisposition—which for a while everyone wanted to attribute every degenerative disease to: *"It doesn't matter what I eat; heart disease runs in the family. Pass the porkchops, please."*

Campbell came to an inescapable conclusion: Eating animals shortened lives—*and so did consuming animal byproducts.* His studies only supported the results of previous epidemiological studies all over the world: cultures with the least animal foods and refined carbohydrates in their diets lived the healthiest, longest lives, all but free of the diseases plaguing Western affluent cultures, like cancer, stoke and heart disease. Sobered by the mountains of evidence, he switched his family to whole food, plant-based diets and then wrote a book to share his lifetime discoveries.

Among his many startling revelations: Diseases traditional doctors gave up on as irreversible and for which they started up expensive drug procedures—maybe even life-threatening surgery—*were* reversible in all but the most advanced cases by switching to whole food, non-animal diets.

His work, and a raft of others by similarly enlightened colleagues, exposed the food industry, government, and bought-and-
paid-for medical colleagues over their arrogant dismissals and
blatant deceptions in the face of overwhelming evidence to the
contrary. Tho, like Lady Macbeth's blood spot, the damning evidence was clear as day, compromised colleagues, marching to the
hypnotic dirges of Meat King and His Dairy Maids—along with
Drug Lord and The Prescriptions—tried contradicting such studies with their own junk science (with a proviso to bury results if
they didn't support their contentions). They displayed a smoke-
and-mirrors caginess the likes of which the wiliest street-corner
shell-game hustler could only envy.

Pitifully, they were not unlike the tobacco industry's spokespeo-
ple who'd lied thru their teeth before a Congressional hearing and
national TV a decade earlier, denying knowing cigarettes were
addictive. That is, until multi-billion-dollar lawsuits made them
change their tune from "Smoke Gets in Your Eyes" to "Brother,
Can you Spare a Dime." Their ill-gotten gains then effectually
paid for bold new anti-smoking campaigns. On one local billboard, for instance, a man starting to light up asks a woman,
"Mind if I smoke?" She counters sweetly with, "Mind if I die?"
(Secondhand smoke killed phenomenal numbers of people every
year.)

Meanwhile, meat eaters, either out of denial, ignorance, or
being too set in their ways to want to change, went along with the
animal-food industries' threadbare assurances. Eaters displayed
the self-destructive irrationality of heroin junkies, refusing to
admit they even had a problem. One bumper sticker spotted in
New York: "I Like Animals. They're Delicious." As I said, some
reality-denying flesh eaters sooner faced devastating, life-savings-
depleting diseases to continue devouring their favorite decomposing animal tissue their bodies ultimately rejected than re-educate
their taste buds. *"Give up bacon and eggs for breakfast? No way.
Steak and lobster dinners? Over my dead body, buddy; pass the A-*

1 and tartar sauce and I'll forget you suggested that."

Not even devastating outbreaks of mad cow disease and bird flu—causing human deaths and untold millions of cows, chickens, turkeys, and geese to be slaughtered ahead of schedule and then destroyed for fear of being infected—inspired all that many, considering, to stick exclusively to safer foods, lower on the food chain. Believing their "high quality" protein diet superior, they continued dragging their state of health down to the Rack and Ruin Café for another Grade A, factory-kill Blue Plate Special.

Someone—I think it was a Korky Fitzwater—once compared animal products to enriched plutonium, with human bodies the reactor plants. Once activated internally, meat and dairy fuel provided large bursts of low-grade energy, the body processing what it could, even as it simultaneously activated a red-alert for their over-acidic, over-rich protein presence stressing the system's easy functioning. But whereas the spent radioactive fuel rods in actual reactors got hauled off, becoming someone else's problem, unassimilated animal fat and proteins *stayed* inside meat eaters and heavy dairy consumers. Their bodies now essentially doubled as radioactive waste dumps, glowing and fizzing and all but guaranteeing to bite them on the ass sooner or later in a body meltdown on a biological level no less spectacular than Chernobyl.

A corrupt system—some called it a *death culture*—forever set profits and power, even at the cost of destroying millions of lives, above serving the common good. *Or what's an anti-universe for?*

No surprise, then, that the medical establishment took over where institutionalized purveyors of cruel and deadly diet left off. Millions checked in to clinics with hosts of degenerative diseases—most linked to long-term diets of animal products and patients completely ignorant of the fact. Nor would they be informed, as diet was all but dismissed by doctors as a health factor.

At its worst, the medical system became like fast food restaurants—*"Can I get you a blood panel with that angioplasty?"*—rushing patients thru and calling for batteries of tests, offering ineffectual and sometimes dangerous drug procedures, keeping them coming back for more of the same (as long as you or your insurer were good for it). And if none of that worked there was the high-tech miracle of invasive surgery—which might buy time (and certainly bought doctors weeklong Paris vacations)—all along ignoring the obvious.

Some colleagues, seeing the light, asked, *"What about prescribing basic preventive health measures like whole food diet? I've heard many have had great success with it in reversing cancers." "If diet's so damn important, Jones, how come they didn't teach us that in medical school? Hell, besides—no money in that. Keep those sprout-munching heresies to yourself if you know what's good for you.*

It wasn't that there weren't dedicated doctors around, those who made positive stands against the blind spots in conventional medicine's disease-oriented mindset, who accented the importance of diet, exercise and positive thinking in preventive healthcare. Even as transformation swept all sectors of society, it affected medicine as well. Physicians such as Andrew Weil heralded the return to natural medicine and healing with bestselling books, integrating the best of conventional medicine with age-old disciplines of natural healing. But change came slowly. Too many physicians—along with nutritionists spouting "meat is one of the essential food groups, and be sure to have four or more servings of whole milk products each day"—had invested too much of their careers into the old system to realize, much less admit, conventional wisdom was sometimes a crock of do-do.

Besides, any doctors hooked on steak-and-eggs meals themselves couldn't very well tell patents such faire was bad for them without hearing a hollow ring to their words. Too many doctors, projecting their own animal-food addiction—which, again, only reflected the almost universally accepted diet—concluded others were just as hopelessly strung out on meat, dairy and eggs, and incapable of change, that it was unrealistic to even suggest giving them up (almost akin to recommending one stop wearing clothes so often). Instead, "cut down on red meat and just eat skinless chicken" was the proffered advice—like telling someone dying of emphysema to limit their daily smoking to half-a-pack a day.

Too many traditional doctors, either in ignorance or denial, ceased to appreciate the body's capacity to regenerate when working harmoniously with nature. They excelled during life-threatening emergencies, to be sure, when they were worth their weight in gold (saving my life a time or two). But for offering effective methods of preventive healthcare they often knew less than their patients. Rather than suggest something as simple as a judicious switch in diet, they recommended the latest expensive mad-scientist drugs from pharmaceutical money machines, saying "we've had some success with this one." (Translation: two in ten healed naturally, probably despite the medicine handicapping the process; no change in five in ten; and three in ten discontinued the drug after serious side-effects developed.) Endlessly two-stepping to the tune of "That Mystifyin' Pill & Procedure Rag," they kept locked into thinking diet was simply unimportant in the grand scheme things.

And it was little wonder: *Medical schools had edited out from the original Hippocratic Oath reference to diet. They'd surgically removed the passage stating, "I will apply dietetic measures for the benefit of the sick according to my ability and judgment; I will keep them from harm and injustice."* I suppose that was too much to ask of mere medical mortals in a world running on hurt and greed.

The meat, dairy and egg industry, in cahoots, then, with physicians, surgeons, government nutritionists and institutional dieticians (not to mention the pharmaceutical industry, forever cashing in on the predictable results of toxic diets), kept up their deceptive show as long as possible.

But by 2012, their goose was cooked—to use an unfortunate but apropos phrase of the time. Momentous class-action lawsuits—again, not unlike the giant tobacco suits—determined that for decades the animal-products industry had known about damning study results conclusively linking their bloody goods and pur-loined reproductive fluids to heart disease and cancer for decades, and yet kept singing the praises of meat and dairy for health. Also, that they'd essentially bribed government and the medical profession to further their grand deception. Whistleblowers had come forward with so much smoking-gun evidence, prosecutors were giddy.

One among the many mind-boggling revelations that came to light: Cow's milk, forever touted as vital to build bones for its calcium content, actually *depleted* calcium from the bones that came to the rescue to help the body alkalinize the acidity caused by the cow fluid's over-rich protein. Leaked internal memos—key ones brought to light by Abe Jenkins, God love him (about to be canned after nineteen and a half years of faithful service and thereby cheated out of a pension)—proved the milk industry was well aware of this and had spent millions to obscure the facts with junk science and misleading ad campaigns. (Years earlier, a court had ordered the Milk Council to quit using one of their popular ads—"Milk. It Does a Body Good"—for being false advertising. Powerful medical evidence had indicated otherwise. But by then their brainwashing campaign had been so successful people continued equating downing bovine nursing fluids with robust health when in fact it was only perfect food for calves.)

Vegetarian Clubs sprouted up in schools across America, and children convinced their parents to quit eating animals. New laws were passed to ease some of the worst animal abuse in factory farms, after constituents pressured their legislators and consumers boycotted target businesses. Vegetarian and vegan cookbooks became best sellers. Former grazing fields were converted to croplands, and croplands once devoted to growing feed converted to grow food. More ethically-minded stock holders divested holdings in companies owning any slaughterhouses and factory farms. The upshot: many a business once making bloody fortunes abusing and killing animals bit the dust, financially loosing their heads not unlike the way unfortunate billions of innocent creatures had lost theirs.

Rejoicing vegans and animal-rights activists around the world—who'd worked tirelessly to hasten the day—knew significant numbers of people were finally waking up to conscious diet. (Read *Rescue of the Animal Kingdom: When Meat Packers Packed It In*, by Clarence Clemstrutter. Comet Press, 2012. Also, for a grand overview, see Dan Dobbler's. *The Rise & Demise of Flesh-Eating Cults on Planet Earth*. Plum Press, 2049.)

World peace now felt that much closer. After the court victory and a hundred-and-fifty-billion dollar, twenty-year settlement, all animal products left on the market—from grisly remains of cows, sheep, pigs, and chickens, neatly cut and shrink-wrapped, to purloined milk and eggs—now carried the warning label:

**The Surgeon General has Determined
the Consumption of Animal Products
is Dangerous to Your Health.**

New billboards sprouted up along freeways: "Plants: Living Food for Living People;" "Got ill? Quit Having a Cow;" and "Dare to keep Kids off Dairy." My personal favorite:

Beef – It's What's Clogging Your Arteries.

☀

The hippie-rainbow counterculture—harbinger of future ways of more natural living in more ways than one—had, of course, decades earlier adopted body freedom and plant-based diets. Among their number in later years were those holding fast to countercultural core values even while conforming to more prosaic appearances and careers. They didn't dwell on such things as nudism and vegetarianism per se. In fact, many thought it weird to make an "ism" out of anything, seeing those who did as symptomatic of society's near-sighted, reductionist thinking, which could never see the forest for the trees for short-sighted quests that isolated and quantified each part of a system rather than grasp its integrated whole. As mentioned, modern nudism had extracted clothesfree living from the larger natural-living value system with giddy nonchalance.

This led my own imagination to wonder *what if?* What if the nature-cure movement—as envisioned by the earlier movement's proto hippies and more far-thinking proponents—*had* transplanted intact and flourished in the United States?

Naturist gatherings then might never have been held in conventional structures, removed from the earth, with smoking in concrete courtyards, cocktails after steak dinners, and disco dancing in glitzy lounges. Instead: deep in the heart of pristine nature, a humbling, earth-grounding hike away from noisy mechanical chariots, with outdoor workshops on fasting, acupuncture, yoga, massage, meditation, vegan nutrition and herbal medicine complementing social nudity as ways to more organic living. Like rainbow gatherings at their best, without the drugs and freeloaders: nary a strong drink or meat-based meal to be found; the camaraderie of singing and live, homegrown music and tribal dancing around cheery campfires, and soaring spirits sailing into starry skies.

The ways and values of our world were corrupted, tho. The divisive, sticky-fingered tribe of Mammon dominated. It didn't surprise me the nature-cure movement—apart from its radical branch—had split almost right from the start into dozens of specialized focuses for the way relentless pressures from omniscient witch doctors of materialistic science kept hell-bent on stamping out the movement in its infancy as a plague of ignorant folk remedies and rank quakery. (Not that there *wasn't* some of that, too: every dicipline had its schemers.) Ardent practitioners and teachers of their respective natural cure methods—including body freedom and plant-based diet—had dug in and battened the hatches to protect their babies from the storm of resistance determined to shut them down—or at least contain the threat to their "health care" monopoly that broke the Hippocratic Oath to do no harm so often you'd think they were racking up frequent-flyer miles.

A look comparing the kinds of resorts allowing nudity dramatized how much freebody consciousness had become orphaned from the original far-seeing vision of natural living. As I said, some nudist resorts, while offering the freedom to be buck-naked around the clock amid more-or-less pleasant surroundings, could feel depressingly mainsream: chlorinated swimming pools; smokers suffered gladly ("park your butts here"); drinkers merrily catered to (*"Name your poison!"*); token efforts to provide non-meat faire (*"soy burger on rye, hold the mayo"*); locations close to droning highway traffic (*"for your travel convenience"*); places shot thru with unsettling vehicle movement (*"What, me walk?"*). While I had no doubt there existed nudist resorts whose owners held fast to advancing deeper naturist values and healing atmospheres, I didn't find any in my limited travels.

In contrast, some of the more spiritually aware and environmentally sensitive mineral springs—like Oregon's Breitenbuch—combined mindful nudity along with vegan meals, healing mineral waters and deep natural surroundings. Another, Orr Springs, tucked near California's redwoods, had one designated smoking

275

spot for the entire place and banned cars from the grounds; free of gagging second-hand smoke and engine-droning, the place was all the more serene, healing and body-friendly.

This isn't to say mineral springs *always* showed a higher consciousness and greater body acceptance. Oh, no. Case in point: northern Arizona's Broken Arrow Springs.

Broken Arrow was a rustic mineral spring resort I vacationed at one summer. I heard it was a spiritually healing sanctuary. Too late, I discovered the place had changed hands and the new owners were shamelessly trading on its venerable reputation by lowering the bar and attracting more mainstream dollars.

Not that the place didn't still offer dramatic natural surroundings, healing waters, a decent gas sauna, plus a dollop of permitted nudity; one could easily imagine the place being a healing retreat. But its restaurant, once offering the finest veggie faire around, now wooed the omnivorous palette full-tilt. Uninspired and overpriced veggie dishes—not even listed on the menu—were offered by request, as if only to appease anyone so picky as to reject the slaughterhouse specials. Adding insult to injury, management procured a beer-and-wine license; guests could now blot out the sorry reality of their sordid pristine surroundings with curative strong drink. And the resort appeared a magnet for those— guests and employees alike—forever bent on voiding poisonous fresh mountain air from their lungs with clouds of good, pure tobacco smoke.

The topper: Twice during my month-long stay—I'd booked ahead, it was non-refundable, and I was too cheap to write it off to experience—the calm was shattered by all-nite quasi-rave parties. Urban partiers, recent refugees from the big city to the neighboring small towns, booked these non-tranquil happenings, apparently wanting to share their lingering inner city angst with the tranquil countryside. Their bacchanalias left mountains of beer, wine and whisky empties in their wake—to be tossed, not recycled— and hung-over, strung-out patrons littering the bathhouse. Irate guests vowed never to return for the ceaseless techno-pop blasting the very place they came to for escape from such energies. During one such brain-numbing nite, I dreamed I was trapped in a canning factory run amok on acid.

Mineral spring or nudist resort (or health spa), each place had its ambiance and focus, attracting its circles of enthusiasts. In a complex and fragmented world, businesses catered to every lifestyle persuasion under the sun. Each found a viable market niche or didn't last. Even so, I couldn't help but find it discouraging so few places tried raising the bar of organic living higher.

Obviously, the original German naturists lived in a simpler, more leisurely paced world: fewer people; worlds more nature yet unspoiled to feel natural *in*; more non-processed and organic foods to feel better for eating, more common horse-sense yet intact to resist unhealthy trends. Living hadn't become so superlocked into super wound-up, high-tech ways.

Hell, like Nuela said, I loved to criticize. Everything was the way it was. At some point I realized it was counterproductive to get upset and bemoan the situation. I was like an early Bob Dylan acoustic folk music fan, yelling "traitor!" when he moved on to electric rock. Or a person thinking once the Haight got overtaken by hard drugs and prostitutes the dream of peace and love was over. Things changed; life went on. Besides, it appeared the counterculture had carried on the more profound, far-reaching ways of naturist lifestyle anyhow.

I saw I'd set myself up for sure disappointment by the way I over-identified with various movements, perhaps seeking in them magic cure-alls for my own sense of incompleteness, of wanting to belong, then feeling let down once realizing their limitations. Why was I looking outside to what others were doing instead of plotting my own course from within?

Maybe that was part of the reason being naked attracted me: it fostered a feeling of oneness, of bonding with nature, of belonging to *some*thing that wouldn't let me down.

EIGHTEEN

Sometimes I like to run naked in the moonlight and the wind,
on a little trail behind our house, when the honeysuckle blooms.
It's a feeling of freedom, so close to God and nature.
—**Dolly Parton**

NOT ALL CLOTHES designers treated the human body with casual disregard for comfort. A handful of the more innovative ones believed clothing should be as body-friendly as possible and came out with creative innovations.

My cousin, Zinny, for instance, went on to more or less re-invent the early bra that Great-Aunt Zoë had helped design, using a simple design of brushed organic hemp to gently support breasts rather than batten them down like a sailing ship's hatches at storm warning. Her black-and-white-striped pattern sold well. She called it—what else?—the Z-bra.

A novelty fashion line, Faux Clothes, started by reform-minded entrepreneurs, carved out a market niche catering to body freedom enthusiasts. Their apparel *looked* like regular clothing at casual glance, but were abbreviated in ways allowing wearers to feel less constricted, more naked. One popular hot-weather outfit: an oversized thin tank-top with short, open leggings attached that extended a few centimeters below the tank's bottom hem; each of the leggings Velcro-ed together loosely around the thighs: Wearers appeared to have shorts on, but in fact were practically bottom-free, thereby enjoying a semi-freebody state while in public with no one the wiser. (As a bonus, the whole outfit came off in seconds flat without a one-legged dance.)

Another faux-outfit: a thin cotton apron, imitating regular clothes, that you draped over your bare front and tucked loosely around the sides while tooling down the highway on long road trips. You *looked* dressed to other drivers, but actually were more naked than when wrapped in an after-shower towel.

✳

After winning much-ballyhooed court cases in several states in more recent years, a growing trickle of proactive women, holding strong feelings on gender equality and body freedom, began going mindfully topfree *beyond* water's edge. Brilliant attorneys had successfully argued against the existing legal inequality, which had often permitted men but not women to freely go about without top cover. They called on Fourteenth Amendment's assurances of equal protection under the law. Now, in a dozen states at least, women could legally be topfree anywhere men could, so long as the intent wasn't overtly sexual.

More women might have broken free of this dress restriction sooner but for inertia taking its toll. If one was kept caged long enuf, one stared awhile at the suddenly open door before walking thru it. Also, men—besides blue-collar workers, surfers and nudists—seldom took advantage of their long-held top-optional freedoms beyond the water except on hottest days. If they didn't, women tended not to either. Anyhow, the ogling attention bare breasts received could quickly neutralize any comforting sense of body liberation a woman otherwise felt.

Women's breasts had forever appeared more the property of others—nursing children, lovers, doctors, clothing industry, pornographers, moral vigilantes, the law, plastic surgeons—than their owners'. Suddenly millions of women were told by the law they *could* be topfree if they wanted. Most, before taking advantage of the new personal body freedom option, had to radically adjust self-perceptions, internalized notions of modesty and acceptable behavior, and gain support from others.

Topfreedom advocates pointed out that the more female breasts were seen in everyday life, the more people would desensitize to the sight—no longer reacting with shock, disdain or arousal—and *re*sensitize to dealing with each other as human beings. The bold encouraged the timid and over-modest and don't-rock-the-boaters to follow unsuit over time: They'd *appeared* acquiescent to the old social norm, but deep inside they'd wanted to liberate their bodies as much as everyone else. Take my niece's friend, Hazel, for instance. A shy librarian, she astounded her family and friends one day by joining other women at a public beach in Chicago and going topfree. She emailed my Zena, who she knew from college days. "I finally said phooey on that clammy Lycra smothering my ta-tas."

The more daring women took advantage of those states' new dress-equality laws in warm weather by driving topfree as well. Since the inside of a vehicle was more a private than public space—one's personal bubble while traveling—people were naturally inclined to want to get comfy. The fewer the clothes, the comfier, with or without air conditioning. During long trips it could make the difference between a pleasant journey and an endurance test.

As many male nudists knew, if you drove topfree it was often an easy stretch—with due vigilance and simple precautions—to drive bottomfree as well without attracting any more notice, especially with our high-speed, high-carriage, tinted-window travel on open highways. One simply stayed calmly alert, with a towel or clothing nearby to cover the lap whenever high-vantage trucks, buses and RVs were close—maybe sit on an undone sarong or keep shorts on down at the ankles for easy cover when needed.

Bare motorists on extended trips had to remember to cover again crossing certain state lines, tho; reports of naked drivers in nude-intolerant regions still inspired high-speed Keystone Kops chases down the highway.

I'd discovered years before, on my empty rural back roads, few things felt so liberating (sex and skinnydipping come to mind) as driving naked. I'd walk out my front door, hop in the car and drive along my back roads, slip out, take a tranquil nature stroll and gather sage along a sandy dry-creek bed, maybe skinnydip in a pond I knew , climb back in the car, and drive back home—all without a stitch. If I had to, I'd put the rush somewhere between being able to sleep as late as you want and quitting a dead-end job after winning the lottery.

❋

I remember the first time Nuela and I drove naked from home to the springs.

"*Purr*-fect weather," I said. We were out on my sundeck on a late Sunday morning in May. Spring had sprung. A huge lenticular hovered over Shasta like a mothership from the Pleiades, come to check on how we were coming along. We were bare as bunnies, sipping apricot-mango smoothies and listening to an old Kansas CD—"Dust in the Wind" wafted from the portable player, gently reminding us how ephemeral life was—while indulging in some reading. She was gobbling up an early Kingsolver novel, discovering Turtle, and I was reading *Grapes of Wrath* for the umpteenth time, re-savoring the "well no—them's two for a penny candies" truck diner scene.

"Is it ever," she agreed. Hey, want to head over to the springs? Should be a congenial crowd there today and I'd love to plunge in that nice cold creek."

I seldom needed coaxing. On nice days the place felt like a Garden of Eden compared to most environs, and there was no finer swimming hole around. "All right. But let's make it interesting: let's stay naked all the way over. Just drape a sarong over your front for passing traffic, like you did that trip last month. We'll park by the cold plunge, so we can get out and jump right in the creek. What do you say?"

"You and your naked challenges. You *really* love driving nude, don't you?"

"Sure I do. It's a rush not having to throw anything on in this weather just because we're leaving home. Think of it as connecting the dots between acceptable nude zones."

"Okay, I'm game."

At times I thought she indulged my whims more than was judicious.

We drove over by way of rural highways. Still in the mood for classic oldies, we immersed in John Denver tunes. We'd keep naked except for the fuchsia sarong she pulled over her front and me a towel over the lap for the few vehicles we encountered en route. We soaked in the sweet sun that poured thru the windows and Nuela started singing along with John, adlibbing shamelessly:

Sunshine on my nippies makes me happy
Sunshine on my loins can make me cry-yyyy
Sunshine on my yoni feels so *loovve-ly*...

"This is like a solarium on wheels," she enthused, after the solar anthem ended. "I love it. That sun almost feels orgasmic."

"Makes you wonder, don't it?"

"It do, indeed, darlin'; indeed it do."

She soon switched CDs and put in an old Doobie Brothers. Their funky a cappella singing in "Black Water" rocked our mobile greenhouse, transporting us to the Mississippi River under a shining Dixie moon.

"But you must have done this now and then, growing up as a nudist, didn't you?" I asked.

"Not since I was a toddler. After that, we'd only be naked in cars on the grounds. Most Floridians wouldn't have taken kindly to nudists taking their lifestyle on the road, oh, no indeed, indeedy not."

"No? I somehow had the impression Florida was pretty much one big nudist colony."

"Hah! You poor innocent. Oh, sure, there're more nude sanctuaries there than in most states, I suppose, but when I left there were places where people *lived* to see you hauled off to jail if you so much as bared a booby."

"I see I was sadly misinformed."

Later she put on Three Dog Night and soon we were fairly dancing in our seats, bobbing in unison as the gospel piano in "Let me Serenade You" rocked us like newborns.

An hour and a listen to the best of The Band later, we pulled up at the springs. A replay of the Doobies and their "Listen to the Music" was bounding out the windows like a joyful force. I cut the engine and stereo, and in their stead the constant white noise roar of Dragonfly Creek flooded the Metro. A dozen people or so were nude sunbathing over on the deck; more skinnydipping in the creek or sunning on nearby rocks. Some looked up, absently checking the latest vehicular intrusion to their naked reverie. I felt badly for that, but it was the way it was there; with parking right next to the bathhouse; I'd have gladly parked further away, like I normally did, and walked over, but for our plan.

Our friend Quincy spotted us and walked over to greet us. Even tho he himself was naked, his eyes popped out when we climbed out the same. "You guys are hard-core, you know that?"

"Zet talked me into it," Nuela admitted. "We drove naked all the way from home. Isn't that a trip?"

"Ah, the advantages of country living," Quincy said, shaking his head in wonder. "City cops would've pulled me over before I got half-way out of town if I'd tried that one. Here, want some oranges? They're from a friend's Chico orchard. No detectable bad vibes."

"Hold that offer; we really want to cool off."

We dove in, and the bracing cold water refreshed us instantly as it enveloped our bodies. Afterwards, we sat on a nearby granite boulder offering snug butt divots, as if designed by nature millions of summers before expressly for homo sapiens' future posterior comfort. The rock's stored sunshine toasted our buns as we slurped Quincy's oranges, juice running down our faces.

I felt flush with triumph for our having made it from one naked zone to another without surrendering to custom and covering up in between. I wanted to believe we'd just stretched the planet's collective body-freedom consciousness a few nanometers, at least.

❋

Our springs, like any place allowing a degree of nakedness, served to show how, trapped inside everyone, there was a nudist wanting to come out. Over the years, it astonished me how many people passing thru there tickled to have stumbled on a place that, besides offering healing waters, allowed them to be naked beyond their bath. Newcomers of all ages tried it and liked it.

I was convinced that in our heart of hearts we were all natural-born nudists. If the world had been a gentler place then—filled with the love and mutual acceptance and reverence for Mother Earth we've since come to know—legions of at-home nudists, not to mention the myriad of practicing nudists, would have been walking about with few or no clothes in nice weather and thinking nothing of it except how natural it felt.

I believed most everybody had a sweet memory, conscious or buried, of being a naked carefree toddler; maybe with family doting on them and thinking how precious it was one could be so innocently unashamed of their bodies. And most everyone also had a linked memory of the time when being naked was suddenly no longer cute, when clothes were thrown on them like bridles over mustangs, breaking their wild and free nature in order to muster into "civilized" society.

But the body remembered. Pure happiness is never forgotten; it remains forever etched in the soul. People were essentially walking around with traumatized cell memories of having been cast from Eden.

On some deep level, we remembered the joy we felt; the elusive innocent feeling vibrated inside us yet, on standby, awaiting reactivation. To rekindle that blissful feeling, millions of people indulged in getting naked privately—sunbathing, skinnydipping, sleeping nude—knowing in their gut they'd been sold a bill of goods, but not knowing what to do about it beyond getting in private naked time and seeking out the few free beaches and nudist resorts.

Now, anymore, individuals needed only nice weather, permission and a safe natural setting to emerge from their cloth cocoons. If the experience also brought up unpleasant repressed feelings to deal with too—as it did me—that was only part of the needed growing lesson.

❀

Whenever weather allowed, more people of both genders favored wearing sarongs, those soft, light wrap-around fringed cloths done in bursts of colors and patterns. Traditionally only women had worn them in Western culture. Now, various men—not gay or cross-dressers—were rebelling against the prescribed two-legged cover-ups called pants. They got free of the apparel that, short of sitting down, required an awkward, stooped over, one-legged dance to don and doff—and often crowded sensitive genitals.

Long the exclusive domain of women, such body cover was thought ludicrous on Western man. This, even tho similar loose wraps were universal in ancient Rome and Greece. Scotsmen, with their skirt-like kilts, were among the recent exceptions. (Historic note of interest: a survey taken about 2002 at last revealed the naked truth on what was worn underneath: two out of three kilt-wearers wore nothing underneath. *Hoot, mon!*)

Someone—a Dudley Morgenstein, I think—came up with a daffy tongue-twister reflecting the new sensitized awareness: *"Generally, genteel gentiles are, towards their genitals, genuinely gentle."*

I loved the sensual freedom sarongs provided. But I dealt with the reactions of less freethinking denizens in my home area. "Is that all for you, *ma'am?*" the redneck checker woman asked me pointedly in my local hardware store. It was the first time I'd experimented wearing a sarong bottom away from the springs. The cloth was a subdued solid color, no blinding fuchsia or lavender floral, but no matter; one didn't stray from gender dress-conformity with impunity, at least not in our not-always open minded region.

"No sir, that's all," I replied in kind.

The checker's dig reflected prevailing thinking. Women, as the more feeling and sensitive being, breathed and dreamed raiment and could dress as colorfully and freely as they pleased. Men, on the other hand—insensitive and unimaginative brutes that they were—stayed shackled to the constrictive gender badges called trousers, symbols of their male dominance, and were deemed unmanly if they dared deviate from the bifurcated mandate. The kicker: women could wear pants if they wanted to and not feel it lessened *their* gender identity, at least so long as the pants were tight enuf to accent their curves. But men in skirts or tunics? Not likely. A Joe Friday world had been telling us, "Just the slacks, man." (A pun for my fellow dinosaurs.)

Even so, some males were now discovering the extravagant comfort of allowing their nether regions to breathe freely. Testes, needing a cooler temperature to be happy campers, are situated outside; jamming them up with tight, binding cloth defeated body engineering and rendered the wearer...well, *testier*. Maybe such a constrictive habit was a carryover from former times when men were always on battle-alert and needed their "family jewels" protected. Anyhow, while many still seemed locked into that mindset, doing daily battle with a hostile world of their own making, others were at last breaking free of it.

I had three different sarongs. Nuela had seven, four of them presents from me; I loved surprising her with a new splash of color to wear. I thought she looked great in every one of them, but she said she felt too much like a zebra in the black-and-white-striped I got her. She used it instead for a wall hanging in the Ch'ien sector of her cabin after she went on a Feng Shui kick. She'd also read in a correspondence chart that black and white were the colors of Spirit. "If that's true," she mused, "maybe that's part of the reason books feel so magical—and why men look so divine in tuxes."

❋

While absurdity abounded in our lives, some things merited serious attention.

Humanity was at a crossroads in those last years of the old world. Accelerating spiritual forces—partly the positive synergy of humanity's expanding spiritual awareness—were transforming our lives. Mankind was deciding whether to become irrelevant as a species or make a grand leap forward: Change or die. Those in influential positions, who chose to stay locked in lower consciousness, with its self-perpetuating greed and insidious control games, stirred up strife to no end. They sent our young off to deadly wars on flimsy pretexts; perpetuated violent diets and the massacre of the animal kingdom; separated couples and families over rigid conformist ideas and oppressive laws; muzzled freedom of speech; despoiled the forests and earth and poisoned our air and water for short-term profit, not giving a damn about the planet that sustained them; they foisted an often-ineffectual medical system that focused on symptoms, not causes...

All right; I've probably dwelled on most of these things enuf already. But maybe I didn't stress the good works of their uncorrupted counterparts, those in high positions who embraced enlightened thinking and helped leverage amazing changes in society. They championed accountable governments and transparent businesses; more pleasant, family-friendly work environments; green architecture, building and remodeling; organic foods and sustainable agriculture; natural healing and preventive health; vital approaches to education; creation of new and relevant jobs at real living wages; and the advent of appropriate technologies and city planning to foster Earth-friendlier living.

Influential or not in the worldly sense, those attuned to the rising spiritual frequency and its interconnected awareness felt a growing sense of oneness. We felt, deep in our bones, the old world had run its sorry-ass course and a quantum leap in human consciousness was, like Henry Mancini's Huckleberry friend of song, "waitin' 'round the bend."

True, the times were chaotic and dizzy, with disaster and heartbreak unfolding everywhere. Man's stepped-up inhumanity—"the corrupt order's having its last fandango," as one friend put it—and the intensifying earth changes wrought havoc of unimaginable levels. But the farsighted saw it as Planet Earth going thru labor pains for the new birth to come.

One of several turning points in raising global consciousness happened the day after Christmas 2005, when a large earthquake triggered a devastating tsunami in the Indian Ocean and hundreds of thousands perished in the ensuing floods. In the past, whenever major disaster struck in faraway countries, too often people only tsk-tsked: it didn't seem real or cause for concern. With that tsunami, tho, it was different, maybe in part because thousands of people from around the planet were spending the holidays in the region when it struck; it was a global disaster. A friend of a friend of mine barely escaped with her life; she intuitively ran for it when she saw the bay tide suddenly being sucked away from shore.

The same thing happened in 2006, when a furious hurricane devastated New Orleans in our own country, displacing more people in a day than the Dust Bowl had in a decade. People everywhere—except perhaps our own government—responded with help, supplies, and dollars.

Disasters brought out the best (and worst) in people. We witnessed a stepped-up global awareness. As we attuned to each other's diverse cultures—each with different ways of living and thinking and being—we became aware of our given culture's limitations and borrowed from the others to fill in the gap: dress, diet, customs, art, music...

Fitfully, as we grew into rudimentary global consciousness, we learned to separate the wheat from the chaff—in everything. This reality-filtering included worldviews people had always accepted as The-Way-Things-Are absolutes: life will always be a struggle; countries can only settle their differences thru bloodshed; the rich will get rich and the poor get poorer; everyone needs to eat animals to be healthy and strong; renewable energy will never be practical; and you must always wear clothes in public.

The more we surrendered our egos and let healing forces transform us, the more we geared thru astounding life progressions. We became more aware of illusionary hindrances, wherever they lurked, and cleared the way for becoming our natural selves— even amid the devastation unleashed on the globe. As a popular music group of the time, R.E.M., merrily put it, *"...it's the end of the world as we know it...and I feel fine!"*

The age-old, frayed habit of mandatory dress was definitely unraveling. All the more so, the further we moved beyond the body-unfriendly industrial era and guilt-based morality. With a renewed Earth connection and more positive mindsets, we gravitated towards new ways of being, fostered finer attunements to our bodies, our environments, and each other.

All in all, the idea of a critical-mass acceptance of public nudity no longer seemed *quite* so impossible. Along with more people wanting world peace—an end to war, hunger, disease, racism, sexism, social injustice, greed, abuse of Mother Earth and her animal kingdom—more people were okay with being peaceably naked in public, thank you very much.

Some people felt some a flash point was possibly at hand, one that might finally dislodge the hidebound notions by mainstream consciousness towards the human body.

If one could happen anywhere, some felt it might happen in that fabled West coast bastion of progressive attitudes and free lifestyles, San Francisco.

The City had already shone brightly twice in history as a beacon the world over—first in the Gold Rush, then Haight-Ashbury; good things often come in threes.

It would come as no surprise if that fabulous, foggy town, sitting on the edge of the world, made even bolder leaps in radical body acceptance than it already had. We know from basic metaphysical law the first collective energies of inhabitants on new land forever stamp that land with its vibration, its resonance to affect each succeeding generation. The first inhabitants of the City and surrounding Bay Area were local Indian tribes whose members often loved nothing better on nice days than to roll in the mud and run around naked.

If that weren't enough: Francis of Assisi, the City's patron saint—upon rejecting all his wealthy father's worldly goods, including the clothes on his back—walked off thru town stark naked in righteous dignity.

It appeared San Francisco had potential for becoming the scene of lots of natives running around righteously naked.

NINETEEN

Not all the Greek runners in the original Olympics
were totally naked. Some wore shoes.
—Mark Twain

PARTICIPANTS IN THE Bay to Breakers
foot race had galloped across San Francisco every spring since
1912. Begun as a way to help lift peoples' spirits after the devastation of the 1906 earthquake and fire, it was also promoted to
draw attention to the town's upcoming 1915 Pan-Pacific Expo; the
race would show the world that its beloved city, with unsinkable
spirit, had risen from the ashes.

The race's predecessor, an annual New Year's event begun a
decade or so earlier, had gone the length of Golden Gate Park. The
new race course spanned the entire town, twelve kilometers, from
the bay, near the Ferry Building, to the breaking waves of the open
Pacific—hence the name. For sheer number of participants, it
grew to be the largest footrace in the world.

As I said, when I first ran it in the mid-sixties, it was a straight-
forward race: everyone ran, or tried to. But times changed and the
event increasingly became a leisurely stroll and city-wide block

party, complete with costumes, mobile refreshment stands and live bands along the way—a madcap holiday celebrating spring, a day when the norm was impishly suspended.

To help suspend it even more, in the late seventies a registered nurse named Lesli Josephson became the first person to run the course nude; she ran it naked two more years.

It was thought no one else had the audacity to run it again *au naturel* until 1986, when one Ed Van Sicklin gave it a try. Seven years later, Sicklin formed a small nude-running contingent, organized as demonstrators, and gained strength in numbers—and an angle. When police randomly busted six of the group of seventeen at the finish line, five of the six pleaded not guilty and hired an attorney—named, appropriately enuf, Stripp—who got their charges dismissed. He had successfully argued it was their constitutionally-protected right to demonstrate in the nude, within limitations. Besides, there was a public outcry—much of the town got a kick out of the naked runners or at least didn't mind—and the frisky city's liberal sensibilities prevailed.

From then on, nude participants were suffered by race sponsors and the law as one of the more exotic participant flavors championed by spectators. Then-race sponsor *San Francisco Examiner* reflected the bemused tolerance in reporting one year that "…it was the naked people who prevailed: Naked nymphs, hula nudes, wizened nudes, nudes in every shade the sun could produce."

Dire warnings released each year, stating naked running would not be tolerated (said maybe to protect the image of corporate sponsors) no doubt scared off many would-be nude participants. Meanwhile, bright-capped demonstrators kept banding together—demonstrating, among other things, how to enjoy being naked in public one day a year. They set guidelines for minimizing friction by staying on the route, not loitering, and keeping their act clean.

With de facto tolerance and popular support, the number of nude participants climbed each year. At century's end, by which time body freedom enthusiasts were joining in from far and wide, some 150 or so people opted to run or stroll naked.

The 2006 run was special, as it came on the wings of commemorating the one-hundredth anniversary of the 1906 quake and fire. From my country home, a world away, I read in the *San Francisco Chronicle* how, despite a cold, clammy start, over 60,000 did the course, and bystanders thronged the route as always, and a scattering of die-hards ran stylishly in nothing.

But it was the harbinger 2008 run, with great weather, in which the number of naked participants passed 300 for the first time. According to Joshua Birdfeather, reporting in *Nude Times* in 2012, "The [2008] event was infused with a remarkable spirit of unabashed naked camaraderie. I believe that race laid the groundwork energetically for what was to come three years later."

✹

As luck would have it—or in total synchronicity, some would say—days before the 2011 race a loose-knit coalition of 900 nudists, naturists, and other sundry freebody proponents from across the country and around the world, came to town to hold a grand symposium on body freedom.

Members brought with them a generous dollop of body-positive energy. Some among them had already helped stretch public-nudity acceptance in their own home regions, thru public naked bike rides, boat rides, nature hikes, and light-hearted naked demonstrations and protests.

To cap their convention, before joining in the run, as most planned to, attendees had won an okay to hold an informal clothesfree picnic and skinnydip at one of the City's clothing-optional spots on the east end of Baker's Beach, at the Presidio's northern coastline.

A ragtag band of Concerned Citizens (insufferable busy bodies), many arrayed in sensible yet stylish Foreverwear—the latest synthetic, derived from recycled low-grade nuclear waste—tried to stop it. It was one thing to allow a thin scattering of naked people to sun their buns at the beach, but 900 at once... The mayor, known to visit a free beach or two in her day, defended it: "So they're naked. So what? Bet most of you were born that way. (Some of you, I've got my doubts.)"

The freebody advocacy group had created a definite stir, I learned on reading the *Examiner*. Droves of vehicles sported bumper stickers and decals that read: **Nudists Have Nothing to Hide**, **Lose your Clothes and Lose your Woes**, **Legalize Your Body**, **Feel Renewed in the Nude**. More politically-minded San Franciscans—many lamenting the passing of the bumper sticker craze—loved it. Especially the one reading:

I'd Rather Go Naked...than not.

The naturist gathering proceeded in the convention center. They covered diverse topics, like changing attitudes and legal issues, and brainstormed stratagems for hastening more enlightened views towards nudity. The keynote speech was "Legalized Nudity in Our Lifetime?"

After, the group had their by-then much-publicized nude picnic at the beach, where they re-anchored their energies thru the elements. There was plenty of volleyball, Frisbee tossing, body painting and skinnydipping. While the Florida contingent couldn't believe how cold the water was, the delegation from Siberia couldn't stop laughing at them.

The *Chronicle* gave the event straight-forward coverage—no smirks or mindless jokes—and included a distant shot of the beach crowd, subtly capturing their pronounced lack of clothes and the apparent innocence of it all. The article stressed the group's obvious comfort and non-judgmental acceptance of one another's uncovered bodies, no matter what shape.

A talk-show host on KGO talk-radio interviewed a spokesperson for the convention gathering, Jill Goodpasture. After articulating the many healthy and positive benefits of being naked more, Jill went on to say, "We sense that society is maybe, just *maybe*, becoming enlightened enough to flirt with the idea of accepting its own physical reality. I know; it's a radical concept: a species learning to view itself and not loose it; imagine. But at times I think we might almost be there."

Word of the gathering and interview reached syndicated radio talk-show host Art Bell, renowned for his Libertarian viewpoints. He piggybacked an hour-long Saturday nite phone interview with Goodpasture between David Icke and the time-travelers' open-line hour. His weekend shows regularly reached five to ten million listeners thru hundreds of subscribing stations across the nation, and more worldwide on the net.

"Think about it," Goodpasture said towards the hour's end. "We interact with the world thru our senses. We don't put cotton in our ears and keep ourselves from hearing pleasant melodies. We don't obscure our vision and impair our ability to experience the delightful nuances of color and light. We'd think it odd to go around handicapping our sense of taste or smell, leaving ourselves all but unable to enjoy the scent of a rose or the savor of a gourmet soup. Yet we regularly mute our largest sense receptor, the skin, with coverings often unnecessary, but for false modesty and outdated morality. It's like going about half deaf or half blind. We essentially all but shut down a critical amount of our capacity for physically interacting with life."

"When you put it like that, it sounds *very* strange indeed," Art said. He appeared in favor of the naturist cause, in a tongue-in-cheek sort of way: he'd intro-ed the set with Moby Grape's "Naked if I Want To," ferreted from his inexhaustible music library.

"I think it's a valid notion: the freedom to be naked—say, when you want to take an evening stroll and *really* enjoy the cooler temperature. Of course, here in the Philippines people would probably wouldn't go for it, but you never know." As bumper music grew, leading to the top of the hour break, he gave his parting shot: "Ha-ha-ha-ha, yes-ss, I think I kind of *like* the idea," adding a final zinger in his signature rapid, running-out-of-air voice, "*but don't tell anybody I said so!*"

Such positive and frank discussions took the public's imagination by storm. A surge of rethinking on the subject of public nudity flooded public consciousness. Along with the predictably raunchy or sensational jokes on local talk radio ("*All-naked radio, all the time...*") and the livid rage of those deeming public nudity an abomination, many were attracted to the idea. They questioned its fading taboo status. Why *couldn't* people be naked more often? Why indeed limit it to a few prescribed areas—public lands and for-fee private ones—often inconveniently distant?

In the Bay Area especially, the beach happening served to take public nudity out of the box long enuf that it didn't go back in easily in the minds of many: Variously, depending on viewpoint, the genie was out of the lamp or Pandora's Box opened.

"I followed the media coverage and something clicked in my mind," Cornelius Bloomsbury, a Daily City flower wholesaler, wrote later in a magazine article.

I'd been nude sunbathing and skinnydipping at Baker [Beach] for years. I'd often wondered if relegating nudity to a few places wasn't perhaps becoming something of a quaint social restraint. Skin cream ads had assured us 'skin is in.' Was it, *really*? I decided I'd find out at the race and get naked on the streets along with my friends. We brought basketfuls of rose petals to strew about the start area and distribute to other baring participants to fling along the way, just for the fun of it: Flower Power revisited.

298

Almost all of the 700 of the 900 symposium members who opted to join in the run/stroll decided to adopt as their costume—no surprise here—the Emperor's New Clothes. A few would rebel against what they saw as a predictable naked conformity and go contrary; they'd participate as mock clothists: painting on "clothes," wearing skin-tone, body-conforming outfits; or dressing in ways that didn't actually conceal the body, like fishnet body suits or transparent coverings.

A more diverse group one could scarcely have imagined—all ages, races, backgrounds, politics and lifestyles. Whether doctors, truck drivers, realtors, actors, massage therapists or flea-circus trainers, they shared a common held belief in body freedom. But while everyone hoped to increase positive body awareness and gain freebody rights, how much and how fast—if at all—to push the envelope of public acceptance without risking negative repercussions had been the subject of endless debate.

Beyond this group, an unrelated, proactive group of a hundred or so freebody activists gathered for the race. Most considered themselves neither nudists nor naturists, but nonetheless believed, like Brit rambler Steve Gough, in the right to be naked if one so chose. They used street theatre, naked protest or other means to make their point. They, too, sensed the time was ripe to give the envelope a decisive nudge, and, to that end, hatched a plan they shared with the more proactive symposium members.

Thus an alliance of divergent energies coalesced in common cause.

※

I was driving down to the City from my mountain home to visit my five old high school friends, with whom I intended to do the race again, forty-five years after my first run. But this time I'd enjoy the surreal rush of leisurely strolling across my old hometown without a stitch on.

Nuela begged off. She preferred working in her vegetable garden—the tomatoes and sweet peas needed attention—and plugging away at her writing rather than deal with the city pressure cooker. Being relatively bodyfree her whole life, she didn't feel the same pull to participate in a "big, crowded city streak," as she put it. I might not have either—I could have a tough enuf time dealing with even towns of 5,000 by then—except I wanted to vanquish my chained-to-clothes memories of the old city. I figured strolling nude across the City free as a fox might do the trick.

"I'll be right beside you in spirit, you know that," she said. "You'll have all your old buddies there; you probably won't even miss me."

I assured her I would.

On the way down I made a special detour.

I wanted a good warm-up dose of being publicly naked. If any place on the West Coast had the jump on being a brave nude world, besides nudist resorts, it was Harbin Hot Springs. There were other nice rural mineral spring resorts en route—Big Bend, Wilbur, Orr—each with unique ambience, healing waters and relaxed atmosphere. But for a mellow, *clothes-what-are-those?* freebody experience, Harbin was *it*. While the entire grounds were not clothing-optional like nudist resorts, the place was more in sync with original German naturist ideas for being down to earth and focused on conscious diet, meditation, yoga, organic gardening, and healing workshops; many older hippie-types and younger neo-hippies helped run the place.

Tucked in gentle wooded hills in Northern California, Harbin had been around in some guise for over a century. Altho a high-volume, 1,700 acre, clothing-optional resort with a focus on holistic living, Harbin often attracted your more sybaritic Bay Area energies.

I was fond of the place. It was where, years earlier, I'd come out of the nudist closet beyond the still-sunbathing, shy-skinnydipping—the same as untold thousands, no doubt. The first time I walked across the courtyard bathing complex naked, part of me felt like an unpaid extra in a pseudo-documentary nudie flick: *They Dared to Bare.*

Harbin's sometimes over-the-top sensual indulgence—a one-time poolside sign, "No Sex in Pool," had said it all—was maybe only par for the course, given the state of American society, at least for California, dubbed "the Future State." For too long we'd hidden behind compulsory clothes that cut us off from ourselves and each other. Possessing amazingly sensitive and receptive instruments, called bodies, we were at long last able to re-sensitize them in such places and feast on the elements. In the process of intentionally coming together without clothes, we enjoyed a good mineral soak and sunbath and shared the simple pleasure of being nude. We accepted and appreciated the way we looked beneath the usually mandated costumes. Essentially, we were learning how to behave normally without clothes.

Getting any voyeuristic or exhibitionistic ya-yas out of one's system was sometimes part of the lesson. You saw enuf naked people and the forbidden-fruit, rapt fascination of objectifying and eroticizing each other's bodies subsided—hopefully. There was often an invisible line between feeling sensuous and feeling sexual, as people once tended only to indulge the senses so richly as a prelude to lovemaking or bandit sex.

It was still easy to cross the line; I still wondered about myself sometimes. I loved Nuela dearly and was always faithful, but if a stunning woman walked along the poolside, moving like a Latin rhythm section and glowing like a goddess, I felt powerless to resist gazing on her beauty. Like a candid cameraman, I'd want to capture every last second of the sight for posterity.

The place hummed with hundreds of visiting members and residents commingled, enjoying the weather, relaxing around the mineral pools, sauna and creek-side camp sites. The 160 or so workers living on the grounds lent the place a sense of community; they strove to tweak the already fine-tuned ambience to greater heights thru new structures, imaginative landscaping and artful signs. I caught dinnertime at the spacious grounds restaurant. Formerly all-vegetarian, it now accommodated omnivores too, but still served imaginative and hearty vegan dishes. I had a rich tomato soup and wild rice with tofu and stir-fried veggies.

That evening I enjoyed soaking silently in the volcanically-heated, outdoor Whisper Pool with dozens of others. I made the *de rigueur* silent gliding entrance down the half-submersed, railed stairway, the sound of the hillside rivulet magically trickling nearby, the moon and stars shining thru the overhanging fig tree's giant leaves.

By week's end, being clothesfree felt so natural I balked at putting them on again in the coed dressing room on departure—the same as untold thousands, no doubt.

I struck up a conversation with one woman as we reluctantly dressed for the world at large. She said, "Once, my girlfriends and I were miles down the road before we remembered we'd forgotten to put our tops on."

Cynics of the time would think, "oh, sure, like I believe *that*," but I could see it happening: Once you get used to not wearing clothes long enuf, it feels artificial putting them back on—part of you *wants* to forget to. Her comment later reminded me how the Amish religious sect referred to venturing beyond their radically different environment as going among "the English," stressing the need for vigilance while around people ignorant or disrespectful of their ways. The more we got used to being naked, the more the textile world felt "English" to us.

302

While at Harbin, I met several others who were also planning to bare for the footrace. We quietly shared our enthusiasms for the event ahead while soaking in the Whisper Pool. "I can't wait," said one man. "My girlfriend and I have been daring ourselves to do it for years."

I gleaned a subtle but definite prescience the run was destined to be important somehow. The times were pregnant; we were in the midst of such mind-boggling, epochal social change, we felt anything could happen on any given day. While our event outcome could have been a headline **HUNDREDS OF NUDE STROLLERS ARRESTED** for all we knew, we somehow envisioned a more positive outcome.

☀

Down in San Francisco, I landed at my friends' out in the Richmond district, on upper Sacramento Street. "Hey, you made it!" Sam greeted me in his arched doorway. He and Gail, high school sweethearts, both the exact same height, had gone on to live together common-law and were ensconced in a spacious, well-kept flat with tall ceilings and curved bay windows. They ran a successful home-based mail-order essential-oil business, and the place always emanated an intriguing bouquet of scents. When I arrived, hauntingly erotic ylang ylang was the current topmost accent, with brilliant tones of lemongrass, lavender and royal rose in supporting roles. We were soon joined by Richard, Jennie and Kate, arriving from the far-flung reaches of the Bay Area. "I had to park *two* blocks away this time," Richard groused good-naturedly.

"Good; you need the exercise," Kate ribbed.

Together we'd formed a six-pack back in the day at Lowell High. We'd sporadically kept in touch over the years. Recently we'd tried for annual get-togethers when we could, and last year opted for a clothing-optional picnic at Baker Beach and included our mates. It was the first time we'd seen the other naked beyond same-sex showers, which was strange, considering how close we felt to each other. It was awkward at first, like having to get to know each other all over again, but then we were past it and got comfy hanging in our birthday suits on the beach. We built sand castles, played Frisbee, and vigilantly kept sand from our sand-wiches—which is not easy.

I was something of a novelty to my friends, having grown up with them there and then gone on to become a reclusive nature boy. They'd elected to stay based in the Bay Area, and kept them-selves more or less citified, altho they got away to nature whenev-er schedules allowed. They envied my tranquil lifestyle ("but what do you *do* there?"); I admired their wired energy and the region's rich cultural ferment ("but you couldn't *pay* me to live here now—wait; yes you could, but it'd have to be a *lot*, and for not very long either, unless it was *really* a lot").

We were perched naked on cedar benches inside the cozy sauna Sam and Gail built in a back room, enjoying the radiant heat and parade of scents. Sam, ever the aroma-therapist, had rigged up a system whereby you selected the desired oil or blend of oils from a wall panel and pushed the corresponding button. A fine spray of essential oil wafted into the room—dispersed by a quiet fan—however frequently you set the timer for. We were currently enjoy-ing his and Gail's favorite, a eucalyptus-lemongrass blend.

"Oh, that's good stuff," Sam said. "We never get tired of it. Hey, sorry we couldn't join you at Harbin, Zet, but we had to bust a gut getting out a big order for a new body-shop chain opening in Kentucky, believe it or not."

"That's all right, guy; duty calls. We'll make it another time." With everyone but me busy in ambitious careers—in part to cover the stratospheric cost of living in the Bay Area—it seemed unlikely. It was a miner miracle whenever we did get together. "The main thing is we're here now."

"Don't you love Harbin's new sauna, tho?" Gail asked

"Oh, yeah"

"Isn't it nice?" Sam agreed. "That old one was a caution, let me tell you. I could never lie down on the sloping benches without my innards protesting something terrible. We've got such a rep for being a purely hot-tub culture here in California—and it's justified, if you ask me. We mispronounce the word as *saw*-na rather than *sow*-na, like most of the world. People probably think we think a sauna's some Japanese hand tool, or maybe part of a doo-wop lyric: 'Sa-sa-sa-sauna-sauna-de-ba-ba-ba-sauna-suana-ba...'"

Inspired by Sam's impromptu singing, we tried stretching his nonsense lyric into a song, but efforts quickly broke down.

Talk turned to the City. We were all proud natives and shared inexhaustible childhood memories: roaming ghostly Sutro Baths; racing down the long slide at Playland-at-the-Beach's funhouse on gunny sacks; riding the electric train across the Bay Bridge; admiring the huge annual City of Paris Christmas tree; hanging off the front outside step of cable cars for a five-cent school-ticket punch, feeling like one was flying; listening to the old-style foghorns, whose rich basso profundo soundings could induce near-mystic reveries... God, the town was a fabulous place to grow up—even if *I* couldn't wait to leave, finally. (It was said every native nursed a love-hate relationship with the place.)

Richard changed the subject, bringing up next day's grand event. It was to be the first nude run and stroll for four of us; Richard and Jennie were veterans of the 2009 event. Kate had planned to do it last year but bailed after a death in the family. Sam and Gail had flirted with the idea for several years and were primed for it now, same as me. Richard and Jennie filled us in.

"I've gotta say, I'm psyched at the thought of us strolling across town *au naturel*," Sam said. "Lends a delicious daring to it all, don't you think?"

"I'll *bet* you're psyched," Gail kidded. "I remember when you took Richard up on that bet to streak down the third-floor hall during first lunch period. Remember, huh?" she poked his ribs.

"I remember. I almost got caught, but, hey, it was an easy ten-spot. Old Grumps spotted me blurring by out the corner of his eye and flung his classroom door open just as I ducked down the stair-well. Oww, it was close."

"Good thing he didn't see me at the other end and ask if I knew who you were. As honor society hall monitor, I'd have been duty-bound to say, 'Yes, sir, I'd know that ass anywhere'—or words to that effect."

"I didn't think you'd actually take me up on that," Richard lamented. "I was broke for a week."

Kidding aside, we all agreed that to be naked and have it be at least semi-okay amid tens of thousands of clothed people—in a place where it could get you arrested any other day of the year—was mind boggling. "I can't think of a nicer way to spend the day," Sam said. "Well, almost none," he added, casting a mock leer at Gail, wiggling his eyebrows.

"*You.*" Gail said, doing an absent, one-quarter blush, used to this routine.

"What I want to know is why *we* should suffer because others cling to denial of their own friggin' reality?" Richard demanded. Like me, he was always good for pointing out society's sundry ills. Unlike me, who shrank from unpleasant confrontations, Richard's warrior spirit *thrived* on calling others on things he thought uncool. "We're all naked under our clothes; it's our fuckin' default appearance, for crying out loud. When some moron yelled at me, 'put some clothes on,' at the last Breakers, I felt like going over and pantsing the guy; I swear to God, I did. It frosts my balls the way people get all smug and hidden behind their clothes and then give us grief because we want to get free of the damn things."

None of us had any doubts how Richard felt on the subject; he was ever the rebel. He'd been pep squad leader at our high school football games: One day he led the packed home bleachers in a special yell, done to a popular "Name Game" nonsense-rhyming song, in which the first letters of various names and words were changed, in turn, from *B*s to *F*s. He warmed us up by having us do *Shirley*, then *banana*, as in the original. When he yelled, "Let's do *Chuck!*"—a conspiratorial glint in his eye—he was rewarded with a rousing, uncensored chorus that maybe helped win the game against Washington but got Richard kicked off the squad. He'd gone on to support environmental causes and was then working for Greenpeace, most recently confronting Norwegian ships for breaking the international ban on whale hunting.

"I mean, the way we we're so damn attached to keeping our bods wrapped, even if it's a hundred degrees out. Our always having to wear clothes is like some four-hundred pound gorilla no one in the room will even acknowledge. The beast could be dressed up in an electric-chartreuse jumpsuit emblazoned with a Clothes R Us logo, wear six-inch heals, purple wig, Elton John sunglasses, and lip-sing Sinatra's "I've Gotta Be Me," and he'd *still* be ignored."

"Well, *there's* an image to give me nitemares," Kate said and laughed. "Poor gorilla. Hey, don't let it get you down, Richard." Kate always wanted to harmonize group energies; she'd gone on to be a respected family councilor. She was more philosophical on the matter: "Look at it this way: they're letting us run naked, aren't they? Or at least they're not stopping us. Now, if enuf of us showing tomorrow do the run bare in a cool way, maybe others might start to come around, maybe even join in. You never know."

"Yeah, right, I can just see that banker who turned me down for a loan the other day because he doesn't like my politics getting naked with us."

"Oh, lighten up, Richard," Jennie said, adding her trilling laugh I loved hearing. (I had wild crush on her in high school, more smitten by her laugh than anything, I think.) Jennie was the brain of our group. "Kate's right," she said. "Lots of people you'd never suspect were even private nudists are probably ripe to come out if they feel it's safe to. Maybe not your banker, probably not your landlord or your Aunt Ophelia either, but lots of others just might surprise you. What it boils down to, I think, is we're all social creatures. We've often dressed for each other; we can be naked for each other too. Case in point: right now."

At that moment a fresh spray of eucalyptus-lemongrass released into the sauna; we quieted a moment to savor the keen scent, made more delightful by Sam ladling water on the stove, instantly superheating the air with a soothing cloud of steam.

Jennie, married and divorced, had gone on to become a successful entrepreneur, designing and marketing her own computer software. Currently she was working on a program matching readers with books-in-print using an in-depth profiling of readers' interests and past favorite novels. She'd shared with me a more abstract overview of the freebody trend by email before my coming down:

> I've concluded [she wrote] that adapting to the simple naturalness of social nakedness—dissociating it from the automatic, hard-wired sexual link—probably involves reconfiguring more brain cells than the discovery the earth was round, centuries earlier. You suddenly *knew* it was round, but your whole life was built around thinking it flat. The same with our ingrained body-negative conditioning—deep as the Mariana Trench, forever linked to sex, reinforced thru millennia of compulsively covering up our bodies. It clings for dear life without something to jar it loose. That's why I think this race is a good thing.

☀

No doubt some of my own keyed-up excitement was symptomatic

of the impossibly-convoluted hang-ups I was still working thru. In part, I think I was overcompensating for having been so emotionally wrapped up inside by wanting to be physically unwrapped outside. Too, I'd internalized the old San Francisco so much I couldn't be in the moment easily there. Too many ancient ghosts pulling me into a vanished past. I needed to free myself to the now.

In the process, I hoped to help build some body-positive feelings in a decidedly un-body-friendly world. Joining in with my friends in light-hearted protest against an oppressive dress code felt like a good way to go—even tho I found the prospect of being naked among tens of thousands of clothed people more than a little daunting. Such a thing in our body-alienated world usually ranked in the top five of one's worst nitemares. Sharing the episode with friends gave me determination to make it a surreal dream instead. Part of me felt like a starry-eyed idealist, refusing to succumb to the ways of a wary, cynical world, but I was with Jennie: we *could* be naked for each other.

☀

My friends told me what I'd already intuited: the City had been in the grip of sweet, magical weather all week; I'd felt the same exotic air at Harbin. Much of Northern California often shared the same weather fronts off the Pacific. The town's acacia trees gave off their heady perfume, songbirds treated my ears to heartbreakingly sweet melodies and the earth was so fertile chamomile and alyssum plants sprouted between the sidewalk cracks. It was a warm, dreamy, sensuous, all's-right-with-the-world kind of feeling, one that made you glad to be alive—and begging to be enjoyed without clothes.

Come Sunday morning and the day of the race, the air felt deliriously enchanted.

We'd all spent the nite at Sam and Gails'. Wanting to get into the freebody zone early, we kept naked for bed after the sauna. In the morning, after showers, we had a naked breakfast of organic oatmeal with soymilk and blackberry soy yogurt, plus Gail's special protein drink. We packed some trail mix, organic energy bars, and vitamin-mineral packets to add to our water bottles for recharging during the day.

Everyone piled into Sam's battered but trustworthy Ford panel van in the garage, jogging outfits on—the floor. Only after parking downtown would we break our dress fast, and then only for a while. Sam and Gail, visible in front, wore abbreviated tank tops and towels over laps to avoid drawing unnecessary attention to our rig, which kate promptly dubbed The Nude-Mobubble.

Looking back, knowing how the deep-rooted taboo of being publicly naked was meeting popular resistance, I think more than a few participants that morning were reluctant to don their running suits after morning showers. They'd rather have stayed naked, like us, and luxuriated in the gift of the day.

We arrived downtown at 7 a.m., dumbfounded to find an unmetered parking place five blocks away (albeit *long* blocks). We piled out—undercover freebodies disguised in clothes—and began the walk over.

The gentlest zephyr caressed us. "Mm-m. Feel that air," Gail said. "Isn't it divine?"

"Couldn't ask for better," I chimed. "Well, maybe one-point-two degrees more," I added, holding up a hand and pretending to gauge a precise temperature reading of the warming air. "Now, point-seven... point-two... there; *perfect.*"

"Holy shit!" Sam said suddenly. "*Look* at that throng."

We'd rounded a corner and a sobering sight indeed greeted us: a sea of people at least thirty thousand strong was spilling everywhere. I'd never seen so many people together on the streets; it might have been a rally to impeach the president.

"Do we *really* want to get naked in this crowd?" Kate asked.

"Don't worry. It'll be all right once we're moving," Richard said, tho I sensed maybe he had concerns too. I think we all did, at first blush. The crowd looked so...*crowded.*

Then, as we merged into the human sea and began to get our bearings, I felt the promise of the Mardi Gras-like spirit of celebratory zaniness filling the air—even with the chaotic milling of tens of thousands all making busy preparations for the race. It was mostly a congenial crowd.

We paid our registration fee and got a numbered identification card to wear, making us official participants and helping support some charity or other—Retirement Fund for Dyslexic Jugglers, for all I remember. I balked at becoming yet another number in our number-crazed world, but it was too nice a day to get upset about anything; I poked two holes in my card and turned it into an unseemly necklace with some string and was done with it.

It was no secret my moods could change like quicksilver, and about then, even tho it was a merry throng, my fledgling freebody enthusiasm wavered. This country boy *knew* he wasn't in Harbin anymore. This was where the rubber met the road, the acid test for putting our bodies on the line. The prospect of getting naked in the teaming city was almost frightening. Coping with the super-concentrated people energies and sensory overload *while* wearing protective textile armor was challenge enuf; attempting to weather it naked suddenly struck me as sheer lunacy. I'd become a city warrior in my younger days, but only after a lifetime of dealing with urban realities and learning to surf the waves of energy; I'd since reprogrammed my circuits 180 degrees and become a country bumpkin. But I was determined to do the progressive side of my family proud and help liberate the City and my memories of it by doing this thing.

Richard had struck a conversation with a twitchy fellow next to us as we stood about, getting our bearings and organizing our bare necessities: sun glasses, water bottles sun block, disposable camera... Richard divulged our intention to run nude, and twitchy said he planned on baring too. But if some of us were nervous at the prospect, he was positively stage-struck.

"I can't believe we're going to do this!" he blurted, working a squeeze ball in his left hand like he was trying to get a grip. "Are you *sure* it's okay? I mean, there's c-cops over there and—"

"Yeah, it's *okay*," Richard assured him, like an older, wiser brother. "Re*lax*. I can't believe we didn't do it sooner. I mean, think about it: We've been like kids asking permission from parental authorities to be ourselves: 'Can I please not wear clothes today? It's so nice out.' 'No, you may *not*. Don't even think about it or I'll send you to your room.' Isn't that the way it's been?"

Twitchy laughed nervously, like someone who'd just paid to hear a nite club comedian savage his every hang-up. "Maybe; I donno. I *still* can't friggin' believe we're doing this!" Richard, patience exhausted, favored him with a withering glance that ended any further conversation. Kate touched the guy's arm to let him know she understood.

I could understand too: For all the private and sheltered-public nudity we'd racked up in our assorted lives, what we were about to do represented a staggering leap to an alternative reality for every first-timer among us. And some of those cops *did* look like they'd enjoy hauling off the first one of us who dared strip on their watch.

By pure chance, we found ourselves settled in next to the naturist contingent, 700 strong. They were still dressed, tho minimally, like us. Maybe we'd been attracted by their relaxed, outgoing ambience, and had naturally gravitated towards them. Decades of having enthusiastically pursued a clothing-optional lifestyle lent them a natural, grounded aura as they stood about, soon to be in their métier.

As it turned out, 300 independent bare demonstrators had networked to join forces with the conventioneers. Many were de facto nudists themselves and veterans of many previous nude runs. They were distinctive by their bright DayGlo caps. Everyone figured, the more the merrier.

You mix 1,000 naturists, nudists and freebody proponents together with 80,000 or so lightly clothed participants on a purely nice day and interesting things were bound to happen—like the naturists deciding they weren't waiting for the starting gun to peel their clothes: One moment they were inconspicuous except for the occasional nude slogan on their T-shirts and tank tops; the next they stood out like unwrapped loaves among a market's shelf of sealed breads.

Absorbing this interesting new wrinkle, I looked over to catch any police reaction. A few cops stared bug-eyed, their universe turning upside down. But their fellow officers seemed at least semi-okay with this unexpected turn of events. Chagrined smiles on a few of their faces led me to think there was maybe a nudist or two among the City's finest. It was too close to the starting gun, and the crowd was too locked and loaded to run, to interfere because people bared early.

Maybe the 1,000 did so only to better catch the gentle morning rays and get in the freebody zone, having little idea what chain of events they would help set into play. Possibly they did it intentionally, wanting to be proactive beyond simply running/strolling nude, and thus give a boost to the efforts of the independent freebody advocates poised along the route. Maybe a little of each; we'd hear both stories.

They'd struck a bold move, in any event: nudity could be contagious. While a naked person could feel self-conscious among clothed people, a clothed person could feel just as self-conscious among naked people—experiencing the same urge to conform. The presence of the large contingent of veteran freebodies, relaxed in their skins, gave our group sudden courage. Richard promptly followed unsuit, then Sam and Gail, then me, Jennie, and finally Kate, who'd hesitated at the last. "Don't worry, Kate," Jennie kid-

313

ded. "Think of it this way: we'll have bragging rights the rest of our lives."

"Fine," Kate said, making a wry face, "but in the meantime I might have smirking clients telling me they saw me nude on the Six O'clock news."

We were all too aware now we weren't skinnydipping at the beach or sunning by a pool or sweating in a dim-lit sauna: We were standing at the edge of a public concrete jungle in broad daylight, amid 80,000 packed people, and soon to run and stroll butt-naked past tens of thousands others lining the route—all dutifully covered with cloth. Getting naked there felt incongruous as hell.

We'd keep our socks and running shoes on—our concrete and asphalt cities were *not* barefoot-friendly—and stashed our clothes in our day packs.

At two meters plus, I was tall enuf, on tip-toe, to look over much of the crowd. I was startled to see we were part of a larger flurry of disrobing going on all about us.

TWENTY

"Clothes separate us from our own bodies as well as the bodies of others."
—Margaret Mead

As THE NEARBY Ferry Building clock's minute hand inched toward the 8 o'clock start time, you could feel the celebratory air ready to burst and flood across the City and saturate the town in festival spirit.

Along with the usual serious runners determined to place were those who had possibly never even run for a bus. They were there to make the event a Mardi Gras procession—with a West Coast twist—by the elaborate, surreal and often comically absurd costumes they fashioned. People's fevered imaginations went into overdrive making them. I admired the portable nine-person Supreme Court bench (six of them dummy figures), whose powder-wigged, august members would yea and nay their collective way cross town, handing down decisions on everything from the dangers of chewing bubblegum and yakking on cell phones in book stores to not placing toilet-paper rolls in the waterfall position.

The unclad contingent—wearing the most outlandish costumes of all in the eyes of conventional thinkers—was about 1,200 strong and growing by the second. As best I could gauge shades of difference in body attitudes, some—like commingled nudists, naturists and freebody demonstrators—stood matter-of-factly at ease, just another day in paradise; others appeared uncertain or a tad indecorous, with "I'm not sure about this" looks on their faces; some appeared to feel a little naughty, like beachgoers daring to take off their swimsuit for the first time; others looked naughty as hell—especially some women, wild grins pasted on their faces, looking like eager participants after three Coke-and-rums at amateur strip nite.

For myself, I sensed the time was ripe to make a stand for positive body acceptance. Even so, I vacillated between the go-for-it camp and the *what-the-hell-am-I-doing?* contingent. What I was about to do just was such a mind-boggling departure from time-honored reality. Downtown San Francisco simply didn't feel conducive to exposing one's tender flesh in, nice weather notwithstanding. No soft earth or flowing creek or peaceful quietude. But friends by my side gave me courage.

And we were in good company. We had the strength of experience and positive nude attitude at our core—dedicated nudists and body-freedom enthusiasts, many of whom felt so strongly everyone should have the right to *just say no to clothes* they devoted parts of their lives to the cause. We also had the strength of numbers: all ages, shapes, sizes, and degrees of fitness; all colors of the rainbow and every sexual persuasion; together we validated we were indeed all naked under our clothes—just as we all suspected.

My initial feeling of vulnerability standing there, fledgling freebody, faded. The nudists' group energy was so open-circuit, it tipped the balance to positive body acceptance among the crowd, fostered an all-inclusive acceptance for each other's nakedness, warts and all. Many people now appeared surprisingly matter-of-fact and unconcerned about being unwrapped—maybe because we were all in the same boat. It was as if, once out of our mandated costumes, we felt authenticated, validated as human beings, each of us unique, each a bona fide member of the human race. With nothing to hide *out*side, it was easier to be whoever we were *in*side. As Kate punned afterwards, "it didn't seem to matter much whether you were an out of shape nude enthusiast or a *buff* buff buff."

Maybe we were growing up.

"Wow, this is great," Gail enthused as she balanced on her haunches and stashed her shorts and tank top into Sam's day pack, along with his. "Something tells me this race'll be a cake-walk."

"You *had* to remind me of food," Jennie said, munching on a carrot. "I want to burn ten pounds."

"It does feel like something weirdly wonderful is happening," I said, inanely channeling Elmer Fudd. "Wouldn't you wace that wascal wabbit over the wainbow, Wachel, to wapidly winnow your waist?"

Kate and Gail both pushed me.

"No wespect."

"It is kind of awesome," Kate agreed. "It almost feels normal, you know?" She re-positioned the one-piece outfit of her number card above her belly, hoping it would be less of a nuisance there. "And the people over there covered up are starting to look…well, *covered up*—kind of like furniture overprotected with plastic covers."

As if hearing Kate's words, participants milling on the widening fringes of our epicenter of unclad humanity, vacillating whether or not to bare, had found themselves being won over, duly amazing themselves and joining unsuit.

And so it began: Like a standing ovation moving from an auditorium's front row to the back, a grand, inexorable human ripple-effect was set into motion, its widening, concentric circles of free-body vibration radiating outward. In a matter of minutes, our unclad contingent had grown to 1,500 strong.

Before the race started it doubled, *and then doubled again.*

"Holy Moley," I said, doubting my eyes. The synergy created by the mass of earnest, naked humanity was staggering.

"You said it," Gail said.

"Is this really happening?" Sam asked.

"I wouldn't have believed it possible," Kate said.

"*Carpe diem!*" Richard yelled, grinning like a pirate.

We truly were seizing the day. Everyone who'd ever sought a fuller sense of being; who'd ever had a fantasy of being naked in public; who'd wanted to shake free of inhibitions or rebel against a lifetime of body oppression; who was already a private nudist and wanted to push their boundaries; who wanted to make a bold affirmation his or her body was all right...were all shucking their clothes, en masse.

Of course, not everyone felt pulled to peel. Actually it was only a minority—maybe one in ten. But one in ten of that mass of humanity was still...*a mass of humanity.*

Unaccountably, people would come to feel all right being publicly naked that day: it felt safe; it felt natural. A bit vulnerable, yes; more than a little surreal, for sure. But there was a magic in the air, the strength in numbers, an amazing easy acceptance of each other, transcending self-conscious fears. People felt daring, exuberant. School was *out* and we wanted to go skinnydipping in the surf across town, and the day was so nice we decided to lose our clothes on the way over.

When the starting gun fired, the air crackled with a million megawatts of electricity.

We waited long minutes before the massive bottleneck of persons in front of us poured out, consoling ourselves with the knowledge we were part of something extraordinary, possibly history-making. Jennie told me later she felt "as if some divine spirit poured over us."

A sea of humanity some 70,000 strong were off—jogging, strolling, galumphing, and otherwise perambulating down Howard Street. Serious runners quickly broke free, the Nigerian who'd won five years in a row taking the lead, feet on fire; others formed straggling running packs trailed him hopefully, out ahead of our more leisurely crowd.

Among the surging mass of humanity starting to thread its way across town were at least 6,000 naked people.

"I happened to be driving nearby when I looked over at a light and saw a solid mass of flesh surging by a block away," a witness, Jamal Abernathy, wrote later in *San Francisco* magazine:

> I hadn't heard of the race and promptly lost all sense of reality the rest of the drive home. It was like something out of an old "Twilight Zone" episode, like an entire town going wild over something in the air. *Why were all these people naked?* I kept asking myself. At the same time, it seemed almost natural considering the nice weather. It was nuts; I was *all* turned around.

Most of our nude contingent went at an easy jog, each hitting a stride, glad to be moving and getting the blood pumping—and wanting to get past the sometimes less-than-scenic commercial district. But this was a fun run for us, not a race, and most of us would switch to stroll-mode after about three kilometers, inspired by looking up Hayes Street hill from its base.

A few, tho, would run the entire length naked, and one or two tough-soled people ran barefoot too, amazing people even more: "Look, he's *barefoot!*" I'd hear a child yelled in astonishment. Lack of jock supports for running men wasn't a problem, as people thought it would be; they didn't realize during running the scrotum automatically pulls the whole apparatus up and in for safety and comfort, like a transforming Batmobile.

Another couple thousand or so of us were in various states of dishabille: topfree, bottomfree, half-sarongs, thongs, tights, hula skirts, pajamas, loin cloths, baby-dolls—every conceivable kind of limited wardrobe.

In the rapid-change dynamics of celebrants' body attitudes, there were dozens of reasons why some elected to keep some clothes on. For many women, just going topfree was a stupendous breakthru in reclaiming personal body freedom. For some men, it went too much against their grain to be fully naked in public; too undignified—and perhaps fears of getting too excited being around one fetching woman too many.

For some people, it was practical concerns: easily burned skin; needing body support; on their moon; testing comfort zones a bit at a time. Those in "sexy" outfits were usually either acting out fantasies—"I dreamed I walked across town in my Maidenform bra (and nothing else)"—or just being camp and showing how absurd some of the stuff was. For yet others it was a matter of not wishing to offend others by obesity, anorexia, skin conditions, surgery scars, mastectomies, missing limbs and the like.

And some, altho maybe already comfortable with their body image and being naked in public, didn't want to feel they were merely conforming to the sudden avalanche of clothes-shedding; they'd wait until they felt their own spontaneous urge to uncover.

Others, tho wanting to, just couldn't bring themselves to break the taboo against being fully naked. Despite the mounting evidence all around them it was okay that day, their internalized rag police just wouldn't let them—at first, anyhow. One young woman, for instance, wearing only a thong bottom the size of a postage stamp, when asked why she kept it on, said, in all seriousness, "Why, I'd be *naked* without it!"

And then there were many who admitted afterwards they'd partly felt like baring but didn't until later because they'd projected self-criticism of their perceived imperfections onto others: not big enuf, not slim enuf, not tight enuf, not built enuf—petty concerns perpetuated by a body-unfriendly society. In fact, they fell well within the bell curve of your average human monkey: maybe a little plump, a little skinny, stretch marks, inertia taking its toll, freckles, moles, hairiness... Just your average human monkey.

While maybe only a handful might have ranked as perfect Greek gods and goddesses that day, many radiated an inner beauty, transforming their outer selves into something astonishing. People who the day before may have believed only the finest specimens of humanity had any business "displaying" themselves were fast changing their tune. They had a revelation: A totally buff person in an ugly mood could be offensive, while a person big as a balloon in a jolly, self-accepting mood could brighten one's day. As an old song went, "You're only as pretty as you feel inside..."

One muscular Adonis got testy, apparently wanting to be admired for his chiseled form and not receiving his due, that or maybe he'd felt resentful having to rub shoulders with all the physical imperfection about him. He started bad-mouthing others.

"If I looked like you, I sure wouldn't be advertising it" he said to one overweight woman, instantly bringing her to tears.

A veteran nudist, big as a mountain, strode over and intervened. He locked eyeballs with Adonis and said with threatening calm, "You know, if the words of your mouth matched your enviable body, maybe we'd be worshipping at your feet, but that's not the case, now, is it, butt face? So put a sock in it." Shocked someone had called him on his behavior—one similarly overweight at that—he clammed up, much to everyone's relief. I learned later the mountain was named Tiny, used to diffusing such situations at Black's Beach in San Diego, on the rare occasions they occurred.

A grand reality check was in progress.

We surged along, hanging a right up Ninth Street, crossing Market and making a gentle left onto Hayes Street and its long, runner-dreaded hill. No sweat at a stroll; we geared down and kept on truckin'. Everyone, whether naked or in some abbreviated outfit, shared a sweet triple-euphoria that day: one part feel-good endorphins surging thru the bloodstream from all the running; one part pure delight in being bare-ass naked, or nearly so, on a beautiful day; and one part rush of empowerment for flouting society's hide-bound notions of acceptable appearance.

All along the route people subtracted clothes, added clothes, traded clothes, gave away clothes, cast off clothes—or stayed bare—according to whims of the moment and how heated each got hiking thru town and after coming to the giddy realization we didn't *have* to wear clothes.

"This is just too awesome," Sam said, holding hands with Gail as they walked along.

"It feels like a dream. Better pinch me," Gail agreed. "No, don't; you'd leave a mark."

"You two," Kate said, again adjusting her ungainly number card. "Now, if we could just lose these damn numbers, I'd be happy. How weird is it? You can be naked, but you still have to wear a *number?* Funny fashion statement, if you ask me: 'Kinder critics voted her stylish in her black-on-white number card,' she said, quoting imaginary fashion writers. 'Jauntily suspended askew from iridescent purple ribbon, together it formed an arresting pendent.' 'A daring understatement,' Gladys Gladstone gushed. But others weren't so kind: 'It's so overdone;' groused Daphne Downer. 'That size card is so *out* this year; she didn't even *try* to accessorize—and don't get me started on those *shoes.*'"

Gail giggled. "Yeah, so it's a *bizzaro* dream. Why humanity's disallowed itself this simple pleasure baffles me."

"Maybe," Jennie ventured, furrowing her brow, "it's because not enuf of us liked ourselves or each other enuf before to allow being so open. We've been so collectively down on ourselves we've kept our bods locked in clothes out of group sado-masochism or something; sort of an "I'm not okay, you're not okay' thing."

"'And the discussion turned serious,'" Richard said in mock commentary tone.

"That," I added, "or we've gotten so used to being 'presentable,' completing ourselves by wearing clothes, that being without them makes us feel not all there, like a tortoise without a shell."

"Maybe," Richard said, weighing in. "but I still think it's the granddaddy of *all* cover-up conspiracies—pun fucking intended. The power brokers of the world want to keep us—The Great Unwashed—in our place with their cunning divide-and-conquer system. They try their damnedest to render us powerless and then snatch away our hard-earned money for clothes in the process. It's like they're taxing bodies with a shame tax is what it is, and wearing clothes is the seal proof we paid. Wear no clothes and it's like, 'He's not paying his taxes.'"

"You know," Kate said, "I think it's *all of the above,* and a zillion other reasons to boot, simple creatures that we are...*not.* Hey, Zet, changing the subject, if I may; where are those cousins you talk about? I'd think they'd make this one for sure."

"Oh, they're bound to be here somewhere," I said, looking around. "Zor said he'd show. 'Wouldn't miss it for the world,' were his exact words. Probably going to parachute down, knowing him. My cousin Allen said he'd like to join in but he was concerned about parading around naked affecting his credibility as a psychologist."

"I can relate to that," Kate deadpanned. "But who knows? Being San Francisco, it'll probably help *my* practice. I can hear my patients now: 'My therapist is so open and self-accepting she strolls naked in public.'"

As Richard predicted would happen, we at last heard a disgruntled spectator yell, "Why don't you put some *clothes* on?" I looked to the source of the discouraging words and spied an intent, thirty-something God Squad type glaring right at us like he was considering making a citizen's arrest.

"That's it," Richard said, starting for him.

It was all we could do to restrain him.

"Killjoy," Richard muttered, after we'd held him back long enuf to cool down some. "Feels so damn smug, hiding behind his polyester, dry-clean-only rags."

"Yeah, we know," Jennie said. "But maybe he'll come out someday—or not. But we've got to show people the impossible is possible, set an example."

"I'd rather set him on his fucking ears," Richard growled, staring daggers in the direction of the spectator, who'd since melted into the crowd, suddenly concerned for his safety.

A nearby clothed stroller snickered. "You nudeniks make it sound like sound like clothes are part of an evil capitalist plot or something."

"Don't laugh, man, it's true," Richard said, now drawing a bead on him.

"How's that?" the man asked, either unaware he was playing with dynamite or thinking a naked man couldn't kick ass, forgetting the opening scene in *Terminator 2* by our former governor.

Jennie, averting certain disaster, pulled Richard away. "Let's just enjoy the day, huh?"

Negative reactions from onlookers were the exception. Granted, some spectators—participants, too—appeared dumfounded so many would dare get naked in public. They probably thought the whole world was turning exhibitionistic. Maybe those mysterious chem trails crisscrossing the skies lately for some unfathomable reason contained something to loosen people's inhibitions. But at least they held their peace.

In contrast, many among the twin rivers of spectators lining the route cheered the sight of us: heroes amid an overdressed world. We were victors, marching triumphantly thru a captured textile town, wearing our non-uniforms proudly. "Yea, naked people!" onlookers yelled. People hooted, cheered, gave thumbs up. A woman screeched in amused disbelief, "Oh, my gawwwwd!" Mischievous teens cooled us down at unexpected moments from their arsenal of Super Soakers, spraying welcome jets of water over us. And some spectators, as happened every year, succumbed to the May madness, peeling off their clothes and joining in.

In fact, it seemed a *lot* of people were joining us, stripping and slipping into a growing river of bare humanity.

❋

The staggered train of serious runners far ahead of us had long since loped up the Hayes Street hill and jagged over to Fell Street. The few nude runners among them were like mythical torch-bearing Olympians—or the foot- and head-winged god Mercury, then moonlighting for FTD florists. After awhile, our huge amalgam of more leisurely paced—costumed, semi-bare and sun-clad—came into view along upper Fell, next to the Park's panhandle, astounding onlookers for the sheer number of happily clothes-challenged.

Meanwhile some of the freebody advocates—rather than join in the run/stroll—had been busy cueing up their plans. They'd borrowed a page from Greenpeace. Having contacted pro-freebody residents by internet beforehand they found some with apartment flats along the route on upper Fell. As anticipated, much of the media had chosen this area to set up in.

When the moment felt right—the crowds reeling from the surrealism of thousands of naked people strolling along a public street, parading around in the nude like it was their birthright or something—activists unfurled their giant banners across the houses' upper stories. **BEING NAKED IS NOT A CRIME** read one seven meters long. Another: **BODY FREEDOM NOW**. The largest, a giant, four-by-fifteen-meter banner, strategically placed across the third story windows of a row Victorian where everyone, especially the media, were bound to see it, proclaimed:

IMAGINE A CLOTHING-OPTIONAL PLANET

Legalize the Human Body.

"Whoa, that'll get people thinking," Gail said, as she stopped to swig some water.

"Imagine…I wonder if they can," Kate mused.

"I hope some day-yy you'll join—" I began singing, before getting pushed again.

"Greenpeace learned that's a sure-fire way to get media notice," Sam said.

"So's walking around starkers," a thoughtful, large-breasted woman, overhearing us, added. "Tell me: Does anyone else feel there're a million eyes on them, like we're in a movie or something? Don't say it's just *me*."

"No," Kate said. "It's not just you, tho I'm sure you're probably getting more attention than some for being, ah, so…*bountiful*. I felt the same way earlier, believe me. Finally I told myself, 'all right, so I'm in a movie. I'm a de facto naked actress, playing a role in a kind of body freedom documentary. Maybe there're oglers catching every bounce and jiggle, probably even some videotaping to jack off to later or hawk to a cheesy video distributor catering to the terminally horny. But this is a needed movie, one that's blowing peoples' minds, one that'll maybe help people get over their damn body phobia.' I told myself all that, and then I started feeling okay."

"Wow, I never thought of it that way."

Kate was still warming to the subject. "Few do, but it's true. Another thing that helped: You know how a nervous speaker is told to imagine her audience naked to overcome stage jitters? Well, I *reversed* that, imagining all the dressed people around us as hiding behind their clothes because they felt embarrassed and self-conscious about their bodies. It sounds weird maybe, but it worked for me."

"No, yeah, I think I see what you mean. Maybe I'll try that. Right now, tho, I still feel, you know...over-exposed."

"Well, then put some clothes on, sweetie; you don't have to prove anything to anyone," Kate said. "No one's trying to be nakeder-than-thou. I know; big-breasted women get enuf grief as it is without showing their puppies, making them feel their main purpose in life is to supply boys with pneumatic joy toys or something. But no more than small-breasted women like me, who've been made to feel they're letting every guy down for not being better endowed. The way I see it, it's all about your own comfort level versus your willingness to go outside it and take risks to gain a stronger sense of self-acceptance and body freedom. If a risk feels too great, go back to your comfort zone. It's okay...really."

"Thanks, I needed that." The young woman stopped to pull over an extra-long, apple-green tank top from her shoulder bag. (Later, she'd remove it again.)

As we soon discovered, the rest of the body freedom activists not yet in the run—the street-theatre contingent—had strategically placed themselves, lightly clothed, among the throng of bystanders lining the route where it wended thru the park on JFK Drive. Their plan, simple enuf, was to disrobe and lightheartedly encourage spectators to join in.

Once we made it to the eastern edge of the park, the City was left behind: It was more or less pure park all the way to the ocean. Naturally, Golden Gate Park was the most relaxed and inviting portion of the route, especially with many roads closed to traffic as they were every Sunday. It felt like the reward for having run (or strolled) the gauntlet of long city blocks.

The park's easternmost area, near the Haight-Ashbury, was a special oasis amid the modest metropolis, being where park creation had commenced in the late 1800s: In their enthusiasm, designers had pulled all the stops. With its verdant grass, lush foliage, winding paths and sun-reflected ponds, I easily imagined the area habitat for faeries, earth spirits and water sprites.

The area had no doubt long inspired urges on nice sunny days to blissfully lose one's clothes, urges actually acted on during the era of flower children with child-like innocence and the forthright grace of a people exercising divine right—*almost as if envisioning the advent of this day some forty-five years earlier.*

Many spectators had chosen this scenic stretch to view the proceedings. As the throng of nude and semi-nude participants surged by, poised freebody activists quietly lost their token coverings and joined in, keeping along the edge of movement. At first glance many still appeared dressed, as underneath they "wore" elaborate body paint imitating clothes. They were both naked and clothed, wearing their bareness as a costume. Others had emblazoned across their fronts and backs colorful body paint messages in swirling lettering: **Dare to Bare! Legalize Humanity...Some Days are Just Too Nice for Clothes...Have a *Nicer* Day—Get Naked!** Yet others were veritable walking works of art, with intricate patterns swirling covering their bodies from head to foot. And some were simply naked, believing the unadorned human body art enough.

As this sprinkling of street-theatre pranksters strolled along, they interacted with spectators, hoping to beguile them to join in.

"Hey, it's *okay* to be naked today."

"Give yourselves something you can talk about the rest of your lives!"

"It's your right as a free American, ya know? Ben Franklin was a nudist—bet your history teacher never told you *that*."

One prankster, wearing only a fresh-woven green laurel on his head, periodically ran and stopped and with out-thrust arm exhorted in mock-oration: "Good people, hear me! You have nothing to lose but your tan lines!" and "Life's too short for a dress rehearsal!" and "If I have but one life to live, let me live it as a human!"

"When he did that, I finally got it," a twenty-eight-year-old woman wrote a year later in *Freebody Times*. "They were like kids playing in the sun, feeling zero shame over their nakedness. I said to myself, *if these people are kooks, I want to be one too*, and I got naked without another thought. My boyfriend was furious. 'If you do this, we're *history*,' he vowed as I climbed out of my shorts and panties. It was funny: suddenly I realized I was better off losing him *and* my clothes."

Among those lining the route that day were many who'd felt tempted to shuck what little they were wearing, but treated the impulse as impossible fantasy. As more and more nude people passed by, many onlookers wrestled with the last vestiges of obedience to the clothes-minded world and its ingrained body-shame and physical self-consciousness. With good-natured encouragements to actually go ahead, they did at last: nude in public for the first time since toddlers. Many undoubtedly experienced a rush suddenly being free of clothes, combined with shivers down their spine for letting the sun's luscious warmth envelop them.

Cousin Zor indeed made his appearance out of the sky, along with two friends. They descended nude, suspended from bright-colored parachutes, drifting down like umbrellas moving underwater, landing softly on Speedway Meadows. Zor's chute was emblazoned in a Day-Glo tie-dye pattern that almost blinded me. The merry troupe quickly folded their chutes and melted into the crowd before any policeman could cite them for floating naked without a license.

I caught up with him. "Hey, Zor, now *that's* what I call making an entrance."

"Cousin! Glad you made it. Zow; *that* was a rush. Feels like the '60s all over again, don't it? 'Hey, check it out, Zet: I took some snaps on the way down guaranteed to blow your mind."

He fiddled a moment with his digital camera and then held up the screen for me to share in the first viewing. Glad I'd thought to bring along my 3X-power reading glasses, I fished them out of my day pack and put them on so the screen would be more than a tiny blur. The first few shots, taken four kilometers high, showed a city stranger than known—a mystical almost-island, in living embrace with the deep-blue sea, ringed with a white foamy necklace. The middle shots showed a thick rope of humanity snaking across town, frayed strands radiating along it. The last shots captured the decided lack of clothes on thousands of people and, finally, their surprise as they watched the group float down.

"Wow. These are gold," I said. You know you could sell those in a heartbeat if you wanted. But I know you; you'll post them free on the Net. Hey, let me introduce you to my friends."

Between the delightful weather, the surge of unclad humanity all around them (becoming more unclad each minute), the sudden bold banners, cheerful encouragements, and naked men dropping from the sky, it was as if many still-dressed people felt gripped by an irresistible impulse to lose their covers.

And the ripple-effect continued outward.

The dissolving lines of spectators merged into the race's contrasting mosaic of flesh tones and cloth dyes. Clothes came off like bargain-hounds cleaning off a sale rack, like lovers too long apart, like students late for gym class. A few, in contrast, disrobed with slow deliberation, savoring the moment of deliverance as they tacitly gave themselves permission.

Pronounced tan lines proclaimed how radical a departure from the norm it was for many.

Newcomers shared the expanses of soft grass along the route with those who'd hoofed it all the way from the Bay—now shucking protective footwear and luxuriating in feeling pliant earth and cool grass on bare feet, nudification complete.

In the more relaxed environment impromptu gatherings erupted, with music, singing, and dancing, mugging for cameras, and generally hamming it up. One group huddled and sang a spirited rendition of "Ding, Dong (The Witch is Dead)"—the witch here no doubt being the Wicked Clothing Authority of the West; afterwards they skipped off, hand-in-hand, singing "We're Off to See the Wizard." Our own group, joined by my cousin and his friends and some others, lined up, linking arms over shoulders, and danced a spirited cancan, kicking high as we could while singing our own accompaniment; the Rockettes we weren't.

Spreckels Lake, along the race route, proved irresistible for skinnydipping and only a few ducks seemed to mind. The lake's Portals of the Past—salvaged frontal columns from sugar baron Spreckels' stately mansion, destroyed in the quake and fire—bore sweet, silent witness to the merriment.

As the contagious waves of body liberation radiated out further, it washed over the entire route's spectators, any distinction between participants and bystanders fairly dissolving. People thronged the park's wide avenue in naked jubilation, fitfully but surely migrating towards the ocean.

The only spectators left were straggles of stunned tourists, a few disbelieving locals, stray pockets of foaming-at-the-mouth religious-righters, and, God love 'em, the Press.

TWENTY-ONE

What is kept deliberately
hidden has an unnatural power to obsess us.
—**Charles Daney**

PEOPLE, BOTH NAKED and clothed,
were glad to give their two cents' worth to the flock of media
reporters on hand. Among the feedback published in the next day's
Examiner was the Question Man column, sound-bite interviews
taken with head shots. People were asked, "What do you think of
all this nudity?"

Barney Combs, yoga instructor: "Zounds, what a
stretch. It feels great!"

Lester Kramden, philosophy major: "I don't understand.
Why are all these people naked?"

Cindy McGee. Clock-maker: "'It's about time."

James Seymour, tourist from Topeka: "I heard San
Franciscans were different, but **this**..."

Julie and Jack Garbsworth, nudist couple: "We flew all
the way from Austin for it."

Scooter Brown, Santa Cruz surfer: "It's like, surreal, but

I could get used to it, like, way-y easily."

(Name withheld) lab animal experimenter: "These people ought to be **ashamed** of themselves."

Terry McMasters, abstract painter: "Pretty surreal."

Fletcher Grimswald, Child psychologist: "Just so much juvenile exhibitionism; people ought to grow up."

G. Yuaryu, self-actualization guru: "A pure-dee affirmation of being alive if every there was one."

Jason P. Bookmaker, accountant: "Seems kind of silly to me, but it adds up to quintessential San Francisco, I suppose."

Algonquin J. Calhoun, attorney-at-law: "Someone ought to **sue** someone over this—here's my card."

As I meandered around I overheard a video interview they didn't use, at least not past the local live feed. A self-proclaimed free spirit told the reporter: "Omigosh, It's *heavenly!* Why don't you join in and find out for yourself?" The reporter, to the astonishment of her cameraperson, did just that, continuing her interviewing in the buff and signing off with, "Naked and loving it, this is Paula Pennington, reporting live..."

For contrast, some reporter caught the opinion of a hopping-mad religious fundamentalist, one Quentin Sedgwick: "It's Sodom and Gomorrah! I tell you, it's Sodom and Gomorrah all over again! God won't stand for it, mark my words!" His outburst drew spirited rejoinders from nearby people: "God *loves* naked people!" "We're *all* naked in the sight of God!" He glared at them in righteous wrath, expecting them to turn to pillars of salt any second.

The closing piece—destined to air that evening for KTVS, Channel 3, a cable feed for nationwide audience—was an interview with a spirited young couple in matching sarongs. "When you think about it," the guy said, "I think we *should* have the right to be naked in weather like this if we want to. I mean, if it means not wearing this," he said, tugging at his sarong, "then..."

334

He didn't finish, as he'd unintentionally pulled off his only cover-ing. He stood naked, looking sheepish a second, then grinned, as his girlfriend had promptly pulled hers off to match. In a burst of giddiness, they ran off hand-in-hand to join the unraveling proces-sion, their brightly colored sarongs held aloft and fluttering in the breeze like exotic body freedom emblems; in the background the banner proclaimed: **IMAGINE A CLOTHING-OPTIONAL PLANET.** The network, deciding this was history-in-the-making (of a sort), would break with precedent and air the clip that evening and not pixelate their nakedness. Capturing the infectious spontaneity of the day, the piece would show at least once or twice in much of the United States and overseas—before being pulled amid fears of obscene network indecency fines.

Meanwhile, back in Golden Gate Park: A tight knot of fundamen-talist tourists who'd earlier raised eyebrows at various nude statu-ary disgracing the park grounds, intending to complain to City Hall, suddenly had living naked people everywhere; it wasn't a Hallmark Moment. Other tourists were beside themselves as well—for running out of film. They knew the folks back home wouldn't believe them. And more than a few tourists joined in (when in Rome…).

People in neighborhoods bordering the giant city park got word of things by cell phone. (*"Jim, remember you said one of these years you were going to do the run naked? Well, you might want to come over here…"*) Others felt the excitement in the air and were drawn over without knowing why.(*"I'm telling you, Carlotta, something big's going on over there. I can feel it!"*) A benefit carwash in progress nearby caught the drift; suddenly its workers felt overdressed in swim suits and continued on in the buff between turning the sprays on each other.

Police faced an unprecedented dilemma: "It appears the whole blinking town is going starkers," as one put it. What should they do?

What *could* they do, with thousands involved? Call up the Guard? Some wanted to, it was revealed later. As it turned out, tho, spirits were high, and most people, apart from being nude, were peaceable. While police did end up arresting a hundred or so that day, it was only those flagrantly disrespecting the rights of others and making rude spectacles of themselves—some drunk or wasted on drugs—who got hauled off.

The overwhelming majority of us were exuberant but law abiding, all things considered. We carried on—happy to savor such delectable body freedom after a lifetime of forced cover-up. Like some impossibly-huge caterpillar, we pulsed towards the ocean.

Among the procession: a young couple pushing their baby stroller, decal on the side reading, "Born Naked—Born Free"; an old couple, each supporting the other along (I overheard them talking: "Didja ever think we'd live to see this, Maude?" "Never in all my born days."); flocks of women friends, saronged and topfree, chatting happily, looking as if they'd been transported to Tahiti without leaving town.

There was the unofficial guest of honor: one of the last living survivors of the '06 Quake. He remembered as a five-year-old sitting on Nob Hill and watching the City burn. Now a hundred-and-ten years young, his tribe of descendents flocked about his wheelchair, proudly taking turns guiding him along. Legend had it as a young man he was a member of the local Polar Bear Club, whose members braved the icy surf every New Year's Day. He'd always defied convention by running into the breakers naked, much to the consternation of town officials. I spotted him later, looking out at all the skinnydippers splashing in the surf with a knowing smile.

The cooling ocean breeze got stronger. We found ourselves singing, laughing, and dancing along. Tunes and rhythms supplied by the many mobile street musicians sprinkled throughout wove an intricate aural tapestry: people played flutes, clarinets, saxes, harmonicas—there was even a nude tuba player, who ompah-pahed as he march-danced along. A troupe of drummers with

336

strapped-on congas thumped infectious rhythms that echoed across town. A mobile piano player aboard an ingenuous contraption peddled along, steering with a knee rudder while plunking out tunes—including a rollicking version of "San Francisco." A college glee club, gleefully naked, reprised the tune a cappella with inspired four-part harmony; as they hit the last three chords of the bridge it sent shivers up my spine. They followed that by singing "By the Sea, By the Sea" and then—shades of Woodstock—led those nearby in spirited rounds of "Row, Row, Row Your Boat."

Our procession pulled towards the ocean as if by magnet, entranced, feeling indeed life was but a dream. My friends and I caught a powerful whiff of tangy salt air and were instantly galvanized, now feeling the sea in our blood. We ran the rest of the way towards the ocean. On of us yelled, "Last one in the water buys dinner!"—I think it was Richard; he was always broke. Cooling air currents caressed our skins as we sprinted the last stretch. A giant old windmill loomed in the distance, one of two long-retired alternate-energy workhorses that once pumped fresh water to irrigate the Park. We dashed across now-closed-off Ocean Highway, down the steps and plowed thru the dry sands and onto the slick. "Wait, I *can't*," Jennie yelled in mock distress a second before we hit the water. "I forgot my swimsuit!"

Race officials, sensing the futility of trying to keep a handle on things, had abandoned the finish-line chutes, set up to clock each runner's time, and stood aside, some in wonder, some in disgust. The spectacle of so much naked humanity pouring out along the long stretch of Ocean Beach was something they'd remember the rest of their lives.

There naturally followed the world's largest skinnydipping party, tho no Guinness official was present to verify. We were so pumped from running, strolling and dancing, the chill ocean water felt great, its liquid magic steeling our newly-liberated bodies and causing tingles of inexplicable joy.

We ended up all chipping in for dinner. We ordered in so we could enjoy the evening dining alnudo on Sam and Gail's back porch, wanting to extend our clothesfree time as long as possible. (A friend had retrieved Sam's van downtown and picked us up at the beach and we dashed into the open side door when the coast was clear.) We basically ordered the same thing to keep things easy. Gail and Sam went to the door to pay the deliveryman, Jay, a casual acquaintance of theirs; he had the presence of mind to not even blink.

"Hey. Let's see what you hungry naked runners ordered now: six foot-longs—I was there naked for it, too, you know; wasn't that something?—six foot longs, baked tofu, avo,-sprout, tomato, red onion, olives on sprouted rye, extra Veganaise and nutritional yeast on two, three with double tofu; plus six large carrot-ginger-garlic juices, am I right?"

"Bring them on!" Richard roared, reminding me of a lion during feeding hour at the zoo.

"I wanted to stay naked for work, too," Jay said after the bill was settled, "but Jude insisted I had to dress. Struck me as unfair, it did. He joked that he'd have to change his deli's name to 'Jude's Nude Food,' otherwise. Well, *Bon appetit!*"

❋

A feature piece in next day's *Chronicle* read:

They dreamed they walked across town in their birth-day suits...but it was no dream...or *was* it? Yesterday a sea of Bay-to-Breakers participants and joiners-in blithely ran and strolled across town nude or nearly so—turning the centuries-old, unspoken social dictate

"Thou Shalt Wear Clothes" flat on its ears.

It's become popular in recent years for a handful of participants to do the race naked, "demonstrating against the absurd U.S. phobia over the naked self," as one organizer put it. At some point, the event transformed from a festive race-and-stroll with a sprinkling of naked people to a body-liberation phenomenon of epic proportions. Perhaps never before in recorded history has there ever been such an en masse breaking free of clothes.

Though the mind-boggling import of the day hasn't sunk in yet, yesterday an estimated 12,000 people— altogether in the altogether—effectively transformed San Francisco into a real Naked City

Talk about The City That Knows How.

And talk people did. Among the flood of letters and emails to the editor printed the next day:

"It's an elusive feeling to describe, strolling across town au naturel. It's easily one of the most exhilarating experiences I've ever had. I heartily recommend it to everyone."

"What I want to know: How come we only do this once a year?"

Until yesterday (a woman wrote) the notion of going naked in public—in the bustling city, no less—I would have deemed sheer lunacy. And yet some sweet intoxication filled the air...as if the muses of old had poured forth from their grand amphorae a magical enchantment to open our hearts and minds to re-discovering the simple joy of enjoying the day free of covering and sharing that delight with others. Eventually I felt so free I joked to friends I wasn't *ever* putting my clothes back on!

An old college sweetheart I hadn't seen in ages was apparently there, for she—sharing my penchant for silly rhyme—signed the following: "We threaded along, among the throng, nude or in thong or bright sarong, singing a song, feeling no wrong."

And finally, this one, which perhaps best captured the import of the day:

...together, we made it feel it was not only okay to be free of clothes—it was natural, the way it should be. We each decided what clothes, if any, we would wear... We felt we were part of history; as if we'd stormed the Bastille; like we'd dumped overtaxed tea into Boston Harbor—we sure dumped our unwanted clothes, anyhow. Only in San Francisco!

TWENTY-TWO

What spirit is so empty and blind, that it cannot recognize
the fact that the foot is more noble than the shoe,
and skin more beautiful than
the garment with which it is clothed?
—**Michelangelo**

ARE YOU AWAKE, ZET?"

I sighed in my half-sleep.

"Zet." My body was nudged gently. "Hey, you."

I wanted to linger in the sweet afterglow of dreamland. The fog lifted slowly. Nuela was snuggled beside me in her cabin bed. I felt enveloped in her soft warmth and the faint scent of patchouli oil, awakening from one pleasant dream to another.

"Mornin', sweetie." We snuggled. Then: "I just had one of the wildest dreams of my life."

"Tell me about it while I make tea," she said, planting a kiss on me and starting to get up, no doubt thinking I wasn't up to anything after last nite.

"Not so fast, you," I said, grabbing her before she could make good her escape. She giggled, pleasantly surprised. To a dream weaver like me, there was something special about making love first thing in the morning, floating along together on right brain after pleasant sleep voyages. The left brain hadn't yet kicked in imperiously with the Concerns of the Day. It was her favorite time too—one of them, anyway.

Nuela juiced a half lemon on the glass reamer and added it to her liter carafe of boiled spring water. This she brought over to the little table by one of her open south windows. The sun was pouring in over her window box crowded with pungent herbs and splashes of flowers. A white nubby cotton cloth of royal-blue fleur-de-lis relief pattern covered the table. Two ceramic mugs, an eye-dropper bottle of stevia sweetener and stir spoon stood at the ready. Completing the setting: picked wildflowers—periwinkle blue, soft red and warm yellow—smiled at us from a mottled ceramic vase her potter friend Lily crafted.

"So. The naked city stroller had nice dreams, huh?" she inquired. I'd already told her all about the race last nite after getting back. I hadn't lingered on the way home; it was great being with my old friends, but I'd missed Nuela like I knew I would.

"In a nutshell, I dreamed—are you ready?—I dreamed there was a quantum leap in body acceptance: The whole bloomin' world was going nudist!"

She burst out laughing. She looked at me and I could tell she was imagining it. "Now *that's* what I call an idea for a book," she said. "Tell me about it. The whole world, you say? Todo el mundo?"

"Si, Senorita." I gave her the dream's highlites, as best as I remembered them. (I wish someone would invent a dream recorder, so we could play dreams back later and share them with others.) Nuela's face grew thoughtful as I finished. "Let's write those down, before you forget them. You know what? I think we really could use this as a theme for a novel. Don't you? 'World goes body-friendly.' We could write it together. Whadaya say? I think it'd be a blast."

"Really? Write a book together?" I could be slow on the uptake. It was a possibility I'd never considered (tho apparently she had). I'd shown her some of my earlier writings and she'd encouraged me to keep at it, thinking I showed promise. The theme was surely a logical one to tackle for two people feeling like we did on the subject. Her enthusiasm was contagious; I found the prospect of collaborating intriguing. "All right, you're on; let's do it. I can see it now: *Brave Nude World.*"

"Or… How about *Nude Awakening?*"

"Oh, yes. So be it. *Nude Awakening* it is. We've got the title. Now all we need is the book."

We plunged to work right after breakfast—or breakslow, as I liked to call it, never wanting to rush thru the first meal of the day if I could avoid it. We tossed ideas back and forth and came up with a format that grabbed us both.

We'd spin a tale in which the City race sparked a quantum leap in freebody consciousness around the world, like in my dream. There'd be serious resistance to the cause, naturally. We'd weave into the plot the pros and cons of public nudity on what had been a perma-dressed planet, brought out thru our main characters, Jake and Iris.

We were psyched. We must have devoted a solid half year at it in our spare time, working "down in the salt mines," as I liked to call the writing process, when you can forget to eat and sleep; we played off each other's imaginations, as we fleshed out the story line, researched, hammered out preliminary drafts.

Then our project got derailed by the death of her middle sister, Nancy, from a car-accident. Nuela had felt especially close to her and was gone three weeks to Florida for the memorial and to be with family. Our happy creative bubble burst, the uncompleted manuscript got unceremoniously stashed in a drawer, put off for a

343

later time that never came. Soon it was forgotten.

After starting this memoir, I remembered it. I rooted thru my ephemera collection of writings, hoping against hope I'd managed to save it when I fled north. I feared it had been left behind, but finally I found it. Saved: the creative souvenir of our union, a precious, if uncompleted, hundred-page novella of our joint foray into story-writing.

I'd forgotten how much we'd put into it. Parts were still skeletal, plot summary yet to be filled out with scenes and characters and dialog, but some of it was pretty good, I thought.

I want to share three extended excerpts from the manuscript here and in the next few chapters, just as we wrote it, sort of story within a story. I think it might help the reader better understand how life was and what we fantasized about—or bring back memories for fellow centurians. (But if an extended fantasy diversion isn't your cup of tea, you can skip ahead to Chapter 25; I promise my feelings won't be hurt.)

[Notes: As a departure point, we first fictionalized my actual naked stroll across town, handing my experiences to Jake. The following sequential excerpts come right after the Letters to the Editor. For dramatic purposes, we upped the number of people participating naked from 12,000 to 50,000. Also, I fictionalized some of my relatives in it and modernized archaic spellings.]

☀

Nude Awakening
by Nuela Gottlieb & Zet Quimby

[First Excerpt]

["...we sure dumped unwanted clothes, anyhow. Only in San Francisco!" the letter to the editor had concluded.]

But it *wasn't* only in San Francisco.

Amazing to relate, the Hundredth Monkey effect took place.

You may remember the story (for a more apt analogy, foods are substituted): Island monkeys once struggled to learn how to peel bananas that grew there so they could enjoy the fruit inside without having to eat the peel as well. Frustration. The more adept and determined finally began figuring it out and teaching others, who taught yet others. The instant the hundredth monkey learned how to peel the banana and better enjoy the fruit, the knowledge was *instantaneously* transmitted to every monkey on the island. Even more phenomenal, this new knowledge simultaneously jumped *over* the sea; monkeys on other islands suddenly knew how to peel bananas too.

Similarly, human monkeys had been wrestling to figure out how to peel away their own banana skins—clothes—and feast on the weather without it being an issue.

Was it possible to remove their "second skin" without suffering discomfort by weird reactions from others beyond a once-a year lark? Over time, many emboldened spirits tried. First one succeeded a while, then another, then small groups, here and in other countries, all determined not to have their personal freedom cramped by an oppressive dress habit, all making peaceful stands for the right to be naked.

That day in San Francisco the hundredth monkey—in this case, maybe it was the 50,000[th] human monkey—peeled away their outer skin. By suddenly activating the spiritual circuit in the Over-

Soul thru which everything is interconnected, the more attuned freebody enthusiasts the world over psychically intuited the break-thru, and, weather providing, peeled away their clothes the first chance they got. Lack of public acceptance, more than lack of personal body acceptance, had been the main thing holding countless people back, and that dam was bursting.

As it happened, much of the nation had also been experiencing dreamy spring weather that day. Serious body freedom advocates in places as disparate as Tucumcari, New Mexico; Harrisburg, Pennsylvania; and Kealakekua, Hawaii, all felt the same spontaneous urge, out of the blue, in synchronicity with people at the epicenter. They gave themselves permission to shuck their clothes wherever there was a modicum of friendly earth or splash of water—sometimes wherever.

It was as if humanity had been playing a game of hide-and-seek [as little Zak intuited a half-century later]. There was the signal in that game that it was safe to come out and reveal yourself; in effect, 50,000 naked people in San Francisco that day had just shouted it, in deafening chorus, to the entire planet: "Olli, olli, Oxen-free-eee!"

A body-liberation wave washed over North America—and the rest of the planet.

Places that hadn't seen so much as a streaker in decades, if ever, suddenly had people unaccountably sunning, picnicking, and playing in the water—nude or topfree or bottomfree—peaceably, casually, delightedly, as if it was the natural order of things.

"I donno, George. They just all of a sudden quit wearing clothes. It's like the town's gone nudist or something. Should we be concerned? George? What are you doing, George? Don't you dare go out that way! Oh, all right. Wait for me. Honestly!"

The more seasonal and private nudists in other, far-flung locales received word of events later in awe, and fitfully followed un-suit, each according to their own state of freebody awareness and resolve to join in the grand cultural shift taking place. We felt strength in numbers, and the numbers were astounding.

Among them was Jake's cousin Rudolph, who surprised Jake by joining in: "I confess it now," he wrote him a year later, from his home in Savannah,

> I used to love getting naked in the woods, sometimes my backyard at nite. About four months after the San Francisco happening I made the leap, like a few others around me had: I took my dog for a walk in the buff, right in broad daylight. It was incredible. I found myself going from 'Omigod, I'm actually naked in public!' to 'hey...*cool*. But you knew that all along, didn't you, Gofer? Yeah, you did.' I really don't know why I felt so self-conscious before.

People who hadn't even been private nudists now began experimenting. They took baby steps at first, like sleeping nude in warmer weather, which allowed them to feel more relaxed with their bare bodies under the bedding, while at the same time still feeling protectively covered. After getting used to this, individuals might stay bare on getting up, rather than automatically reaching for a robe. Beginning to feel at ease unclad, a person would do their ablutions, fix their morning coffee or tea, maybe take it out on the back deck to more fully enjoy the gentle morning sun. Once acclimating to this breakthru, they might take it to the next level and venture nude to the mailbox, perchance greeting a neighbor or passersby with a cheery "Isn't it a *great* day?"

Others expanded their comfort zone more gradually. Maybe first they'd wear oversized tops or brief bottoms around the house, doing everyday things—vacuuming, chatting on the phone, feeding their pet mongoose—and eventually expanded their unclad comfort zone by venturing outdoors in their back yard, maybe do nude yoga or tai chi, garden, clip their nails, have a primal scream.

One popular exercise, long advocated by nude proponents, was to undress and stand or sit in front of a floor-length mirror each day, consciously and non-judgmentally viewing one's body in its entirety, until a person could accept the sight of himself without inwardly flinching. It had helped Jake at one point in his growth: He went from feeling shocked at seeing his naked self, to feeling okay, to thinking *you handsome devil; now, if you just worked on your pecs and glutes a little...*

People living in body-friendly regions at some point took the leap, like Rudolph had, daring to take a clothesfree stroll in town. Some wore footwear, others went barefoot. As Jake's brother Myron—then going by Zarathustra after getting into a classical kick—penned:

> We'd walk 'round the block and down to the dock; by the flock we'd grock—not wearing a sock or Rebok (or smock or frock, or any silly schlock)—weathering the shock of any mock or hock from cocky jock." Thus Zarathustra sprach. [Okay, this we might've deleted.]

As the paradigm shift in body attitude took deeper hold in society, many surprised themselves by becoming enthusiastic freebodies in record time. One instant devotee, a gourmet chef, wrote: "I liken the extravagance of feeling to savoring a ten-course feast after having endured an interminable diet of bread and water." Another report, from a house architect: "One day I woke up and realized how much sunshine brightened my mood when I experienced it nude, so I started designing homes that maximized solar exposure for easier clothesfree living. I always encourage clients to include a solarium if they possibly can, as there's nothing like it in winter." And from a home realtor:

I grew up feeling mostly disconnected from my body. Once I allowed myself to be naked more, I experienced an integration of body, mind and spirit I'd rarely, if ever, felt, outside the boudoir or massage studio. I loved being freebody, but had to limit it to inside, shades drawn, as I had no backyard and lived in one helluva squirrely-minded berg. Finally I couldn't take it any more and moved to a warmer, body-friendlier town. Location really *is* everything.

Many said everyday nudity was almost as much fun as sex, for the sheer physical pleasure and profound sense of enhanced well-being it offered. Some went so far as to say it was *more* fun than *bad* sex at least (but then, too, so was flying a kite or a good bowel movement). Tons of feel-good endorphins surged thru people's bodies as they discovered the simple pleasure of feeling at ease in their exposed skins beyond the bedroom, bathroom and locker room for the first time since toddlers.

One retired high school history teacher shared her epiphany after she'd been going clothesfree a while. She recounted how

> ...I suddenly felt I'd been enslaved by clothes my whole life and hadn't even known it; like chains always on me, binding me to a subtly weird servitude. When my neighbors and I recently got together for a clothing-optional summer potluck and got to talking, we realized many of us had experienced the same revelation: a heavy burden had been lifted from us and *we were literally enlightened.* One of us compared it to the sudden ability to move about freely while talking on a cordless phone after having had movement restricted your whole life by a short tangled cord.

It felt too weird for others, tho, trying to break the time-forged compulsive-dress shackles and fine-tune their body image. Not even in the nicest weather and relaxed places. Society's internalized judgments and individuals' ingrained force of habit put up a fight and won; their Inner Nudist was beyond reach.

Like Jake's rich Aunt Velma. As Jake related to Iris, "My aunt told me in no uncertain terms that if I didn't stop sending her free-body literature she was cutting me out of her will. I probably should've known better, but I thought the old bird might come around, judging by all the sensuous Fragonard and Boucher painting repros on her wall. Go figure."

For others, it was more a matter of not being sensitive to their bodies. Everyone was different. Whereas some found wearing needless clothes burdensome, others seemed divinely happy in their clothes, enjoying the hand-in-glove fit between their bodies and apparel. They derived no extra comfort going without them—just the opposite, in fact. They kept to the time-honored habit of always dressing, regardless of everything, never so much as walking thru their empty, curtained house naked after a shower even. And then there were those—possibly the majority—that were simply used to wearing clothes and never gave the custom a second thought.

Not uptight about nudity per se but opting not to indulge in it themselves, this number formed the nude-tolerant ranks that made it easier for others to enjoy the new personal freedom.

A curious thing: For the countless people who did adapt and embrace a freebody awareness and lifestyle, going nude quickly became habit-forming; *what felt weird was putting clothes back on*. People were out-and-out delighted how liberated they felt.

Jake's Southern California cousin, Bev, for instance, emailed him: "*Wow!* I had no idea. Apologies, Jake. Ya know, I always thought you weird for wanting to go naked and all. My husband talked me into giving it a try at a resort last Memorial Day weekend, and damn if it doesn't add a new dimension to life. (Don't get me wrong, Cuz: I *still* think you're weird—just not about that.)"

✹

The sporadic nudifying of America and far reaches of the planet spread like a cloudburst across a parched flood plain before thunder-struck authorities could fathom what happened. Many of them, happily resigned to compulsory dress, thank you, may as well have been in some parallel universe for all their understanding of what was unfolding. Having forgotten they were human monkeys, the phenomenon had by-passed them completely; they were clueless. Their initial bafflement—*"This can't really be happening, can it? All right, that's not funny, Bill; put your pants back on"*—caused a critical time delay in responding, letting the new personal liberty to take root that much deeper before the loyal clothed opposition responded in force.

Before long, the open-minded among of the population no longer bought into the thinking wanting to be publicly/socially naked was aberrant, kinky or socially irresponsible. Realizing with a start their freedom to simply *be* had been systematically suppressed for ages—to the point people didn't even *realize* it— people got naked with a vengeance. Some removed their clothes with calm mindfulness, some with wild abandon, some with pure defiance—tearing them off and ritually burning them—but all with a newborn conviction they were within rights as human monkeys to enjoy the day without custom-mandated costumes if they so chose.

People felt, with a mysterious certainty, that the clothes-minded world was at last unraveling.

The transforming energy afoot was aided and abetted by both the freedom-loving press and the more oppressive media, whose negative spins and dismissive downplaying ("...clearly a concerted effort by exhibitionistic malcontents to undermine the way of life of decent, hard-working Americans everywhere") were so sad one almost felt sorry for them.

The more progressive television networks scrambled to boost their ratings in a new competitive war to integrate casual nudity into their shows—as had been accepted for years in Brazil, Germany, the United Kingdom, Japan and Australia. Such faire was shown fitfully at first, as far-right forces threatened sponsor boycotts if the networks didn't start kowtowing to good old-fashioned body shame again. Soon, tho, the number of viewing consumers who *did* appreciate candid, tasteful freebody scenes now and then became so great, TV execs told the self-appointed morality police where to get off. In one later-published response to a protesting viewer's letter, a network executive had written back:

Dear Mr. Kadiddle,

Regarding your expressed displeasure in our broadcasting occasional tasteful nudity, claiming even private recreational nudity is '…an abomination, something that would never happen in Mr. Rogers' neighborhood,' you should know: Mr. Rogers in real life began every morning with a brisk nude swim in his lap pool. *Now* will you be my friend?

TWENTY-THREE

How do you know what you know until you've written it?
Writing is knowing. What did Kafka know? The insurance business?
—**E. L. Doctorow**

Nude Awakening
by Nuela Gottlieb and Zet Quimby

[Second Excerpt]

PEOPLE WANTED TO believe they had finally and forever thrown off the yoke of textile tyranny—that they'd triumphantly established body freedom rights for the oppressively over-wrapped masses everywhere, yearning to breathe free.

But nothing comes easy. Lamentably, the Bastille hadn't fallen. It had weakened, but stood defiant yet, a wounded lion (nattily dressed in sharkskin), continuing to visit withering stares and threats of dire penalties on public nudity, wherever it lurked.

The order of wise and benevolent body-phobic powers dedicated to legislating people's lives had gone thru shock, denial, fury and resolve in rapid succession. As they sometimes displayed a

353

talent for being obtuse, it was no surprise they hadn't seen it coming. Organized nudism had always struck them as the provincial domain of an aging population with dwindling memberships. They were lulled into thinking it ludicrous a freebody culture could ever threaten to go mainstream, that nudism would forever remain the unthreatening fringe pastime of a few harmless kooks, content to play nekkid volleyball in their gated grounds and bronze in the sun on certain remote beaches, most a pain to reach anyhow.

Meanwhile, the textile industry—like a trillion silk worms stuck on spin cycle—continued cranking out their daily tonnage of garments to cover our shame and line share-holders' generous-cut pockets.

Too late, they realized new generations had been quietly integrating increased body freedom into their lives, becoming casual freebodies, cultivating positive body attitudes, informally stretching the envelope further each year. Most hadn't bothered to join any organizations touting it, such outfits perceived as too fuddy-duddy or too nudity-focused, or both. But freebody seeds had been germinating underground and had now sprouted into the light of day.

Regrouping, textiled leaders knew they had to do something — *fast*—to scare the pants back on people. If not, their whole power game might come undone, their enforced dress code exposed as an indecent sham. The American Powers That Were burned the midnite oil trying to figure some way to call on the Patriot Act, with its enhanced powers to regulate our lives. If they couldn't dream up a case linking being naked to a national security threat (*"'Naked Arab terrorists trying to demoralize us'...no, I don't suppose they'd buy that..."*) then, by God, they'd go another route. They hastily cobbled together a federal anti-nudity policy.

Serendipitously, the new law of the land was so rife with legal loopholes you could drive a fleet of Segues thru them. In some regions the law had so little support from otherwise law-abiding

citizens, it would long prove ineffectual.
The law was promptly nicknamed The Unbareable Act.

☀

Public nudity became not unlike Prohibition of the 1920s: Then, altho drinking alcoholic beverages was illegal, it didn't stop millions from blithely ignoring the fact and drinking in merry abandon, feeling a shared spirit of delicious conspiracy all the while. They'd concluded making alcohol illegal just because some couldn't handle their liquor was unfair to the rest, who could; similarly, freebodies felt that just because some couldn't handle nudity shouldn't mean the rest had to stay uncomfortable to accommodate their denial.

Even as the Feds had earlier focused on busting liquor manufacturers, distributors and floating speak-easies, they now focused on easiest targets: obvious exhibitionists, voyeurs, and the more disruptive, in-yur-face activists who wore their nudity like a military uniform. The anger of the last could turn off less-confrontational body freedom proponents. Most people simply wanted the freedom to be themselves, covered or uncovered, not force anything on anybody. Even so, some admired their willingness to go to the mat in pushing for universal freebody rights.

For awhile chaos ruled supreme. Peoples' minds scrambled to reconfigure age-old attitudes towards nudity, working to dissociate the automatic linkage to sex. A flurry of sick-day calls went in as employees took time out to enjoy what was seen as a temporary holiday from clothes. People thought it wouldn't last, that it was some temporary aberration—like a legendary public pay phone in Tonasket, Washington that in the 80s had suddenly allowed free long-distance calls: everyone who knew about it practically lived in the booth, leisurely talking for hours to friends and family around the world, before the glitch was caught. Public nudity was the same, people thought; a matter of time before it ended. Beaches got so packed with people wanting to try out nudism that overnite presses scrambled to publish guidebooks listing off-the-beaten-path body-friendly spots.

More than a few traffic accidents happened at first, as various people lost control of the wheel on seeing nude and semi-nude people casually strolling down the street. But since this initially surreal sight was far more likely to occur in tolerant regions—in which drivers themselves might be nude—it wasn't as bad as one might have thought.

Humans can be amazingly adaptable to changing conditions, even if they involve overhauling age-old, hardwired thought patterns. In this case it took longer, but more-aware people adjusted faster, no doubt due in part to the increasing vibratory frequency of the planet then being reported by credible geo-scientists. Not resisted, this increase, while requiring stretching one's accustomed comfort zone to keep a handle on things, was conducive to speeding personal growth and fostering deeper heart centeredness. That in the process people at times felt like madly spinning 78-rpm records or caffeinated New Yorkers at rush hour struck slower-paced people like Jake as lamentable. But he figured it behooved an awakening people to ride the global change as best they could in order to not be thrown off the merry-go-round of global consciousness emerging.

Those who had truly gotten themselves together, who appeared to have cracked life's secret code, refused to be caught up in such breakneck currents; they maintained a constant 33 1/3 pace in their lives. Such holy-stoned people always radiated a powerful and peaceful aura, even in the midst of a rushed city: It was as if they were strolling along a mountain trail on the first day of spring, leisurely enjoying the varied splendors of nature. Supernatural beings, they kept intact a mighty vision of a positive future and helped anchor the world thru stormy times to come.

✻

State and county policies were in flux; enforcement varied from region to region, despite the ostensibly all-powerful federal stance. Some states, long down on nudity, showed a Barney Fife eagerness to comply with new policies, while others, with more open-minded traditions, told the Feds where to get off.

So it was that in places not so enamored with Federal meddling discreet freebodies were almost invariably left alone, and in more conservative regions, marching lock-step with Washington, even the most low-key and considerate could be treated roughshod—put thru the wringer and hung out to dry.

As for the brash...Jake's Cousin Bo finally picked the wrong town to parachute into and he spent a week meditating inside a jail cell in Dime-a-Dance, Texas. "I'll never forget the look on their faces when townspeople saw me coming out of the sky," Bo said. "The tie-dye chute alone fried their synapses, but when they realized I was naked too, their jaws dropped to the sidewalk. They served some tasty cornbread in that jail; I asked for the recipe, but they wouldn't give it to me."

Until federal law could be enforced, authorities had a thorny legal problem on their hands. They'd always depended on age-old custom to discourage people from going nude instead of having *specific* anti-nudity statutes on the books. Now legions of lawyers and legal aids unearthed every obscure law and ordinance they could find and bent current ones into legal pretzels in their efforts to stem the naked tide: "Public disturbance," "indecent exposure," and "lewd conduct" statutes were zealously invoked like the fate of the universe was at stake. To enforce them they ignored making any distinction between the new wholesome nudity and the earlier salacious sort. Because prurient charges wouldn't stick, droves of cases were dismissed.

357

Even so, in the first year thousands, most caught up in notorious surprise government sweeps, ended up getting arrested—"Lose your Clothes, Go to Jail" was the message brought to the listener as a free public service by the Ad Council—and hauled off to the nearest station. (Jake and many of his friends got to know how it felt to be caged like an animal.) These were in contrast to people acting irresponsibly: a naked drunk person was arrested for drunk-in-public, not naked-in-public. But for every ten arrested for the high crime of wanting to catch some rays unwrapped, a hundred more came forward to rally for their release—nude, of course. Jails couldn't hold them all; something had to give.

Authorities shrank the offense to a fine.

Nude support came from a few elected officials, some of whom were freebody enthusiasts themselves and sympathized with the movement. Any politician risked vote trades in Congress, even re-election, for voicing her pro-body-freedom stance. One day a Vermont representative walked into session barenaked, protesting his colleagues' latest proposed repressive bills; he was hooted into sudden oblivion.

Tho such elected supporters lacked the numbers to do much, they served to help legitimize the cause by reflecting the credibility gap that had emboldened multitudes of citizens to disregard anti-freebody ordinances. The situation was much like the droves of vehicle drivers used to ignoring highways' posted speed limits: Even tho they faced a high fine if caught, people then couldn't drive *fast* enuf. Now it seemed they couldn't get *naked* enuf.

Fitfully, in some crazy-quilt way, going bare gained a de facto legitimacy in more open-minded regions. The nude-friendly helped bolsters efforts. While opting to keep under wraps, they defended the right of others *not* to, so long as their behavior remained otherwise socially responsible.

Jake's rhyme-crazed friend Zero wrote a loopy poem in his

journal, trying to capture the mood of light-hearted rebellion:

We chose no clothes: no pose or shows in rows of bows or SuppHose—none of those; from toes to nose, they froze our flows. One grows and flows and glows out of clothes. We arose from repose, with dozy-does, to expose the woes of our uptight foes and their mandated clothes. With this doggerel prose—as awkward as clothes—I hereby disclose that we chose no clothes.

Millions of people "got away with it"—as long as they weren't in the wrong place at the wrong time, kept their wits about them for quick cover-up when need be, and observed commonsense bounds of liberalized propriety. Unclad people in more freethinking regions were almost guaranteed hassle-free nude recreation at beaches, rivers, lakes and public parks, both in town and country.

Many larger towns, tho, with hectic environments, concrete surfaces, and strait-laced politics, could be un-conducive to feeling comfortable in *clothed*, let alone naked. Perforce, in such regions most out-of-doors social nudity still occurred in the friendly arms of nature and on private property.

Also, people in many smaller towns, often more set in their ways, were not as inclined to suddenly let it all hang out. A town near Jake was a case in point: the place catered to an upscale tourist trade, so authorities were quick to discourage any nudifying of Main Street. While skinnydipping was a venerable institution for many nature-loving locals and visitors alike at nearby lakes and streams, in town only the quieter, off-the-beaten-path neighborhoods felt safe for shucking clothes as people went about their days.

"I drive thru that berg naked now and then just to try evening things out," Jake told Iris. He spoke with an offhanded casualness that belied his dedication to the freebody cause. Only last month he'd helped found the Transparent Planet Society as an offshoot of NAKAD, or the National Association for Kicking Apparel

Dependency.

In some larger cities, tho—those with good city-planning, free-thinking traditions and lots of nice weather—nudity became *fashionable*. People got into going naked or in fanciful states of dishabille in the course of their everyday lives. Elaborate body paint became the new status symbol for some—painted by exclusive body artists—to replace showing off expensive clothes. (Would people never learn?) Others, with money to burn and body shame to lose, and who wanted to keep up with the naked Jones's, fast-tracked at intensive workshops guaranteeing "Prude-to-Nude in One Week—or a new outfit on us." Some, wanting to overcome their clothing obsession, attended support groups for recovering clothes addicts: *"Hi. I'm Bob, and I'm a clothing addict." "Hi, Bob."* Others, with bad diets and over-sedentary lifestyles, were inspired to clean up their act and upgrade their hygiene, taking pride in getting fit so they could join the fashionably nekkid.

Sometimes entire neighborhoods became effectively clothing-optional zones. On especially nude-worthy days one might rise, take a stroll, have a vegan breakfast at the New Age Café, splash in the park creek, sun a while, and later join a block party, all without a stitch on. ["Big wow, we can do that any time," I can hear readers saying. But remember, the thought of doing such things then was...well, *unthinkable*.] Some freebodies carried along light cover-ups in case the sun became either too intense or scarce, or in the unlikely event of a surprise Fed sweep.

A person learned to savor the freedom of answering the front door unclad, as there was a good chance the visitor was nude as well and, if not, it didn't matter—unless it was their Aunt Gertrude from Omaha paying a surprise visit, or a zealous door-to-door crusader from the Clothes for Decency League.

Inevitably, people began waging friendly contests to see who could stay nakedest the longest. One long hot summer a determined couple was close to breaking a local record of two months, one week, when their luck ran out—their minivan broke down on the road passing thru a backwater town boasting the sign:

NO CLOTHES
NO SERVICE

One among the endless parade of reality TV shows predictably tried exploiting the freebody trend. Perhaps the nuttiest in a *long* line of contenders was *Naked Island*, which pitted opposing team players—picked for their obvious love of apparel, often models and other clotheshorses—going cold turkey on a tropical island. Bare but for straw hats, sunglasses, and *lots* of maximum sunblock, players scrambled thru inane challenges to earn clothes. In a sort of reverse strip poker, the first team to earn complete outfits got to go on to the next round of competition. Iris was marginally amused watching them conflict between wanting the prize, wanting to cover, and—as producers realized too late—wanting to stay uncovered. The show cancelled after four episodes because too many had "nuded out," suddenly breaking their clothing addiction and *wanting* to stay naked, prize money or no.

☀

A surprising number of people in colder climates took to going clothesfree more often. Birds of a feather—in places like Boulder, Colorado; Bennington, Vermont; and Madison, Wisconsin— enjoyed nude skiing, hiking and swimming. Even people in coldest Alaska and Minnesota luxuriated in going naked more often inside their super-insulated homes. It appeared the colder the climate, the more popular sauna get-togethers. People ran out into freezing weather, bodies steaming, and rolled naked in the snow or cold-plunged in nearby water, emboldened by each other (*"C'mon, I dare you!" "I will if you will." "You're on!"*) and the hot room awaiting them after.

Skeptics in warmer climates didn't believe such reports. They shivered at the thought of being naked in anything less than 72°F. [26°C.] weather, determined by scientists as the minimum temperature for inactive nude comfort. But a body can acclimate to even the coldest clime. Living an active outdoors life kept the circulation pumping, and finishing baths and showers with cold rinses kept the skin cells closed for lower-temperature tolerance. Some believed it was all in the mind anyhow—that people psyched themselves into thinking it was too cold not to wear clothes, and so it was.

The radiant sun's power to warm amazed Jake. In his region, which got chilly in winter, he learned to stretch clothesfree time: He tacked up a thick reflective space blanket along the wall of his south-facing sundeck and onto the angled half-sheets of plywood propped on either side of where he'd sit. So long as a full sun shone and no wind blew, it didn't matter if the thermometer read below freezing; he still baked like a potato.

Jake upgraded his scene when a solar-applications company came out with the first-generation model of a portable mini-solarium kit. After "easy assembly," requiring half a day and supreme patience to keep from loosing it, the kit became a wheel-able, raised-bed, glass-enclosed, insulated space for one or two persons, to enjoy soaking in the rays while reading a novel while sipping a lemonade, or making love. It could be below freezing out, a foot of snow on the ground, but with the pregnant sun giving birth thru the glass, a body could feel whisked to a tropical island beach.

Acquaintances of his, without handy sundeck or portable solarium, came up with yet another way to soak up precious wintertime sun. They employed moveable greenhouses many owned yet rarely thought to employ as such: *their vehicles.* Ideally they had a van, minivan or such, with lots of glass and plenty of room for getting comfy in, but any enclosed, insulated vehicle with enuf glass would do. They parked their fossil-fuel beasts in a sunny level spot (private property or nude-friendly public place), let the sun get it toasty, got naked and—*voila!*—instant freebody oasis. Such solar enclosures came complete with sound systems, opening windows for moderating heat and air flow, and 12-volt outlets for electronic gadgets.

One freebody home-biz operator, Buz Dinklestrum, got completely set up in his extra window van with wireless computer and cell phone and worked in the buff every sunny workday all thru winter (He drove enuf between such use to keep the battery from going dead.) "All that sweet sunshine kept my energy up better than coffee ever could," he said. "And my heating bill down."

The May 2012 issue of *Reader's Digest* published scientific evidence of the health benefits of judicious amounts of sunshine, helping popularize and legitimize nude sunbathing. The article revealed how the sun's Far-infrared energy absorbed a few centimeters below the skin surface, helping increase circulation and oxygen supply to damaged tissue. People realized then why sunshine felt so good; it penetrated *inside* the body. The discovery came as no surprise to true believers who always felt better for having nothing between them and old Sol.

Another article, in *Time*, announced new findings suggesting a link between skin cancer and faulty diet. Scientists speculated the true culprit was perhaps not too much sun, but dead food, both animal and vegetable. Void of life-supporting enzymes, such faire over time debilitated the body's functioning to the point it couldn't assimilate solar rays efficiently. Result: skin cancer. A stack of studies suggested that when its owner fed it right with live plant foods, the body *thrived* on sunshine. Scientists, hedging their bets, still cautioned on the wisdom of limiting sunbathing to the gentle rays of morning and late afternoon, as depletion of the protective ozone layer could make the sun's intense mid-day rays draining and possibly hazardous to health, regardless of diet.

Soon after these articles and a flurry of others came out, people who once thought nudism distasteful or just plain weird started practicing it like the latest fad. They'd drink in the sunshine— maybe an organic carrot juice too—wherever they could, back yard or city park. "*Doctor's orders,*" they'd say, smiling like they'd just rediscovered the wheel.

Many discovered a bonus to more freebody time: unexpected emotional and mental boosts. While traveling—two months after total remission of his prostate cancer soon after switching his diet—Jake stumbled on a revealing personal journal a friend shared, describing one such transformation. The woman writer had apparently been a strict body-phobe, not even liking her former husband to see her naked, even tho "...my friends were always assuring me I had a nice figure." It turned out both her best and worst early childhood memories were fused together by a single life-altering incident: she was toddling around naked in the yard on a nice afternoon, doting mom by her side, treasuring the magic of the sun and caresses of the warm breezes one moment; the next, an uptight neighbor was growling something mean to her mom and she suddenly felt her clothes being yanked onto her "like a trussed-up calf." She remembered futilely trying to pull them off again while railing in protest to her equally distraught mom.

She was a latent freebody about to reclaim her freedom:

> Not long after the San Francisco happening, I was in the park, wistfully watching a toddler running around naked, giggling and laughing at the playful attentions lavished by the mom, herself topfree. Suddenly it triggered a flood of memories. I had an epiphany. I rushed home, peeled off my clothes, went into my back yard

and started dancing my ass off to my favorite music like I'd never danced before—completely blissing out. I'd regained a long-lost part of myself."

There were myriad reasons why people were attracted to the notion of foregoing clothes beyond bed and bath, reasons formed by varied life experiences, unique physiologies, sensitivities to various climates, and formative-year environments. Having had a lifetime of experience with nudity, *everyone* was a natural-born expert on the matter, each with pronounced feelings and opinions.

Some felt more self-accepting and peaceful naked. Some felt a profound sense of simplicity and integration. Some felt more creatively juiced and lucid-thinking—Victor Hugo gave his clothes to his servants with orders not to return them until his day's writing was done. The reason one woman gave for going bare: the greater sense of wholeness it allowed her for being able to see and feel, to *sense* her full body. With clothes hiding much of her, she said she felt part of her was missing, felt cut off from herself. "If I can see and feel myself," she explained to Iris—taking an informal survey for an article idea she had—"I'm all there. Otherwise it's like in that old Ronald Reagan movie, when the guy who's just lost a leg cries, 'Where's the *rest* of me?'"

Some felt more real, more sensual, more childlike, more alive... Some felt all of the above and more. While there were as many complex blends of feelings and attitudes about nudity as there were people on the planet, *virtually everyone said it made them feel better*.

The more freebody people became, the more they grew and tuned into deeper, unexplored regions of themselves, integrated body, mind and spirit, discovered what made them tick.

✺

Then there were the crudists, people who acted out their body repressions nude wherever clothed people were, mocking them like monkeys in a zoo, baring their buttocks, proffering "whadayagotahide, huh?" taunts, and otherwise delighting in making clothes-wearers uncomfortable.

Such crudists, along with the over-the-top public-sex proponents, who tried to legitimize their behavior under the guise of freedom of expression, caused endless grief to mutually-accommodating freebody advocates. Even tho it was a misguided minority confusing liberty with license, repressive media made tons of hay from every such incident, trying to prop up their weakening reality framework. They painted the entire freebody movement with the same broad stroke: buncha deviant exhibitionists; sex-crazed sensualists; what do you expect out of San Francisco; no decent citizen; blah, blah...

Media voices changed their spin as it became apparent many otherwise upright, taxpaying citizens were ardent freebody advocates. Now they shed crocodile tears, saying that it was truly regrettable a few spoiled it for the many and everyone had to suffer for it, blah, blah...so keep your shirt on—and your pants too. And, hey, your shoes too, while you're at it...damn hippies. mumble, grumble...

On what was dubbed *the Nude-Lewd Scale,* people on one end held outlooks so twisted they invariably equated public nudity with sex orgies, projecting this attitude onto everybody out just hoping to soak up some rays and maybe socialize a bit without being needlessly packaged. At the other end were those with holistic views of their earthly temples; they accepted the naked self as one's unique and beautiful human identity in the natural order of things and for the life of them couldn't understand why people made such a fuss over whether one was clothed or not.

Shifting consciousness migrated towards the latter mindset, shaping a new bell-curve. The latest survey in the United States revealed, as in the earlier poll, that 80 percent of people still had no objection to freebodies at designated beaches ("as long as they *keep* it there, for God's sake!"), but by now, in addition 40 percent believed in the right to be responsibly naked *anywhere*.

Nude proponents maintained it was group therapy on a massive scale. They stressed how, along with their clothes, nudists threw off trunk-loads of body-shame, false modesty and chronic body insecurities. They claimed increased body acceptance—one's own and others—made social nudity pleasant, therapeutic and self-validating, made people feel more human and alive. Shucking clothes bespeaking income, status and lifestyle allowed people to feel more honest, sensitive and accepting of each other as generic, "no brand" members of the human race: no bees in the bonnet, nothing up the sleeves, no ants in the pants, no knickers in a knot.

Advocates readily admitted increased nudity wasn't a panacea for the world's problems, but believed it was good for easing a few. People were more likely feel better about their bodies and be happier in their skins, thus making more positive contributions to society.

Opponents naturally denied or downplayed any validity to these arguments. They pointed out that, whereas in primitive places even so-called heathen natives oftentimes wore loin cloths, now people were so much worse for showing no modesty at all. To this charge it was pointed out that, if indeed humans had some innate modest tendency to publicly cover their genitals—and the point wasn't conceded—the tendency was eclipsed by being buried under too many clothes for too many years *not* to get totally free of them for a while. Only then could people begin to strike a new comfort-zone balance.

✺

People inaugurated Body Freedom Day, a celebration observing the anniversary of the historic San Francisco run. Every May 22nd, freebody enthusiasts celebrated the day with naked gatherings at beaches, parks and private lands.

Fresh attention was focused on issues at hand: learning to gauge the appropriateness of being naked in a given social situation; nude etiquette, the extra importance of good hygiene. Veterans had a chance to compare notes. It offered newbie nudies a chance to muster into the freebody lifestyle; being among kindred spirits provided needed structure to help integrate their radically shifting realities. The focus on all things freebody served to educate the masses; enthusiastic new converts were won over and more than a few chronic resisters at last succumbed.

Raw and living food enthusiasts—many freebodies as well—had food booths offering gourmet vegan food and held workshops on freeing up one's insides of unwanted vestments thru fasting, colonics and new diet. "Get naked *inside*, too," they encouraged. "Loose your animal food 'clothes' and feel even better."

Booths offered the latest in body-friendly apparel, skin paints, pamphlets and books, CDs and artwork. One booth specialized in signs, both printed and wood-routed; offerings included POSTED – NOW ENTERING A FREE-BODY ZONE, ANOTHER BODY-FRIENDLY HOME, and a tongue-in-cheek, twin storefront set: WE DO NOT DISCRIMINATE AGAINST NAKED PEOPLE, sold together with WE DO NOT DISCRIMINATE AGAINST CLOTHED PEOPLE.

Another specialized in oversize T-shirts, window decals and bumper stickers. Some of the more humorous messages offered included:

Save Your A/C - Drive Naked!
Don't Arrest Me I was Born This Way
Eat Beans, not Beings
More Tactile, Less Textile
If you Want to Wear Fur, Stop Shaving

Bare to Be Different

More serious slogans:

Be Kind to Animals. Don't Eat Them
Emancipate Yourself from Textile Slavery
Torturing one Animal is Cruelty, Billions a Way of Life
Government Has no Business Setting Dress Codes
Animal Liberation equals Human Liberation
Heart Attacks: God's revenge for eating his animal friends

Iris suspected some of the vending-booth owners maybe weren't that much into the freebody cause. She got a clue on noticing how many hired young nubile women and hunky men to vend their stuff buff.

Her suspicions were confirmed on buying a T-shirt saying "Wear Apparel at Your Own Peril." The irony of having to *wear* the thing to make the statement tickled her sense of humor. When the pretty but nervous nude blonde vender handed her the packaged shirt and change, she confided, "This is the first time I've ever done anything like this."

Iris was instantly concerned. She'd always believed it should always be a free-will choice whether or not one wore clothes. Required nudity on the job, or anywhere, was just as bad as required clothes, in her book—probably worse: forced clothes made you physically uncomfortable, but required nudity could be devastating if you weren't ready for it.

"You're not comfortable doing this, then?"

"Not really," the vender admitted. "I mean, I suppose I *could* be. I don't know. I'm here to make money. My rent's due and the pay's decent. This stuff's been selling like crazy and—whoops, here comes the boss," she whispered. Then: "*Will there be any-*

thing else for you?"

"No, but thanks," Iris said, playing along, giving her an encouraging smile. She pointedly didn't glance at the boss as she walked away; she sensed his funny-money smile, even so.

Nude enthusiasts threw picnics, lectures, workshops, dances and concerts to celebrate the day. Honors were presented to actors, writers and directors who'd done tasteful, nonsexual nude scenes in their films, helping the public gain healthier body attitudes. Popular acts participated. One year a music group calling themselves Barenaked Ladies finally lived up to their name.

A favorite comedian did an instant-classic routine. He came on stage fully dressed and affected supreme shock at seeing a mostly naked audience. He then let himself be coaxed thru lightning-fast banter with them to gradually shed his clothes. Coming full-circle towards the end of his act, he spotted a dressed confederate in the audience and launched a surreal nude-fundamentalist diatribe over how he dared to be so offensive as to wear clothes.

"I cannot fathom how you can stand there and not feel God judging you for hiding the glory of His handiwork. Have you *no* shame, man? God will not be mocked. Come forward, my son, lose your disgraceful clothes, and be baptized in the living sunshine."

☀

Iris never wore the shirt. While she admired the wit and artistry of the era's T-shirt designers, she realized she disliked wearing a message on her body; it made her feel like a walking billboard. Besides, it offered guys an excuse to stare at her. And most artwork, no matter how exquisite, used paint that irritated the skin and kept cloth from breathing. Plus, she reasoned, if it was warm enuf to just wear a T-shirt, it was warm enuf to just wear a tank top, and, if not, the shirt's cleverness and artistry were wasted underneath an outer layer. And anyhow, the booth owner put a weird vibe on the transaction. (Iris, a double-Libra, seldom had just *one* reason for any decision in life; she could—often did—weigh the pros and cons of most anything ad infinitum. She was in annalytical heaven years ago, when her Advanced Comp. teacher told the class to do a compare-and-contrast on two book's viewpoints on a subject.)

She really didn't know why she bought the thing—caught up in the excitement of the day and wanting a souvenir, she supposed. After the T-shirt sat unused in her dresser drawer a year, she donated it to Salvation Army. She wondered if its new owner—perhaps grabbing it for one-twentieth the cost—would appreciate the message, or just wear it for a necessary shield, not bothering to read its message, as some people didn't. Or if it would sit unworn in that person's dresser, too.

She thought how all the money people spent on clothes never worn—or worn only once—would probably erase the national debt.

TWENTY-FOUR

A writer should concern himself with whatever absorbs his fancy, stirs his heart, and unlimbers his typewriter.
—**E. B. White**

Nude Awakening
by Nuela Gottlieb and Zet Quimby

Third Excerpt

DURING THAT TIME of fast-shifting body attitudes, people flocked to lakes, rivers, beaches, resorts and mineral springs. They tested the waters of social nudity for the first time. There too, the already acclimated pursued their free-body lifestyle in peace.

Nude-friendly public waterfronts installed open outdoor showers; people who at first felt on stage rinsing off nude in open view (*"Ohmigod, everyone's watching!"*) soon accepted them with barely a thought. Soaping down one's nether regions, tho, was usually still reserved for private; individuals didn't want to give even the *appearance* they were playing with themselves.

A steep learning curve loomed for beginning social nudists (not to mention closet nudists). It was one thing to sunbathe or sauna naked in public, remaining perfectly still and low-key—Nudism 101—another entirely to move about freely, around others, doing everyday things, unconcerned about parts of one's anatomy bouncing and bobbing, sagging and dragging. Leaving behind a lifetime of inert public nudity was scary at first for anyone getting shut of a lifetime of body suppression. Both Jake and Iris knew that all too well. Those who'd accepted their bodies but still equated all nudity with sex felt they were starring in their own R-rated movie—*X*-rated ones in nude-intolerant regions. Lingering warped perspectives made voyeurs and exhibitionists of many.

One taste of how free and newly integrated it made them feel, tho—plus how much more open others were to them out of uniform—and newcomers took to it like ducks to water. The sheer exuberance felt—walking and running and working and playing and dancing in the buff, without any undue self-consciousness— was better therapy than money could buy. Long before, Iris had found carefree nudity to be as dramatic a difference over mere nude sunbathing as color-motion photography was over black- and-white still frames.

The two-sided coin of voyeurism-exhibitionism, corruptly mint- ed in people's minds for bodies too long hidden, was at last rolling towards oblivion. Socially-responsible public nudity diffused and transformed the worst of pent-up, unnatural fantasy-mania and body objectifying. The once-twisted mind-state of society had perhaps unwound enough to move past its antiquated attitudes. People were still only human; there were still the casual appraisal and open admiration of one another's bodies. But it was just that— casual and open—not the creepy or judgmental scrutiny that once put a crimp in anybody's efforts to enjoy a few rays unwrapped.

The freedom to be you: a novel concept in those times of budding self-awareness, when still-prevailing negative forces appeared to have zero interest in whether you were an authentic human being or a brainwashed automaton, so long as you danced to their shop-til-you-drop siren song.

☀

[The following summarized list was slated for mustering into the plot somehow. I include it here for its analytical insights.]

In time, long-forgotten baby memories of total, unself-conscious innocence—of being naked and fully open to life—re-surfaced, and then people *knew* it was a good thing. People who'd initially resisted the new, super-relaxed dress codes were won over for very different reasons:

Sunscreen, body paint and temporary-tattoo makers were ecstatic as business went thru the roof.

Less washing and drying to do, a definite boon for every family with a passel of kids, and a big plus in times of time-crunches, water shortages and overloaded sewage-processing plants.

Fewer clothes to buy, another boon for families—and everyone else. People were glad to stop helping finance new yachts for clothing corporation CEOs and their ingrate offspring.

As clothing production cut back, the glut of material and human resources once dedicated to supporting an over-clothed world were freed up to better use.

Planet Earth was spared being poisoned by so many insecticide- and pesticide-loaded cotton fields (the main clothing material) plus the toxins created producing polyester, Dacron, nylon, Ban-Lon and on and on.

"Clothesfree," and "Clothing-Optional" became magical phrases for luring related business, no less than "Fat-Free" and "Sugar-Free" had been in attracting certain grocery shoppers.

Thrift shops and new-to-you stores did record business as they were inundated by clothes from those needing fewer, which they sold to die-hard clothes-junkies ever wanting more.

Energy needs plummeted in hot weather. People discovered in foregoing clothes bodies self-regulated easier. Clothed, people had to set energy-guzzling air conditioning units to 72°F. [26°C.] to be comfortable; naked, they could be comfy—depending on humidity, air flow and activity—up to the 90s [high 30s]. Air units gathered dust or become geranium stands, as people often felt fine with just a fan on, thus easing the energy crunch and helping avoid rolling blackouts and grid meltdowns.

People who regularly skinnydipped—or at least finished showers cold—kept comfortable with lower thermostat settings in chillier weather, again helping save energy.

The porn industry, pants on fire, was going down in flames. Changing consciousness towards the human body fostered healthier attitudes. They could no longer exploit body alienation. Flashers went the way of the dinosaur; exhibitionists and voyeurs were endangered species. Sundry strippers in nude-friendly regions started looking for new lines of work, while the more talented exotic dancers happily discovered they were still in demand (once they lost any gratuitous bump-and-grind), as people grew to enjoy tasteful performances of graceful freebody dance.

The pleasure of lovemaking was enhanced. While losing that sudden *yum, we're naked!* rush, always good for churning hormones to a fine froth, going bare for long stretches beforehand away from the boudoir enabled couples to gain a more exquisite physical sensitivity and fine-tuned equilibrium not otherwise possible. It always took awhile to lose the shadow effect of clothing muting one's sensual receptivity. Being nude a long time beforehand was like slow-cooking in a crock pot: it brought out the more subtle flavors of food rather than nuking it in a microwave. According to tantric yoga, it takes about twenty minutes for a couple's energy fields to fully merge; already being nude and in freebody homeostasis could only help the process.

Workers discovered that if, on coming home after a hard day's work rather than "slip into something more comfortable" they simply slipped *out* of whatever was *un*comfortable, the day's stresses melted more readily. Those working in more fulfilling and creative fields that supported, not eroded, body integrity found this easiest. Such work conditions allowed a person to stay relatively tuned in to her body comfort rather than numb down to cope with un-bodyfriendly work conditions. (Those who usually felt uptight from work had little desire—beyond sex and hygienic needs—*to* get naked; the discomfort their clothes created—like a permanent Band-aid—matched the discomfort of their headspace.)

Growing numbers of people who earned a living from home had it made. Individuals worked more contentedly in the nude—on their phone, at the computer, packaging shipments, doing inventory, whatever—around the clock if they wanted to. No one to say *boo*. Non-machine piece-work assemblers, feeling greater ease nude, got more work done; writers, taking their laptops out to sundecks, felt moved to more inspired thought; farmers working the soil and orchardists harvesting fruit felt an extra-rich connectedness with the earth, imparting more harmonious energy into the food stream.

Absenteeism declined as relaxing dress codes made working more pleasant—especially workplaces in more progressive warm climes that inaugurated Clothing-Optional Fridays. Business owners discovered productivity increased and air-conditioning expenses plummeted. (At mineral spring resorts and health spas, bathhouse attendants might go as bare as the bathers—except for an employee armband or cap—making work more pleasant and helping put arriving customers into a relaxed freebody zone faster.)

Rapes decreased. Since rape was sparked in part by a crazed obsession to reveal what was concealed, the drop was shown linked to more open body-acceptance. Other violent crime dropped as well, tho links weren't as conclusive. For one, warm-weather domestic disturbances declined as couples and families felt more comfortable and relaxed out-of-clothes. Even some non-violent crime rates went down—notably clothes shoplifting.

Businesses showing solidarity with freebody enthusiasts garnered loyal support. A common sign in front windows of stores: **NO CLOTHES, NO PROBLEM.** Restaurants wanting to cater to everyone offered clothing and non-clothing sections, providing fresh sitting towels for the bare-bottomed who didn't bring their own: *"Party of five? Clothing or Non-Clothing? ... I know it is, but they make me ask."*

Inevitably, there were strong misunderstandings over what body freedom was all about. A quick-response team of activists worked on damage control by those foaming at the mouth over the spreading body liberation. It was easy for people undergoing sensitive healings from feelings of shame and self-objectification to feel blown away by stony-hearted nude-intolerance, and some adopted militant attitudes in return, demonizing clothes and their wearers.

Freebody proponents launched campaigns to try to head off at the pass any negative reactions from those thinking some kind of socially-mandated nudity was in the offing, one determined to make them feel ill at ease for wanting to keep covered. They stressed it should be everyone's right to wear as little or as much as they wanted without it becoming an issue either way. Plugging into PR efforts one summer, Iris's studio co-worker, Luangela, came up with a slogan that soon appeared as part of a public-service ad campaign in nude-friendly media outlets:

Wear it or Bare it - It's Every Body's Choice.

Others went overboard in other ways: Jake's cousin, Gaspar, a hard shell Baptist, went fundamentalist-nudist; he said he wanted to put the fun back in fundamentalism. He kept getting arrested for nakedly expounding the virtues of nudity and attendant evils of clothes in town squares throughout the Bible belt—gaining brief notoriety as "the Naked Preacher"—before finally being given an involuntary vacation.

☀

The clothing industry was predictably up in arms, their inventory buildups an embarrassment of stitches. Their spoken argument:

"It's throwing people out of work and slowing the economy." Their unspoken lament: "How the hell can we compete with *that?*" Many clothing concerns bit the dust—and good riddance, people said—as people quit wearing their too-constrictive, synthetic, uninspired, overpriced, skin-irritating sweatshop offerings.

Freebodies, when they did wear clothes, opted for loose-fitting, organic fiber, natural-dyed, body-friendly clothes. They still enjoyed clothes—maybe even more, since they were becoming friends, not keepers. People wanted skin-friendly clothes, clothes that let them breathe and move freely, that were easy-on-easy-off—like wrap-around skirts, sundresses, kilts, sarongs, saris, muumuus, pareus, lava-lavas, tunics...and, for minimal cover-up, reinvented loin cloths, "...*in a dizzying rainbow of colors, only $9.99, while supplies last*." Savvy clothing concerns had responded with new lines to match changing tastes and thrived. Also popular: over-the-shoulder totes to hold light cover-ups and bare necessities for the newly pocket-less and vending machines that offered temporary biodegradable cover-ups for sudden temperature and mood change—"*sorry, no color choice*."

For years it appeared a never-ending battle between those thinking a legal, universal clothing-option was all but a *fait accompli* and those vowing adamantly, "Not gonna happen. Throw 'em in prison sweatshops. *That'll* teach 'em." Two popular anti-freebody T-shirts: **No Nudes is Good Nudes** and

**I'll lose this shirt
when you
give me a word
that rhymes with 'naked'**

☀

Until lawmakers fixed the loopholes in their anti-nudity statutes, more tolerant states, as mentioned, believing federal government had no business setting dress codes, complied only with the *letter* of the law. Cops went thru the motions of responding to finger-wagging complaints, but if they determined nude but otherwise socially responsible people at least wore sunglasses, sandals, a hair beret—*anything*—they winked and told them to have a nice day. Technically, they weren't naked.

Julie, a friend of Iris's, wanting to enjoy a naked lunch in the park, was apparently out of luck one day after someone complained: no ankle bracelet, no nail polish—even her wedding ring was at the jewelers for cleaning. The peace officer reluctantly began writing her up.

"Wait a sec," she said, "I've got my radio on!"

"Nice try, but I don't think that'll fly... Say, wasn't that a Marilyn Monroe line?"

He was almost done when Julie remembered. "Wait—seriously. I just remembered: I'm wearing *contacts*."

He stopped writing, peered into her eyes to determine she indeed was, tore up the ticket and grinned. "*Have a nice day.*"

☀

[End of Excerpts]

There you have it. I know Nuela would be tickled to see our joint effort in print after all these years.

TWENTY-FIVE

*There comes moods when clothes of ours are not only too irksome
to wear, but are themselves indecent. Perhaps indeed he or she to
whom the free exhilarating extasy of nakedness in Nature has never
been eligible (and how many thousands there are!) has not really
known what purity is– nor what faith or art or health really is.*
—Walt Whitman, A Sun-bathed Nakedness

WHAT REALLY HAPPENED after the nude
run across San Francisco? Nuela and I had super-revved our imaginations, visualizing the possibilities of a quantum leap in radical
body acceptance. But meanwhile we were left with more prosaic
realities.

A dress habit thousands of years old wasn't about to change
overnite. One day of local naked celebration in San Francisco did-
n't give us more than the barest foothold in reversing socially
accepted body suppression on the global level.

In our caterpillar world, any substantial body freedom was yet
in chrysalis stage.

But we'd definitely pushed the proverbial envelope. The event had planted seeds of freebody awareness far and wide, with media helping, if only offering up a pop culture piece de jour spin in the vein of "those wild San Franciscans" comic relief because the event was too big a story to ignore.

I think possibly more people were freed up from more oppressed feelings that day than anytime since the collapse of the Berlin Wall. In the aftermath of that day, droves of people came out of the nudist closet. They felt freer to be naked more often, both at select beaches, mineral spring and resorts, and around their own homes.Progressive-minded people had had their urges to be naked validated.

Liberal cities with pleasant climates began allowing greater topfreedom at their pools and public beaches. And full nudity at designated free beaches—while still vulnerable to the vagaries of shifting politics, prodded by control freaks and high-minded body-phobes insisting we keep wrapped up, like merchandise—became so popular it took more than rinky-dink, oh-the-shame morals campaigns to ban unwrapping at them now.

Flocks of freedom-loving people, wanting to live a more natural life, shook the dust from their uptight burgs and headed to places more open-minded. A minor miracle unfolded in such places as its denizens, whether budding freebodies or not, had a more live-and-let-live philosophy about being discretely naked during nice weather.

In some of these regions naturist-leaning Christian church congregations blossomed. They naturally believed the naked state had the potential to bring people closer to the divine state. Tho accepting the teachings of Jesus, church members dismissed as poppycock the notion Original Sin was related to nudity per se, insisting it was all about separation from God. As the head of a Christian nudist community in Florida, David Blood, said: "The Bible very clearly states that when Adam and Eve were with God, they were naked. When people are right with

384

God, they do not have to fear nudity."

Naturist Christians held faith in humanity's inherent goodness when allowed to unfold in a free and nurturing environment—one free of guilt-drenched, projected judgments zealously attributed to a wrathful God. Church leaders held clothing-optional services, performed nude weddings and river baptisms, and set up intentional clothing-optional communities. As the founder of one community stated, "We are made by God, and in the image of God: why should we be ashamed of His handiwork?"

Encouraging changes, while not as dramatic as the ones we'd envisioned, were definitely in the wind. Like Nuela said, a clothing-optional world couldn't be built in a day. There was an organic growth rate to social changes, no less than to a pomegranate tree.

※

All this perhaps begs the question: Why *weren't* we more ready to let people be their naked selves?

This was a question Nuela and I had given plenty of thought to as we hammered out the story. We tried wrapping our minds around the many reasons why what happened in San Francisco in 2011 wouldn't play in Pretoria any time soon.

We'd jotted down a bushel full when we were away from our computers on the road, doing a hot springs tour of the Northwest. Again, I want to share what we came up with. (She had such a personable handwriting style I feel her presence just looking at her script; the cursive tales on her *Y*'s make me want to swing on them like a kid on monkey bars. In contrast, I needed a translator to decipher some of my own scribbles.)

Fourteen Reasons Why We Kept Our Shirts On

1. Some, coming from the older school and perhaps not anti-nudity per se—comfortable naked in private—couldn't fathom people wanting to be *publicly* naked: It didn't compute. They thought it an unhealthy trend, one to be discouraged.

2. Many who enjoyed being naked in private were too modest, too law-abiding, or too locked into enjoying their accustomed forbidden-fruit mindset to want to come out—unless or until public nudity became fully legal and accepted.

3. In an age of maddening conformity, people often tried distinguishing themselves from the crowd by the clothes they wore. It was as a Tunick photo-shoot volunteer said: "People *think* they're revealing themselves when they take their clothes off; they're not. They're revealing themselves when they put clothes *on*." We become artists—good, bad or indifferent—by the way we paint the canvas of our bodies with clothes, accessories and, with women, make-up. People love to dress up.

4. Resistance, actual and potential, from one unlikely business sector: nudist resorts and associations. Some resorts were concerned about loosing revenue if one could suddenly be naked in lots of places—not unlike Nevada casinos initially losing business after other states legalized gambling after it had long been the only one allowing it.

When one association said of a sporadic burst of public nudity in Germany, "They are hurting the nudist cause," some viewed this as a conditional support of body freedom, as if wanting to keep nudism a niche lifestyle for people with bucks, on their grounds. Or otherwise keep their tightly-organized brand of social nudity dominant, rather than generically available to everyone, everywhere. Whatever the case, it was easy getting so insulated inside nudist organizations members cried foul whenever people went outside them. (Some didn't realize such structures served as temporary but crucial scaffoldings only, enabling the gradual, focused building of more enlightened body attitudes.)

5.   The sight of unclad people could only be bad for business—with notable exceptions, like the multi-billion-dollar nude travel and recreation industry. Running the material world required material-ed people. Our naked selves might be closer to images of our divine selves, but the business world had no use for such divine reminders unless it helped sell Buicks, beers or boob jobs.

The business arena thrived on intense competition. Workers girded their loins, gritted their teeth, and launched into the battle fray, dressed from head to foot in Power Clothes; a naked business person could lose that edge in a hurry. Even if some could conceivably keep their drive intact naked, others would be incapable of taking them seriously—clearly the wrong kind of naked ambition. Businesses priding themselves on transparent operation thought opaque a good thing on this score. Businessmen daring to simply loosen their constrictive ties to breathe easier on hot days were seen as fudging on the game rules' strict decorum. Image was everything.

6.   Many, if not most, people felt clothes improved people's appearance. "Let's face it," a friend once told me, "people look better with clothes on." We were so used to seeing bodies covered in nicely uniform, colorful fabric we were uncomfortable seeing one another's plain, unwrapped selves, complete with moles, hair, scars and the like. Frequently, the only naked bodies we saw apart from relations (*"Seeing my husband naked is enuf, believe me."*) were for titillation: porn, movie actors, models and strippers. It was easy to become overcritical of everyday, less than "teen perfect" bodies (which Americans, at least, seemed to worship as the ideal figure, maybe linked to being so used to despoiling virgin lands).

Such sentiment was somewhat understandable in light of how many let their bodies go to wrack and ruin thru bad diet, lack of exercise and living in toxic, body-unfriendly environments. Lack of beneficial doses of sun further eroded the body's health. Hidden, tho, it didn't much matter *how* our bodies looked beyond our heads and, sometimes, limbs: Raiment covered a multitude of binges. As a result, many otherwise open-minded people felt conflicted between wanting to allow people the freedom to go uncovered and wanting to preserve the accustomed habit of seeing them only when mercifully covered in cloth.

7. Some feared public nudity would remove too much mystery. Keeping bodies hidden for all but your lover kept the experience of shared nudity more special and intimate, people thought. If everyone could always see everyone else's physical goodies, as it were, lovemaking would feel watered down. Also, partners' eyes might get turned. Men, often more easily aroused visually, would scarf up the continual eye candy feast of naked women, their gypsy pheromones dancing thunderstorms of errant lust. Some men didn't want to tempt fate—or involuntary salutes—being bare around them, nor did possessive partners, realizing this all too well.

8. The time-honored game of conceal/reveal in luring and keeping mates would be rendered obsolete. Many women had too much time, money and energy invested in alluring lingerie and other enticing apparel to look their ravishing best in to want to give them up willingly. Men hooked on such titillation agreed; so did shareholders in companies like Gloria's Secret and Ooh La La, Limited.

9. Both sexes might feel less secure if their every self-perceived body flaw was visible right from the start, before even saying "hi," let alone trying to win over a prospect with their personality.

("How can you charm the pants off someone if they aren't wearing any?" one wit wanted to know.) In a depth-challenged culture that idealized a fictional air-brushed level of physical perfection, body coverings helped level the playing field.

10. Fewer women than men felt comfortable with it. Women often appeared more receptive to sensual delights and would've loved nothing better than the world to be enlightened enuf for them to be freely nude when they felt like it. But our world wasn't enlightened yet. It was ingrained in male-dominant societies that no self-respecting woman revealed herself to anyone other than her partner, lest she lose honor and virtue by becoming the object of other men's lust.

Even more free-spirited women, not buying that, could feel uncomfortable nude in public if it did attract unwanted attention. As a result, often it was only women enjoying, or at least not minding, being such objects of random male lust—either to reinforce feelings of desirability, make a living, or indulge in the cheap thrills of astral sex—who publicly bared, thus reinforcing the nude-sex link in the public's mind. (It had come as a revelation to men like me, and some women too, lagging on the freebody learning curve, that many women who did appear bare or topfree in public, far from trying to lure a lover or indulge in self-gratifying exhibitionism, simply wanted to enjoy time without clothes beyond isolated situations.)

A survey of the time revealed some 98 percent of women felt somehow dissatisfied with their bodies. Nine in ten were uncomfortable even talking about their vaginas. They'd succumbed to Madison Avenue and the petty body-image angst of a body-alienated culture. They'd "let their figures go," or, more commonly, felt at a disadvantage without fashion aids to enhance an appearance they felt would be wanting otherwise. Knowing how much males constantly appraised their forms, and traditionally having had their self-esteem wrapped up in trying to please them, they'd become their own worst critics, the least accepting of their own bodies.

For whatever reasons, many, if not most, women were duly alarmed at the prospect of their unadorned selves being seen.

11. A lesser but still significant number of men also felt uncomfortable unwrapped in public. Some simply felt too vulnerable or awkward, having grown up less body-attuned than women. Others had become as obsessive about their bodies as women, dissatisfied with anything less than hardbodies. The thinking: if they didn't have anything worth showing off, they'd better keep it covered.

A shallow culture objectifying body parts and pursuing "bigger is better" thinking could be as merciless critiquing a man's staff as a woman's breasts. For some, it was too unnerving a thought having one's penis dangling there for frank assessment by every smirking girl and size-comparing guy. Then there was George's Seinfeldian concern of "significant shrinkage!" after a cold water dip. Anything with such shape-shifting unpredictability was perhaps best left under wraps.

(The rising consciousness of *people's* liberation lessened these concerns for both genders over time. Men worked thru socially-imposed gender-role issues and got in tune with their suppressed receptive sides. Women tapped their assertive warrior sides, taking back their bodies and enjoying social and public nudity, refusing to let any idle male lust crowd their comfort zone.)

12. Children, of course, were a huge concern. Toddlers, not yet socially conditioned, were natural freebodies. All thru clothing-mandated history, they served to remind parents how to feel relaxed naked, and the world how innocent nudity could be. Oddly enuf, tho, the same parents who delighted in embarrassing their kids by showing naked baby pictures to total strangers felt shame and mortification over naked pictures of them taken when older—

as if their bodies had lost every shred of wholesomeness and integrity on coming of age.

Many parents—even those who were maybe comfortable nude as family at home and with friends and simpatico strangers away from home—remained too skeptical about the state of humanity to ever think of endorsing any universal clothing option. They were concerned about the safety of their kids if allowed to run naked among the sexually precocious of their peers, not to mention any pedophiles still lurking. (My own grandniece, Zoey, Zak's mom, had a close call as a toddler at a free beach after her mother let her wander out of sight. When she went looking and caught up with her, she found a suspicious man hovering over her daughter with obvious designs. The man darted away on her approach like a wolf chased off at the last from easy pickings.)

Even more freethinking parents often set strict parameters on where, when, and with whom their older kids could be naked (if at all). Children entering teen years, with sudden body changes, weren't always keen on the idea anyway. Some who *did* take to it often became closet nudists in their own homes. Parents either thought their kids' raging hormones better controlled if kept under wraps, or, feeling body-alienated themselves, simply couldn't deal with seeing their own kids undressed; it could even spark incestuous desires.

Others, on a more even keel, were concerned only about the flack uptight neighbors might throw at them—report them to child services, even—for letting their kids run around naked, even if simply to cavort thru a sprinkler on their own lawn on a hot summer day. My friend Brenda's toddlers used to play happily naked on the front lawn of their Santa Barbara home until a neighbor raised a ridiculous stink over it and ended that childhood fun.

The U.S.'s penchant for periodic witch hunts over various perceived crises of varying actuality was deeply ingrained in our national psyche. It was then manifesting in at times off-target, ineffectual protection efforts against a real child-abuse problem.

391

Parents allowing themselves and their kids body freedom in their own home were considered morally reprehensible by extreme right-wingers, as if the parents were turning them on to heroin, sinking to incest or "God knows what."

13. Inertia prevailed. While more people came to feel safe fore-going cloth when weather, whim and circumstance allowed, yet another basic reason the overwhelming majority still resisted was *sheer force of habit.*

Millennia of keeping our torsos securely encased made us feel it the natural order of things, nudity the unnatural. We were like institutionalized prisoners: We were so used to being locked up in our clothes we no longer wanted to live on "the outside."

Clothes were our adopted second skin, our constant friend, our security blanket in an unkind world, intimately bolstering, caress-ing, enveloping our bodies, providing private, safe, customized mini-climates. Our bodies became used to such always-there, pro-tective companions—they were our *bodyguards.* (The fact we equated bared backsides with a feeling of self-conscious discom-fort is brought home by the word "embarrassed," used to describe that feeling.) People had become *addicted* to clothes, evidenced by the manic enthusiasm generated over the prospect of going shopping for a new fix.

Most everyone enjoyed immersing in water nude—if only pri-vately in tubs and Jacuzzis—the sensation being akin to liquid clothes for the pronounced, all-enveloping pressure it exerted on the body, even as it became all but hidden under the water's sur-face. But many of the self-same people had little or no interest in adapting to the subtler—but no less pleasurable—sensations of their bodies being enveloped in warm air and sunshine. It involved re-adjusting some long-established equilibrium and experiencing initial discomfort for the easier likelihood of being seen by others. It weirded everyone out, so why risk it?

For whatever causes, clothes were habitual. People had become so wed to clothes it was almost as if we'd taken a secular vow to always wear our habits—and were shocked at the thought of being seen out of them. The Order of the Perpetually Clothed?

14. By far, the biggest objection to the idea of making clothing optional in the old world revolved around a perceived sense of threatened decency. The fading social order saw its time-honored sense of propriety under direct assault whenever increased body liberty dared show itself. Since the only time its members got together without clothes in mixed genders was for sex, the turn of events in San Francisco clearly reflected a moral breakdown of society—nothing less than a hedonistic retreat into shameless exhibitionism.

   This perception of unseemliness was fueled in part by advocates of open sex. It was always a fine line how far couples could share open displays of passion before hearing cries of "get a room!" No question, it was easier getting carried away making out naked. Without consideration of others' reasonable sensibilities nude *could* be rude.

   One time, Nuela and I, feeling amorous, found ourselves swept past the point of no return while at an Oregon beach. We found what looked like a secluded tall-grass patch above the shore and were on the home stretch when we heard what turned out to be a Girl Scouts troupe approaching. We rolled ourselves over into our blanket and feigned simple snuggling, but too late, I think. The scout leader favored us with a withering glare and some of the girls giggled nervously. It left us feeling chagrinned and put a definite crimp in things.

TWENTY-SIX

> *...Nobody told me there'd be days like these*
> *Strange days indeed (most peculiar, mama)*
> **—John Lennon**
> **"Nobody Told Me"**

I GUESS THAT'S IT," Nuela said, looking around. We'd finished loading her luggage into the side door of the rental minivan she'd soon drive to Sacramento International. In a material detachment I could only marvel at, she'd pared down her belongings to what could fit into three luggage cases, one a smaller carry-on. We'd held a huge yard sale at a friend's in town and made three runs to Salvation Army, but inevitable dribbles and drabs of accumulated belongings remained. "Keep or donate whatever's left, or leave them for Carla; I'm sure she could use a lot of them."

"I can't believe you're really leaving." I said, stating the obvious. I knew she had to follow her inner guidance, but it didn't make parting any easier.

After a decade-long roller-coaster ride together with more ups than downs, Nuela and I were splitting in a basically friendly break. I'd proved myself couple material after all. We'd made a tight team, so much so many people took us for a married couple.

We'd always tried to give each other enuf space to pursue independent interests and relations. Maybe it was how I sometimes begrudged her spending time with others, to the detriment of our own quality time (I felt) that strained things now and then. Part of me knew it was my only own insecurity, prompting abandonment issues, but I couldn't always overcome it.

In any event, she'd felt an irresistible urge—out of the blue—to up and move to Australia. She said she wanted to learn the ways of the Aborigines and write a novel based on their lifestyle, something in the spirit of *Mutant Message Down Under.* She was impulsive that way; it was that trait that brought her into my life in the first place. Now it was the trait that was taking her away from it. She'd sold her homestead to Carla, a retired forester from one of her yoga classes.

"I know, sometimes I can't believe I'm leaving either. You know how much I've come to like the Shasta area—and its residents." She turned and gave me a long, silent hug. I felt the now-familiar yet still indescribable oneness course thru me; I was still wandering who she was, really. "You'll be okay," she said, looking deep in my eyes, "Remember, we're always together, no matter where each of us is."

"That'll be small consolation on a cold winter nite."

She laughed and pushed me away. "I know you; you'll find someone else to keep you warm before long."

"Maybe. But I sure got used to you. You know my addictive personality."

"All too well, sweetie; all too well. Tell you what, if you don't find somebody new and you ever get tired of being a stick-in-the-mud Northwesterner, you can always fly over and try finding me in the outback; maybe I'll still be available."

I laughed ruefully. "Like I can see myself doing that." She knew I wasn't over-fond of flying. Our trips together had been the first time I'd been on a plane in seventeen years and I hadn't flown since.

"You'll be *fine*. I'll email you as soon as I get to Melbourne.
We shared a last hug and kiss. Then she was gone.

I'd feel her residual energy traces in my cabin for months after. I'd
miss her more than I thought it possible to miss someone. In our
ten years together we'd only been apart two or three times and
never for longer than three weeks.

But I finally moved on. I became a bewildered single for a while
and then, as she predicted, met someone new, and when I least
expected it: doing my wash at the laundermat.

Two years later a package arrived in the mail, bearing all kinds
of exotic kangaroo and koala bear stamps. I read her new novel in
one sitting. I felt her close in my heart again, now in a nice, nonat-
tached way.

But I'd've sworn I recognized myself in a quirky tribesman
character, having trouble making his boomerang come back.

☀

Nuela and I, tho we'd liked to imagine otherwise, knew it might
be a long while before universal acceptance of either body freedom or vegan diet came about. Millions had changed their lives,
embracing radical body acceptance and dietary consciousness,
but many more millions hadn't. So long as people kept wrapped
up in the vicious circle of strife, hurting each other, slaughtering
their animal brethren, trying to monopolize the food stream,
plundering the planet, building un-bodyfriendly habitats—forever keeping Mother Nature on the run and ourselves from staying connected with her—such things as radical body freedom
and vegan diet would remain about as popular as nudists and
tofu burgers at a methodist pig roast. Separated from nature, we
were separated from ourselves; separated from ourselves, we

were separated from nature.

One nice Sunday morning I tore myself away from my church of the living wilderness that was home, got dressed, and drove to town to meet my friend Sally, who was concluding a service at the Our Lady of Perpetual Perplexity Church. I waited in my car in the dirt parking lot out back, trying not to feel like a heathen for not wanting to go in. I felt the presence of God a hundred times more in the glory of his creation than the inside of any manmade church—no matter how beautiful the stained glass work or majestic the organ music and choral singing. I suppose I've always been something of a primitive; I just had little use for organized events in my life—especially religious ones, most especially *indoor* religious ones on nice days when all of nature was singing in the sunshine.

Trying to keep a positive frame of mind, I imagined the church as The Church in the Wildwood—after a hymnal song of that name from my childhood. To me, the song always evoked an image of a congregation happily communing—inside a church, yes—but deep in the bosom of pristine nature, a place so pure and unspoiled it was the land *around* the simple rustic church that made it feel holy. I was learning to appreciate how God was in everything and everyone, but it sure was easier appreciating the fact gazing on a redwood tree than staring at a Coke machine. I looked around and thought, *well, this isn't too bad.* Even tho within earshot of an interstate highway, the grounds had an honest dirt parking lot and a little grassy area dotted with trees, and, to top it off, the murmur of a nearby creek. Always pulled to moving water, I got out and started towards the sweet sound, thinking maybe I'd wade in the water and sit beside it and meditate a while. It wasn't to be: unapologetically blocking my way was an eight-foot-tall chain-link fence, growling "Keep Out" to one and all.

That said it all to me: It was the freaking *fences* of the world,

symbolizing the prevailing divisive mindset, which made it challenging to be our natural selves. Our living habitats were fenced
off, slabbed over, parceled off, closed in, locked up, shut down,
under surveillance and chemically treated. We had Mother Nature
on the run at every turn—and thus, ourselves too.

Someone once wrote, "Love is when you feel safe being naked."
The outdoors of most towns and cities rarely qualified (tho, after
diligent search, I'd discovered three skinnydipping spots within
the city limits of my own nearby towns). Inviting natural places
could be few and far between, and not many of us want to ditch
the first line of defense between us and an unkind world.

Of course, that didn't faze dedicated urban body freedom warriors. They kept taking it to the street, protesting for the right to be
responsibly naked anywhere, anytime. First, people had fought for
the right to be socially naked on their own private properties, then
at designated clothing-optional public spots, and now, anywhere at
all. "The best thing to do," one anonymous person wrote sardon-
ically,

> would be to designate everywhere as clothing optional,
> and we could leave little fenced-in areas for the prudes
> to prance around in. Call them 'Prudist Camps.' They
> could peer out of their fences and indulge in their offen-
> sive 'I'm offended' behavior whenever they saw a natu-
> ral person walk by, without bothering the rest of us.

Naturally—or unnaturally—such warriors were seen by many
as weirdos and shameless exhibitionists rather than champions of
personal liberty.

We'd gain few far-reaching, iron-clad legal rights to safeguard
freebody rights on public lands beyond existing free beaches and
various municipal pools. True, people were sometimes freer to go
about more *semi*-naked than before, but being completely nude
remained too much a slap in the face of the antiquated sensibili-

399

ties of a clothes-minded world, too much to expect our real, unadorned selves could actually be free of oppressive judgments and censuring. Dare remove that token bit of cloth pledging fealty to Babylon and you were in big trouble, bub.

Freebody lifestylers were a long way from receiving equitable treatment under the law. The Spirit of Justice statue in the Department of Justice's Great Hall may have been half-naked but she was half-clothed too. A case was slowly working its way to the Supreme Court to decide whether the Constitution covered being uncovered. Prospects looked bleak, tho, with the decision resting on nine people super-glued to long black robes.

❋

Things looked about the same over the likelihood of cruelty-free diet becoming universal. Despite the 2012 wake-up call with the historic class action lawsuit, vegan consciousness wasn't spreading as fast as optimistic advocates hoped. True, a growing stream of more conscious individuals went vegetarian—while an estimated 20 million Americans were vegetarians in 2001, by 2013 the numbers had swollen to 60 million, or about one in six, including an estimated sixteen million vegans, with similar figures in other countries

Even so, a veritable Mississippi River of people kept tearing away at their favorite decomposing flesh, numb or indifferent to the reality of the act's inherent violence to their fellow sentient beings. People kept in denial or ignorance how it devastated their health, perpetuated world hunger, and reduced the livability and sustainability of our planet. The same way millions kept smoking after proof-positive the habit was a sure form of slow suicide, so it was with the legion of meat eaters either keeping in denial or not giving a damn.

The pain and suffering behind that succulent curried lamb—the

400

bloody reality of the billions of sentient lives taken each year for people's dining "pleasure"—went ignored among those still hooked on carcass-consumption. Like heroin junkies, they cared only about getting their next dead-critter fix. The dark humor behind a Texas bumper sticker spoke volumes: "Eat Low on the Food Chain. Barbeque a Vegetarian." As did another: "Proud member of PETA: People Eating Tasty Animals."

People knew an abiding peace on Earth couldn't come about until (among a thousand other things) we stopped slaughtering members of the animal kingdom entrusted to our care because we refused to shake free of an ancient violent habit.

Hell, we couldn't even stop killing each other.

True, we'd made a historic breakthru. In the wake of the meat and dairy industry lawsuit, millions of people woke up, forsaking eating animals, and droves of lacto-ovo vegetarians gave up all animal byproducts as well. That suit had only come about due to diligent efforts of many over long decades to educate people and encourage businesses to change.

A decade earlier, for instance, The Humane Society mounted a successful campaign. They convinced the Whole Food Market and Wild Oats Marketplace natural food chains—plus a few other large conventional egg buyers—to only stock cage-free chicken eggs, thus saving millions of chickens from a tortuous existence in cramped indoor cages. And more people raised free-range cattle and buffalo, free of the hormones, antibiotics and chemical feeds and inhumane conditions of factory farms.

But these were only baby steps. It was still injurious, exploitative, and resource-wasting animal food people ate, still painful deaths feeling creatures suffered after their "useful product life" had ended, still environmental degradation spreading over the face of the planet.

People might forsake red meat, even poultry, but you didn't try taking away their dolphin sandwich—*tuna* sandwich, actually, but, as vegans pointed out, what difference did it make? *Either all life was sacred and deserved to live, or we were playing god, say-ing you, you and you are treasured animals, worthy of protection. But you, you—and especially you, ya crazy gobbler—prepare to die; you're slated for our buffet platter at the Women Against Violence charity luncheon next Saturday.*

And so it was that the majority of people kept eating animals and their reproductive fluids and kept dying before their time— their animal-residue-laden bodies failing them, the anguished cries of all the innocent beasts they'd devoured echoing inside them, even as they went to join their number in death.

There was a poetic justice to it all—death begot death. But that was small consolation for all the needless suffering experienced by humans and animals alike.

It was a pity more people never connected the dots: For instance, I felt that a leaning towards violent novels, movies and TV shows was an obvious reflection of violent diet. As people avidly turned the page or kept eyes fearfully glued to the screen, their bodies and minds resonated with the fright and death of the slain sentient beings they'd devoured, having absorbed the horror of the animals' demise with every bite. Similarly, I saw the way meat eaters' habit of relishing the mayhem and violence of certain bone-crunching war games among spectator sports reflected the mayhem and violence coursing thru their bodies from such cruel diets.

Unreasoning people adamantly refused to see the cause and effect on either issue, to look at entrenched ways in a new light. And so it was that while a remnant of humanity spanned giant leaps in body liberation and conscious diet, the rest, deceived by modern-day sadducees, kept locked into the wrong-headed, oppressive cultural habits of old. Content to live in the unconscious ways of their forefathers, they missed out on the global transformation underway

TWENTY-SEVEN

For what is it to die
but to stand naked in the wind
and to melt into the sun.
—**Kahlil Gibran,**
The Prophet

PERHAPS NOTHING IN our lives could have prepared us for the changes to occur on Planet Earth. No matter how much we anticipated something momentous in the wings—thinking whatever it was couldn't happen soon enuf if the planet were to survive—what actually happened defied most people's wildest imagining.

Terminally obtuse rulers had tried, with dwindling success, to assure people there was nothing to worry about during those final days of the old world. Even as ices melted and seas rose, temperatures climbed, and hurricanes and earthquakes and volcanic eruptions unleashed. Only lifetime members of the Flat Earth Society and Egyptian Fish of Denial League could possibly have doubted *something* was about to happen

It was almost as if to erase any doubt from anyone's minds that Earth changes had finally come to a head, permanently preempting our regularly-scheduled existence.

☀

As it turned out, the historic day-after-Christmas tsunami of late '05 had served only as a wake-up call for the far more catastrophic tsunami to come. The first tsunami was caused by quake; the second by an unwelcome visitor from space.

As everyone knows, late one nite and without warning (beyond radio predictions from psychics few heeded), a rogue asteroid, nearly two kilometers in diameter, slammed into the Pacific. The impact and displacement of trillions of tons of water in the ocean's bowl set off unimaginably towering, three- to four-kilometer-high waves, inundating the sleeping West Coast and much of the entire Pacific Rim. Any tsunami warning sirens were too little, too late. The shockwave of the asteroid's impact carried to the sea floor, then activating tectonic plate movement, in turn triggering a chain reaction of further devastation thru earthquakes and volcanic eruptions.

I'd received an unmistakable dream premonition a few months beforehand that my homestead would soon no longer be safe. Reluctantly I moved north, to the mountains of eastern Washington State, well before the time the asteroid kersplashed into the mighty deep.

For a while I'd thought to go down with my ship rather than move, like Harry Truman and his umpteen cats when Washington's Mount St. Helens blew in 1980. But I felt I had deeds to do yet and so left my home of thirty years. I pared down belongings to what fit in my panel van, sold, gave away or abandoned the rest, and got out of Dodge. It broke my heart to part from my painstakingly gathered collection of mostly useless belongings. (Yes, I still got emotionally attached to stuff I had no earthly use for: broken lamps I'd never fix; tools I'd never use; and obscure books I'd likely never read unless stuck on a desert island.) But I did manage to save my family's journals and albums—which, as the family's ad hoc archivist, had found their way into my possession—and a box of well-loved books I couldn't imagine being without, along with practical items like food, clothes, bedding, silver coins and other trade-ables, and tools I did use.

If I'd stayed, I'd likely have been swept into oblivion. For even tho the valley was hundreds of kilometers inland and over a thousand meters above normal sea level, a mountainous ocean wave poured thru like a cross-country tour, flooding all in its path. If, by miracle, I *had* survived that, the poisonous gasses released from Mount Shasta erupting soon after would have claimed me for sure.

Untold millions perished overnite; millions more the following days. We hadn't anything to compare it to. In a matter of hours, more people died than in all modern wars combined.

Survivors, shaken, numb with grief and scared senseless, struggled to salvage pieces of their lives.

The world over, people worked together to deal with the common disaster. A growing sense of unity emerged: We were no longer separate, isolated countries and peoples. In the face of widespread devastation, we attuned to the reality of being fellow crew members aboard the same fragile blue-and-white Christmas ornament whirling majestically thru space.

As every school child knows, that series of catastrophes, staggering as they were, served only to brace us for the truly epochal planetary polar shift yet to come.

Within days, over two-thirds of Earth's inhabitants perished.

I'd never experienced anything close to the fright and awe I felt: my hair turned white overnite. Our sphere went catawampus, stars swam thru the sky; screaming, 600-kilometer-an-hour jet stream winds touched down and nite seemed to last forever *when the planet stopped spinning.*

Even those among we survivors, convinced the world was only going thru a radical realignment—that it wasn't the end of the world—were shaken to our core. Nobody took the certainty of drawing their next breath for granted. We knew the world would spin again, in fresh gyroscopic balance, but whether with us or without us was the question. The series of events and the Biblical devastation it wrought dealt a sledgehammer blow to the sensibilities of all who lived to tell.

Earth underwent a complex recalibration my non-scientific brain could never quite understand—tho my seventh grade grand-nephew later tried explaining it to me.

When the planet commenced turning again—an eternity and two days later—a golden calm prevailed; the birth travails were over; a happy, bouncing Earth, sporting new magnetic poles, emerged.

Ready or not, we were given another chance to redeem our fallen trust and become wise stewards of the planet.

I sensed the hand of destiny on me. A profound gratitude and absolute wonder spread thru me for being blessed to witness our home planet's grand new chapter in life and fresh flowering of humanity. I slowly absorbed the reality of old familiar land formations having slipped forever beneath the waves and new ones emerging in their stead from the briny deep, glistening wet like newborn babies.

I'd sorely miss many of those now with us only in spirit.

Years flew by before I learned who among family, friends and acquaintances had survived. Communication systems and records were obliterated, travel of any distance all but impossible. I'd run into Kate a few years later; she'd been vacationing in Canada and talking on the phone to Sam and Gail in San Francisco an hour before the comet hit. She thought Jennie made it, but didn't know for sure.

Mom survived the comet, but was lost in the shift. I wish she could have lived to see the new world; she would have fit right in. My sister is alive and well, still in Brazil, adjusting to the new, cooler climate. I still don't know what became of my brother Clyde; he was in the Bay Area the last I knew, but we'd lost touch long ago. My brother Jason had moved to New Zealand; as Edgar Cayce predicted, it had become a new land of opportunity.

I'm not sure what became of Nuela. We'd kept in touch by phone and email, but lost contact after the splash. I could be wrong, but my senses tell me she's alive and well; she would've received guidance warning if she'd needed to get out of harm's way, and longevity ran in her family, same as in mine. She'd be a spry 106 now.

Mount Shasta and the land around it transformed to an isle, one of a new archipelago of islands left after lower lands bid adieu and slipped beneath the waves. The region was uninhabitable for years because, even after the eruption, poisonous gases kept seeping out.

After it was safe to, I decided to move back, along with new-found family from Washington. It felt dreamlike using a sailing ship to reach the shores of the once-landlocked mountain, but by then much of life had become dreamlike. Together we built a cluster of new shelters, salvaging lumber from the ruined buildings scattered over the countryside like driftwood on the shore after a storm. A few old acquaintances who'd also evacuated in time chose to move back too: people get attached to this old mountain. It looked different with many of its forests flattened into kindling and its northwest side blown out like some giant being thought it edible and took huge scoops out to sample. But it was still the Big Rock Candy Mountain. I tried finding my old place for a while, but the topography had changed so radically I gave up. Those silver dollars are probably still buried somewhere.

In time, our new community grew and integrated. New trees stretched heavenward. One fall equinox we christened the place Earth Haven.

❋

A whole new world unfolded before us.

After the shift we survivors were forced back to basic survival mode in our long struggle to salvage and rebuild civilization. Mutual survival depended on everyone working together, each pulling his or her weight. Everyone realized this.

Needless to say, whether or not one was wearing clothes was the *last* damn thing on anyone's mind.

In the aftermath of the travails that gripped the planet, that once-seemingly inalterable pattern of human behavior, mandatory-compulsive dress, observed and enforced for endless generations, was jettisoned like so much surplus baggage. It went the way of centralized electric power, combustion engines and Hostess Twinkies

We embraced body freedom more easily, as our living environments gained in body-friendliness. We naturally shaped current habitats with an eye to nurturing and sustaining its dwellers amid nature. If a person could time-travel here from three generations ago, she'd think she was on another planet: absent the noise and crowding; gone the blinding lights and blaring ads; the empty and cruel food and toxic beverages; the soulless abodes in sad cities; the madman's pharmaceuticals and cut-happy surgeons; the working at odds with each other and mindless duplication of effort—

and the blind compulsion to always wear clothes.

As it turned out, the universal acceptance of our bodies became a mere footnote in history, even as it was gained. Having made peace with Mother Nature and each other, we'd made peace with our biologic selves as well.

When work, weather or occasion demand, we freely wear apparel; when weather, leisure or spontaneity allow, we freely wear nothing. Clothes are our friends now, never our keepers—especially since returning to fashioning more homemade raiment: It's easier feeling good wearing a hemp sweater lovingly knit by a close friend than synthetic apparel of chemical dyes cranked out by some anonymous exploited worker in a far off sweat shop.

The entire issue, in the grand scheme of things, is irrelevant now. While it was perhaps understandable people long denied the right to go freebody would go hog-wild, as we did the day of the race, we can't help but see such enthusiasm as a bit funny-sad now. It seems it was always the way thru history, tho: the pendulum of social conditions swung from one extreme to the other in every popular struggle to correct a long-term injustice. Then, the fundamental right to be clothesfree was a valiant cause in the minds and hearts of many, *as it was a right denied*. Body freedom was one of scores of keen social issues we grappled with, but one most dismissed as too absurd and frivolous to merit attention. Even tho it brought to the fore extremes of basic acceptance and non-acceptance of one another.

Proponents could become impatient for the rest of the world to see the light, tho they knew it was a matter of time. That it came in our lifetime was a pleasant surprise: Some would sooner have thought the skies turn green, loan sharks turn honest and pigs soar thru the air before we ever let people walk about freely naked. Those legions of body-phobic, "nattering nabobs of negativity," led by priests, politicians, and the posh panoply of power panderers—claiming public nudity interfered with their right to be spared the unspeakable spectacle of spying unwrapped specimens of their species—have by now mostly left their once impressively wrapped bodies.

Of course, we still love to dress up. Witness our current enthusiasm for the newest line of hi-tech apparel, and with colors that change to complement shifting moods. Or the line that changes thermal and water-repellent properties, according to how hot or cold or wet it is. Just two of the latest in humanity's age-old love affair with body coverings.

Thankfully, we've come to strike a natural balance. The change didn't happen overnite. Ultimately it took new generations, not yet born in those last days, to lead the way. Unfettered by the self-conscious body shame and sexual exploitation of their elders' world, the young set the bar ever higher, encouraging the rest of us to rid ourselves of any lingering vestiges of negative body attitude.

It was the same with vegan diet. Those once-hardcore meat eaters who hadn't died before their time or during the Earth changes finally saw the light—learning to resonate with the higher frequency and now-universal awareness of the grand interconnectivity of everything. The irrationality of brooking violence or exploitation toward man or beast became clear as day.

With each new generation, the once iron grip of cruel diet faded to memory among those of us who'd lived thru it. And, as the reader knows, there are more than a few of us centurions around now. That our current average life expectancy is now 141 years is as much due to a mindful diet and conscious living as it is to our many medical advances. Over 2,300 years after Hippocrates said, "Let food be your medicine and medicine your food," we finally adapted his wisdom.

The planet is still healing, its countless wounds knitting slowly. The vibrational scars from the systematic slaughter of billions of animals (let alone the endless deadly wars among man) remain with us and can be felt by the more psychic children. It gladdens me how we periodically do healing ceremonies on sites once slaughter yards; planting trees, singing, and praying for animal spirits to be at peace, asking their forgiveness for our millennia of enslaving, mistreating, and killing them.

Earth heals a little more with each passing season, along with its torn ozone layer. No magic wand was waved to make everything all right; no *Extreme Makeover: Planetary Edition* came along from another galaxy. We're still working to undo the effects of endless planetary abuse.

But believe me, it's a relative paradise compared to how we once lived—so peaceful that in gentle weather many now feel naturally inclined to go about without coverings.

Of course, we've developed social patterns on where and when we opt to go freebody: whenever nicer weather allows, most always by the water, for indoor and outdoor leisure and recreation, and sometimes for eating, shopping, and casual meetings; seldom in colder weather, at formal affairs, or work environments in which safety and sterile conditions are paramount concerns; almost never at costume parties.

These are logically-formed conventions, but even these are a bit flexible, allowing for individuals' whims and idiosyncrasies. After a long hot sauna and icy cold plunge, for instance, one might be comfortable naked walking about awhile in even the chilliest weather. In our Herculean effort to rebuild the world, we realized the importance of honoring individuals' rights to be themselves, no matter how odd or eccentric, so long as they contributed to the common good and didn't infringe on the rights of others.

Old fossils like me, who remember how things were in those beleaguered times, treasure being free to let the morning sun warm our bones as we munch on a fresh-picked apple.

Epilogue

I wish I could send this writing back in time; I really do. Let early 21st century people know a new world is just around the corner—that their wanting the option to be naked will soon be considered reasonable, their desire not to exploit the animal kingdom universally embraced.

Wouldn't that be something? So often they felt they were tilting at windmills, bucking the tide rebelling against the tyranny of the indomitable Textile Empire and mighty Meat Machine, scarcely daring to believe either would ever topple. They could use some good news. Advocates of body freedom and natural, whole food diets must have felt at times they were stranded on some strange flesh-eating, textile-obsessed planet.

I heard a stir scientists are maybe getting close to a breakthru in teleportation and time-travel technology that would enable precisely such a thing. But I'm not holding my breath. Even if this book *were* sent back, people then were so skeptical they'd surely dismiss it as a hoax—and I wouldn't blame them. I doubt I'd have believed it myself. In our insufferable omniscience, we were so sure we knew what was possible and what was not. Anything not in line with the dominant worldview of reality was rejected out of hand.

But maybe a few would believe it and take heart.

An old man can dream.

✷

To help gain yet a better perspective on nudity and dress, some of us are putting together a historical exhibit at Earth Haven's community center. It will coincide with the 50ᵗʰ anniversary of the historic 2011 Bay-to-Breakers run. We intend to show thru photos, film snippets, and text of the times how very different things were then regarding body attitudes. We've unearthed pieces that will leave you dumbfounded: some will make you laugh, others make you want to cry.

We'll document Body Freedom Day and some of the many freebody pioneers and unsung heroes who helped lead the exodus from forced dress over time.

Gourmet snacks will be provided. My great-great-grand-niece, Zara, is catering; her little brother Zak will help out.

Someone found a battered old sign to post by the entrance to pique interest:

Nudity Prohibited
Violators will be Prosecuted

I understand it once greeted beachgoers at a bygone beach on the Florida coast called Paradise Cove.

We're hoping the exhibit will be ready by next summer solstice.

Sources and Further Reading

Adams, Carol J. *Living Among Meat Eaters: The Vegetarian's Survival Handbook.* Three Rivers Press, 2001.

Aron, Elaine N., Ph.D. *The Highly Sensitive Person: How to Thrive When the World Overwhelms You.* Broadway Books, 1996.

Barcan, Ruth. *Nudity, a Cultural Anatomy.* Berg, 2004.

Boutenko, Victoria. *12 Steps to Raw Foods: How to End Your Addiction to Cooked Food.* Raw Family Publishing, 2002.

Brown, Lester B. *Plan B 2.0: Rescuing a Planet under Stress and a Civilization in Trouble.* Earth Policy Institute, 2006.

Campbell, T. Colin, Ph.D, with Thomas M. Campbell II. *The China Study: The Most Comprehensive Study of Nutrition Ever Conducted and the Startling Implications for Diet, Weight Loss and Long-Term Health.* Benbella Books, 2005.

Cinder, Cec. *The Nudist Idea.* Ultraviolet Press, 1998.

Cousens, Gabriel, M.D. *Spiritual Nutrition: Six Foundations for Spiritual Life and the Awakening of Kundalini.* North Atlantic Books, 1986, 2005.

Donanelly, Arlene. *Naked States.* Documentary video on Spencer Tunick's nationwide photo shoots, Juntos Films, 2000.

Droulliard, Harvey. *The Spirit of Lady Godiva,* Anecdote Productions, 2002.

Goodson, Aileen, Ph.D. *Therapy, Nudity & Joy: the Therapeutic Use of Nudity Through the Ages.* Elysium Growth Press, 1991.

Kennedy, Gordon. *Children of the Sun: A Pictorial Anthology; From Germany to California 1883-1949.* Nivaria Press, 1998.

Halweil, Brian. *Eat Here: Reclaiming Homegrown Pleasures in a Global Supermarket.* The Worldwatch Institute. W. W. Norton & Company, 2004.

Hartman, William E., PhD. *Nudist Society: An Authoritative, Complete Study of Nudism in America.* Crown Publishers, Inc., 1970.

Kern, Ken, Ted Kogon, Rob Thallon. *The Owner-Building and the*

Code: Politics of Building Your Home. Owner-Builder Publications, 1976.

Keyes, Jr., Ken. *The Hundredth Monkey.* Public domain. 1982.

Latteier, Carolyn. *Breasts: The Women's Perspective on an American Obsession.* Harrington Park Press, 1998.

Marcus, Erik. *Vegan: The New Ethics of Eating.* Revised edition. McBooks Press, 2001.

Radetsky, Peter. *Allergic to the Twentieth Century: The Explosion in Environmental Allergies – from Sick Building to Multiple Chemical Sensitivity.* Little, Brown and Co., 1997.

Regan, Tom. *The Case for Animal Rights.* University of California Press, 1983, 1985, 2004.

Robbins, John. *The Food Revolution: How Your Diet Can Help Save Your Life and Our World.* Conari Press, 2001.

Robbins, John. *Diet for a New America: How Your Food Choices Affect Your Health, Happiness and the Future of Life on Earth.* Stillpoint Publishing, 1987.

Singer, Peter. *Animal Liberation.* Ecco, 1975, 2002.

Smith, Dennis Craig. *Growing Up Without Shame: Social Nudity – It's Effects on Children.* Elysium Growth Press, 1986, 1996.

Spiegel, Maura and Lithe Sebesta. *The Breast Book: an Intimate and Curious History.* Workman Publishing, 2002.

Stepaniak, Joanne. *The Vegan Sourcebook,* second edition. Lowell House, 1998, 2000.

Storey, Mark. *Cinema Au Naturel: A History of Nudist Film.* Naturist Educational Foundation, 2003.

Weil, Andrew, M.D. *Heath and Healing.* Houghton Mifflin Company, 1983, 1995.

Yalom, Marilyn. *A History of the Breast.* Ballantine, 1997.

Zanluv, P. *Transparent Planet.* Lightyear Press, 2037.

Acknowledgments

I'd like to acknowledge the State of Jefferson; I sometimes drive like an old man; and that a local, decades-running penny-saver ad, reading "Two side by side burial plots...will not sell separately," is surely fodder for a novel. Also, I'm lysdexic, astounded I didn't find occasion to use the word *minutiae* until now, and astonished my grandfather, born in 1850, could have been a drummer boy in the Civil War.

Forever indebted to The Naturist Society, of Oshkosh, Wisconsin, from whose quarterly periodical, *Nude & Natural: The Magazine of Naturist Living,* an abundance of quotes, facts and information on all things nudist was freely gathered. In many ways, this book exists because of the inspired, lively writings of TNS's talented contributors—notably that force of nature, Mark Storey, who also lent enthusiastic support to my writing efforts.

Some of the book's bumper sticker, banner and T-shirt slogans are original; others borrowed; credit here for the latter to whoever brainstormed them: you know who you are. Thanks to Bill Pennington, who coined the apropos phrase *clothes-minded.*

For their early support, thanks to Candace, Tamy, Dolores, Ingrid, and Elizabeth. For suggesting reworking the novella, my thanks go to Cheryl. For later support, thanks to Marian Blue, for her spirited book-doctoring; and Dr. Eve Thompson, for generous encouragement. Also, thanks to Ernie of C.O.S, Alison, Obie, Jonathan, Nada, Otto, Jessie, Victor, Rick, James, Annie, Stella, Val and Sola, for their interest, sharing and feedback.

Interest in the politics of food was born toiling in the vineyards of Seattle's all-volunteer Capitol Hill Food Co-op with a redoubtable group of co-workers during the latter purple haze days. It was furthered by serendipitously stumbling across such books as Jim Hightower's *Food for People, Not for Profit*, John Robbins' *Diet for a New America* and T. Colin Campbell's *The China Study*. Reading Gordon Kennedy's heartfelt and illuminating work, *Children of the Sun* fired the idea of tying conscious diet and body freedom together in the story.

Kudos to nude group photographer Harvey Droulliard and crew, whose futuristic photos and daring poses also inspired the work. Thanks to Charles Daney for his collection of pithy quotations—some of which head the chapters—and his *Weekly Nudesletter*, which provided invaluable research material; and to the computer technicians who helped me figure out my newfangled laptop all the way from Bombay.

Undying gratitude goes to my book designer, Marie-Josée Wells, who took on the daunting task of breathing the work to life and demonstrated amazing patience and understanding for an erratic wordsmith. Thanks to Tracy Tuttle for a great cover.

Special thanks to participants of the Bare-to-Breakers race, World Naked Bike Ride, and other positive nude events, for setting the example of radical body acceptance and helping inspire the project; and to vegetarian and vegan advocates everywhere, for helping show the way to a real happy meal.

Web Sites

body freedom:
naturistsociety.com   The Naturist Society. Worlds of info.
aanr.com   American Association for Nude Recreation.
clothesfree.com   International Nudist Association. (U.S. based)
fcn.ca/inf   I.N.F. International Nudist Federation. (Europe-based;
   choice of languages.) Defends interests of organized naturism
   in 30 countries.
bodyfreedom.org   Experience Nakedness Project; Body Freedom
   Collaborative. Colorful, fun site.
fcn.ca   Federation of Canadian Naturists (FCN)
spencertunick.com   Photographer of huge nude-groupings
   around the world. Amazing photos.
barewitness.org   Scrapbook of bare messages of peace around the
   globe. Astounding photos.
Baretobreakers.com   Informs and organizes runners/strollers for
   San Francisco's real-life annual nude demonstration.
naturist-christians.org   Naturist Christians
worldnakedbikeride.org   Info on annual, multi-city naked bike
   protest of oil dependency and body oppression.
barefooters.org   Society for Barefoot Living.

animal rights and vegan living:
vegan.com   Daily updates, in-depth info "for both vegans and
   vegetarians."
rawseattle.org   Support and information about raw food diet.
navs-online.org   Promotes vegetarian living, sponsors regional
   and national conferences, publishes Vegetarian Voice.
peta-online.org   People for the Ethical Treatment of Animals.
   Works to stop animal cruelty globally.
far-musa.org   Farm Sanctuary, promotes vegan diet, advocates for
   well-being of farm animals.

ABOUT THE AUTHOR STUART WARD JR, an expatriate San Franciscan, grew up in a Victorian bearing souvenir ceiling cracks from the 1906 quake. He lives in upstate California in a self-built rustic home, where he's lived off-grid 28 years. He's been vegetarian 37 years, vegan for one, and a body freedom proponent for ten. He's labored a half decade at a clothing-optional mineral springs, and has contributed to N, The Naturist Society's quarterly. This is his first novel.

ABOUT THE WORK Ward offers: "John Lennon once said he sang of peace and love because he felt so much hate and anger and hoped to change by focusing on the opposite. I wrote about body freedom in part to try dissolving my body hang-ups by visualizing a more enlightened, body-positive world. And, by blending radical body acceptance and conscious diet, I hoped to strike a balance between pursuing inner and outer body harmony by offering a more expansive view of natural living."

The work is an expanded re-imagining of his novella, *Body Freedom Day: When a Clothed-Minded World Unraveled,* which, in turn, evolved from a short-short penned 35 years earlier. The two-stage, three-year project began life on a Royal desktop manual typewriter and soon migrated to a Presario laptop computer— generated 99 percent by sunshine.

Notes

Notes

Notes

Notes